TERRA STANDS ALONE

BOOK THREE OF THE THEOGONY

Chris Kennedy

Theogony Books
Coinjock, NC

Chris Kennedy/Chris Kennedy Publishing
2052 Bierce Dr.
Virginia Beach, VA 23454
http://chriskennedypublishing.com/

Publisher's Note: This is a work of fiction. Names, characters, places, and incidents are a product of the author's imagination. Locales and public names are sometimes used for atmospheric purposes. Any resemblance to actual people, living or dead, or to businesses, companies, events, institutions, or locales is completely coincidental.

Ordering Information:
Quantity sales. Special discounts are available on quantity purchases by corporations, associations, and others. For details, contact the "Special Sales Department" at the address above.

Terra Stands Alone/ Chris Kennedy. -- 1st ed.
ISBN 978-0990333531

As always, this book is for my wife and children. I would like to thank Linda, Jennie and Jimmy, who took the time to critically read the work and make it better. Any mistakes that remain are my own. I would like to thank my mother, without whose steadfast belief in me, I would not be where I am today. Thank you.

Author's Notes

Note: When more than one race refers to a planet or star in Janissaries, the same name is used by both races in order to prevent confusion. Also on the topic of planet naming, the normal convention for planets is to take the name of the parent star and add a lower case letter (i.e., Tau Ceti 'b'). The first planet discovered in a system is usually given the designation 'b' and later planets are given subsequent letters as they are found. In order to prevent confusion in Janissaries, the closest planet to the star in a star system is given the letter 'a', with the rest of the planets given subsequent letters in order of their proximity to the star.

STARGATE MAP

Ssselipsssiss Space
|
Gliese 832 (Lizard Orbital Station)
|
Tau Ceti   Ssselipsssiss Space   Mrowry Space
| | |
Kepler 78 — Ross 248 — HD 40307   —   83 Leonis   —   61 Virginis (Grrrnow)
|
Kepler 22 — WASP 18 — Gliese 221   Gliese 163 — Gliese 676 — Mrowry Space
|
Gliese 667 — Epsilon Eridani (Domus) |
| |
61 Cygni — Gliese 581 — GD 61 (Elspeck) — Mu Arae — Aesir Space
| |
Lacaille 8760   Fomalhaut
| |
Kapteyn's Star   HR 8799
| |
Vulpecula 452   51 Pegasi (Archonis) — Archon Space
| |
Solar System (Earth)   55 Cancri (Clarion)
| |
Ross 154   HD 10180 (Malak) — Gliese 777 (Depsi)
| |
? — Lalande 21185 — Gliese 876 — 54 Piscium (Olympos)
| |
COROT-7 (Drakon)   Hooolong Space
|
Drakul Space

"You can ask me for anything, except time."

— Napoleon Bonaparte

Prologue

The president watched as the battlecruiser emerged from the stargate. Within seconds, light flared as the first of the antimatter mines guarding the stargate detonated alongside it. Designed for stargate penetration, the ship's shields absorbed the blast, and its lasers began firing as the battlecruiser's crew tried to fight its way clear.

Unlike the static minefields of old, though, this minefield was mobile; each of the 50 pound devices had a motor that gave the mine a final burst of speed toward its target. As the inner layer of mines attacked the warship, the next layer moved inward, filling in the spaces of the mines that had detonated or been destroyed. Flashes showed that some of the ship's lasers found their targets, but space is big. The mines, comparatively, were *very* small, and the asymmetric nature of the threat made them extremely difficult to counter. The battlecruiser was caught in a web of mines and a second mine exploded. A third mine exploded seconds later, overloading the warship's shields with its 215 megaton blast.

A second battlecruiser emerged from the stargate in time to see a fourth mine detonate alongside the first battlecruiser, engulfing its engines in the explosion. 30 anti-ship missiles, launched from canisters at point blank range, followed closely after the explosion. Power-

1

less, the ship's crew was unable to defend itself, and the missiles hit the center of the ship from opposite sides, ripping it in half.

The second battlecruiser was unable to go to the first ship's aid, as the second warship's emergence had triggered the next layer of mines. Its crew tried to avoid the fate of the first ship and successfully eliminated over 30 of the mines as they approached. Unfortunately for the crew, the minefield numbered in the tens of thousands, and it was not long before one got close enough to activate. Again, the first detonation was absorbed by the ship's shields. The second and third mines exploded nearly simultaneously, their blasts overlapping to knock out the battlecruiser's shields. The ship's crew tried to make it back to the safety of the stargate by flipping the ship end over end, but the ship's path was blocked by the emergence of the battleship that followed the battlecruisers into the Solar System.

Over 1.5 miles long and massing over 4 million tons, the battleship was better prepared for the minefield; it had an improved tracking system that could find and target the mines. It also had over 150 lasers and gamma ray lasers (grasers) of various sizes with which to defend itself. As the crew identified the missile canisters for what they were, counter-missiles leapt out from missile ports to preemptively target them. Working in concert, the battleship's crew methodically tried to cut its way out of the minefield.

Programmed to target the aft end of a ship, one of the mines reached the back of the second battlecruiser, and power on the ship died as its engines were destroyed in a massive explosion. Another mine struck the front of the ship, vaporizing a 45 feet long section of its hull and splitting a large seam down the starboard side. Fluids, people and equipment were sucked out of the ship as it tumbled out of control. Worried that the ship might make it past the minefield, the defenders launched five more missiles from the periphery in a coup de grace that destroyed it.

Although several mines exploded alongside the battleship, none succeeded in breaching its shields. Seeing that the battleship might make it through their defenses, the Solar System's guardians activated all of their manual defenses, and anti-ship missiles began launching at the invader from all sides. Each canister only held one missile, but the defenders had over 1,000 of the large canisters, and they launched 250 missiles at the battleship. From a range of only a million miles, the battleship's crew only had seconds to intercept the missiles accelerating at over 100,000 times the force of gravity (100,000 G's).

Counter-missile missiles leapt from ports all around the battleship, and counter-missile lasers retargeted on the incoming ship killers, but there wasn't time to stop them all. 87 missiles from the first volley made it through the ship's defenses. Almost half of these spent themselves on the battleship's redundant shields, but the battleship's shields finally failed, and the Terran missiles tore gaping holes down its sides.

Seeing that they were incapable of stopping all of the weapons arrayed against them, the battleship's crew rotated the ship to retreat to the safety of the stargate. Flashes of light could be seen down the length of the battleship as another volley of 250 anti-ship missiles struck home, killing its defenses and its defenders. As the ship accelerated back toward the stargate, one of the missiles hit the aft end of the ship, knocking out one of its four engines.

The battleship neared the safety of the stargate, but two more mines were in its path and detonated alongside it. One hit the middle of the craft, taking a 100' bite out of its side. The other mine functioned as intended and struck the back of the ship, where it knocked out two more of the warship's engines and caused the fourth to go out of line. Already screaming at maximum power, the remaining engine skewed the ship as the off-center thrust spun the ship in a circle. Its crew and the system's defenders watched in horror as the massive ship hit the stargate sideways, and an invisible knife cut the ship in half. The aft end of the ship entered the stargate and went through, while the front half spun off to the side of the stargate, unpowered and out of control.

The general in charge of the briefing turned off the recording. "As you can see, Mrs. President," he said, "we were successful in stopping the Drakuls from entering the system; however, it looks like part of their ship made it back to the other side of the stargate. They are going to know that there is a civilization on this side, and they will probably come through next time in much greater force. If they do, we are going to be in trouble... just stopping those three ships used up over half of the defenses we prepositioned at the gate."

Chapter One

"**G**eneral Quarters! General Quarters! All hands man your battle stations. Launch all alert fighters! General Quarters! General Quarters! All hands man your battle stations. Now launch all alert fighters!" Calvin rolled out of his bed. What? Another drill? It seemed like all they'd done since they got back was drill and drill and drill. As he started throwing on his flight suit, he realized with a start that the voice hadn't said, "This is a drill." There were only two things that they'd call general quarters for, a loss of pressure or actual combat.

Drakuls, he thought, lacing up his boot. A shiver went down his back. The Drakuls were the Terran's worst nightmare, a race of 10-feet tall bloodsucking frogs that were headed toward the Earth. The Drakuls must have come through the stargate. That was the only reason they'd launch the fighters.

"Attention all hands," said a voice over the intercom; "make preparations to get underway. The *Vella Gulf* will lift in 10 minutes. I say again, the *Vella Gulf* will lift in 10 minutes."

The squadron commander for the *Vella Gulf's* 12 fighters, Lieutenant Commander Shawn Hobbs, or 'Calvin' to his aviator friends, had the closest stateroom to the squadron's ready room, so he was the first one there, aside from the three officers that had been watching a Tri-D movie on the ready room's Mrowry TV.

5

"What's up, Clarisse?" he asked the duty officer, Lieutenant Clarisse Boudreau.

"Ops just called, sir," said the Canadian officer, "and we've got Drakul ships coming through Stargate #1. Two battlecruisers and a battleship so far, eh? The defenses are responding and Skywatch has asked for all available ships to get there ASAP."

"Shit," said Calvin, "it's just us. The *Terra* hasn't returned from Epsilon Eridani yet, and the battlecruiser is still being fixed." The *Terra*, the Earth's newest (and only) battleship, had just taken its first crew aboard, and they were on a short cruise to get everyone trained. The fleet's other acquisition, a still unnamed battlecruiser that the *Vella Gulf* captured on its last mission, was also unable to lift, as maintenance crews were still repairing the graser holes that the *Terra* made through its bridge and galley.

The only Terran defenses still in-system were the *Vella Gulf*, a 3,000 year-old cruiser, and its complement of 12 space fighters. There was another cruiser, but it was a Mrowry ship, not Terran. A race of felinoid warriors that looked like Bengal tigers, the Mrowry had been a space-faring nation since the beginning of the Neolithic age on Earth. Even if the Mrowry cruiser joined them, two cruisers versus one of the battlecruisers wasn't a fair fight. And the battleship wouldn't even notice as it drove over them. "Damn it," said Calvin, shaking his head. "I can't wait for a battle where we're not fighting ships that are bigger than we are. Is the *Emperor's Paw* responding?"

"Yes sir," replied Lieutenant Boudreau. She looked at her watch. "The Mrowry are going to be lifting in about 15 minutes."

"Good," said Calvin. At least they wouldn't go to their deaths alone.

"Hi Skipper," said Lieutenant Sasaki 'Supidi' Akio as he entered the ready room. "I'm ready to go when you are." The Japanese man was the officer that normally flew with Calvin as his Weapons System Officer (WSO), the person who operated the navigation, communications and weapons systems for their space fighter. Ever since being crewed with Calvin, Supidi had exhibited an almost unnatural ability to show up whenever Calvin needed him.

"They said to start launching as soon as we're ready," said Clarisse. "Skipper, you've got *Asp 01* and Guppy, you're in *Asp 02*."

Calvin looked at the two other officers that were in the ready room, Lieutenant Terry 'Guppy' Gupton and his WSO, Lieutenant Martyn 'Tinman' Sinclair. Both had just checked into the squadron the week before. Although they had both received their implants and downloaded their training, neither had actually flown in the fighters yet. Their whole experience with flying space fighters was a two-hour flight in a simulator. There was also the whole love/hate relationship, as Gupton was from Australia and Sinclair from New Zealand. Their relationship was mostly good-natured...most days.

Still, they flew well together in the simulator; when things got ugly, they melded into a good team. "He's not half bad...for an Aussie," Sinclair was heard to have said afterward. Still, if there were Drakuls coming through the gate, the time for Earth-borne conflicts was well past. "Man up *02*," Calvin said. "We'll try and take it slow at first, but we've got to get out there."

"Yes sir!" they chorused, and the four men left to get into their fighters.

Bridge, Drakul Ship Mangler, Ross 154, December 8, 2020

Captain Bullig hated most of the things about his life. He especially hated his ship, which had been built by one of the conquered alien races. The Overlord had given him command of it as punishment; the nine feet high ceiling was far too low for his 10 feet height. He had to walk around the ship stooped, which made it uncomfortable to go anywhere. While a new bed had been installed in his cabin, the room itself was only nine feet long, so he was unable to stretch out. He hated the race of giant caterpillars that had built the ship. The only thing they were good for was dinner.

He hated this star system. The star known as Ross 154 was a red dwarf that had two planets in its habitable zone (the distance from the star where it was warm enough to have liquid water, but not so hot as to boil it off). Unfortunately, both of the planets were barren, as Ross 154 was also a flare star. The star would flare up every few decades, reaching out to cook off anything growing on the two planets. This occurred across the star's spectrum, from x-rays to radio waves, sterilizing the planets at an unpredictable rate before the star subsided again to its normal luminosity. It was a waste of prime real estate that could have been used to support a civilization worthy of conquering. He hated being stationed here.

"The battle group is proceeding to the stargate," said his communicator.

"Good," said Bullig. "I hope they all die miserably." He had petitioned to be included in the Drakul exploratory force, but had been denied. He hated all of the crews that had been picked to go, while he stayed behind on this side of the stargate. The *Mangler* was the system's picket. Its crew's mission was to wait behind and, if an enemy came through the gate, to run back to the High Command and warn them.

"Why is that?" asked Commander Chark, the *Mangler's* executive officer (XO). "Don't you want them to go and find new planets to pillage and plunder?"

"No," said Bullig, "I want *me* to go and find new planets for *me* to pillage and plunder. Waiting here on the chance that we'll need to run back to the High Command is not a worthy task for a warrior. I want to *KILL!*"

The ship's steward brought Bullig a punch bowl full of one week-old hatchlings. When he was in this kind of a fury, the crew had learned that it was better to give him something to take his anger out on, rather than the bridge crew. They were already starting to run short-handed, and they'd only been in the Ross 154 system for three weeks.

"How will the battle group dying miserably help you?" asked the XO as Bullig pulled a struggling hatchling out of the bowl by one of its hind feet. It screamed as he let it dangle. He let it sway in front of his face for a couple of seconds so that the hatchling could see what was coming.

Born self-aware, the hatchling knew it was about to die, and it screamed harder, eliciting a smile from Bullig. He threw it into his mouth and bit down, sucking its blood through his hollow incisors. One week was about the right age, Bullig thought. Any older and they had a tendency to bite you back. He chewed up the husk and swallowed it.

"If they die miserably," Bullig said, "that will mean that not only did they find us a new race to conquer, but they also found one that would put up a fight. The race that built this ship surrendered every time we came into a system where they were. Where is the fun in that?"

"It isn't much fun fighting a race that won't fight back," agreed the XO. "They were, however, quite tasty."

"Indeed, they were," said a calmer Bullig as he sucked on a second hatchling.

"The battle group is entering the stargate," said the communicator. "They passed on a message for you sir, but I don't think you want to hear it."

"No, I probably don't," said Bullig. The commanding officer of the *Destroyer* had been a hatchling with Bullig. He never missed a chance to let Bullig know that he was 'going places' while Bullig sat behind watching the stargate. "Tell him that I said to find a new wife and kids while he's on patrol," ordered Bullig, "because I'm going to kill and eat the ones he left back home."

"Sorry, sir, his ship has already gone through the stargate," said the communicator.

"It doesn't matter," replied Bullig. He smiled at the XO. "I'll still do it, of course."

"I hope they find some more of those short humanoids," said the XO, looking at the tactical display. "You know, the ones that opened the gateway for us to come into this universe. They didn't fight very well, either, but they also tasted good."

"Psi-something, I think they called themselves," said Bullig, who had been given one of them as a present. As it was one of the last ones the Drakuls had, he had played with it for a while before finally eating it. "Psilons or Psiclants or something like that. You are right; it would be nice to find a few more of them."

Bullig reflected on his civilization's progress in this universe and wondered if they'd find any more of the...Psiclopes...that's what they were. The gods definitely had a sense of humor. The Drakul race in this universe had been wiped out, but a Psiclopes scientist trying to link collapsed black holes into stargates had opened up a dimensional doorway to the Drakuls' home world in a parallel universe. As luck would have it, the doorway opened at a Drakul military base and over 2,000 soldiers and sailors came through the gate before it closed. The Drakuls captured a nearby spaceport and the two cruisers that were there...and then feasted on the sailors that previously crewed them.

He was only a new recruit then. After they found out their race had been annihilated in this universe, the High Command decided to go slowly. They flew the two captured cruisers to a nearby navy yard of a felinoid race and captured the battleship there. They had then taken the battleship and the navy base's Class 6 replicator and had run to the end of civilized space, where they began building up their power.

20 years ago, the High Command finally decided it was ready to go on the offensive. The first three systems were easy. Two were inhabited by the caterpillar race and easily subdued; the other was inhabited by the Psiclopes. No challenge to any of them. Although the Psiclopes were technologically advanced, their defenses were minimal, and there were barely eight million of them on the planet. The XO was right; at least they tasted good.

The fourth planet they attacked was inhabited by a race of winged humanoids. Three easy conquests made the Drakuls over-confident, and the High Command only sent a battle group made up of four battlecruisers, because that was all it had taken to subdue the first three systems.

When the battlecruisers didn't return, the High Command sent a full squadron of eight battlecruisers. Those ships also didn't return, so the High Command sent a fleet of eight battleships, accompanied by two squadrons of battlecruisers and two squadrons of cruisers. This fleet successfully captured the system; however, it was like putting a stick into an anthill, and the winged humanoids returned in force with a fleet of their own. The Drakuls were forced to withdraw from the system, and each race heavily reinforced its side of the stargate. The two fleets probed each other, but neither side was able to fight its way back through the stargate. A long stalemate followed.

Having grown tired of the standstill, the Overlord had recently killed the High Command and promoted a new one. Rather than follow the failed policies of their predecessors, they came up with a new plan; they decided to open up a second theater of war. By sending ships through a different stargate, they hoped to find another way around that would let them come from behind the winged humans and take them by surprise.

While they built the ships required to fight a two-front war, the High Command sent a destroyer down this stargate chain to explore it, but the destroyer hadn't returned. The battle group that just left was supposed to scout down the chain of stargates and find out where it went.

"I've got gate activation," called the defensive systems technician, or defender. "Based on mass, it looks like one of the battlecruisers is back already."

"Which battlecruiser is it?" asked Bullig. If it was the *Destroyer*, it would be his classmate, coming back to let him know that they found and enslaved a new civilization. He hoped it was the *Destroyer*...even though he hoped it wasn't.

"It's the...no, it's not either of the battlecruisers," said the defender, "although it has about the same mass as one of them. It's weird sir. If I didn't know any better, I'd say that the radar image looked like the back half of the battleship. It only appears to have one engine working and that one is at full power. The ship is spinning around in circles and is in danger of running back into the stargate again."

The defender paused. "It *is* the *Slayer* sir," he said finally. "Or, at least it's what's left of her. I'm getting emergency beacons that identify the ship as the *Slayer*."

"Communications!" called Captain Bullig, "are you able to reach anyone aboard the ship?"

"No sir," said the communicator, "I have not been able to reach anyone."

"Nor will you," said the defender. "Its artificial gravity is out, and it's making a 30 G turn. Anyone that's still on that ship is probably plastered onto one of the walls."

"What about the artificial intelligence (AI) onboard?" asked Bullig. "Can you reach it?"

"He won't be able to," replied the defender. "The part that came through the stargate is from aft of the bridge. All of the processors for the ship's AI are in the front half of the ship, wherever that is."

"It looks like you got your wish," noted the XO.

"Yes," said Bullig with a smile, "it looks like I did."

Chapter Two

"**D**amn, Supidi, it looks like we missed it," said Calvin. They had been orbiting in the vicinity of the stargate for two hours, but nothing else had come through it.

"Do you suppose they learned their lesson this time?" asked the Japanese officer. "First the destroyer and now this? Having only half of a battleship come back has got to be bad for morale."

"Who knows how Drakuls think?" asked Calvin. "For all I know, they'll look at that as competition and think that attacking us is fun." He thought about it a few seconds and added, "I'm not challenging them, mind you. I hope they stay on their side of the stargate for at least another couple of years. Now that we have a replicator and can build our own ships, if they'd just give us a chance, we could be ready to give them a lot of fun by then."

Bridge, Drakul Ship *Mangler*, Ross 154, December 8, 2020

"**F**inally, some competition," noted Captain Bullig with satisfaction as the shuttle returned with a couple of survivors from the battleship. The other shuttle had already returned with a full load of dead bodies. No sense letting that much fresh food go to waste, he thought. "Let's go take a look and see what's there."

"But Captain," said Commander Chark, "the forces on the other side of the stargate just destroyed two battlecruisers and a battleship. Whatever is there will likely destroy us as well! Our duty is to report to the Overlord." He looked around the bridge for support. No one met his eyes.

He never saw the blow from Captain Bullig that hit him in the side of the head, knocking him to the deck. "You are new on the crew," said Captain Bullig, leaning over him, "so I will tell you this once. This is *my* ship. *I* am the Captain. My word is law." He looked down at the XO. "Do you have a problem with that?"

"No, Captain Bullig," groveled Commander Chark. "I don't have a problem at all. Whatever you say is good with me."

"Excellent," said Captain Bullig. "Remember that." He turned to the helmsman. "Begin acceleration toward the stargate. Full speed ahead."

The XO crawled to the back of the bridge, where he stood back up next to the communications station. "Madness," he said under his breath. "The Overlord will flay us alive for violating orders."

"No," said the communicator in the same low whisper; "madness is contradicting the Captain on the bridge of *his* ship. How do you think you got your position? He killed the last two XOs for the same thing. The only thing that saved you was the low ceiling. He couldn't use his killing punch. The Overlord is a long way away, and who knows if we'll ever make it back home. The Captain is *here*. It's best you remember that. Besides, he usually knows what he's doing; he has gotten us out of many bad situations."

"If he's such a good Captain," said Commander Chark, "why is he on this ship and not one of the ships that just went through the gate?"

"Simple," said the communicator. "He didn't know his last XO was a second cousin of the Overlord. Being on this ship is his punishment for killing him."

Asp 01, Stargate #1, Solar System, December 8, 2020

"Asp 01, this is the Vella Gulf," the radio blared. "All ships are to return to the Vella Gulf for refueling."

"Roger that, Vella Gulf," replied Supidi over the radio. "We are returning to the ship." He switched to the tactical frequency used by the squadron. "All Spacehawks, we are to return to the ship for refueling. Join up on us." The squadron gathered together and headed back to the ship with feelings of both disappointment and relief. Although they were disappointed that they missed out on the action, they were even more relieved that a bigger force hadn't come through. With a good portion of the system's defenses depleted, most decided it was better that way.

Bridge, Drakul Ship *Mangler*, Ross 154, December 8, 2020

"Five minutes to stargate," said the helmsman.

"Battle stations!" ordered Captain Bullig. "Cease the drive. Rotate ship. Engines to full after rotation!"

"Rotating ship," said the helmsman. "Engines coming to full."

"Initiating battle stations," added the defender. A blue light began flashing, and a horn began to wail.

"You're going to go through the stargate...backwards?" asked the XO.

"Of course," said Captain Bullig with a laugh. "We might get trapped there and destroyed if we didn't. That might make the Overlord unhappy, and we definitely wouldn't want that." He gave another laugh and then was serious again. "Open all weapons' hatches and extend all laser mounts."

"Hatches opening," called both the attacker and the defender simultaneously. "Mounts moving." Both of the technicians had missiles and lasers; the defender was responsible for the ship's counter-missile lasers and missiles, while the attacker ran the *Mangler's* anti-ship missiles and lasers.

"Transit in five," said the helmsman. "Four...three...two...one... mark!"

TSS *Vella Gulf,* Stargate #1, Solar System, December 8, 2020

"I heard a piece of the battleship made it back through the stargate," said Calvin. All of the crews had swapped out when the space fighters came back to refuel, and fresh crews were now manning them. "Is that true?"

"Yes, it did," said Captain James Sheppard, the commanding officer (CO) of the Terran spaceship *Vella Gulf.* "Skywatch said that the back half of the ship made it through." Skywatch was the Strategic Command's Joint Functional Component Command for Space. Located at Vandenberg Air Force Base in California, Skywatch's Space Operations Center was responsible for the system's defenses until the newly-formed Terran Space Force was able to take over that function.

"We've got to go through and get it," said Calvin. "If one of their ships comes along and sees it, they will know that we're on the other side of the stargate."

"I said the same thing," said Captain Sheppard. "Skywatch is worried about what happens if we go through the stargate and find out that there are Drakuls waiting for us. We are the only Terran ship in the system right now, and they don't want to lose us."

"Lose us?" asked Calvin. "We're going to lose our anonymity if we don't go get it."

"They said—" Captain Sheppard answered.

"*Skywatch reports another gate activation!*" interrupted the communications officer. "They have a single transit inbound. It's a small ship, cruiser-sized or smaller."

"Launch the alert fighters!" ordered Captain Sheppard. He looked over to the offensive systems officer (OSO) seated at the operations station. "Let me know when you have a firing solution!"

The *Vella Gulf* was positioned 7.5 million miles from the stargate, just inside the 8 million mile range of its missiles. It took light and radar 40 seconds to cross that distance. Skywatch had a radar station next to the gate that used a faster than light radio system to transmit what it was sensing, so the *Vella Gulf's* crew was aware that the intruder had entered the system almost 30 seconds before it was able to see it with the ship's sensors.

"VAMPIRE!" called the defensive systems officer (DSO), using the codeword for enemy missiles. "I've got missiles being launched!" The intruder wasn't so handicapped; the *Vella Gulf* would be visible to the enemy's optical sensors upon entry. A good crew entering a new system could often fire a volley or two of missiles before the defenders were able to reply, even with the time it took for the systems (and personnel) to settle out after a stargate transit.

The intruder obviously had a good crew.

Bridge, Drakul Ship *Mangler*, Solar System, December 8, 2020

"**M**inefield!" yelled the defender as the *Mangler* entered the system stern-first. "Minefield defenses on automatic!" With the flip of the switch, the ship's counter-missile batteries and counter-missile lasers began firing autonomously, as fast as their targeting systems could find and identify the mines.

"We should be OK for a few minutes," said Captain Bullig. "Look for ships and try to get their identification. Helmsman, stand by for emergency thrust."

"How are we OK if we're in a minefield!" screamed Commander Chark. "We've got to go! Helm, emergency thrust, now!"

"*Belay that order!*" roared Captain Bullig. "They won't have mines next to the stargate. The mines will be further away, so that the defenders have time to identify any intruders prior to activating their minefield. Besides, the enemy wouldn't want their mines to accidentally fall into the stargate. We are in no danger from mines."

"Contact!" called the attacker. "Optical systems show a ship located to starboard!"

"Fire all starboard batteries on that line of bearing," said Captain Bullig. "Get as much information on it as you can." He looked at the helmsman. "Emergency thrust, *now!*" he said. "Take us back through the stargate!"

The helmsman pushed the button that his claw had been hovering over, and the ship shuddered as its inertial compensators tried to keep up with the thrust of the emergency power setting.

Missiles roared away from the ship on the bearing of the enemy ship. Without radar or laser targeting, the missiles would have to find the ship using their onboard systems. They wouldn't have their normal range, thought Bullig, but maybe they'd get lucky.

The screens flashed as the first mine intercepted them, but the force of its explosion was absorbed by the shields. A second volley of missiles left the ship.

"Transit in three," called the helmsman, "two...one...mark!"

The *Mangler* was gone. It had only been in the Solar System for 56 seconds.

Bridge, TSS *Vella Gulf,* Stargate #1, Solar System, December 8, 2020

"Missiles inbound!" called the DSO. "I have 10 vampires inbound!"

"Defend the ship, DSO," said Captain Sheppard. "You are cleared to engage."

"Cleared to engage, aye," replied the defensive systems officer. "Missile hatches open. Laser hatches open; mounts extending." The ship's lasers were normally stored inside the hull to prevent damage to them during transit and were physically extended when needed. "Standing by to launch counter-missiles." He watched his screen as the missiles continued inbound. "6 million miles...5 million miles...launching counter missiles." He pushed a button. 27 missiles leapt from their tubes and raced to meet the incoming missiles at over 100,000 G's.

"All fighters launched and proceeding on mission," reported Calvin, getting the word from his operations officer via his implant.

"I've got a second volley being launched," said the DSO. "10 more inbound."

"I've got a solution on the Drakul ship!" called the OSO.

"*Fire!*" ordered Captain Sheppard. "Take them out!" Almost immediately, he could feel the rumble as nine large ship-killers launched.

"Second volley of counter-missile missiles away," said the DSO. "Intercept of first volley." He paused, watching his scope. "Four missiles still inbound." He moved a switch and pushed a button. "Launching missiles at second volley. Second intercept of first volley; all missiles destroyed."

"Skywatch reports that the intruder just transited out of the system," called the communications officer.

"*Fuck!*" swore the OSO, losing his target. "Do you want me to abort our missiles?" With no target, the missiles would just be a hazard as they would continue to run until they found a target or ran out of power.

"Yes," said Captain Sheppard with a sigh. "Abort the missiles."

"Second volley intercepted by counter missiles," noted the DSO. "Six vampires remaining." He paused. "Second intercept of second volley at 1.2 million miles...three missiles remaining," announced the DSO. He pushed a new button, enabling the lasers. "Damn it, these missiles are good. Lasers firing at the second volley." He grabbed the microphone to transmit on the ship-wide intercom system. *"All hands, brace for impact!"*

Bridge, Drakul Ship *Mangler*, Ross 154, December 8, 2020

As the ship reentered the Ross 154 system, a loud '*crack*' was heard from the back of the bridge. None of the crew turned to look; they already knew what had happened.

"Set course for Drakon," said Captain Bullig, looking up from the body of his former XO. Commander Chark's head hung at an odd angle, facing straight behind him. Blood spurted from two puncture wounds in his neck. Captain Bullig added, "Maximum speed," and then went back to feeding. Combat always made him hungry.

Bridge, TSS *Vella Gulf*, Stargate #1, Solar System, December 8, 2020

"Two missiles remaining!" called the DSO. "Now one. No! NO! *NO!*"

Everyone braced for impact. There was a flash on the screens, but no impact.

"What happened?" asked Captain Sheppard.

"The last missile acquired one of the fighters launching from the ship," said the DSO. "It hit *Asp 03* before the lasers could get it. They're gone."

Calvin got the word from the squadron at the same time. "That was my new XO, Lieutenant Commander Mike Fuller and his pilot

Lieutenant Jean Baker," he said. He shook his head. "I knew them both from flight school...they just checked in last week."

Chapter Three

"The Drakuls came through stern-first, with very little forward velocity," said the intelligence officer, who had viewed all of the data, "and they never quite made it into the minefield. By the time that Skywatch could get the mines moving to intercept them, the Drakuls were already gone."

"Well, they obviously got a good look at us," said Captain Sheppard.

"Yes, they did," said the intel officer. "Although the Drakuls' systems wouldn't have had time to lock onto us and get precise measurements, the Drakuls will have almost a full minute of video of us to look at. They may very well be able to identify the ship."

"What good will that do them?" asked Calvin. "The Drakuls are from another universe. Even if they captured some sort of identification database, the *Vella Gulf* is 3,000 years old. It is unlikely that we'll be in it."

"It's impossible to know," said the intel officer with a shrug. "Based on our analysis of the Drakuls' attack, their cruiser has one more missile tube in its broadside than we do. That will be something to consider if we ever go up against them again."

"You mean *when* we go up against them," replied Calvin. He looked at Captain Sheppard. "Has Fleet Command given us permission to go through the stargate after them?"

"Actually, we just got our orders," replied Captain Sheppard. "We are supposed to go back to Earth for a strategy conference and then on to Domus. Fleet Command wants the *Terra* back here ASAP."

President's Conference Room, Terran Government
Headquarters, Lake Pedam, Nigeria, December 11, 2020

Calvin was amazed at the progress that had been made on the new governmental headquarters. It had only been six months since his last visit, but in that time the entire headquarters building had been completed, as well as several of the ministerial buildings. He especially appreciated the shuttle landing pad that had been built next to the headquarters. All he had to do was fly in, land and walk over to the meeting. No pesky rental cars or baggage claims. The only thing better would be once they got the transporters working. He had heard that all of the airline and car companies were already fighting the implementation of transporters...and there wasn't even a single person who could use them yet. It figured.

Sitting down in the president's conference room, he checked his watch. He was 10 minutes early, which was right on time as far as he was concerned. You definitely did *not* want to be late to meet the president of the new world government. Looking around, he saw that he was one of the most junior people in the room. There were plenty of 'stars' denoting admirals and generals, and even a few captains walking around carrying coffee for them, but he didn't see anyone else below the rank of captain. He shrugged. The former Chief of Naval Operations for the United States, Admiral Wright, had asked him to attend, so here he was. When the head of the Terran Fleet Command tells you to jump, you ask how high. But only once you're already on the way up.

He looked at his watch. Five minutes to go. He began amusing himself by trying to figure out who else was attending the meeting. He knew who Terran President Katrina Nehru was as he had seen her on the news many times. Previously a member of India's Parliament, she had risen to take control of the world-wide government that had been formed when the aliens had announced their presence. He didn't see her here yet. That wasn't a surprise; Calvin was pretty sure her schedule was even busier than his. He only had to worry about trying to save the planet; he didn't have to figure out how to get all of the former nations to cooperate. He shuddered. That was a job he did *not* want.

He saw a dark skinned man he didn't recognize standing by the table, and he did a facial web search via implant on him. Got it. Masood Khalil from Pakistan, the secretary of state.

Before he could move on to the tall exotic woman standing next to him, a window opened up in his mind, indicating an incoming call. It was from Steropes, one of the three aliens who had made first contact with the Terrans two years previously. Calvin's experience with him had been mixed. Although Steropes had proven himself as someone to be reckoned with in combat, he had also lied and withheld information that might have been helpful to the Terrans. The three aliens, or 'Psiclopes' as they called themselves, had been found to be playing both sides for their own advantage. This included putting Calvin into bad situations to see how he would react, all in the name of some research project they were conducting. To say that their relationship was 'strained' was an understatement. A big understatement.

Still, Steropes' last conversation with Calvin had been to give him what appeared to be a sincere apology for everything he had done. Calvin decided to accept his call.

"*Hi Steropes,*" he said, as the window changed to show a picture of Steropes. "*I'm kind of busy right now. What's up?*"

"*I know you are,*" said Steropes. "*I heard that the Terran president is holding a meeting to determine the diplomatic and military way forward. There are two things that* must *be decided today. The first is that you must accompany the* Vella Gulf *in its mission to the Archons. You* must."

"*Huh,*" said Calvin. "*I didn't know that a mission had even been agreed to yet. I think the military command is trying to pull back all of our ships to defend the Earth. It's obvious that the Drakuls have found us.*"

"*It hasn't been agreed to yet,*" said Steropes, "*but it will be. There is no way that you can hold off the Drakuls by yourself. Ask Solomon. I asked the artificial intelligence to run some simulations, based on all of the information we have. It's all about ships; you don't have enough, nor do you have the capability to make enough of them before you are overrun. I am hopeful that someone will see this, as your civilization will be destroyed if you do not seek additional aid.*"

"*I don't know,*" said Calvin. "*I haven't been included in the planning, but I heard that the president is going to ask the Mrowry for aid.*"

"*I talked to Captain Yerrow,*" replied Steropes. Captain Yerrow was the commanding officer of the *Emperor's Paw*, the ship that had returned to Earth with the *Vella Gulf* on its last mission. He was also the crown prince of the Mrowry. "*He reiterated they wouldn't be able to send aid. He plans to tell the president that at the meeting.*"

"I'm surprised he even spoke to you," replied Calvin. *"They don't like you guys at all."*

"No, they don't," admitted Steropes. *"However, they do like their empire, and having you take some of the burden of defending it from them would be beneficial. I told him about the simulations I had run, hoping to get him to provide assistance to the Earth. He was greatly disturbed...but still did not believe that they would be able to do anything for you."*

"OK," said Calvin, *"I got it. Convince the president of the world, who doesn't even know me, to release one of only three ships we have available to defend our planet. We're supposed to go on a journey to a star system that we have never been to, talk to a race that we have never met, and get them to provide aid against our common foe. Have I got all of that right?"*

"Yes," said Steropes, *"that is correct."* Calvin shook his head, for a culture that had made so many tremendous advances, sarcasm usually went right over their heads.

Calvin laughed. *"There shouldn't be any problem, then. What's the second thing? Get the Chinese to come along?"* To date, the only major nation that hadn't joined the Terran World Government was China, who was holding out for a number of reasons.

"No," said Steropes, *"it is much easier than that. You must take me along with you when you go."*

"WHAT?" asked Calvin. From the number of heads that turned to look at him, he realized that he had spoken out loud in his surprise. He made sure that he only spoke over the implant as he continued. *"You guys screwed us. Why in the world would we take you along with us? So that you could find out more of our secrets to use against us? You've got to be out of your fucking mind if you think I'm going to put you into that kind of position of trust again. Besides, aren't you building up your media empire? Can you afford to leave that?"*

Calvin had seen that the Psiclopes were working to start the first implant shopping and entertainment network. When Calvin had first turned on his implant, there had been selections for Shopping, Entertainment, News, Sports, Education, Military, Search and Tools, but Shopping, Entertainment, News and Sports had been grayed out. When he had asked why that was, he had been told that they weren't at a 'civilized' planet that had access to all of those networks. All of the grayed out selections had become active a couple of weeks ago. When Calvin had asked someone about them, he had been told that the Psiclopes had started a new entertainment network.

"You have me confused with Arges," said Steropes. *"With more and more of the Terrans getting implants, and no one in the government or military ever going to trust him again, Arges decided to start an information and shopping implant network. He sold a bunch of his heirlooms to build up some capital and bought a run on the Class 2 replicator on the moon. He used his time to make several artificial intelligences that he is using to run the networks. He has both an internet and an implant marketplace that already have more traffic than the Terran Shopping Network. He is hoping to be outselling Amazon by the end of the year."*

"And people are actually coming to him to get the news?" asked Calvin.

"You'd be surprised," said Steropes. *"People want to hear what he has to say, regardless of what the topic is. Not only is his news network outperforming CNN, he has people calling all of the time to give him secret information about various programs, both legal and illegal. If he wanted, he could leak more secrets than Wikileaks and Edward Snowden combined."*

"That's not good," said Calvin, who knew that the Psiclopes lived to collect information they could use later. To them, information was the best currency. Calvin would have to say something to whoever ran the world government's version of the FBI...or maybe the sen-

ate...or someone. Arges obviously needed to be reined in. "*Why are you telling me this?*" Calvin finally asked.

"*I'm telling you because I am not a part of it,*" said Steropes. "*As you know, my wife Parvati believed in doing the right thing. Over the last several months, I have had a lot of time to contemplate the meaning of life, and I believe that she was the one on the right track. I have rededicated my life to following in her footsteps. I want to go because I want to help you. It is the only way to make up for what I have done. If you will let me go, I will give you the benefit of my 5,000 years of galactic experience. I will not hold anything back, nor try to slant things to make you choose one path or another. I give you my word that I will only tell you the truth from now on.*"

"*The truth, huh?*" asked Calvin. "*That would be pretty refreshing...maybe even enough to let you come with us if we end up going to meet with the Archons. There's only one problem.*"

"*How can you trust me?*" asked Steropes.

"*That's the one I was thinking of,*" agreed Calvin. "*You've lied and skated around the truth so many times, it's second nature to you. How can I know you will only tell the truth? I'd ask you to swear on it, but I have no idea what is important enough to make it a meaningful vow.*"

"*I will swear on the soul of Parvati,*" said Steropes. "*Someday I hope to meet her again; the only way I will ever do so is to make all of the wrong things I've done right again.*"

"*OK,*" said Calvin, "*Let's try this once. Tell me about the Archons.*"

"*What would you like to know?*" asked Steropes. "*I have been to their home planet once and have interacted with them on several occasions, including twice here on Earth.*"

"WHAT?" For the second time, heads turned. Calvin waved them off with another apology. Steropes must really be serious, he thought. He's never been this forthright before. "*When were the Archons here?*"

"*They were here around 1500 B.C. and then again around 800 B.C.,*" said Steropes. "*We asked them to come and help with different invaders that had come to your planet.*"

"*Would I have heard of either of these?*" Calvin asked.

"*Yes,*" Steropes replied. *The rakshasas were so horrific they still exist within Indian lore.*"

Calvin ran a quick internet search and found that the rakshasas were creatures from Hindu mythology. They were reputed to be insatiable cannibals who liked drinking blood from human skulls. Yuck. Some were thought to have the ability to fly or to change their shapes at will.

"*Geez,*" said Calvin. "*Another creature that wants to eat us?*"

"*That is correct,*" said Steropes. "*They are nasty, disgusting creatures. Unfortunately, one of their powers is the ability to charm individuals. We asked the Archons to come and help us get rid of them, because they are not easily influenced.*"

"*Wait a minute,*" said Calvin. "*The race that we're going to go ask for aid isn't easily influenced?*"

"*That is correct,*" said Steropes. "*As a race, they are some of the most single-minded people I have ever met. They do believe in doing the right thing, though, so they came and helped rid Earth of the rakshasas, but not before the rakshasas had eaten enough people to make it into Hindu mythology.*"

"*What else can you tell me about the Archons?*" asked Calvin. He was enjoying getting straight answers from a Psiclops for a change.

"*The Archons are another of the founding races of the Alliance of Civilizations,*" said Steropes. "*They are humanoid in appearance and are about seven feet tall with long, white-blond hair.*"

"Tall and white hair," repeated Calvin. *"Got it. Anything else?"*

"Yes," said Steropes. *"They also have wings."*

"Wings?" asked Calvin. *"Seven feet tall with wings? That sounds just like..."*

"Angels," answered Steropes. *"Yes...they look just like angels."*

"Enough," said Calvin. *"I don't think I want to know any more."* He noticed everyone was moving toward their seats; the meeting appeared to be about to start. Sure enough, everyone stood as the president walked in. *"Look, I've got to go,"* he said. *"The president is here."*

"So I can go with you?" asked Steropes hopefully.

"I don't know," said Calvin. *"I don't make the decisions."*

"But you'll ask them for me?" Steropes asked.

"I don't know," replied Calvin. *"Let me think about it."*

"OK," said Steropes, disappointment heavy in his voice. He played his last card. *"Once, you trusted me to fight alongside you inside a Mayan pyramid,"* he said. *"I told you I would be able to help, and that I would save Terran lives. I don't know how many lives I saved that day, but it was probably most of the platoon, if not all of it. You trusted me then; I would ask that you trust me now, if for no other reason than in remembrance of that day."*

"I remember it," said Calvin. *"Like I said, I'll think about it."* The window to Steropes closed.

The conference room had filled up while he was talking with Steropes, Calvin noted. The space itself was unlike any other he had ever been in. At its center was a table which could easily seat 20 people to a side. Behind it on both sides, the floor of the room sloped upward, with 10 rows of stadium seating. It was almost like a mini-parliament. The leaders could sit around the table, with plenty of room for their staffs or other experts that might be needed. Although most of the people at the table had implants which would translate any Terran language, all of the seating in the room had jacks that allowed users to plug in and get a running translation of the conversation, provided by a small artificial intelligence that had been replicated for that purpose. It also kept notes and logs of all of the conversations within the room, unless told not to.

At one end of the table sat the leaders of the Terran Government. In addition to the president seated at the head of the table, Calvin also recognized the vice president, the secretary of state and guessed that the tall woman he had seen earlier was the speaker of one of the houses of parliament. Their staffers completely filled all of the rows behind them and encroached into the seating of the other participants.

On one side of the table sat several members from Epsilon Eridani. The planet Domus in that star system supported two races, which had come together to form their own world government so they could join the Republic of Terra. Calvin could see the princesses from both of the planet's races in attendance. One of these was humanoid, with members that could generally pass as human, although they tended to look a little more Cro-Magnon. The other race, the kuji, was a race of lizards that looked like six feet tall versions of the tyrannosaurus rex. As the kuji were unable to sit comfortably in the Terran chairs, an enterprising craftsman had built a modified stool with a back that let them relax without getting their tails caught up.

Calvin could also see Second Lieutenant Contreras in the seating behind the kuji princess. Previously a member of Calvin's platoon, Contreras had become good friends with the princess after he saved her life. He was currently serving as the head of her security forces.

On the other side of the table sat the Mrowry contingent, led by Captain Yerrow and Commander Andowwn, the commanding officer and executive officer of the Mrowry cruiser *Emperor's Paw*. Although Captain Yerrow had served as the executive officer of the TSS *Terra* when it had first been acquired by the fleet, he had relinquished that position to a Terran officer once there were a sufficient number of implanted humans.

The Fleet Command staff sat at the end of the table opposite the president, led by its head, Admiral James Wright. Calvin had met Admiral Wright during the Sino-American War of 2018. Although their working relationship had been strained at first, the admiral was aware of most of Calvin's accomplishments and looked in on him from time to time, like admirals will often do for their prodigies. Several representatives from the *Vella Gulf*, the only Terran spaceship currently in-system, sat with the staff. Calvin had originally been invited to sit at the table, but had been moved to the first row of the stadium seating when the Terran government higher-ups had claimed a greater number of seats than expected. He had moved a little higher on his own accord as more and more 'stars' had come in.

"Thank you all for coming today," said Terran President Katrina Nehru. In addition to the hidden microphones and speakers that transmitted her voice, it was also being sent over the implant network so Calvin had no problems hearing her, even though he was at the opposite end of the room and removed from the table. She looked around the crowded conference room and smiled. "I guess that one of the perks of being president of the world," she said, "is that when you ask for a meeting everyone shows up on time." Several polite chuckles could be heard throughout the room.

"I asked for all of you to come here today," she continued in a more serious tone, "so that we could formulate a coherent strategy for the defense of the Solar System. Admiral Wright, could you please give us a status report?"

While Admiral Wright began summing up the battle at Stargate #1, Calvin had a thought. *"Solomon, Calvin,"* he commed to the artificial intelligence (AI) onboard the *Vella Gulf. "Are you receiving me?"*

"I am receiving you," answered the AI. *"I am currently orbiting overhead. What can I do for you?"*

"I understand that Steropes had you run some simulations," said Calvin. *"Is that correct?"*

"Yes," replied Solomon, *"I did not have any prohibitions on that, and the ones he asked me to run were not of a classified nature. Am I no longer allowed to interact with him?"*

"No," said Calvin, *"it's OK to talk to him. His status is still being evaluated. Can you tell me about the simulations?"*

"Certainly, Calvin," answered Solomon. *"He asked me to run simulations on when the Drakuls would be likely to return, and what size force they would show up with. Based on information I received from the* Emperor's Paw, *I tried to answer those questions for him."*

"And what did you determine?" asked Calvin.

"There are several caveats I must make before I give you the results," advised Solomon. *"First, there is not much data on the new Drakuls on which to base the simulations, so I used historical data from the original race of Drakuls. They may act differently, but I cannot control for this. Second, I have no access to their order of battle, other than what the Archons had passed on to the Mrowry as of two years ago. They may have more ships or less than what I am using, which would speed up or slow down their fleet's movements. Third, I do not have access to the current situation at 54 Piscium, where the Drakuls and the Archons are fighting, which would also be a major factor in their planning. These things will have a major effect on the simulation's outcome."*

"*Got it,*" said Calvin. "*With those caveats, what did you determine?*"

"*The Drakuls will be back between five and nine months from now,*" said Solomon. "*They will return with at least one dreadnought, eight battleships and 16 battlecruisers, as well as a number of smaller ships. A host of cruisers will lead the assault, sacrificing themselves to clear out the Terran minefield. They will be met by two to three Terran battleships and five battlecruisers. The battle will be fierce, with neither side asking for or giving quarter. The Terran forces will be destroyed, and the Drakul forces will still have two battleships, five battlecruisers and eight cruisers left over. The Earth will be conquered and become a pastureland for Drakul food harvesters.*" Damn, thought Calvin. If they brought a dreadnought, Terra was in trouble because dreadnoughts were bigger than anything Terra had in its inventory. Way bigger. He doubted they could stop one if it showed up.

"*Is that a sure thing?*" asked Calvin. "*How many times did you run the simulation?*"

"*I ran it 3,869 times,*" said Solomon. "*In over 30% of them, the Drakuls also destroyed at least part of the planet during the battle, launching missiles at it to split the focus of the defending forces.*"

"*So,*" Calvin asked, "*How many did we win?*"

"*None of them,*" replied Solomon. "*In most cases, all of the Terran spaceships were destroyed within the first hour.*"

"*Damn,*" said Calvin. "*Did Steropes ask you about what happened if we got aid?*"

"*Yes, he did,*" replied Solomon. "*If the Archons respond with aid, you were more likely to survive the initial assault.*"

"*How likely?*" asked Calvin, noticing that Admiral Wright was finishing up.

"*If the Archons respond with aid, you have a 5% chance of surviving the initial assault,*" replied Solomon.

"*Thanks,*" said Calvin. "*I've gotta go. Could you please push that info to Admiral Wright of Fleet Command? Tell him it's something I said he needs for this discussion.*" Calvin knew that the admiral had gotten his implants a week ago. A gift from the Psiclopes, implants allowed recipients to download information directly to their brains, as well as to talk to each other via a special communications network. Calvin doubted that getting bad news in the middle of a briefing was one of the reasons the admiral wanted them.

"Thank you for the recap of the battle," said President Nehru. She looked around to see if there were any questions. When she saw none, she asked, "What are Fleet Command's intentions to ensure that we are equally successful next time?"

The admiral didn't answer. When she looked down the table she could see his eyes slightly unfocused and a frown on his face. She recognized the look of someone that just got implants carrying on a conversation. The fact that he took the call in the middle of a presidential meeting meant that it was either incredibly important, or he had requested information about the topic of conversation from someone outside the conference. With a start, his eyes focused, and he realized that everyone was waiting on him.

"I'm sorry, madam president," he said, trying to recover. "I...um...asked for some simulations to be run to project what the Drakuls would do next, and I just got the results." He took a breath and released it, trying to put off the news as long as he could. "They're not good," he said finally.

The president frowned. "Could you please be a little more specific on what 'not good' means?" she asked.

"The AI onboard the *Vella Gulf* ran several thousand simulations on what the Drakuls would most likely do, based on historical information and the data passed on to us by the Mrowry," Admiral Wright explained. "The AI thinks that they will be back in force, as early as five months from now, with enough ships to break into the system and subdue it."

President Nehru noticed the Mrowry officers nodding their head, which she had been told was a practice that both races had in common. "I see you nodding your head, Captain Yerrow," she said. "Do you have something to add?"

"I'm sorry to be the bearer of bad tidings," replied Captain Yerrow, "but we ran the same simulations onboard our ship. The results were the same, with one small difference. Our AI only gives you four months before their return." There was a general intake of breath from around the table and plenty of scared looks, especially from the civilians.

"Well, that outcome is not acceptable to me," stated the president in a matter-of-fact tone of voice. "I will not be both the first and last president of this republic. There are always choices and options. What did the AIs say we could do to ensure our survival? Do we need more mines? More ships? What do we need to do or build?" The matter-of-fact voice gave way slightly at the end, Calvin saw. He couldn't blame her; he felt the same way.

"Barring help from an outside source," said Captain Yerrow, "it is nearly certain that you will be overrun. Like Admiral Wright, we ran our simulation several thousand times, and the outcome was always the same. For the record, even if you receive outside aid, it is still unlikely that you will defeat them."

"Unacceptable," said the president, the steel back in her backbone. "If it is friends we must have, then it is friends that we will get. What aid can we expect from the Mrowry?"

Captain Yerrow and Commander Andowwn looked at each other, talking via implant. After a couple of seconds, Captain Yerrow turned to face the president. "I do not know what aid my father will be able to send," he said. "It is unlikely to be much, if anything."

"Well, what about if you stayed here?" asked Masood Khalil, the Pakistani secretary of state. "Would your ship help turn the tide against the Drakuls?"

Captain Yerrow gave the Mrowry version of a smile. It involved a lot of teeth and was very intimidating up close. "One cruiser, no matter how good it is, will not stop a Drakul battlecruiser, much less a battleship. Our lives would be better spent trying to make it back to ask my father for aid. In all honesty, should we actually be successful and make it back, there is not much of a chance that he will have aid to spare. When we left, we were being hard-pressed on all sides."

"Then we will have to go to the other race that is currently fighting the Drakuls," said the president. "What do we know about them?"

"They are the Archons," said Captain Yerrow. "I do not know if you will have any more success with them than you will with my father, but aid is more likely to be found there than at our capital of Grrrnow."

"Then we will go there, as well," said the president. She looked at the secretary of state. "Put together a mission that goes first to the home world of the Mrowry and then to the home world of the Archons. Make sure that your best person is on it."

"Just like the *Vella Gulf's* last mission," said Khalil, "our best ambassador remains Juliette Ricketts-Smith. She did good work on their last mission and has the benefit of already having been to the stars once."

"Great," said the president. She looked around the table at the Terrans and the delegation for Domus. "So we are agreed that the *Vella Gulf* will go to meet with the Archons?" She saw heads nodding around the table. She looked at Admiral Wright. "Until they get back, that leaves us with a battleship, a battlecruiser and the Mrowry cruiser until we can get the new replicator making ships?"

"That is correct," said Admiral Wright.

Before he could add anything else, Captain Yerrow cleared his throat. "I'm sorry, but we will not be staying here. When the *Vella Gulf* leaves for Grrrnow, we will be taking the *Emperor's Paw* back to our home world, too."

"I see," the president said. "I guess Terra stands alone, then."

"Not alone," said the prince. "I will be leaving as many of my warriors as I can spare to help train the crew of the *Terra,* and the rest of us will be with you in spirit. I will also leave some pilots to help train your pilots in space fighter combat, but it is imperative that I leave. I know for sure that my father will not aid you if I am not there, as your civilization is unknown to him. If there is any aid to be had, it will only be given if I am there to vouch for you."

The president had previously served as the chairman of the upper house of India's parliament and was used to making decisions. "Go with my blessings, then," she said, "and help convince your father to send whatever aid he can. If you can also do something to help with the Archons, I would appreciate that, as well." She looked at the rest of the group in attendance. "What other things can we do to help improve our readiness? What aren't we doing that we should be?"

"If I may," said the only person seated with Fleet Command wearing civilian clothes. Calvin recognized Andrew Brown, the person who ran the Fleet's Material Management Network. Also known as 'Replicator Command,' its sole purpose was to ensure the Republic of Terra's two replicators ran as efficiently as possible. The replicators were alien devices with the ability to rapidly assemble anything they had the blueprints for. They functioned somewhat like transporters in that they broke things down to their most basic level and then reassembled them. You couldn't get something for nothing, though; whatever material you wanted the finished product to be made of had to be loaded into the replicator first. Before coming to work for Replicator Command, Andrew Brown had been the plant manager for Boeing's Airplane Programs Manufacturing Site in Renton, Washington. Although no human had experience running replicators, he had a wealth of experience managing massive aircraft production facilities.

The Republic of Terra had a Class 2 replicator that the *Vella Gulf* brought back from its first mission and a Class 6 that it brought back from its second. Although the Class 2 was only able to build things up to the size of a space fighter or shuttle, the Class 6 was enormous. Just over a mile long and about 1,500 feet in diameter, it could build anything up to the size of a battleship, if you had about two and a half months to do it. The Terrans didn't have that kind of time. Both the *Terra* and the *Vella Gulf* also had smaller replicators onboard that could be used for making things for their ship's company, like the crew's combat suits, weapons, and implants. The *Vella Gulf* had one of the smaller replicators; the *Terra* had three.

"Yes?" asked the president. "You are...?"

"I'm Andrew Brown, ma'am," he said. "I run the replicators for Fleet Command. I'm not sure if it's my place to say it or not, but the best thing that you could do to help us would be to get China to come onboard with us. They have a wealth of materials we need to build more ships. If we're going to stand alone, we're going to need to stand together as a planet, *with* the Chinese."

"We have tried repeatedly to do that," said the president, "but they don't want to be a part of this. They won't even talk to us. They have withdrawn to their country and won't receive our diplomats. Do you have some insight into how we can get them to join us?"

"No ma'am, I don't," said Brown. "I'm no politician. I just make airplanes...well, now it's space planes. You asked what we needed; we need access to their resources."

The Terran government staff all looked at each other in frustration. They had *tried* to get China to join the government. Repeatedly. But whether it was because of their recent loss in the war with America, or because it was later found that they had been led astray by one of the Psiclopes and they were embarrassed by the loss of face, they hadn't wanted to participate in the world government.

An awkward silence followed as they spoke among themselves via implant. Finally Calvin couldn't take it any longer. He stood up. "I think I have an idea that might work," he said in a loud voice, "but it involves using Steropes to help convince them." Several heads immediately began shaking, including all of the Mrowry. The Psiclopes had broken the trust of the Mrowry and had thrown the universe into the state of war it was in; the Mrowry wanted nothing to do with the oath breakers.

"Well, here's the deal," said Calvin before anyone could say anything that couldn't be taken back. "I think he can convince them to join the government. We need the resources that the Chinese have, whether that is the rare Earth elements they have stockpiled, which we need," Brown began nodding his head, "or whether it is their manpower. Right now, nearly 20% of Earth's manpower is sitting idly by, when it could be working to build the things the Earth needs to defend itself. *We need the Chinese!* For those of you that don't know me, I'm Lieutenant Commander Hobbs. I was heavily involved in the war against the Chinese when they invaded Seattle. They shot down my airplane and killed many of my friends. If I can say that we need them, we need them."

Calvin looked at the end of the table where the Fleet Command leaders and the commanding officer of the *Vella Gulf* sat. "If I can make this happen," he said, "Steropes is going to want to come with us on the trip to meet with the Archons. I want him to come; I think his experience will be extremely valuable."

Now the Terran heads were shaking, too. Everyone in the room had bad experiences with the Psiclopes. He tried again. "I've been in combat with him," said Calvin, "and I know him better than anyone. He says that he wants to help us, and I believe him. He's even willing to tell us about all of the shady deals Arges is currently putting together. I want to bring him, and I will personally vouch for him."

Admiral Wright had come to rely on Calvin's judgment. It had served him well during the war, and he knew that Calvin was an excellent judge of people. While the admiral didn't believe the rumor going around that Calvin was the reborn spirit of the Greek god Zeus, he knew that Calvin was often in the center of things when they went to shit, and had always come through them smelling of roses. If Calvin thought that the little bastard was salvageable, Steropes could go with him. At least that meant there was one fewer Psiclopes in the Solar System, which made his own life easier. "OK," said Admiral Wright. "If he can convince the Chinese to join the world government, and you want to vouch for him, he can go."

"Thank you sir," said Calvin. "I'll get right on it." He turned to leave.

"Calvin?" asked Admiral Wright.

"Yes sir?" asked Calvin, turning around.

"I hope you know what you're doing," said Admiral Wright.

"Yes sir," said Calvin. "Me too." He turned and left. If nothing else, Calvin thought, at least it gets me out of this meeting.

Transporter Room, TSS *Vella Gulf*, Earth Orbit, December 11, 2020

"Thanks for joining me," said Calvin as Steropes beamed in. He had been waiting for the Psiclops to join him in the *Vella Gulf's* transporter room. The room was a circular space about 25 feet in diameter. It had a raised platform with 12 circular metal plates covering about 2/3 of it and a control console on the right as you entered the room.

"No problem," replied Steropes, stepping off the platform. "It's good to be back on the *Vella Gulf* again."

"As it turns out," said Calvin, "the meeting went down pretty much as you thought it would. They are going to send the *Vella Gulf* to the home world of the Archons."

"Archonis," said Steropes.

"What?" asked Calvin.

"Archonis is the home world of the Archons," said Steropes. "That is where their capital is."

"Oh," said Calvin. "I guess that's where we're going then."

"Will I be allowed to come?" asked Steropes.

"That is still to be determined," replied Calvin. "I'll be honest with you; there are a *lot* of people that don't want you around."

"That is understandable," acknowledged Steropes, "although I wasn't the one responsible for most of the things of which the Psiclopes have been accused. It is all guilt by association."

"Be that as it may," replied Calvin, "the sentiment remains. I did, however, get them to give you a chance. If you can help me with one thing, you'll be allowed to accompany us."

"What is the one thing?" asked Steropes. "Slay a dragon? Storm a castle? I've done those things, but not in a couple thousand years, so I'm probably a little rusty."

"No," answered Calvin. "Nothing like that." Maybe the Psiclops *did* understand sarcasm, after all. "I'm hoping that combat won't be necessary...although there is a chance that it might if we screw this up. The Terran government wants China to join up."

"Really?" asked Steropes. "Let me guess. You are short of some element and want China to join because they have it?"

"Well, resources are certainly part of the reason why," admitted Calvin. "It would also be nice to have their billion inhabitants working with us. If we're going to be overrun shortly, we need everyone we can get. We especially need the Chinese. Can you help with this or not?"

"Of course I can help," replied Steropes. "The Psiclopes caused this problem; it is only right that we fix it. It may actually be easier than you think to fix. May I use the transporter a moment or two? There is something I need to get."

"Umm, sure, I guess," said Calvin. "Why are you asking me?"

"Because I am currently banned from using the transporter, by order of the *Vella Gulf's* commanding officer," replied Steropes. "I need someone to authorize me to use it again."

"That is true," said Solomon, the *Vella Gulf's* AI. "He is currently prohibited from using the transporter without authorization. I only transported Steropes up because you said it was all right."

"Solomon, I have authorization from Admiral Wright to accomplish this task," said Calvin. "Steropes is authorized to use the transporter."

"Thank you," Steropes said. He went back over to the transport platform and stood on one of the grids. After a couple of seconds, he appeared to stretch toward the ceiling and then vanished.

Calvin waited a couple of minutes, but nothing happened.

He waited another couple of minutes, wondering if he had made a mistake by granting Steropes complete access to the transporter. If he had gone somewhere unauthorized and was into mischief...

"Hey, umm, Solomon...where'd he go?" Calvin finally asked.

"Steropes is currently in Nepal," replied Solomon. "I believe there is a cave high up in the Himalayas that the Psiclopes use to store their items. He is returning."

On the transporter platform, one of the grids appeared active. A smear appeared that initially went from floor to ceiling, but coalesced into Steropes, holding a bundle wrapped in plastic. He took off the plastic to reveal a very normal-looking briefcase.

"What is that?" Calvin asked.

"It's a briefcase," Steropes replied. "It's also the answer to your problem. If you would please join me here on the platform?"

"Wait," said Calvin. "We're not beaming somewhere, are we? I can't beam, can I? I haven't been surveyed or scanned or whatever it is. Fleet Command said that no one was to beam until we got scanned, so that we didn't lose anyone unnecessarily." When the Terrans had first taken control of the *Vella Gulf*, the Psiclopes had told them that a person needed to be surveyed by some sort of molecular scanner prior to using the transporter. That ensured the person being transported would be reassembled correctly at the other end of the trip and would end up where he was supposed to be. Too high and you would fall to the floor; too low and your body would become mixed with the ground. If you ended up beaming into a space that held an object, it would become part of your body. All of these were painful; most of them were also fatal.

"Well, yes, it would be better if we had done that first," said Steropes, "but the chances of something bad happening are less than 1%. The Psiclopes have made this trip on a number of occasions, so it is pretty safe. Unless you're really, really unlucky, everything will be fine. Do you want to get this done, or not?"

"I've got a bad feeling," said Calvin. He stepped onto the platform and walked over to the pad indicated by Steropes. "Are you sure about this?"

"I'm almost positive," said Steropes with a smile.

"Almost?" Calvin asked as he stepped onto the grid.

"Initiate," said Steropes. Calvin felt stretched...

President's Bedroom, Beijing, China, December 11, 2020

And then he was in a bedroom, judging by the snoring, although it was hard to tell in the dark. "Damn it," Calvin said as he fell six inches to the floor.

"See?" asked Steropes. "Nothing to it. Unless you were really unlucky, nothing bad was going to happen."

There was a grunt close by. The snoring stopped, and a light turned on. Calvin saw that he was indeed in a bedroom, a very ornate and well-appointed one. "What is the meaning of this?" a voice asked in Chinese. A man sat up in the bed. Calvin recognized him. The man was Jiang Jiabao, the President of the People's Republic of China.

Seeing Steropes, the man yelled, "You!" in a very loud voice.

Steropes quickly said, "Yes, we would like to talk to you privately." He held up the briefcase. "I have the pictures for you."

Someone began beating on the door. "Are you all right, Mr. President?" a voice asked.

The president hopped out of bed and walked quickly to the door. He motioned Calvin and Steropes to move to where they couldn't be seen, and then he opened the door, just as the armed guard outside was opening it with a key.

"I am fine," said the president. "I was just having a bad dream. I will probably watch TV for a little while to relax before going back to sleep. Good night." He closed the door and locked it. Reaching up, he turned on what looked like a genuine Mrowry Tri-D TV that was mounted on the wall. They may have withdrawn from politics, but their espionage network still seemed to be functioning quite well, Calvin noted. The president turned and motioned for Calvin and Steropes to join him next to it.

"Those are my pictures?" he asked Steropes.

"Yes," agreed Steropes. "All of them."

"And what do I have to do this time?" the president asked.

"Wait a minute," said Calvin. "What is this? Blackmail?"

"Yes," answered the president, "they have been blackmailing me. You expect me to believe that you weren't part of it? Wait! I recognize you. You are the American hero that stopped the attack. Of course! You're in on it."

"No, Mr. President, I was completely unaware of this before now," replied Calvin. "I was just at a meeting of the Terran government, and we need your nation to join us if we are to have a chance of defending our world. There are aliens coming that will destroy us all. I knew you were deceived into attacking the United States, and that the Psiclopes had something to do with it. I asked Steropes if he might know of a way to get you to join the Terran Federation. He said that he did, and then he beamed us here, but he has yet to tell me why."

"Arges was blackmailing him," said Steropes. He turned to the president. "I never knew what leverage Arges had over you Mr. President, but something he said to me after we were banned from the *Vella Gulf* got me thinking. He said something like, 'well, I can still make the Chinese dance,' or something like that, so I knew he had something. It wasn't hard to figure out what, once I asked the *Vella Gulf's* AI a couple of questions. Personally, I am sorry he did this to you." He handed the president the briefcase.

"Don't you want me to promise to join before you give me this?" the president asked. "What are you not telling me?"

"I am not hiding anything," answered Steropes. "I am here to right a wrong that was done to you. I can't make what Arges did right, but I can at least remove the hold he had over you."

"So I am free to choose to join or not, as I alone decide?" asked the president.

"Yes," said Steropes, "although I hope you will choose to join. The need is dire. We expect the planet to be overrun sometime within the next six months."

"Then we had better get moving," said the president, tossing the briefcase onto the bed. "Although we withdrew politically, we have kept tabs on what was going on, and we are aware of the Drakul menace. We knew that you would need us eventually, and have been mining and storing all of the raw materials we could. I knew that one day the need would be terrible enough that you would come to us; I wanted to be prepared for that day."

"You wouldn't happen to have any thulium," Calvin asked, "would you?"

"That is one of the so-called 'rare Earth elements?" the president asked.

"Yes, it is," Calvin replied.

"Then we should have at least a ton of it," the president answered. "We have at least a ton of all of them. There's just one thing."

Calvin's eyes narrowed. "What's one more thing?"

"I will give you all of these things," the president responded, "and we will join the world government, but I want one thing in return. I know that you are about to leave on a mission. I want my son to be part of it. He has about 2,500 hours of flight time in tactical jets. I think he would make a nice addition to your squadron."

"Umm, I don't have any say in that," Calvin replied. "All of the manning is done by a selection board."

"You were able to get the government to let Steropes go along with you," the president said with what could only be called a sly grin. "I think you ought to be able to get Fang in, as well. See what you can do. I would hate for all of the thulium we have stockpiled to go to waste."

Transporter Room, TSS *Vella Gulf*, Earth Orbit, December 11, 2020

"**D**amn it!" Calvin swore as he fell a foot to the floor of the transporter room. "This shit's no fun. I'd almost *rather* take a shuttle than beam someplace if I'm going to fall every time I transport."

"Sorry about that," Steropes replied. "I asked Solomon to aim a foot high. Better you fall a little bit than materialize too low. Until you get surveyed, it was just a good precaution."

"Wait a minute," Calvin said, "You told him to aim a foot high? I only fell about six inches when we beamed down. If I'd have materialized a foot lower..."

"It would have been really painful," answered Steropes. "Good thing you weren't really unlucky today, isn't it?"

"Fuck!" swore Calvin. "That's not funny. You could have killed me!"

"It was very unlikely," Steropes replied. "Solomon's beamings are within a foot of 'on target' in 99.3% of transits. You were fine. Besides, we needed to do it."

"We did," Calvin agreed. "But next time, how about telling me, so that I at least have a say in whether or not I kill myself?" Calvin asked.

Chapter Four

"Hey Skipper," Calvin said. "What's going on? I just heard that we're not leaving on time."

"That's true," said Captain James Sheppard, the commanding officer of the *Vella Gulf*. Recently promoted to captain, he had also been named the ship's permanent commanding officer. Sheppard had returned from the last mission as the ship's acting commanding officer, a position he assumed when all of the officers senior to him left to take command of the newly acquired, larger ships. "We were just starting our final checks when we got word from Fleet Command that we needed to wait for the shuttle that's coming up. They also said that we would need to take on additional fuel, but neither message said where it was coming from, nor where we were supposed to put it, since our bunkers are already full. I guess we'll find out when the shuttle gets here."

"I wasn't aware there was a shuttle coming," Calvin replied. As the squadron commander for the ship's space fighters and shuttles, normally he was aware of all of the flights into or out of the *Vella Gulf*. He mentally checked the daily flight schedule again. Nope, not there. "The flight isn't on the flight schedule. When is it due in? Where's it coming from?"

"I don't know where it's coming from," Captain Sheppard replied. "I wasn't told. But it should be here soon."

"Solomon," Calvin said, "can you tell me the point of origin for the shuttle that is coming?"

"My sensors show that it left from the area of Alice Springs, Australia," replied the AI, "however my records do not show a facility of any kind in that area."

"Hmmm...," said Captain Sheppard. "I've heard rumors about—"

"The shuttle is here," advised Solomon, before Captain Sheppard could say anything else. He looked over to see a faraway look in Calvin's eyes as he communicated with someone via implant.

"The shuttle only had one person on it," reported Calvin. "The squadron said the lieutenant's name is Peter Finn. Apparently, he's some kind of special combat systems engineer that brought something up for us. The lieutenant has asked if the senior officers would meet him in your conference room for some sort of presentation."

CO's Conference Room, TSS _Vella Gulf_, Earth Orbit, December 13, 2020

Calvin and Captain Sheppard walked into the conference room to find the lieutenant already there, which was surprising because he had about four times the distance to travel. As the lieutenant turned around, Calvin could only think of one word. Nerd. He was medium height with dark hair slightly longer than regulations permitted, and he had thick-rimmed glasses that would probably have worked better at birth control than condoms. If he had seen the Sun in the last decade or so, it wasn't apparent from the pallor of his skin. He also looked like he was about 16 years old, far too young to be in uniform, much less a lieutenant.

Before either could say anything, the lieutenant walked over and stuck out his hand to Calvin. His walk was weird, Calvin noted, almost like he was dragging his right foot. "Good afternoon, Lieutenant Commander Hobbs," he said, his speech faster than normal. "It is such a pleasure to meet you. I have read all of your reports. Very exciting. Did you really kill the god Quetzalcoatl with a spear? Of course you did. It was in the report. You have always had access to the best and newest equipment, so it was really surprising that you used a spear to kill him. I wish that I could have been with you when you first met the aliens. It must have been really cool to be the first person to get to use alien technology."

"Who's the new guy?" asked army captain Paul 'Night' Train, walking into the room. Night was the XO of the special forces platoon that Calvin commanded, in addition to his job of being the *Gulf's* squadron commander.

"I don't know," said Calvin. "He hasn't stopped talking long enough for us to find out anything about him."

"Oh! Of course! We need to introduce everyone so that I can get on with my work," said Lieutenant Finn. "I must confess to being a big fan of yours. I can't imagine going to all of those places and doing all of those things. Of course, now I guess I will be going to new places and seeing new things, too. I just don't know about all of those adventures. I'm not sure that my heart will be able to take it. I'm just..."

"*What the hell are you talking about?*" growled Night loudly. He had received a wound to his voice box earlier in his career that made his voice sound gruff at the best of times. When he was annoyed, it only got worse. Like now.

"Oh! I'm doing it again!" Lieutenant Finn said. "I just get so excited sometimes that I can't help myself." He turned to focus on Night. "Oh, my goodness! Lieutenant Paul Train! Now Captain Train! The man they call 'Night.' You singlehandedly killed 27 Ssselipsssiss onboard the *Emperor's Paw*, giving you the all time record for extraterrestrials killed. The way you took down that dinobear on Keppler-22 was nothing short of amazing, too. I just can't imagine being in the same room with both of you."

Night held up a hand. "Do you have a death wish?" he asked.

"No," said Lieutenant Finn. "Why would you ask that? If anything, it would seem that you are the one that puts yourself into positions from which there is no escape, leading one to infer that—"

Night held up his hand again. "Then. Shut. Up." Night said slowly. "Or. I. Will. Kill You. Myself."

The threat worked; the lieutenant stopped talking.

Captain Sheppard used the pause to regain control. "I'm Captain Sheppard," he said. "What was so important that we needed to wait for you?"

Lieutenant Finn blinked. "Didn't anyone tell you?" he asked.

"No," Captain Sheppard replied, "Until you got here, we didn't even know you were coming."

"Oh! I get it," he said, looking around furtively. "It's a military secret, of course. We wouldn't want the word to get out that we've got it, now would we?" He looked around the room as if looking for spies.

"This ship is quite secure," said Captain Sheppard. "Whatever it is that you've brought for us, you can talk about it here."

"Really?" he asked. "Oh! OK. As promised, I've brought your stealth modules."

CO's Conference Room, TSS *Vella Gulf*, Earth Orbit, December 13, 2020

Realizing that it was going to take a while to get anything coherent from the lieutenant, Captain Sheppard called for the rest of his staff and seated everyone present at the conference table. While they were waiting for the rest of the officers to get there, they made small talk, and Lieutenant Finn explained his walk. He had been born with a tibial torsion, or twisted shin, and had dealt with it all of his life. Although the doctors thought they corrected it as a child, the twisted shin had been a recurring problem throughout his life. The doctors had no idea why.

When all of his officers were present, Captain Sheppard asked the newcomer, "Now, who are you, and who do you work for?" The lieutenant took a deep breath. "Slowly," Captain Sheppard added.

"My name is Lieutenant Peter Finn," he said, "and I am a systems engineer with the Development Section of the Office of Planning & Development (OPD)." As he looked around the table, he saw nothing but blank stares. "You haven't ever heard of OPD?" he asked.

Everyone shook their heads. "We've been kind of busy," said Captain Sheppard. "You know, fighting aliens and such. Trying to save the world."

"Oh! Yeah, I forgot," the lieutenant said. "It's hard to keep up with fleet developments when you're out of the system. Right." He paused. "You know what Department X is, though, right?"

More blank stares. "Keep trying," Captain Sheppard urged.

"Maybe I should start at the beginning?" the lieutenant asked.

Everyone nodded. "That would probably be helpful," Captain Sheppard agreed.

"When the fleet was formed," explained Lieutenant Finn, "Admiral Wright realized that we were going to need a unit that looked at the new alien technology and tried to figure out how it could be made to work for us, so he created Department X. Its main mission is to exploit all of the alien technology that we acquire." He smiled. "On behalf of Department X, I would like to thank you for bringing back so many new toys for us to play with." More blank stares.

"Don't you know what you've done for Terra?" Lieutenant Finn asked, disbelief in his voice.

"Well, let's see," said Calvin. "We've brought back a couple of ships and a couple of replicators. I guess the ships have new weapons and systems, stuff like that?"

"No," said Lieutenant Finn. "No, no, no, no, no. That's not it at all. Let's take the replicator on the moon. What does it do?"

"It makes our space fighters and shuttles," said Calvin. "I know Replicator Command also uses it to make some of our stuff if it's too big to be made in the replicator onboard. But it's only good for making things that it has a blueprint for in its data banks; you can't just think of things and get it to make them."

Lieutenant Finn was aghast. "Oh! Has no one ever told you..." he wondered. Finally, he slapped his forehead with his palm. "Sorry, I forgot, military security again. I'm still new to all of this military stuff. I only completed MIT a couple of months ago." He paused and pursed his lips. "Do any of you know how many blueprints the Class 2 replicator has in its data banks? Anyone?"

"A couple hundred?" Calvin asked.

Lieutenant Finn shook his head. "A couple of hundred *million*, maybe. We're still counting and categorizing. It may be a billion. It may be more. The bigger replicator, the one that can make a battleship, has *billions* of blueprints inside, and they are all state-of-the-art. It has the blueprints for all of the pieces to make a super dreadnought, if you wanted to take the time to assemble something three miles long. It would probably be easier to make the pieces for a Class 8 replicator, put the replicator together, and then have *it* make the super dreadnought. At least that way, you could make more super dreadnoughts if you wanted...and if you had all of the materials required. The Planning Section of OPD is working on how to do that; you'd have to ask them about it." He stopped talking, having lost his original point.

"So, we brought back lots of things for you to play with?" Calvin prompted.

"Oh! Absolutely," Lieutenant Finn said. "We have been going through the data banks trying to find things that we need or could use. When I read your last mission report, I got interested in the stealth fighters that took out the Ssselipsssiss battleship. Cool stuff, right? I wanted to be the person to figure that out, and they normally let the smart ones pick out their own projects to run with."

Lieutenant Finn did seem smart, thought Calvin, even if he didn't appear to have the common sense of most farm animals. "So, did you figure out the whole stealth thing?" Calvin prompted.

"Well, sort of, mostly," said Lieutenant Finn. "It involved a lot of new concepts and technology that our science had never come up with, and probably wouldn't have for some time. It's going to be really hard to explain. I barely understand it, so I'm pretty sure that you won't. Sorry. No offense. I'll try, though. Do you all understand the concepts of matter and energy?"

Everyone's heads nodded. At a basic level, that information was simple physics that had been downloaded to everyone as part of their basic implant package.

"Ok, so matter is the stuff that everything is made of, right?" Lieutenant Finn asked. Seeing heads nodding he continued, "Energy, however, is a property that matter has. The same amount of matter can have different amounts of energy, which lets it exist in different states. Water vapor, water and ice are the same matter, just with different amounts of energy. Are you with me so far?"

Heads nodded again. So far, pretty basic stuff.

"OK," said Lieutenant Finn, "here's where it gets complicated. Energy is more of a relative concept, and scientists always speak of energy values as being 'positive' in nature. In the past, they have always eliminated solutions that gave rise to negative energies as unphysical. Even though there is antimatter, no one ever thought that the existence of antimatter implied the existence of anti-energy. But it's there and it exists, even if it shouldn't."

"I'm not saying that I understand that," Calvin said, "because my brain doesn't understand how you can create anti-energy, but what I'd like to know is what happens when you get energy and anti-energy together. Matter and antimatter don't mix well together."

Lieutenant Finn clapped his hands happily. "See! That's just it. You've given me some wonderful toys! No one *knows* what happens. The stealth modules generate some sort of anti-energy that absorbs energy directed at it. The combination of energy and anti-energy ought to blow up, or react, or do *something*, but all we've been able to determine is that the two just vanish. Perhaps they blow up in an anti-universe? I don't know. All I know is that the stealth module works."

"We're happy to have made your life a little better," interrupted Night. "Are you getting to the point where I give a shit about theoretical physics? How does this help me kill Drakuls?"

"Oh! Help you kill Drakuls?" asked Lieutenant Finn, looking puzzled. "It doesn't help you kill anything."

"Then please tell me," growled Night even more dangerously, *"why the fuck are you wasting my time?"*

"I'm here to help you get where you need to go," said Lieutenant Finn.

"How are you going to do that?" asked Captain Sheppard.

"I figured out how to adapt the fighter stealth modules to work for a cruiser-sized ship. I'm going to make you invisible."

Bridge, TSS *Vella Gulf*, Earth Orbit, December 16, 2020

Captain Sheppard looked at the black Bengal tiger's face on the view screen. "We're finally ready to go," he said. "How are things coming over there?"

"We are just finishing up," replied Captain Yerrow. "We are sending your Lieutenant Finn back over in a shuttle. Although he was very helpful, I have to ask, does he *ever* stop talking?"

"Very rarely," Captain Sheppard replied with a grin.

"We will be ready to go in a few minutes," said Captain Yerrow. "Before we go, we had an idea that we wanted to discuss with you."

"What is it?" Captain Sheppard asked.

"We were looking at the star charts," Captain Yerrow replied, "and there are two ways to go after we reach Epsilon Eridani. One way is longer but safe; the other way is shorter, but it goes through Ssselipsssiss space. We were originally going to go the long way around to get to Grrrnow, but it is much quicker if we go the other way. We didn't think it worth mentioning previously because of the danger of running the Ssselipsssiss blockade. With the new stealth modules, though, we think that going through Ssselipsssiss space is the better option."

"Why's that?" Captain Sheppard asked.

"Well, not only is that way much shorter and faster," explained Captain Yerrow, "but going that way also allows us to find out what forces the Ssselipsssiss have on the other side of the stargate from the system that the Mrowry control. The intelligence gained could be extremely valuable in planning our nation's strategy. It may be that this info could permit my father to send ships to your aid."

"If that's the case," Captain Sheppard replied after a few seconds of thought, "then we need to try it."

"That's what I thought, too," Captain Yerrow agreed. "We can discuss it further as we go. *Emperor's Paw*, out." The front screen went black and then changed to show the Earth.

Captain Sheppard stared at the picture on the screen. It would be a while until he saw that view again, he thought while he digested what he had just heard...if ever.

Captain Sheppard turned to Calvin. "Do you have all of your folks aboard?"

Calvin nodded. "I do," he said. "Our newest member, Lieutenant Jiang Fang, shuttled up about an hour ago, along with the rest of the replacements. We'll have to get him his implants while we're underway, but I checked, and we have the supplies available."

"How did you get the Chinese to join the world government?" asked Captain Sheppard. "How did you even get a meeting with their president? I thought they withdrew from the world's politics. Did you just take a shuttle down and land in Beijing?"

"Umm, I'd really rather not talk about that, sir," Calvin replied. "Let's just say I made a few calls and leave it at that."

"And you're sure about bringing Steropes?"

"No, I'm not," said Calvin. "He's changed since he found out about the Drakuls capturing his home world. He seems angry, and yet he's worried about making things right. Those two things are a dangerous combination."

"You think he wants to go kill Drakuls?" asked Captain Sheppard.

"Without a doubt," said Calvin. "Wouldn't you? What I'm more worried about is that he wants to get himself killed in the process. I don't mind him dying that much; I'm more worried about having someone with a death wish in my platoon. When they go, they usually take out the people around them."

Squadron CO's Office, TSS *Vella Gulf*, Stargate #2, December 16, 2020

"Knock, knock," said a female voice from the door. Calvin looked up to see a Royal Air Force (RAF) Lieutenant Commander that he didn't know standing at the door. He looked at her uniform and saw that the woman was a Weapons Systems Officer (WSO).

"Can I help you?" Calvin asked.

"Actually, I'm here to help you," said the officer, her voice full of quiet competence. "My name is Lieutenant Commander Sarah Brighton. I'm your new XO."

Calvin stood up and offered his hand. Calvin found himself looking nearly eye-to-eye with her; she nearly matched his six feet. "Good to have you here," he said, "the circumstances notwithstanding. I've heard lots of good things about you."

"They're all lies," said the newcomer with a smile. "The truth is far worse."

"Well it *is* good to have you," said Calvin. "I didn't think you'd make it in time."

"I was lucky enough to catch the last shuttle up," the officer replied. "I also brought the last of the replacements with me." She indicated several people standing in the passageway outside Calvin's office. The first two people he could see looked identical.

"Aw, crap," Calvin said looking at the pair of flight-suited officers. "I've already got one set of twins in the platoon that drives me crazy. Please tell me we didn't get another set."

"OK," replied Lieutenant Commander Brighton. "We didn't get another set of twins. Those two are cousins; they just look alike. They do have the same name, though, Paul Mees. One of them goes by "Rob" to keep things simple."

"Which one is that?" asked Calvin.

"Damned if I know," replied the XO. "There are two others," she added. "The first is Lieutenant Brett Dylan Fox, our last WSO. He's RAF, too. He started out his career in admin and ended up on the staff of an aviator. The general got him a shot at taking the aviation test, and he aced it. He's never looked back, having been a test pilot in both jets and helicopters. The other person is Lieutenant Matthew Kamins, our last pilot. I don't know a lot about him, other than he's from the German Navy."

"We're all set then," replied Calvin. "The squadron's got all of the personnel that it is supposed to. With the addition of the extra days, Replicator Command was even able to make us a replacement Asp fighter to take the spot of the one the Drakuls blew up. I don't know how they did it, but we're deploying with a full squadron."

Bridge, TSS *Vella Gulf,* Stargate #2, December 16, 2020

The stargate loomed in front of the ship, a giant mass of nothingness. Made from two black holes that had been linked together by an ancient civilization, it transferred a ship from one place to another instantly...or as close to instantly as anyone had ever been able to prove. No one knew how they worked, and only one person had ever been close to figuring them out. He wasn't telling; he had died when Drakuls came through the semi-functioning gate that he had created.

Captain Sheppard looked at the gate on the view screen. Terra stood alone against a tide of Drakuls, and its only hope was for him to find and bring back aid. No pressure there.

Captain Sheppard was first and foremost a naval officer, and the U.S. Navy had a long tradition of getting the mission done...somehow. It wasn't always pretty, but naval officers always figured out a way in the end. From everything he had heard as mission prep, though, it looked like this mission had more riding on it than any other mission in naval history...as well as the smallest chance for success. Terra needed aid from the Mrowry, but even their crown prince thought it unlikely they would get any. They might get aid from the Archons...but they were an unknown race that owed them nothing. That seemed like a long shot, too. According to both the Mrowry and Steropes, there wasn't anyone else close by to ask. He took a deep breath and let it out slowly. They'd find a way. They had to.

Time to get the show on the road. "Sound General Quarters!" he ordered. Also called "battle stations," the General Quarters announcement was made to signal that battle or the threat of damage was imminent. When the call was made, the crew would report to their combat stations and would close the ship's airtight and fireproof doors to keep any potential damage from spreading. Since the first stargate transit the *Vella Gulf* made under Captain Deutch, it had become standard practice to set General Quarters prior to transit, as well as to man up all of the space fighters. You never knew what was waiting for you on the other side of the gate.

"Aye aye, sir!" said the duty engineer, seated next to the helmsman at the front console. He was responsible for all of the damage control systems. He turned on the General Quarters alarm. *Bong! Bong! Bong! Bong!* sounded the bell. It was followed by the engineer's call of "General Quarters, General Quarters, all hands man your battle stations!"

"Helmsman, full speed ahead!" Captain Sheppard ordered. "Contact the *Emperor's Paw*," he said, turning to the communications officer. "Let them know we're making the jump. We'll see them on the other side."

Chapter Five

In the Presence of His Majesty, Drakon, COROT-7 System, December 20, 2020

Captain Bullig walked down the empty stone chamber, hoping that neither his knees nor his bowels betrayed him. To bring the Overlord bad news was usually a death sentence. The Overlord didn't just shoot the messenger; he usually ate him...piece by piece while what was left of the messenger was forced to watch.

As Captain Bullig had narrowly escaped a similar fate his last time here, bringing bad news a second time was *not* what he wanted to do. That was why he had violated the Overlord's orders and had gone into the Solar System; he had been hoping to find *some* good news that he could use to save his life. Violating the Overlord's orders was similarly fatal, though, so it was a desperate gamble. He had known the deck was stacked against him, but it was his only chance.

And it was the slimmest of chances.

Only one thing scared Captain Bullig, and that was the Overlord. Fully 14 feet tall, with fangs that stuck out over four inches, he was covered in scars from all of his battles and fights to achieve supremacy. A veteran of over 200 duels, he had won every fight he had ever been in. He had also killed every opponent he had ever faced, usually by dismemberment; surrender was not an option.

The greeting hall was empty, so the Overlord had obviously heard that Bullig was bringing bad news. It did no good for minions to hear bad news, so the Overlord cleared the hall when he knew it was coming. Bullig's meter-long boots made slapping sounds that echoed loudly in the empty hall. Bullig had to cross 200 feet from the entryway to the platform that the Overlord's throne sat on. He could feel the Overlord's eyes on him the whole way. He knew not to look at the Overlord, as the Overlord had a habit of licking his lips as people approached with bad news. If he saw that, he would...he didn't know what he'd do. Run? Cower? Beg? Wet himself? None of the options were particularly helpful. He very carefully looked at the Overlord's feet, which wasn't hard as the platform that held the Overlord's throne was nine feet high. The better to overawe his subjects...as if that was needed.

He marched up to within 20 feet, then got down on his knees for the next 10 feet, and then on his stomach the last 10 feet. Without looking up, he played his one card. "I have come from the Ross 154 system, and I bring you good news, your honorable majestic graciousness!"

"Good news?" the Overlord asked in a booming voice that echoed in the hall. "I was told that you brought bad news. I heard that our fleet there was destroyed, and that *you* violated my orders."

Bullig wasn't surprised that someone from his crew had sold him out. When one of the Overlord's enforcers pulled you aside to 'ask you a few questions,' you told them everything you knew. Bullig was dead if his plan didn't work.

"As far as the fleet being destroyed," he said in as strong a voice as he could muster while lying on his stomach, "that much is true. The exploration force went through the stargate, and only half of the battleship *Slayer* came back through. It appears nearly all of them were killed."

"And you consider the loss of one of *my* battle groups to be good news?" asked the Overlord.

"I do not consider their loss to be good news," replied Bullig; "however, I do consider the fact that we have found a worthy enemy to be good news. That is why I left the system where I was stationed." He definitely did *not* say that he violated orders. "I wanted to take a look inside the system and see if they were worthy of your majestic attention. I figured that the battle group would have cleared out any mines that might be near the stargate, and I was right. The system is inhabited by a species of soft and tasty-looking bipeds. We collected enough of their transmissions in the short time we were there to find out that they call themselves, 'humans.' They appear to be quite warlike in nature. Although the only ship we saw was a cruiser, they also had fighters, so there may be at least one spacecraft carrier nearby. We were not there long enough to see any other ships. Even though the battle group had cleared out many mines, there were still a lot of them remaining."

"What is the state of their technology?" asked the Overlord.

"They will be a challenge to defeat, but not too difficult, oh honorable majestic graciousness," said Bullig. "They should provide our fleet a little fun. Their technology is fairly old, and it is not of a caliber that should cause us to lose too many ships. In fact, their cruiser was much like what the ancient Eldive had in our old home world before we conquered and ate them. The main planet in this 'Solar System' is called 'Dirt.' It must be good dirt, because there appears to be about seven billion people on their planet."

"Well done," said the Overlord. "You know...I think I may just let you live, after all."

Bullig's ear holes twitched. His plan had worked!

"In fact," mused the Overlord, "I think I will have you lead the attack into this 'Solar System.'"

Bullig's ear holes twitched even more. His plan had worked even better than he had thought possible! He was going to get promoted to admiral and would direct the attack! He'd send in the cruisers to absorb the mines and then go in with the heavy forces to kill the humans. Life was great!

"Yes," continued the Overlord. "You know the system; you should lead."

Bullig would get his pick of the spoils! He could retire in comfort!

"You know the way," said the Overlord, making up his mind. "Therefore, you will lead the attack. You will command the first ship that goes through the stargate."

Bullig sighed. His life was over.

Bridge, TSS *Vella Gulf,* Lacaille 8760, December 25, 2020

"Good luck," Captain Peotr Barishov said from the front view screen, "and Godspeed. We will hold the system until you return. Just don't take too long, da?" The Russian captain commanded the TSS *Septar*, the battlecruiser acquired on the *Vella Gulf's* second mission. Formerly a Ssselipsssiss warship, its crew had surrendered to the Terrans after the battleship *Terra* put a four-meter hole through its bridge, vaporizing its commanding officer.

The *Vella Gulf* had rendezvoused with the *Septar* in Lacaille 8760, and Captain Sheppard had relayed Fleet Command's instructions for the *Septar* to return to Earth at its best speed. It would be almost a week in transit, having to pass through both the Vulpecula 452 and Kapteyn's Star systems. Until its return, there would not be any ships in the Solar System to defend Earth, a fact that had many politicians (and admirals) more than a little nervous. Not that the battlecruiser would do much to stop a battleship or dreadnought if one of them showed up.

"Thanks," replied Captain Sheppard, "and good luck to you as well. We'll go as fast as we can. *Vella Gulf* out." The view screen went black.

The *Septar* was in many ways symbolic of what was both good and bad about the Republic of Terra, Captain Sheppard realized. When the Terrans brought the ship back to Earth, the nations had been unable to agree on a name for it; every politician wanted to name the battlecruiser after some aspect of their nation-state. The Terran government had finally decided to name the class of battlecruisers after oceans, but then couldn't agree on which ocean to start with.

Finally, the kuji representative from Domus said in frustration (after the third hour of argument), "Well if you can't agree on one of your oceans, name it after ours. The *Septar*." Her outburst caught everyone by surprise. Before anyone could say anything else, the humanoid princess from Domus called out, "I second that!" Recognizing a break in the impasse, everyone else agreed, and the ship was christened the TSS *Septar*. Although that took care of the problem at hand, it did nothing to solve the problem of what to call the next one.

Many people left the meeting almost hoping that the Earth never built another one.

The Republic of Terra was similar. While on the surface all of the nations appeared to go along with each other, that was just a thin veneer. The alliance was so new that trust had yet to form between the nations; it wouldn't take much to pull them apart again. A nation born in war, the states of the Republic of Terra didn't trust one another yet, and people still thought of themselves as members of their former nations first. Those that thought of themselves as Terrans usually only did so as a distant second. The new nation needed time for everyone to grow together.

He wondered if they would get that time.

Chapter Six

"**O**h, what fun it is to ride in a one horse open sleigh!" Calvin sang loudly, if not particularly well; the other 200 voices drowned him out so no one knew or cared whether he was on key or not. Being away from home on Christmas was always hard for military members, even if they *were* on a mission to save the planet. If it was the last Christmas that humanity was to experience, the men and women of the *Vella Gulf* would have liked to have spent it with their families.

Recognizing that, Captain Sheppard had commissioned a sing-along to take everyone's minds off of being away from home, and nearly all of the off duty personnel came to sing. Even the men and women from religions that didn't celebrate Christmas seemed to enjoy the camaraderie.

An outgrowth of the U.S. Navy, the Terran Space Fleet had kept most of the customs and traditions of that service, including the tradition of being 'dry.' No alcohol was allowed on board, except for a small amount kept under lock and key for 'medicinal' purposes. For Christmas, Captain Sheppard had decided morale needed a boost, and he had made an alcohol ration available; each member of the ship's crew received two beers.

Looking around the mess, Calvin decided that the (admittedly bad) singing and the (too few) beers had worked their magic; at least for a little while it looked like morale had improved. As he walked out of the mess, he saw that someone had made a Drakul doll and had hung it by a noose from the ceiling next to the door. Pinned to it was the note, 'Merry Christmas, Drakul scum. Now die!' That wasn't really the kind of Christmas spirit that Calvin had grown up with, but he could appreciate the sentiment nonetheless.

Chapter Seven

Chapel, TSS _Vella Gulf_, 61 Cygni, December 28, 2020

As the last bars of the recessional music finished playing, the congregation began filing out of the ship's chapel. All except for one, Father Zuhlsdorf saw. Calvin remained seated in the second row.

Calvin watched as the last person left the small room and then approached the chaplain where he stood waiting by the altar. "Can I help you with something?" asked Father Zuhlsdorf.

Calvin looked troubled. His eyes searched the room before finally coming to rest on the chaplain. He sighed. "I don't know, Father, but I hope so," he said.

Father Zuhlsdorf continued to wait patiently, allowing Calvin to get to what was bothering him in his own time.

"You're probably aware that I'm not a big church-goer," Calvin said finally.

"Well, I know that I haven't seen you here many times previously," the chaplain replied.

The chaplain was being charitable; Calvin knew he had _never_ attended mass on the _Vella Gulf_. "I've been a bit troubled lately," Calvin said, before pausing again. "It's this whole 'hero spirit' thing."

"I've heard the Psiclopes talking about that in the past," Father Zuhlsdorf said. "I imagine that being an acknowledged hero is a lot of weight to bear...if you believe in it."

"That's just it, Father," said Calvin, "I don't know what I'm supposed to believe. The Psiclopes are an advanced civilization; you would think that they ought to have all of this stuff figured out. They think that they can follow a spirit as it is reincarnated over and over, and that I was Zeus in a former life. And if that's not bad enough, they're pinning the whole survival of the Earth on me. They think that my actions will either save or destroy the Earth...*and* they believe that it's more likely that I will fail."

"That *is* indeed a lot of pressure," said Father Zuhlsdorf, "but once again, it's only a lot of pressure if you believe it..."

Calvin looked up at the chaplain.

"...and I do not," finished the chaplain.

"You don't?" asked Calvin.

"Of course not," replied the chaplain. "Their religion goes against many of the key tenets of my faith and what I believe." He paused. "And that's what it comes down to; it's all a matter of faith and what you believe. What *they* believe isn't what's important; what's important in your case is what *you* believe." He paused again. "So Calvin, what do you believe?"

Calvin sighed. "I've thought about it a lot since we left Earth, and I just don't see how everything they say is possible. It sounds like the Psiclopes just make up stuff so that their people can feel good about the future. It's a lot easier to live your life knowing that if things go badly, there's always going to be someone that will come along to save you. In the end, I guess it really doesn't matter. All I can do is all I can do, no more and no less, regardless of whether I am a normal human being or some ultra-powerful spirit. At the end of the day, all I can do is my best."

"That's all we can ever do, my son," replied the chaplain.

"Thanks, Father," Calvin said getting up. "That helps a lot."

Bridge, TSS *Terra*, Epsilon Eridani, December 31, 2020

"**D**on't come back with less than a dreadnought for me!" Captain Lorena Griffin joked. The commanding officer of the battleship TSS *Terra*, Captain Griffin was in charge of the largest ship in the Terran fleet. On the *Vella Gulf's* last mission, the Mrowry had given the Terrans the battleship, as well as the Class 6 replicator that was assembling it, rather than blow them up to keep them from falling into the claws of the Ssselipsssiss.

Although brand new and state-of-the-art, the *Terra's* crew was as green as any battleship crew that had ever been to the stars. There were a few Mrowry advisors that had stayed with it to help bring the *Terra's* crew up to speed, but they were few and far between. The Mrowry were going to stay until the next ship went back to Mrowry space, whenever that was. When they volunteered, they did so knowing that they were on extended duty...an extended duty that might very well result in a life sentence. It was a tribute to the leadership of their crown prince that when Captain Yerrow had said it was important and asked for volunteers, over half of the crew had volunteered.

The *Vella Gulf* had just arrived in the Epsilon Eridani system, bringing with it the news of the attack on Earth and the *Terra's* recall 'at its fastest possible speed' to aid in the Earth's continued defense. As she gave the orders that would return the *Terra* to Earth, Captain Griffin said a silent prayer for the safe, speedy and successful return of the *Vella Gulf*, which would be continuing on in its search for aid against the Drakuls. While the *Terra* was an extremely capable ship, even with the addition of the Mrowry, its crew was still too green...far too green for what they would likely be called upon to do.

Come home soon, *Vella Gulf*, she thought, and please bring friends.

Cargo Bay, *Shuttle 02*, Domus Orbit, January 1, 2021

Calvin looked around the back of the shuttle's cargo compartment. In addition to several large pallets of materials to be used in the ship's replicator, they were also returning to the *Vella Gulf* from the planet with several new members for the platoon and a combat cameraman.

"Y'all strap in back there now, y'hear?" said the shuttle pilot in a Southern drawl over the craft's intercom system.

Master Chief looked over to Calvin with a curious look on his face. "I thought a couple of the Domans were flying the shuttle," said Master Chief. "Did someone else swap out?"

Calvin sighed. "No," he said. "The two crewmen are kuji. Unfortunately, someone introduced Tex to a recording of some country comedian and told him that, with a name like Tex, he needed to have a Southern drawl." Calvin shook his head in disgust. "If I could find out who did that," he added, "I'd cheerfully have him shot."

Master Chief nodded his head toward two people sitting in the back of the shuttle by themselves. "Please tell me those two aren't another set of twins for the platoon," he said. "The Gordon brothers are enough for one army, much less a single platoon."

Calvin leaned forward to see where Master Chief was looking. "No," Calvin said. "Those two aren't twins; they're cousins. They just look alike. You don't have to worry about them in any event. They're part of the squadron, not the platoon." He pulled up the roster in his head. "Their names are Sean and Phil Ventura. They are the second set of cousins we got in the squadron; I said the same thing when I saw the first set." One of them punched the other. Hard. As they watched, the second Ventura punched the first one back. If anything, it was harder than the punch he had received. "Lieutenant Park Ji-hyun, who was here training them, said they fight all the time on the ground," Calvin said, "but apparently they make a great team when you put them in the cockpit of a space fighter together. It's almost like they can read each other's minds."

"I've had enough of that mind reading bullshit for a lifetime, sir," said Master Chief. "What ever happened to keeping your thoughts to yourself?"

Calvin laughed and nodded to the other group of Domus humanoids. "Those three are the ones coming to the platoon. Lieutenant Contreras spoke very highly of them. He said they are his star pupils."

"I talked to Captain Smith while we were there," replied Master Chief. "He said that *Mister* Contreras called them 'the Three Caballeros.'" Despite being a career SEAL, Master Chief O'Leary had never been a big fan of authority, especially 'colorful' authority, and Contreras was as colorful as they came. "He also said they were hard workers and would make good additions to the unit. From left to right they are Corporal Craig Cuillard, Corporal John Stump and Corporal Weldon Owens. Like most of the humanoids here seem to be doing, they all took Terran names when they signed up."

Seeing everyone looking at them, Corporal Cuillard said, "We are the Three Caballeros."

"Gluck ab!" they all yelled simultaneously.

"You've got to be fucking kidding me," Master Chief said. He looked at Calvin. "Can you *please* add Lieutenant Contreras to the list of people that need to be shot when we get back?"

Platoon Gym, TSS *Vella Gulf,* Domus Orbit, January 1, 2021

"Good to see you back in the gym again, sir," Master Chief said as Calvin walked in. "It's been a while."

"Yeah, I know," Calvin replied. "It's good to have some time to myself so that I *can* get back into working out again."

Calvin looked out over the gym floor where the platoon was exercising. Many of the faces were still new to him. The platoon had come back from the previous mission with a *lot* of holes in its manning. Some of the holes had been because they left personnel behind as security forces and trainers on a couple of the planets they visited; others were due to the combat that had occurred there, too.

It had taken a while for the Board to meet to replace them. It hadn't met until the end of November; by the time the results were posted, it had been the first week of December. Most of the new recruits hadn't even been onboard when the *Gulf* went to help defend the stargate, and it had been a scramble to get them onboard, implanted and modified before the cruiser left for Archonis.

The Psiclopes had given the Terrans a variety of upgrades in return for the Terrans' help in getting them back to their home planet. In addition to the implants that allowed them to download training and communicate via a mind-to-mind radio system, the *Vella Gulf's* medibot had been qualified to do a variety of things, like making their vision sharper and their reflexes faster, as well as making them stronger and giving them better endurance. It was a standard part of coming to the platoon now. Check in, visit the medibot and get your implants and modifications.

"Checking on the newbies?" asked Night as he walked in.

"Yeah," said Calvin. "I'm trying to put names to faces, but am coming up blank on a few of them."

"Well, let me help you," Night said, turning to look out over the expansive gym floor. The *Vella Gulf* had originally been built by an avian race called the Eldive; they had used the room as a place to stretch their wings. It was large enough for most of the activities that the platoon needed to practice. They had even been able to put in a small pistol range.

"How about the guy on the pistol range with Corporal Sanders?" Calvin asked. "He looks familiar, but I can't quite place him."

"He ought to look familiar," replied Master Chief. "His brother was in the platoon during the war. Do you remember PFC Trevor Hall? That's Corporal Patrick Hall. He's Mad Dog's brother."

"Is he as good a soldier as Mad Dog?" asked Calvin. "I didn't get to know him very well, but he seemed like a good guy."

"Yes and no," hedged Master Chief.

"What's that mean?" Calvin asked with a laugh. The soldiers on the pistol range put down their weapons and pressed the buttons at their stations that would bring their targets back to them.

"Well, he's got the eyes of an eagle and the reflexes of a Mrowry," said Master Chief. "Also, his personnel reports indicate that he was an excellent pilot and an expert with edged weapons, even *before* he got implanted."

"So what's the problem?" asked Calvin looking over Corporal Hall's shoulder as he pulled his target off the line. The target was almost new, with only a few holes in the outer rings.

"It doesn't matter what type of ranged weapon you give him," replied Master Chief. "He can't hit the broadside of a barn. It's a good thing he's an expert with bladed weapons; I hear that he's the worst shot in all of Africa."

"Hey! I'm working on it, Master Chief!" Corporal Hall exclaimed.

Master Chief looked pointedly at his target, a look of utter disdain on his face. "Keep working," he said.

"I think you already met the new Ground Force Leader, Master Gunnery Sergeant Joan Kinkead, right?" asked Night as the group moved away from the pistol range. The platoon was broken down into two 'forces,' a Ground Force and a Space Force. Although both concentrated in their area of expertise, they also cross-trained in the other area so that they would be ready for anything.

"Yeah, I met her a few days ago when she checked in," replied Calvin. "I told her that we get all of the hard missions, and she just laughed. Her comment was, 'Try being a Marine Corps drill sergeant while raising eight kids. That's hard. This shit's easy.'"

Master Chief laughed. "That sounds like her," he said. "I knew her from before; our paths crossed a couple of times. The person who she's talking to is the new Squad 'B' Leader, Staff Sergeant Michael Burke. I don't know him, but he seems like a good leader."

The conversation was interrupted by a tremendous noise from the firing range behind them. A cyborg had come in and stood at the range with one foot behind him as a brace. The eight-foot tall half-man/half-machine had old-fashioned pistols in both hands and was firing them both simultaneously. The pistols looked bigger than normal and sounded like cannons going off. Each also had an extended magazine that looked like it could hold about 50 rounds. The speed at which he fired them made it seem like they were automatic machine pistols, even though Calvin could see his fingers working the triggers. He finished and brought the target back. Unlike Corporal Hall's, the entire black part at the center had been shot out, leaving a hole in the center of the target.

"Nice shooting, Staff Sergeant Dantone," Calvin said. Also known as 'The Wall,' Staff Sergeant Dantone had been mauled by an extra-terrestrial (ET) during their previous mission. The medibot had not been able to save anything except his brain and some of his spinal cord, so it had turned him into a cyborg, encasing the brain in a robot body. The cyborg turned around and Calvin could see that he looked very different from the last time Calvin had seen him. The red-haired wig that he was wearing was especially noticeable.

"Thank you sir," said the cyborg, "but I'm not The Wall. My name is Staff Sergeant Steve Randolph. I used to be a combat engineer, specializing in demolitions; unfortunately, my partner made a mistake one day a couple of months ago. They couldn't save most of my body, but my brain was still good. One of my doctors knew that the medibot on the moon could do a cyborg conversion, and they offered it to me. With a choice between being a 100% disabled vet and being able to kick ass, I chose to come and kick some ET ass, sir!"

"Welcome aboard," Calvin said.

"Thank you sir," the cyborg said.

"What are you shooting there?" Calvin asked.

The cyborg handed one over to Calvin so that he could see it. "It's a modified Israeli .50 caliber Desert Eagle. I never had the strength to one-hand it effectively before." He smiled. "Now I do."

Calvin could see what he meant. The pistol was huge. He chuckled. "You'll fit in just fine, I think," he said, handing the pistol back to the cyborg. "We're big fans of overkill here." The cyborg turned back to the range and began refilling his magazines.

"Oh, there's The Wall," Calvin said, looking around the room. The other cyborg was standing to the side of one of the practice areas with his right arm in the air while someone Calvin didn't recognize worked on some part of his mechanical body. The cameraman that they had picked up on Domus was standing nearby taking photos. "Who's the guy working on him?" Calvin asked. "He seems a bit...older...than the rest of the group."

"He *is* a bit older," Master Chief replied. "He started out in Grey's Scouts in Rhodesia when he was younger, but he's still in great shape. He's one of those 'jack of all trades' kind of guys that every unit needs. He's also the best cyborg mechanic there is going. When he got out of the military, he went into robotics and now has about a million degrees in robotics and that 'cyber' word that means robotics."

"Cybernetics?" asked Calvin.

"Yeah," replied Master Chief, "that thing. With two cyborgs in the unit now, I'm glad we got him. If they break, hopefully he can fix them. His name is Sergeant Mark Hopper. He goes by the name 'Hoppy.'"

"Someone went way out on a limb for that call sign," Calvin noted.

Master Chief shrugged, "He said that's what he's always been called, even before he got into the army. I guess his friends weren't very imaginative." He looked at the cameraman. "Was the photographer your idea? Not getting enough TV time?"

"No," replied Calvin. "I've had all of the publicity I need for this lifetime and several more. His name is Bob Jones; he goes by the nickname 'Danger.' I didn't know we were getting him until we were on Domus. There was a combat cameraman doing a show on the new members of the Terran Republic, and the Domans hired him to do a 'real Terran news show' on the war."

"Wonderful," grumped Master Chief. "We obviously didn't have enough distractions already, what with cyborgs, baby dinosaurs and talking cats walking around. We needed to have a movie camera for all the boys and girls to preen for, too. Just fucking wonderful."

Night cleared his throat. "If Master Chief is done, you can also see the two new medics we got working out with swords over on the other mat. The woman is Paige Julia Lawrence, and the man is Ray Jones."

Calvin raised an eyebrow.

"Yes, that makes three people named Jones," replied Night. "This one is easy to remember; he goes by 'Doc.' Both he and Lawrence had prior careers they gave up when the Drakuls showed up. Lawrence had been working on biowarfare defense, doing some sort of DNA sequencing shit that's way over my head. Jones was working with SWAT, but was also a prior Marine corpsman. Both have some interesting side skills."

"Cool," said Calvin.

"And that just leaves the three corporals over at the bench press that you already met," said Master Chief, "Corporals Stump, Cuillard and Owens. Cuillard is the one working out on the bench."

"Don't you mean 'the Three Caballeros'?" asked Calvin.

Master Chief growled. "Sir, please don't start that shit, too; it only gives them big heads."

As Calvin looked over, he saw that Cuillard was doing presses with 225 pounds, and the other two were counting. With a shock he realized that they were in the 90s.

"94...95...96...97...98...99...100." The man set the weights down. He didn't seem fazed or tired in the slightest. Corporal Owens took his place and began pumping out the repetitions.

"Not bad," said Calvin. "Obviously they got some pretty good endurance modifications from the medibot."

"They ran out of something they needed to do the bio-modifications on Domus," said Master Chief. "Those three got their implants but didn't get their mods; they get them next week."

"Really?" asked Calvin. "Holy *crap!*"

"Yeah," agreed Night. "They're brutes."

Bridge, Drakul Ship *Destruction of Olympos*, COROT-7 System, January 3, 2021

Captain Bullig stretched. If he was going to die, he thought, at least he was going to do it in style. Although the Overlord still obviously bore him a grudge, even the Overlord had seen that Bullig needed more firepower to break into the new system and had given him one of their new dreadnoughts to use as his flagship. Built in the 54 Piscium system by some of their feeder races, the ship was made for Drakuls. Built on the Mrowry dreadnought design that was in the replicator they had captured, the feeder race had expanded it so that the ceilings were 15 feet high. Unlike the *Mangler*, he could move about freely without crouching everywhere he went.

Although he had disagreed with the Overlord's policy of allowing limited freedom for some of the members of captured species (he had only disagreed to himself; disagreeing with the Overlord publicly tended to decrease one's lifespan significantly), this was one example of where they were helpful to have around. Drakuls were warriors and didn't have time for things like building.

He couldn't wait for the rest of the fleet to be assembled. This was going to be fun.

Chapter Eight

"When do you advise turning on the stealth package?" asked Captain Yerrow from the view screen. The ships were close to the stargate that would take them into the Ross 248 system. It was possible that the enemy waited on the other side.

Captain Sheppard looked at Lieutenant Finn, whom he had asked to join him on the bridge.

"Oh! You can turn them on at any time you'd like," answered Lieutenant Finn. "The only problem is going to be fuel consumption. They eat helium-3 like it's chocolate."

"I do not know what chocolate is," replied Captain Yerrow, "but I have seen how quickly a space fighter's stealth module consumes its fuel. Still, I think it would be prudent to turn it on prior to going through the stargate, in case there are any Ssselipsssiss on the other side. It would also be good to ensure they are operational prior to that."

"I agree," said Captain Sheppard. "Why don't you turn your system on for five minutes, and we'll check you out. Then you can do the same for us."

"That is a good plan," agreed Captain Yerrow. "We will do so. Yerrow out."

The screen blanked and then became an image of the *Emperor's Paw*, paralleling them five miles to starboard. As the crew on the *Vella Gulf* watched, the *Paw* shimmered and then disappeared.

Captain Sheppard nodded. "All systems try to find the *Emperor's Paw*," he ordered. "Let me know if you have any success."

The offensive systems officer and defensive systems officer both looked but were unable to find the *Paw* on their systems. A tight smile began to creep across Lieutenant Finn's face.

"Ummm," said Steropes, who was manning the science station.

"Yes?" Captain Sheppard asked. "Can you see them?"

"See them?" asked Steropes. "No, I can't see them." He paused. "However, I am getting some sort of weird gravity transient. It's like there is something periodically there, but I can't lock in on it."

Lieutenant Finn looked crushed. "That has been a recurring problem," he said. "The stealth system is really good on all forms of energy, like radar and laser. It produces a field that drinks them right up. Gravity is different, though; there's no energy to absorb. It's one of the four fundamental forces, and the only one that acts on all particles with mass. I've worked to try to make the shields provide a buffer against it, but it is wildly imperfect. It is rather like trying to play baseball with a soccer ball; you can do it, but it doesn't work very well."

"Perhaps it might have been helpful to tell us that prior to now," chided Captain Sheppard. "We might have been able to work something out."

"Oh! I did report it to my superiors at Department X before we left," said Lieutenant Finn, "but they said the mission had to go, regardless, so it didn't matter. I'm sorry; I thought you knew. Just don't get close to any of the enemy ships, and it shouldn't matter.

You have to be fairly close to the stealth ship in order for them to see the gravity transient."

"How close?" asked Calvin.

"If you are outside of 50,000 miles from a stealthed cruiser, it is unlikely that you'll see it," replied Lieutenant Finn. "A stealth fighter can't be seen from more than about 10,000 miles."

"So," Captain Sheppard said, "as long as we don't let them in close, we're OK?"

"Yes," said Lieutenant Finn, "we should be."

Bridge, TSS *Vella Gulf*, HD 40307, January 11, 2021

"I guess this is where we'll find out how well your system works," said Captain Sheppard.

"Yes," said Lieutenant Finn, who was uncharacteristically quiet as his big moment approached.

His system had worked as intended, with two small glitches. The first of these was that the system had dropped for about five seconds when they entered the Ross 248 system from the WASP 18 system, due to the mechanical disorientation caused by going through the stargate. Happily, there hadn't been any of the Ssselipsssiss in the system to see it. The other problem they would have to deal with was that the stealth system did nothing to prevent the signal associated with a stargate activation. When a ship entered a system, the stargate emitted an electromagnetic pulse. The magnitude of the pulse was proportional to the speed and mass of the ship going through it. The faster or larger the ship was, the bigger the pulse it gave off. If they entered the system going any faster than their slowest speed, the Ssselipsssiss would know that something had just entered the system, even if they couldn't see the ship. Going that slowly would leave them vulnerable to any of the enemy's weapons and especially vulnerable to mines.

As planned, the Mrowry had transited into the HD 40307 system first, with the *Vella Gulf* following them 10 minutes later. As they had feared, there *were* Ssselipsssiss in this system, as two of their battleships, eight battlecruisers and eight cruisers were positioned around the system's other stargate into the 83 Leonis system. Although the star system had several planets, none were habitable, even if the system hadn't been a war zone.

Their entrance into the system had been noticed by the Ssselipsssiss fleet. When the lizards had subsequently been unable to determine who or what had entered the system, they had detached two of their battlecruisers to investigate. The two battlecruisers had been easy to avoid, and the *Vella Gulf* had transited the system without being seen. With their stealth shields up, the crew of the *Vella Gulf* had no idea where the *Emperor's Paw* was; they just had to assume that they were proceeding as planned. Space was large, so they probably wouldn't run into the Mrowry ship, even if the Terrans took exactly the same route. Probably. They hadn't had any spurious gravity readings, so they thought...hoped...that the *Paw* was where it should be.

As they approached the Ssselipsssiss fleet, the answer to the question of how well the system worked would determine whether they lived or died. Everyone was tense; conversations were held in whispers, as if the lizards would hear them across the intervening miles.

Captain Sheppard frowned. "I was actually hoping that your answer would be, 'Shouldn't be a problem, Skipper. It'll work perfectly.'"

"I would like to be able to say that," replied Lieutenant Finn, "but anything mechanical rarely works correctly the first time you try it. This one is especially hard because the modules were grafted onto two different types of ships. I've read everything I could on the *Vella Gulf*, and I'm pretty sure ours will work. I didn't have as much material on the *Emperor's Paw*. I hope it works for them...but I can't be sure it will."

"The lizzie ships are moving," said the defensive systems officer (DSO).

"Where are they going?" asked Captain Sheppard.

"I don't know," replied the DSO. "They appear to be randomly moving around."

"Steropes? Ensign Sommers?" asked Captain Sheppard. "Any ideas?"

"We were just discussing it," said Ensign Sara Sommers, who was manning the science station. "We're pretty sure they know two ships are in the system; they just don't know where. There are three stargates out of the system, the one we came through, the one going to Ssselipsssiss space and the one we're headed to. They can probably guess that we're trying to go toward Mrowry space, and they are either trying to find us or cut us off, or both."

"What do you want me to do, Skipper?" asked the helmsman.

"Power levels on the enemy ships coming up," said the DSO. "It looks like they're preparing to fire on something. It's not us though; we're still out of range."

"Got it," said Captain Sheppard.

"Gate activation," both Steropes and the DSO said simultaneously. "Looks like a transit out," added the DSO; "I didn't see anything come in. The lizzies are going crazy now. I think they're looking for us." The DSO paused. "What the..." he muttered. "Now they're firing their lasers *all* over the place."

"They are trying to find us," said Steropes. "They're hoping that we'll fly through one of their laser beams, and it will spotlight us."

"Solomon," said Captain Sheppard, "Are you watching the Ssselipsssiss?"

"Yes, Captain Sheppard, I am," replied the AI.

"Good," said Captain Sheppard. "Please analyze their patterns. If we were to make a high speed run from here to the stargate, what are the odds of their hitting us with one of their lasers?"

"The odds are minimal," answered Solomon. "The beams are very narrow, and they have a lot of space to cover. Even if they concentrated all of their weapons on the area near the stargate, they would still have less than a 2% chance of hitting us."

"Thanks, Solomon, that's pretty much what I thought, too," replied Captain Sheppard. "Helmsman, all ahead full to the stargate."

"All ahead full, aye," said the helmsman.

The ship began accelerating toward the stargate.

"Shit!" swore the DSO. "One of the battlecruisers just changed direction. We're going to pass about 26,000 miles from it."

"All ahead flank," said Captain Sheppard.

"Increasing to flank speed, aye" replied the helmsman.

"The odds of detection have increased to 57%," Solomon noted, "based on the probability of gravimetric detection."

"Noted," Captain Sheppard said.

"The lizzies are going crazy," the DSO said. "They are firing everywhere. One of the battlecruisers just hit one of the battleships, and the battleship shot back at it, too. Neither penetrated the other's shields, but still. It's crazy, sir."

"Five minutes to stargate," the helmsman said.

"Entering detection range of battlecruiser," the DSO said.

"Four minutes to stargate," the helmsman said.

"They know we're here," the DSO called. "All laser batteries are firing in our general direction."

"On screen," said Captain Sheppard. The AI indicated where the laser beams were being fired in relation to the *Vella Gulf*. Lieutenant Finn was pretty sure he was happier not knowing. There were a *lot* of lasers firing in their direction.

"Three minutes to stargate," the helmsman said.

"We're hit!" the DSO said. "Glancing shot, starboard shield. Shields at 98%, but they're going to know we're here." He paused. "Yep, they've got us," he added. "All of their weapons are refocusing in our vicinity. The battlecruiser is turning to port to unmask its broadside."

"Two minutes to stargate!" the helmsman said.

"All ships turning toward us and accelerating," the DSO said. "We're hit!" Everyone on the bridge could feel the extra energy around them as the shields absorbed it. "Battleship hit! Stealth is down. Shields at 78%."

"Permission to fire?" requested the offensive systems officer (OSO). Many of the *Vella Gulf's* systems were covered with the stealth modules, but not all.

"Permission granted," said Captain Sheppard. "Fire at will!"

"One battleship, four battlecruisers and four cruisers giving chase," Steropes noted. "It appears they mean to chase us into the next system."

"Missiles launching, both sides," noted the OSO. The crew could feel the ship shudder as the missiles blasted out of their tubes. "Lasers and grasers firing," he added.

"*Minefield!*" the DSO called. "Mines appear inactive," he added a few second later, "probably because of the ships following us."

"One minute to stargate," said the helmsman.

"Two hits on our aft shields," said the DSO. "Shields are at 12%. We'll lose them with the next hit. *Missiles inbound!*"

"Standby to launch all fighters as soon as we emerge," Captain Sheppard ordered.

"Launch all fighters on emergence, aye," Lieutenant Commander Brighton repeated.

"We're hit!" called the DSO. "Aft shields are down."

"Laser hit at Frame 220 aft," the duty engineer reported. "Damage control crews responding."

"Counter-missile lasers and missiles firing," added the DSO. Only the OSO sitting next to him could hear him mutter, "C'mon baby, get me to the gate..."

"Ssselipsssiss ships definitely intend to follow us," Steropes advised. "The battleship and two battlecruisers are continuing to accelerate. They will catch us in the next system."

"We're not going to stop all the missiles!" called the DSO. He dialed up the ship's intercom system. "*Missile impact in 10 seconds,*" he transmitted. "*All hands brace for shock!*"

"Five seconds..." the DSO said under his breath. "Four...three...two..."

The ship hit the stargate and jumped.

Bridge, TSS *Vella Gulf,* 83 Leonis, January 11, 2021

"Emergence," Steropes called. "Launching probes."

"All space fighters launching," LCDR Brighton added.

"*Minefield!*" the DSO yelled.

Asp 01, 83 Leonis, January 11, 2021

Asp 01 launched as soon as the *Vella Gulf's* systems stabilized from the transit, right into the middle of a minefield. A *large* minefield, Calvin noted. He was an expert on mines, having laid or help lay a number of minefields during his career. The Terran mines were relatively small, massing only about 23 kilograms, including the five kilograms of antimatter that gave them their explosive force. The Mrowry mines were much bigger than their Terran counterparts, massing over 200 kilograms. Calvin didn't know whether the difference was because they held more explosives, had additional tracking capabilities or whether they incorporated some other offensive or defensive measure...nor did he want to find out. As his fighter separated from the *Vella Gulf,* the bigger ship blinked back into stealth mode, leaving the fighters nothing to look at but the mines. All he could think of was getting a long way from them, as quickly as he could.

"*All Spacehawks follow me*," he commed as he began a max acceleration transit toward what his sensors said was the closest edge of the minefield. The 11 other space fighters, seeing the threat, turned to follow Calvin's ship, trying to stay as far away as they could from the mines.

As Calvin evaded the mines, which didn't seem to be active, he saw the true nature of the threat. Several battleships and a larger number of battlecruisers and smaller vessels were arrayed around the largest spaceship he had ever seen. It had to be one of the dreadnoughts or super dreadnoughts he had heard of; the craft measured almost two miles in length. He hoped the *Emperor's Paw* had let the crew aboard the behemoth know that the *Vella Gulf* was coming or this was going to be the end of their mission. With that much firepower aimed at it, he doubted the *Gulf* could even make it back through the stargate before being destroyed. As Calvin's system registered another stargate activation, the largest vessel began launching missiles.

"Sir," said his WSO, Lieutenant Sasaki 'Supidi' Akio, "the Mrowry are launching at us."

Bridge, TSS *Vella Gulf*, 83 Leonis, January 11, 2021

"Sir!" the DSO called, "the dreadnought is launching missiles at us!"

"Understood," said Captain Sheppard. "Rotate the ship. Prepare to launch counter-missile missiles. Let's try to remember that they're our friends, even if they don't know it yet."

"Most of the tubes are blocked by the stealth modules, sir!" said the DSO.

"I know," said Captain Sheppard. "We'll do what we can to defend ourselves." He turned to the communications officer. "See if you can contact the *Paw*," he directed. "As soon as you can, please."

***Asp 01*, 83 Leonis, January 11, 2021**

""Terran Ship Vella Gulf and all of its fighters, this is the Mrowry dreadnought Night Hunter," commed a voice from the giant spaceship. "Please vacate the area around the stargate while we deal with the Ssselipsssiss that followed you through it. I say again, please vacate the area around the stargate so we can deal with the ships that followed you through it." The voice sounded like it was used to being obeyed. As Calvin watched, the missiles from the dreadnought rocketed past his fighter to impact the shields of the battleship that had entered the system behind him. Within seconds, all of the Mrowry ships were firing, and a tremendous amount of ordnance was headed in his general direction.

While Calvin would have liked to turn and fire the missiles he carried as well, he realized that it was far more important to get out of the way of the missiles aimed at the lizard battleship, most of which were larger than his fighter. He hoped the Gulf was out of the way. His new hi-def stereo was still aboard it.

The second volley of missiles from the dreadnought knocked down the battleship's forward shields, and missiles began impacting the front half of the ship. The battleship's crew was handicapped as they could only employ the missiles and lasers on the front of their ship, its 'chase' armament, while the dreadnought and its accompanying ships were already broadside to the battleship and pouring fire into it from all of their main batteries. Waiting within its effective laser range, the dreadnought began lashing the lizard battleship with its 5-meter aperture grasers and 4.5 meter lasers, quickly rendering the battleship's chase weapons into scrap metal.

As the fighters cleared the minefield, the battleship began to turn, not to the side to unmask its main batteries, but to go end-over-end so that it could begin decelerating. Realizing that it was in an unwinnable fight, its crew was trying to run. They would never get the opportunity, Calvin saw, as the first two mines detonated close aboard. The first mine exploded with a nearly 400 megaton blast that knocked down the battleship's aft shields; the second wiped out most of its engines and engineering spaces. The salvo of missiles that arrived just after the mines exploded turned the aft section into a pile of junk metal that matched the front of the ship.

As the weapons magazine onboard the battleship blew up, tearing the ship in half, a Ssselipsssiss battlecruiser emerged from the stargate, followed almost immediately by a second battlecruiser. Seeing the Mrowry fleet arrayed against them, within seconds both flipped end-over-end to flee; however, like the battleship before them, they didn't get the opportunity. The dreadnought shifted fire smoothly from the remains of the battleship to the first of the battlecruisers. Not built to withstand the sole focus of a dreadnought's main battery of energy weapons, its shields were overloading before the first round of missiles had even launched. The dreadnought kept up the fire, and the battlecruiser's shields failed as the first volley of missiles arrived. The battlecruiser's counter-missile batteries were successful in eliminating several of the dreadnought's missiles, and several of the other missiles tracked off to obliterate pieces of the battleship that were in their way. The other 25 missiles hit the battlecruiser, wrecking it beyond repair. One of these was a direct hit on the bridge, which eliminated any further central control of the ship's actions.

The second battlecruiser drew the focus of the Mrowry battleships and battlecruisers. Although their weapons were smaller than the dreadnought's, there were more than enough to do the job. Outnumbered more than 10 to one, and outclassed by the three battleships, the battlecruiser's shields were down within four minutes of entering the system, and the ship was racked by more than 40 anti-ship missiles two minutes after that. With command and control out, and its engineering spaces decimated, its captain did what many previous Ssselipsssiss captains had done when they realized they were in an unwinnable fight. He detonated the core of the ship's drive system in a massive explosion.

The dreadnought continued to punch 16 feet wide holes into the remains of the first battlecruiser for another minute until air and fluids stopped venting from it, and then a pause came over the battle group as it waited to see if any additional ships would come through the stargate. Calvin used the time to look at the 8,200 feet long dreadnought on the WSO's system. As the massive ship's capabilities became clear, Calvin looked at Supidi and said, "We have got to get some of those for us!"

Chapter Nine

Bridge, TSS *Vella Gulf,* 83 Leonis, January 11, 2021

"It doesn't look like any more of the Ssselipsssiss are coming," noted Captain Sheppard. "Recall the fighters, please, and ask Lieutenant Rrower to report to the bridge."

"Recall the fighters, aye, sir," said Lieutenant Commander Brighton.

"Lieutenant Rrower to the bridge, aye," added the operations officer. Lieutenant Rrower was the senior Mrowry officer onboard the *Vella Gulf.* Having served in combat with the Terrans on a couple of occasions, he was the logical choice to have onboard the ship as their liaison.

Several minutes passed by in a tense silence.

"Sir!" the communications officer called. "We are being hailed by the *Night Hunter.*"

"Put it on the front view screen, please," said Captain Sheppard. The screen split into two, revealing two nearly identical Mrowry standing on their bridges. Both of them were royalty, as they were completely black in color. The only difference visible between them was that the one on the right wore the uniform of an admiral; the one on the left was Captain Yerrow.

The admiral spoke first. "Welcome humans to Mrowry space," it said. "We gave you some time because Captain Yerrow guessed that your Lieutenant Commander Hobbs would be in one of the fighters that you just recovered. Is he currently back and within viewer range?"

"Yes, I am," said Calvin, walking onto the bridge along with Lieutenant Rrower. "I'm Lieutenant Commander Hobbs. Is there something that I can do for you?"

"No," said the admiral. "There is actually something that I wanted to do for you. I wanted to thank you. As I understand it, I have you to thank for returning my brother to me."

"It was hardly me alone," replied Calvin. "The entire crew of the *Vella Gulf* and the *Emperor's Paw* all did their parts. I didn't do any more than anyone else."

"Your modesty becomes you," replied the admiral; "however, my brother told me briefly about your idea to use the battleship that was still in the replicator to destroy the lizard battlecruiser. In all of my time fighting them, I have never heard of a Ssselipsssiss ship surrendering before. Well done!"

"Thank you, but I didn't do that all by myself, either," said Calvin. "In fact one of your officers, Lieutenant Rrower, was instrumental in running some of the cabling that made it possible."

"He did, did he?" asked the admiral. "I will have to speak with him about it and get his side of the story." The admiral turned to look at Captain Sheppard. "Regardless, I am Admiral Krrower, and on behalf of the emperor, I welcome you to Mrowry space. You are indeed very welcome, even if you hadn't come bearing my brother. Any ally in a storm is welcome, and we are in one of the worst storms ever."

"Thank you," said Captain Sheppard. "We greatly appreciate your taking care of the Ssselipsssiss ships that were following us."

"It was our pleasure," replied the admiral. "Actually, I was just talking with my brother, and he thinks that by splitting the forces on the other side of the stargate, we ought to be able to go through and finish off the remaining forces there."

"Without a doubt you could finish off the ships that are there," said Captain Sheppard. "There is only a battleship and some battle-cruisers remaining. The problem will be the minefield. It was rather extensive when we went through."

"We have been preparing for an opportunity such as this, and we have many mine clearance craft to send in ahead of us," said Admiral Krrower. "We just didn't know what enemy forces were on the other side of the stargate. Now that we know, and have already destroyed some of them, we are going to go through and capture the system. We have enough mines and other area denial weapons to ensure that once we take that system, barring a major offensive by the Ssselipsssiss, we won't give it back up to them again. They got the system by surprise; we will *not* let them surprise us again."

Captain Yerrow finally spoke. "I would like to stay here for the assault. There are many members of my former battle group whose spirits cry out for revenge. I would like to help get it for them."

"As much as I would like to go to battle with you again, brother," said the admiral, "this is not the time. Word of your demise has already gone back to Grrrnow. You need to get back to the capital as soon as possible, not only for our parents, but also so that all of our subjects can see that the heir is alive and well. Now is not the time to have people restless and worried about the succession. This war is not close to over; there will be plenty of time for us to fight together."

"You are right, of course, admiral," said Captain Yerrow. "We will head back now to prepare the way for the humans. *Emperor's Paw*, out." His half of the screen went blank, and the picture of the admiral expanded to fill the screen.

"My brother also told me that you are here to request aid in your fight against the Drakuls," the admiral said. "I am very much afraid that we do not have any aid to give, as we do not have enough assets for all of our borders, much less to send to a nation that we did not know existed until today. It is not that I don't *want* to help you; I just do not have any ships that I can spare. I can, however, send you forward with some indication of our support and good will, as I will send my son along with you. When he's not getting into trouble, he will serve you well as an ambassador of our civilization. Hopefully he will be able to ease your entry into relations with the Archons. They can be...difficult....at times."

"Thank you," said Captain Sheppard. "When will he be available to travel? Our need is urgent, and we must be off as soon as we are able."

The admiral looked at Lieutenant Rrower where he stood next to Calvin. "I am ready to go whenever they are ready to leave," Lieutenant Rrower said. "My things are already aboard this ship."

"Good," said the admiral with a nod. "Make sure you call your mother when you stop on Grrrnow."

"Yes, father," said Lieutenant Rrower.

The admiral looked back at Captain Sheppard. "Good luck," he said. "I look forward to speaking with you in better times."

"Good luck to all of us," agreed Captain Sheppard. The view screen went blank.

"So, you are the son of the admiral and the grandson of the emperor?" asked Calvin.

"Yes," Lieutenant Rrower answered with what Calvin had come to recognize as the Mrowry version of a shrug. "I am 13th in line for the throne. Well, 14th now, since one of my uncles had a son while I was in your system. I'm expendable. I'm looking forward to continuing on with you. Your race is...interesting. You are learning things that we forgot long ago. I think it is time that we relearned some of them."

"I don't get it," said the ambassador, trying to understand Mrowry society. "If Captain Yerrow is the crown prince, how is it that his younger brother outranks him and can order him around?"

"It is a matter of positional authority," said Lieutenant Rrower. "My father is in the military full time and has been promoted past the crown prince, who has other ceremonial duties that take some of his time. Still, we are warriors first, so he must continue to spend time in command to show his worth. If he cannot command the loyalty of a cruiser's crew, how could he hope to command a nation spanning many star systems?"

"Good point," said Calvin. "I wonder how we could get that practice implemented back home?"

Bridge, TSS *Terra*, Earth Orbit, January 14, 2021

"We are doing everything possible to prepare additional defenses for the stargate," Admiral Wright said on the front view screen. "We are making additional mines and missile launchers as fast as we can. The replicator should finish the next battlecruiser tomorrow, giving us a second one of those. Going forward, we ought to be able to pump them out much more quickly, too."

"Why is that?" asked Captain Griffin, the commanding officer of the *Terra*.

"The battlecruiser was held up in the replicator for 9 days, blocking all progress, because it needed about 100 pounds of protactinium," replied Admiral Wright. "We didn't know ahead of time that we were going to need any. Protactinium is naturally radioactive and highly toxic; however, the aliens have some way to treat it that makes it safe to handle. Protactinium is used for some of the superconductive circuits in the fire control system, so we couldn't do without it. We had to put down a civil war in Zaire to get it; that's the only place it's mined. Until we could, the missing 100 pounds held up the 800,000 ton ship."

"Well, we need that ship and a lot more like it as fast as you can get them out here," said Captain Griffin. "In the meantime, there's one other thing that we can do to prepare."

"What's that?" Admiral Wright asked.

"We need to take the *Terra* through the stargate," Captain Griffin replied.

"I don't think the government will go for that," Admiral Wright said, looking puzzled. "Why do you think you need to do that?" he asked.

"Because," Captain Griffin said, "all other things being equal, I'd much rather fight them there."

"OK, I'll ask again," said the admiral. "Why is that? All of our defenses are on *this* side of the stargate. If you go through it, you lose all of that protection and support."

"I'm sorry sir," Captain Griffin said, "but I've got a lot more ex-perience in fighting space battles than you do. We've *got* to go through the stargate and see what's there. It doesn't make sense not to. There might be a battle group waiting for us there, but it would be a lot better to fight the Drakuls in a place where they can't shoot missiles at Earth while we're fighting them. Having to choose be-tween saving the planet and finishing off one of their ships would be a bit distracting, don't you think?"

"That's true," the admiral replied. "I see what you mean; I'd ra-ther fight them there, too, if I had a choice. But our defenses are *here*."

"The defenses are here *now*," Captain Griffin agreed, "and that's the problem. We need to go through and attack them in the other system if we can. If we go through and find ourselves overwhelmed, we beat a hasty retreat. But if we can go in there and take the system from them, we get the ability to fight a defense in depth. We can mine the other stargate in the system and make them have to bleed twice to get to the Solar System. Hopefully, we can buy enough time for the *Vella Gulf* to bring aid. Even if it doesn't, it will at least give us more time to build ships of our own. If we let the Drakuls get into this system, all hope is lost. Perhaps if we hit them now, we can de-stroy at least a part of their force before it gets to be too large for us to beat."

"You are in command of our only battleship," Admiral Wright said. "We absolutely cannot afford to lose you."

"How about if I do the same maneuver the Drakuls did," asked Captain Griffin, "where I enter the stargate backwards? That way I am prepared to exit back to the Solar System if needed. I can get a quick look. If it's good, I'll continue in-system and will mine the other stargate. If there are too many Drakuls, I'll run rather than engaging them in battle. How is that?"

"That might work," said Admiral Wright thoughtfully. "That just might work..."

Chapter Ten

Bridge, TSS *Vella Gulf*, Grrrnow, 61 Virginis, January 15, 2021

The 61 Virginis system almost felt like home to the Terrans. After all of the systems they had traveled through, the star known as 61 Virginis was the most Sun-like one they had seen. Similar in composition to the Sun, it was just a tiny bit smaller, with only 95% of the Sun's mass and 85% of its luminosity.

Five planets orbited the star. The three planets closest to it were too hot to be habitable; the other two, however, were both habitable and inhabited. The fourth planet, the capital planet of Grrrnow, was remarkably similar to the Earth, although five times larger. The fifth planet, Grrrshow, was a little smaller and cooler, but still habitable.

"We are being hailed by the planet," said the communications officer. "We just received a message that the emperor has asked that you meet him at his private estate. They sent the coordinates."

"Then I guess that's what we'll do," replied Captain Sheppard, looking at the image of a super dreadnought in orbit over the planet on the front view screen. The ship was almost three miles in length, with missile and laser ports running down its sides. "I'd hate to make them angry."

Emperor Yazhak the Third's Estate, Grrrnow, 61 Virginis, January 15, 2021

The emperor looked like a bipedal black panther. His sable coat was a midnight black so deep that it shimmered, with only a few white hairs here and there. He gave off a hunter's aura so strong that ambassadors from many of the meeker races had a hard time being in his presence. Even the Terrans could feel it. "Welcome to Grrrnow," he said as the Terran delegation was brought into his solarium. "I am Emperor Yazhak the Third. I understand that I have you to thank for returning my son and granddaughter to me. The empire rejoiced to find that the rumors of the crown prince's demise were greatly exaggerated."

"Thank you for your welcome," the ambassador replied. "I am Ambassador Juliette Ricketts-Smith. It is good to finally meet you, as we have heard much about you from your son."

"Good to see you again, too, grandson," said the emperor, looking at Lieutenant Rrower. "I understand that you have had an interesting last few months."

"Yes, grandfather," Lieutenant Rrower agreed. "When you suggested that I broaden my education with a tour of duty in the fleet, I don't think that you planned anything like the last cruise of the *Emperor's Paw*. It was, however, both exciting and educational. I believe that it has helped me to grow as both a leader and an officer."

"Combat has a way of doing that," agreed the emperor. "For those that survive it, anyway," he added. He looked back to the ambassador. "Who else have you brought today?"

The ambassador turned to the rest of the Terran contingent and introduced them. "This is Captain Sheppard, the commanding officer of the cruiser *Vella Gulf*." Captain Sheppard bowed. "To his right is Commander Anita Collins, the *Gulf's* executive officer, Lieutenant Commander Shawn Hobbs, who leads our forces that go off-ship, and Steropes, who has taken on the role of advisor for our society."

"All of you are very welcome here," the emperor confirmed. "I never thought I'd say it, but even you are welcome here," he added to Steropes. "My son says that you have put aside the ways of your civilization and have decided to participate in society again."

"I know that my civilization has many things to atone for," Steropes said. "It is impossible for me to make up for all of them, but those things that I can do, I will. I intend to help the Terrans in their current struggles and will do whatever I can for them. The loss of Olympos has caused me to rethink many of the things that we did in the past, and the reasons for why we did them. Perhaps it is also the close association I have had with the Terrans over the centuries; I think some of their values may have rubbed off on me."

"Regardless of what your civilization has done in the past," the emperor said, "I was sorry to hear about the loss of your home world. I would not wish a Drakul invasion on anyone."

Steropes nodded, overcome by emotion.

"Now, as I understand it," the emperor said, turning back to the ambassador, "you have come looking for aid in your fight against the Drakuls." The Terrans nodded. Before any of them could say anything, the emperor continued, "I am sorry, but is not possible to send you anything at this time. My son tells me that you would make an excellent ally, and, if given time, you will be able to stand on your own feet. Unfortunately, we are pressed on all sides. I do not know what has changed with the Ssselipsssiss, but something seems to be driving them toward us, and it is all that we can do to hold them back. Even the *Emperor's Paw* is needed immediately, though it is but a cruiser. It is being re-provisioned and will leave tomorrow for the front lines with the super dreadnought in orbit. That will leave the capital undefended for the first time in memory. I'm sorry, but we don't have any ships to spare. I fear that we won't be able to defend the planets we already have, much less yours."

"Your son told us that would probably be the answer," the ambassador said, "but we still had to ask. Our need is great; the peril is dire. The Drakuls have already found our planet, and it is only a matter of time before they show up in force. Terra stands alone, and it is unlikely that we will be able to turn them away without outside aid."

"Then you must go on to the Archons, who are also fighting the Drakuls," said the emperor. "It is unlikely they will be able to do anything for you either, but it is your only other option. While some of the minor races might be able to send a ship or two, that is not what you need. You need several capital ships to defend your stargate."

"We understand," the ambassador replied. "That is where we will go next."

"I will be continuing on with the Terrans," Lieutenant Rrower said. "My father is sending me with them to help with the Archons and to learn all that I can from them. I would also like permission to go into combat with them if that becomes necessary. I have worked out with their troops, and I believe that I could help them."

"That makes sense," the emperor said. "Do try not to get yourself killed." He turned to the officers from the *Vella Gulf.* "Is there anything else I can do for you?"

"Is that Clowder Rock," asked Calvin, gazing out the window at a large rock formation about half a mile away.

"Yes, it is," the emperor replied. "How do you know of it?"

"It's a long story," said Calvin, "but we were told to look for formations like it. When we have more time, I would like to take a walk around it."

"I'm sure my granddaughter, Princess Merrorritor, would love to show it to you," the emperor said. "She has a special connection to it and goes on walks there as often as she is allowed."

President's Chambers, National Assembly Building, Abuja, Nigeria, January 16, 2021

"I appreciate your coming here today to explain it to us," Terran President Katrina Nehru said. "Why do you think it so important to take our only battleship through the stargate?" Not wanting to make the decision without consulting the civilian controlling authorities, Admiral Wright had requested a meeting with the key governmental decision makers. The president, the vice president, the heads of both houses of Parliament and the secretary of state had come to the president's chambers to meet with Captain Griffin and the admiral.

"There are four reasons why it's so important," said Captain Griffin, who had prepared for that question. "The first is a matter of convenience for me. I would much rather fight the Drakuls anywhere other than this system. If we have to fight them here, it will already be a desperate, last ditch fight. If we fail to control this stargate, we have nowhere to fall back to; if we lose this stargate, we lose Earth. Taking another system down the chain of stargates gives us options. It allows us to fight on our terms, rather than on theirs."

"The second reason is similar to the first," continued Captain Griffin. "If we fight them here, all they have to do to distract us is start shooting things at Earth. If they launch missiles at Earth, we will be forced to decide whether to try to stop the missiles or continue fighting their spaceships. That is a sure roadmap to failure. Even if we focus on their ships first, we won't fight as well, knowing that our homes and families are in jeopardy."

"That makes sense," said Amanda Silva, the speaker of the lower house of parliament. "All things considered, I'd much rather they weren't shooting missiles at the Earth."

"Agreed," said Captain Griffin. "Third, we need to know what is in the next system. There are a variety of tactical and operational reasons for going through the stargate. Maybe the Drakuls have something there like a replicator that we could capture and bring back, which would aid in our defense of the system. Maybe there is something there that would be detrimental to their war effort if they lost it, like the refueling point necessary for them to continue their fight into our system. There are a number of things that might be there that would help us or hurt them. It's worth taking a look."

"Finally," concluded Captain Griffin, "it buys us time. If we can control the next system, it will take them time to make a system entry there, and then additional time to regroup and do it again into our system. That will give the *Vella Gulf* extra time to find aid. Captain Yerrow didn't think that his father would be able to send us aid. If that is true, then the *Vella Gulf* will have to go all the way to Archonis. That will add nearly a month both ways, plus whatever time is needed to organize their assistance. Best case, we are going to need to hold for at least three months before anyone shows up to help. Best case. Worst case, the *Vella Gulf* comes back without any assistance. The additional time will let us better prepare our defenses here. If we have to defend the system by ourselves, we'll at least be in the best possible position to do so."

"I think I understand all that," said Masood Khalil, the secretary of state, "but as I also understand, you command our most capable ship. If we lose you, won't the Drakuls be able to pour into our system, nearly unchecked?"

"Our destruction would significantly degrade Earth's defenses," acknowledged Captain Griffin; "the *Terra* is our most capable ship. However, I feel that it is better to use that advantage where I can fight the ship like I know how, without having to worry about defending the Earth at the same time I'm trying to kill Drakuls. I intend to use the same maneuver the last Drakul spaceship used on us. I will go through the stargate backwards; that way, I'll be able to run if needed. While the risk of losing the *Terra* is there, I think I can sufficiently minimize the danger. We need to know what's in the next system, and if we can take it, we will have more options for dealing with the Drakuls in the future."

"I am not a military person," President Nehru said, "nor do I have much experience in military matters. Still, what you said makes sense; those are compelling reasons to go through the stargate and take a look." She looked at Admiral Wright. "If you think there is reason enough to do it," she said, "send the *Terra* through."

Chapter Eleven

"Rotate ship!" ordered Captain Griffin.

"Ship rotating, sir," replied the helmsman.

It had taken longer than Captain Griffin wanted to get permission to attempt this maneuver. The Terran government wanted to be careful with their only battleship, Captain Griffin knew, but they were being *too* careful. If she had to fight the Drakuls, she wanted to do it as far away from the Earth as possible. How could the leaders not see that? If you don't want Earth to get hit by a nuclear weapon, don't let anything carrying a nuke get into the system. Duh. By waiting until they came through the stargate to engage them, the Terrans were giving up the initiative. She knew they couldn't win that way.

The *Septar* was close by. If the *Terra* didn't return in an hour, the battlecruiser would follow them into Ross 154. Captain Griffin hoped she wouldn't need the warship sooner than that, but if there were any Drakuls in Ross 154, she intended to destroy them. She wouldn't fight a suicidal battle against long odds, but if she could get into the system, damn it, she was getting into the system, and she was *by God* going to hold it for Terra. It was the only way they could buy the time they needed.

"How are we doing on our line-up for the stargate?" she asked.

"We're nominal to profile," the helmsman answered. "We're headed straight into the stargate."

It was a lot different piloting a battleship than a cruiser, Captain Griffin thought. There was far less margin for error, as the crew of the Drakul battleship found out when it tried to flee the Solar System during the Battle of Stargate #1. She looked at the stargate on the view screen. It looked like they were headed into it. Breathe, she thought. Just breathe.

"Five seconds to stargate!" called the helmsman.

Please God, just don't let there be anything bigger than a battleship there, Captain Griffin prayed.

"Three..."

And God, if you could make it where there wasn't anything bigger than a battlecruiser waiting, Captain Griffin continued, I'd surely appreciate it.

"Two..."

"For Terra!" someone yelled. Captain Griffin realized that she was the one who had yelled it.

"One..."

The universe expanded to infinity as the ship entered the stargate.

Bridge, TSS *Terra*, Ross 154, January 19, 2021

"System stabilizing," said the Mrowry sitting at the science station. "Launching probes." He sent out a variety of probes to expand the ship's sensor network, looking for any evidence of energy or power sources. He didn't have to look far for the system's other stargate; it was no more than an hour away at normal speed.

"Clear here," called the DSO.

"I'm not showing any targets, either," said the OSO.

"They are correct," agreed the Mrowry science officer after another couple of minutes searching. "I do not see any evidence of the enemy in the system."

Captain Griffin sighed. She had been keyed up for a fight. After all of the buildup, the lack of an enemy to fight was tremendously anticlimactic. Even though it was better that they didn't have to fight to get into the system, her adrenaline was at an all time high, and it would take a few minutes for her to relax again.

"Proceed to the other stargate," she ordered. "We've got a lot of mines to place."

Bridge, Drakul Ship *Destruction of Olympos*, Lalande 21185 System, January 30, 2021

Captain Bullig considered his fleet's disposition on the tactical plot. Arrayed defensively around the stargate to Ross 154, the ships appeared ready to go. He had just received word that the Overlord had recalled some of the ships from the Kepler-62 system to join his fleet, as they were no longer needed there. Although the planet wasn't 'pacified' yet in the sense that all of the local life forms had been rounded up and led to the livestock pens, the ships weren't required for the control of the planet. He had heard that the creatures there were hard to see and even harder to capture, but they were delicious if you could get one in your grasp.

With the addition of the two battleships and three battlecruisers that were on the way, he would have the dreadnought, six battleships, 18 battlecruisers and 18 cruisers. That ought to be more than enough to acquire the new food source. The ships from Kepler-62 should arrive in four to five days; the assault could begin in less than a week. He shivered in anticipation.

Chapter Twelve

"Welcome to the 51 Pegasi system and Archonis, the home world of the Archons," Steropes said as they entered the new system.

"About damn time," LCDR Sarah Brighton, the squadron's XO, said. "We've been chasing this wild goose for months; it will be nice to get some resolution."

It had taken the *Vella Gulf* more than two weeks to get from Grrrnow to Archonis, traveling through five systems along the way. The systems of Gliese 676, Mu Arae, GD 61, Fomalhaut and HR 8799 all lay in their rear view mirror. Although the journey hadn't been dangerous, since the systems were controlled by either the Mrowry or the Archons, all of the crew was conscious of the passage of time. They needed to find aid and get it back to Earth ASAP!

"There is something that you need to know prior to dealing with the Archons," Steropes added. He paused. "Well, several things, I guess, if I am to be totally accurate."

"What do I need to know?" asked Captain Sheppard.

"The Archons are difficult to work with during the best of times," Steropes explained. "While the race generally believes in doing good things and helping others, they can sometimes come across as rather haughty. They have the reputation of knowing what is best for outside civilizations, regardless of what the outsiders might think.

Once they have decided something, they are very difficult to sway from their point of view."

"But they listen to reason?" Captain Sheppard asked.

"Sometimes," Steropes replied. "It is usually a matter of finding the right argument to convince them. Sometimes the subtle approach works best; other times you need to hit them in the head with a brick. It is impossible to know what will work with them on any given occasion. The only thing that's certain is that they will have a strong opinion of what is best, which may or may not match up with your view of what is best."

"Got it," Captain Sheppard said. "What else do we need to know?"

"Second," Steropes replied, "you need to know that it is very difficult not to go along with their point of view."

"Why is that?" Calvin asked.

"They are empathetic transmitters," Steropes replied. "Empaths are highly sensitive people who can perceive emotions in other people and feel what they feel. In the case of the Archons, rather than feeling your emotions, they are able to transmit their feelings to you, where you perceive them as your own. When they argue a point with you, not only will *they* believe that they are right, their aura will tend to make *you* believe that they are right, too. It is hard to convince them of anything other than what they believe in; by the time the argument is over, most outsiders have come around to the Archon view."

"We're being hailed by the planet," the communications officer interrupted.

"On screen," Captain Sheppard replied. He turned back to Steropes. "You said I needed to know several things," he said. "What is the third?"

"The third is that you will be culturally biased and predisposed to believe them," Steropes replied. He nodded to the front screen. "They look like angels."

Captain Sheppard turned to look at the front screen and found himself looking at an angel. If it wasn't an angel, it certainly *looked* like an angel. Over seven feet tall, the Archon was humanoid in appearance and impossibly beautiful by human standards. The Archon's flowing hair was nearly snow white, matching the feathers in his wings, which extended up beyond his shoulders. It also had the bluest eyes that Captain Sheppard had ever seen. The commanding officer didn't need the Archon to transmit anything to him; he was awed at just the sight of it.

"Welcome to Archonis," the alien said. "We have had word of your coming and the High Archon will meet with you when you arrive at the planet. I am Admiral Jeremiel, the commanding officer of the Archon ship *Righteousness*, currently in orbit above Archonis. If you need anything prior to your meeting with the High Archon, please let me know." He nodded, and then the transmission ended.

"That was kind of abrupt," Calvin said.

"That is the nature of the Archons," Steropes said. "They are interested in whatever they are interested in; at best, the other civilizations are distractions that keep them from focusing on what they feel is important. At worst....well, you can imagine; it's not pretty."

"You were correct in your description," Captain Sheppard said. "I almost felt like I should bow down to them, or kneel...or something."

"They *are* intimidating," Steropes agreed. "It is even worse when you are near them. You have yet to feel their aura. It is quite daunting."

Bridge, TSS *Vella Gulf,* 51 Pegasi System, February 1, 2021

"The star in this system is 51 Pegasi," Ensign Sara Sommers noted. "It is a Sun-like star located about 50 light-years from Earth. Like our Sun, 51 Pegasi is a main sequence star with the characteristic yellow hue of a G-type star. It is a little older and more massive than the Sun, and it has two planets. The first of these is a Jupiter-like planet that circles the star so closely that the planet's average temperature is 2200°F."

"Too hot for me," the helmsman muttered.

"The other planet is Archonis," Sara continued, "which is located just slightly further from 51 Pegasi than Earth is from the Sun. Since 51 Pegasi is a little bigger and hotter, Earth and Archonis are similar; they also have similar atmospheres. The only difference is that Archonis is a water world. Over 90% of its surface is covered in water."

"They must be able to get metal from somewhere," said the DSO, "because the ship that is in orbit over Archonis, the *Righteousness* I think they called it, is a dreadnought almost two miles long. Whatever you say to them when you're down on the planet, please be nice."

Spaceport, Archonis, 51 Pegasi System, February 1, 2021

The Terrans' shuttle touched down at the spaceport, and the boarding ramp came down, giving the Terrans their first look at the Archons waiting for them. Although they spoke with Admiral Jeremiel on entering the system, they were unprepared for meeting them in person. Steropes had warned the Terrans that a feeling of awe was common when anyone first met an Archon; his warning didn't do the feeling justice.

Calvin and Night were the first two people off the shuttle, and they were immediately overwhelmed by the five Archons that stood waiting for them. Standing just over seven feet tall, all of them looked like angels. They were uniform in appearance, with hair and wings of white. They were also dressed in white, with robes that appeared to glow or shimmer, and they were naturally phosphorescent like some of the deep sea fish on Terra. They were so beautiful that they were hard to look at.

Several guards stood further back. Mirror images of the first group, the only differences were that they were dressed in white powered armor, not robes, and held laser rifles. They looked ready for trouble and gave the impression of being ready to deal with any threat.

The Terrans also experienced the Archons' nature as empathic transmitters for the first time, and the force of their personalities threatened to overwhelm the Terrans. The Archons were annoyed at having to stop what they were doing to greet the Terrans, and Calvin and Night found themselves feeling annoyed at having to come and meet the Archons.

"*Wow,*" commed Calvin to Night. "*Five minutes ago, I wanted their help. Now I'm pissed off that I had to come meet them.*"

"*No kidding,*" Night replied. "*I was just wondering if I could take them all before their guards responded.*" He paused, looking around. "*For the record,*" he added, "*I think I can.*"

One of the Archons stepped forward. Spreading his arms, he said, "Ye are welcome." With his greeting, the Terrans felt more welcome than they had ever felt previously in their lives. Might as well make the best of this, Calvin decided, having suddenly lost the feeling of annoyance.

"Thank you," said the ambassador, stepping forward. "I am Juliette Ricketts-Smith of the Terran Republic. We are very happy to be here and are looking forward to establishing ties with your civilization."

"We are looking forward to learning more about the current state of thy civilization," said the one that had spoken first. "My name is Gabriel, and I am the benefactor for all messengers arriving here. Please come with me so that we can go somewhere more comfortable. The High Archon has asked for you to meet with him in his chambers." As Gabriel spoke with them, the Terrans realized that the day *was* rather warm. Meeting with the High Archon in his chambers *would* be better.

"As you can see," Gabriel said, "our planet is a water world. The main bureaucratic offices are on a nearby island; we will take a short shuttle flight to get there." He indicated a large, open-topped transport that was sitting nearby. A driver/pilot was sitting in the front seat at the vehicle's controls. Four rows of benches allowed seating for about 20 behind him. Calvin realized that the seats had no backs, which would have been difficult for winged creatures to sit on. The way the benches were built, the Archons were able to stretch their wings behind them. Lacking wings, there was plenty of room for the Terrans, although they weren't able to lean back and relax.

The group boarded the transport and was on its way. The vehicle's open top gave the Terrans a great view of the surrounding countryside and oceanic panorama, allowing them to see all of the flora and fauna native to the planet. "It is interesting that all of the creatures here have wings," Calvin remarked to the Archon sitting next to him.

"It was necessary to survive on this planet," replied the Archon. "As you can see, nearly all of the land on this planet is within a few miles of the ocean. In the depths of the ocean is the hafgufa, a terrible creature that would come up onto land to capture its prey. Life on land here long ago developed wings to allow it to escape the hafgufa, whether that was to fly to another island or just to hover until the creature returned to the water. Now that we have weapons, the remaining hafgufa no longer trouble us."

As the hovercar continued on its flight, the Terrans saw a small herd of what were definitely pegasi, a griffin riding on the thermals and something that looked like a winged horse with the head and upper body of an eagle.

"What is that?" Night asked, pointing at the unknown creature.

One of the Archons looked to where he was pointing and said, "That is a hippogriff."

"A hippogriff?" asked Night. "I thought those were mythological creatures."

Calvin shook his head. "Not anymore."

High Archon's Chambers, Archonis, 51 Pegasi System, February 1, 2021

"Ye are welcome," greeted the High Archon, causing a warm glow that put all of the Terrans at peace. At seven and a half feet tall, he was the tallest Archon the Terrans had seen. The emotions he transmitted were similarly strong.

"Thank you," said the ambassador. "We have travelled a long way to get here, and your warm greeting is greatly appreciated."

"Yes," said the High Archon. "I understand that ye have come from Earth, 16 stargates from here, in order to ask for our aid."

"You have me at a disadvantage," said the ambassador. "You seem to know a lot about us; we, however, know almost nothing about you."

"Thy planet is not unknown to us," said the High Archon, "as we were called by the Psiclopes to defend it from the rakshasas. Nasty creatures, those rakshasas." He looked at Steropes and then back to the ambassador. "I can see why the Psiclopes would care about defending thy planet," he added. "Ye do look similar to them, although a good bit taller."

"That is true, I guess," the ambassador allowed, not wanting to disagree.

"I had my aide look up all of the information we had on thy planet," the High Archon explained. "Apparently our ancestors visited it on two occasions; once to drive out the rakshasas and the other to help with the capture of a shape shifter that made it to thy planet."

"Yes," agreed Steropes. "I was there for both of those occasions, and your assistance was instrumental in allowing the Terrans to grow and develop unhindered. Both the rakshasas and the shape shifter would have reduced them to little more than slaves on their own planet."

"Thank you for your previous assistance," added the ambassador, "even if we did not know it at the time. We are already in your debt, but find ourselves in a similar position once again, as we are about to be overrun by the Drakuls."

"They are also nasty creatures," the High Archon said with a sniff, "and if it were in my power to give you aid against them, I would. Unfortunately, I am not the one to talk to for military matters. I am the benefactor for civil administration; for military assistance, ye must talk to Grand Admiral Michael, who is in charge of the fleet. He is the benefactor for all things military. He is currently in the HD 10180 system, defending it against a Drakul invasion of our own. Although I am not an expert in warfare, it seems to me that the battle there has become very static of late. He may be able to send some ships to thy planet, but ye will have to travel there to ask the question. I realize that ye have already traveled far, but ye must go another two systems to seek the aid ye desire."

Chapter Thirteen

Bridge, TSS *Atlantic*, Ross 154, February 2, 2021

"Terra, all of our mines are placed, and we're empty," radioed the Septar's communications officer. "We're going back for another load."

"Roger that, Septar," transmitted the Terra's communications officer. "Godspeed and hurry back!"

"Don't start the party without us!"

Captain Adler smiled. The longer the Drakuls gave them, the better prepared they became. The TSS Atlantic had entered the Ross 154 system an hour previously and was inbound to the stargate with a load of missile launchers. Each launcher was nothing more than a cruiser-sized anti-ship missile in a box, with a small communications and navigations suite that would allow it to stay in place for about five years.

The battlecruiser Atlantic was making its maiden voyage to bring the load of missiles. The government had finally decided to name the battlecruiser class based on the number of countries bordering each ocean, and the Atlantic Ocean had more than any other. The name didn't matter to Captain Adler; he was just happy his ship was finished in time for him to fight the Drakuls with it. He wouldn't mind a little time to train his crew prior to battle, too, if he could get it.

Every moment of every crewmember's day was spent in training, trying to master the ship's systems. If not to master them, at least to become proficient with them. Hell, thought Captain Adler, if we could just figure out how to launch missiles, that would be great. The ship didn't have a motto yet, and he idly wondered how, "There's plenty of time to sleep when you're dead!" would sound.

Bridge, Drakul Ship *Destruction of Olympos*, Stargate to the Ross 154 System, February 5, 2021

Captain Bullig didn't have to be onboard the first ship to go into the Ross 154 system; the Overlord had only specified that he lead the assault into the system of the new food source. As the last battlecruiser moved into position, he smiled. They were ready.

It would be interesting to see how the new food source had prepared for his return. Based on what had happened to the last force that had gone up against them, he figured it would be something nasty. He sent his forces through the gate accordingly. He wouldn't be on the first ship if he didn't have to be.

"Commence the assault!" he transmitted. The first battleship began its attack run, followed by the rest of the fleet. As the *Destruction of Olympos* started to pick up speed, he grinned from ear to ear. He had waited a long time to lead a conquering force.

The first battleship made the jump.

Bridge, TSS *Terra*, Ross 154 System, February 5, 2021

"Stargate emergence!" called the DSO. "Drakul Battleship! Mines are being activated. Launchers are coming online."

"Cleared to fire," said Captain Griffin. "All weapons. Let's show them what we've got."

The crew of the *Terra* had been waiting for this moment. Not anxiously awaiting the arrival of the Drakuls, but not quite dreading it, either. As each load of mines was placed and each layer of box launchers was added to the stargate's defenses, the Terrans had become more and more confident they could hold the gate.

Waiting within laser and graser range, the *Terra* began firing as its mounts came online. Hatches opened down the length of its starboard side as the *Terra's* missiles indicated their readiness and then roared off in search of their targets.

Within a minute of the battleship's entrance into the system, the first of the Terran mines detonated, far closer to the stargate than they were normally placed. The Terrans had hoped to hit the ship before its shields stabilized, but they didn't succeed. The battleship's shields were in place and absorbed the blast, as they did the explosions of the second and third mines, as well. Counter-missile missiles and lasers began firing from both sides of the battleship in an effort to keep any more mines from reaching it, but a fourth mine activated. Although it didn't breach the shield, it was all the battleship's forward shields could take, and they collapsed.

A second battleship entered the system in time to see the first round of missiles impact its comrade, and nuclear fire enveloped the ship from both sides as it was hit by 17 missiles from the first box launcher salvo and another 25 missiles from the *Terra* that made it through its defenses. Its aft shields failed as well, and the battleship was defenseless against the *Terra's* energy weapons. The 16 grasers in the starboard broadside drilled four meter holes into the Drakul invader, while the *Terra's* 12 lasers added their own 3.5 meter holes.

After firing twice at the first battleship, the OSO could see that there was little to be gained by hitting it again. Its bridge was open to space in at least two places and all four of its engines were out. It floated powerless in space. Seeing this, the OSO shifted targets as the *Terra's* shields absorbed the first volley of laser fire from the second battleship. Before he could fire, a third battleship entered the system.

"Damn," muttered the OSO, "I'm falling behind. Maybe this will help." He triggered three waves of box launchers as the first mines came into proximity with the second battleship and detonated along its sides. Missiles hit the ship from both sides, and two more mines detonated alongside it. The battleship's shields collapsed.

No longer able to stop the Terrans' energy weapons, the lasers and grasers of the *Terra* struck home on the second battleship, augmented by the weapons of the battlecruisers *Septar*, *Atlantic* and *Pacific*, and the Drakul battleship began venting atmosphere in a number of places.

The death throes of the second battleship gave the third battleship's crew the time it needed to stabilize their systems, and the Terran ships were forced to defend themselves from the incoming missiles it launched. Making matters worse for the Terrans, the first Drakul battlecruiser entered the system, followed closely by a second and a third.

The Terran battlecruisers ignored their counterparts and continued firing at the second battleship. With a wave of missiles from the *Terra* and two more waves of box launcher missiles, the battleship was finished, its magazines detonating in a cataclysmic explosion that would have been spectacular in atmosphere. The *Terra* shifted fire to the third Drakul battleship.

A fourth battlecruiser entered the Ross 154 system, followed by a fifth and a sixth. "It's getting a little crowded in here," noted the DSO, who was starting to lose the battle against incoming missiles. As more and more ships entered the system, all of them targeted the *Terra* as the biggest threat. The OSO couldn't kill the invaders fast enough, despite using the last two waves of box launchers to breach the third Drakul battleship's shields. Several mines also struck the battleship, with two detonating next to the giant ship's engines. Powerless, the ship absorbed the next round of battleship missiles from the *Terra* without destroying a single one; 34 missiles, each bigger than a space fighter, detonated along its length. Lasers and grasers sought out critical areas, and the battleship was quickly rendered into scrap.

The *Terra* shifted fire to the Drakul battlecruiser engaged with the *Septar*, and its weight of fire quickly turned the battle for the Terran battlecruiser. The Drakul battlecruiser it was fighting lost its shields and then its bridge to the combined energy weapons of the *Terra* and the *Septar*. The OSO on the *Terra* shifted fire again to the battlecruiser that the *Pacific* had engaged. As the prepositioned mines came within range of the enemy battlecruiser fleet and took their toll on the battlecruisers' shields, the OSO started to feel confident that he could hold the stargate.

Until the Drakul dreadnought entered the system.

Recognizing the dreadnought for the threat it was, all four Terran ships immediately shifted fire to it in an effort to knock down its shields. The Drakul vessel did not return fire immediately; instead, it focused its weapons on the mines that were moving toward it. The dreadnought eliminated all but one of the mines before they could detonate. The one that did activate did not appear to have much effect on the behemoth's shields; the OSO barely noticed a fluctuation in them as the mine exploded.

Having eliminated the closest threat, the dreadnought fired at the *Atlantic,* which had the misfortune of being in full view of one of the dreadnought's broadsides. Although the dreadnought was not as long as some of the other nations' dreadnought classes, it still massed over seven million tons and was much wider and taller. Its broadside included 48 dreadnought-sized missile launchers and 35 lasers that were each 5.25 meters in diameter.

All of these fired at the *Atlantic.*

It was impossible to tell, even later in the slow motion replays, how many of these hit the *Atlantic* and how many were absorbed by its shields, but the answers were easy enough to comprehend without replay. Too many and not enough. The *Atlantic* was hit by at least 35 of the dreadnought's missiles, each of which was nearly half the size of a frigate-class warship, and at least 25 of the lasers. As the sensors cleared, the Terrans got their first look at what was left of the *Atlantic.* Five pieces were all that remained, blown apart so thoroughly that all were open to space. As the crews of the other ships watched, a last missile, launched later than the rest of the broadside due to some technological glitch, arrived at what was left of the Atlantic, obliterating the largest piece.

"Holy shit," someone said. It was hard to tell who; everyone thought it.

"*Retreat!*" commed Captain Griffin. "*All ships retreat to the Solar System at flank speed.*"

Captain Griffin looked again at the remains of the *Atlantic,* which had been shifted to one of the smaller monitors and sat back in her captain's chair. The battle had been going so well, she thought, before the arrival of the dreadnought. They had all fired at it several times and not made a dent in its shields. She knew that all of their defenses combined weren't up to the task of defeating the dreadnought. They didn't have anything that could.

If the *Vella Gulf* didn't get back with something big, they were doomed.

Bridge, Drakul Ship *Destruction of Olympos*, Ross 154 System, February 5, 2021

They had chased off the food source's pitifully few ships, and Captain Bullig savored a hatchling with a smile. Although an unpleasant surprise for the first several battleships that went through the stargate, it had been a fierce and surprisingly vicious fight to gain entry into the system. Totally enjoyable. His smaller craft were now scouring the remains of the ships that had been destroyed to gather the rest of the harvest. He was especially looking forward to seeing what the new food source tasted like. The battlecruiser they had destroyed should yield many samples. Hopefully, some were still relatively intact after the explosive decompression of the ship. He hadn't meant to hit it *quite* that hard...but the destruction of the battlecruiser had been impressive and would be a memory that the food source would take back with them to their home system to make them fight better next time.

"Aren't we going to give chase?" asked his new XO. "We could probably destroy at least another one or two of them before they get away."

"No," replied Bullig, savoring another hatchling as he enjoyed the afterglow of battle. "Let them take back word of our great victory to their system, where they can cower in fear until we are ready to finish them. I'm sure the destruction of their battlecruiser will be great for morale when it is played on their news services." Like a cat with a mouse, he wanted to play with them for a while. Like the cat, he realized that once he destroyed his prey, all of the fun would be gone from it forever.

He smiled outwardly, although he knew he was going to have to send back for more ships to break into the food source's home star system. The Overlord would not be pleased with that, but it was necessary; if they had this many defenses in the outer system, they would have even more in their home system. Maybe even enough to destroy a dreadnought. He needed more ships. Perhaps he should send some samples of the food source to the Overlord to make sure he got the ships he wanted. It would take a little longer than he had planned before they could conduct the next attack, giving the food source more time to prepare, but that was all right. Without the challenge, where was the fun? He just needed to figure out a way to keep from dying in the next assault. What was the good of conquest, if you weren't around for the pillage and plunder that inevitably followed?

"The minions have returned, Captain," said the communicator.

"Good," Captain Bullig replied. "Bring them here."

He needed to learn more about the next system to prepare for the assault. As the command ship for the Drakul fleet, the *Destruction of Olympos* had a few members of the feeder races that it carried to do the things the Drakuls either could not or would not do. Playing with computers was one of those things, so he had sent some of the minions to the battlecruiser he had destroyed to see what they could learn about the new feeder race.

The first group he sent had reported that they weren't able to break into the computer system onboard the battlecruiser. After he had eaten two of them in front of the others, the rest of the group decided they would like to go back and try again. Apparently, watching their comrades get consumed jogged something loose in their minds, giving them new ideas for how to get into the computer systems.

His master at arms brought two of the worm creatures onto the bridge. They were shaking in fear. He chuckled, deep in his throat. This is what he lived for.

"So, were you sufficiently motivated to break into their systems this time?" he asked the taller of the Hooolongs.

"Yes, your lordship," replied the Hooolong. Its four eyes looked in four directions at once, unconsciously looking for a way to escape the danger it knew it was in. None of the eyes looked at Bullig, and he laughed again. "We were able to break into the Terran's computer system."

"Wait," Bullig said, stopping him. "The Terran's computer system?"

The Hooolong moved its head in a circular motion, indicating assent. "Their main planet is called Terra in their language. They consider themselves to be Terrans."

"What did you find in their computer systems?" asked Captain Bullig.

"We found a message to the ship called 'Septar,' which we believe was one of the ships that fled the system," said the smaller of the two. "The message ordered them to continue bringing mines to the stargate until the minefield was at least twice as strong as the one in Ross 154, which we believe is the system we are currently in. We tried to cross-check this with the ship's ephemeris, but it was damaged beyond salvation."

Captain Bullig made a hungry noise at the back of his throat.

"And that's why we searched the bridge," the taller Hooolong said quickly, "until we found a star chart, which confirmed that we are in Ross 154. The message that we found was two months old, so we do not know what happened in the interim, but as of two months ago, the minefield in the next system was supposed to be at least twice as strong as this one. It also referenced box launchers; there were supposed to be three times as many of them."

Hmmm...thought Captain Bullig...twice as many mines and three times the number of box launchers. Based on the number of ships defending Ross 154, he didn't expect that there would be many ships in the next system. Even though the enemy forces had been vastly inferior in this system, they had still managed to inflict a number of losses on his force.

"Good," he said, looking at the taller one. "I will let you live."

Both of the Hooolongs slumped in relief. "I only said that one," Bullig said. Before the smaller Hooolong could move, he grabbed it and bit through the large artery below its eyes. Slurping happily, he continued to work out his plan to capture the next system...Terra. He could do it with the ships he had, but there would be a large number of casualties, and he didn't want to be one of them. The Overlord had been specific that Bullig was to be in command of the first ship into that system. He would be, but for him to survive the assault he would need a few more ships...

Chapter Fourteen

"**S**ystem entry," Sara said, having picked up the habit from Steropes. "This is the HD 10180 system, which includes the Archon planet of Malak. It has two stargates in addition to the stargate we used to enter the system. The first of these goes on to the Gliese 777 system, and the other goes into 54 Piscium. Both of these systems are inhabited. The Archon fleet is currently stationed around the stargate to the 54 Piscium system."

"Holy shit," said Calvin, looking at the tactical plot as the information came in on the assembled Archon fleet and its flagship, the super dreadnought *Holy Word*. "That thing is enormous! You could put the entire Terran fleet into one end of the *Holy Word,* and it would rattle around inside it. And there are three more almost as large!" Three miles long, the ship massed over 10 million tons and was over half a mile wide. Most of the bridge crew was speechless. They had thought that the *Terra* was immense. Until now. "They have ships like that," he continued, "and *they* can't break into the Olympos system?" He shook his head and then added simply, "fuck."

"Indeed," Steropes said. "What you aren't taking into consideration is that each ship has to go through the gate one at a time. As the super dreadnought emerges, I imagine that the Drakuls have a similar collection of vessels on the other side of the stargate waiting to turn

143

it into scrap. This fleet is enormous and could do a devastating amount of damage if it could get into the next system. The problem is getting it into the system unscathed."

Calvin looked at the hologram of the defenses arrayed around the stargate. "What are these things?" he asked, pointing at a collection of things that looked like asteroids.

"They are orbital fortresses," said Lieutenant Rrower, who had been to the front previously. "They are asteroids that have been hollowed out and turned into fixed battle stations. They can absorb a lot of damage and still remain functional, as all of their important systems are buried deep inside."

"Couldn't the Archons send one of those through to precede an assault? They would be great for breaking into a system."

"It wouldn't work," Lieutenant Rrower said shaking his head. "They have small engines for station keeping but not big enough to go through the stargate. Additionally, they are too wide to go through. Pieces of it would get cut off if they tried it."

"OK," agreed Calvin, "If you can't take them through the stargate, I understand why you would have them form a ring in front of the stargate. But what about this group that is right in front of the stargate? It would seem that a ship entering the system would run right into them."

Lieutenant Rrower showed his teeth in the Mrowry version of a smile. "Exactly," he said. "Early on in the war, the Drakuls tried to come through the stargate at a significant portion of the speed of light. That way, they hoped to break through the minefield and away from all of the ships that were positioned nearby."

"Isn't that dangerous?" Captain Sheppard asked.

"Very much so," agreed Lieutenant Rrower. "The margin for error is very small. If you miss the entryway even a little bit, the stargate will slice your ship apart."

"Did it work?" asked Calvin.

"Actually, it did," replied Lieutenant Rrower. "Five ships made it through. If the Drakuls had been prepared to exploit the opening, they could have done some significant damage. As it was, they only sent through cruisers, and the Archons were able to track them all down and destroy them. It was lucky that they weren't ground assault ships, or the planet would have suffered greatly. One cruiser did fire a number of missiles at the planet from long range. Most were intercepted, but two made it to the planet. I understand there was a significant loss of life."

"After that, they moved some asteroids to block the stargate?" Calvin asked.

"Yes," Lieutenant Rrower replied. "A couple of weeks later the Drakuls tried to send another battle group through. The battleship that came through first did an excellent job of destroying the first asteroid when it ran into the rock at almost half of the speed of light. The ship was completely flattened. The next couple of crews misjudged their entrance, and only portions of their ships came through the stargate. By the time the fourth ship came through, the Archons already had the next asteroid in place."

Calvin studied the plot a little longer and then asked, "Are there also asteroids in front of the stargate on the Olympos side of it?"

"Umm, no, I don't think so," Lieutenant Rrower said. "The star is very close to the stargate in the Olympos system. *Very* close. If you try to go too fast through the stargate, you're probably going to run into the star. Any of the largest ships, like the dreadnoughts and super dreadnoughts, are too massive to make the turn if they come out going fast. Their momentum will take them right into the star. That's why the system is so easy for the Drakuls to defend; every ship has to come through slowly, making them very susceptible to the defenders and the minefield there. It's also why the Drakuls only sent cruisers through the first time they tried their high speed entrances. Getting by the star and into the stargate at that speed is incredibly dangerous. It takes both skill and a large portion of luck."

"Sir," called the communications officer, "the *Holy Word* just called. They asked if you could shuttle over to meet with Grand Admiral Michael."

"Please tell them that we are on our way," replied Captain Sheppard. He looked around the bridge. "We've come a long way for this conference. Let's not keep the grand admiral waiting!"

CO's Conference Room, Archon Ship *Holy Word*, HD 10180, February 7, 2021

The Terran delegation filed into the conference room onboard the *Holy Word*, the flagship of Grand Admiral Michael. All of them were in a bad mood. They could feel that they were wasting the Archons' time, which would have been better spent preparing the defenses of the system. Calvin looked around the room disconsolately. It was bigger than a similar Terran conference room. The table in the room would have seated close to 30 Terrans comfortably, but was only made for 20 Archons. Although the Archons were only a little larger than the average Terran, the Archons' wings took up a lot of extra space.

An Archon wearing the uniform of a grand admiral entered the room, followed by nine others of lesser ranks. He took a seat at the end of the table and indicated that everyone should be seated. "Welcome to the front lines," the Archon said in a deep voice. "I am Grand Admiral Michael, the admiral in charge of this front. As I understand it, ye have come looking for aid in thy own fight against the Drakuls. Unfortunately, I do not have aid to give. A week ago, maybe, but not anymore."

His aura overwhelmed the Terrans listening to him; they were crushed.

"Why is that?" asked Captain Sheppard, fighting his feelings. "What changed?"

Grand Admiral Michael looked to one of his staff and nodded. "I am Captain Raziel," replied the Archon Michael nodded to. "I run fleet intelligence." He paused and then continued, "A couple of days ago, a deep reconnaissance ship returned from a survey behind the Drakul lines. What the crew found was very disturbing."

Captain Raziel's aura was nearly as strong as Grand Admiral Michael's, and all of the Terrans found themselves worrying about what the ship found.

"The reconnaissance ship discovered that the Drakuls were building a new orbital fortress," the intelligence officer continued. "The station is a hollowed out asteroid, to which they have added a large number of lasers and missile sites. We've seen them build things like this before, but this fortress is different because it has four stargate-capable engines, and it is smaller than their normal fortresses. Usually, the Drakuls modify large asteroids so they can withstand a lot of damage. This asteroid is only two miles in diameter. If ye put these two facts together, it looks like they intend to send it through the stargate."

"Wait a second, sir," interrupted Calvin. "I didn't think that the Drakuls did anything innovative. Did something change?"

The intelligence officer looked intently at Calvin, as if sizing him up, before nodding his head as if conceding a point. "Yes," he finally said. "Something has changed with them. This is only the latest in a string of new concepts and improvements they've come up with. We don't know whether they have become smarter themselves, or whether some new entity is helping them, but this is just the latest example of Drakul innovation. They have built an asteroid fortress that is mobile, and we believe they are going to use it to attack into this system."

"If they can get it through the stargate," Captain Sheppard said, "what effect will it have on the war?"

"It is enormous," said Captain Raziel. "There are so many weapons systems on it, if they can get it through the stargate with even half of them intact, it will break the blockade here."

"And that," interjected Grand Admiral Michael, "is precisely why we cannot afford to loan you any ships. We need every one of them here in order to try to stop this monstrosity when it comes through the gate."

"Can't you do something else, besides just sitting here waiting for it to show up?" asked Calvin, not wanting to give into the feelings of despair washing over him. "How about attacking through the stargate and destroying it before they're ready?"

"That is not possible," Grand Admiral Michael replied, causing another wave of hopelessness to hit the Terrans. "They have too many ships waiting on the other side of the stargate, in addition to an enormous minefield. We have enough mine clearance vessels that we could probably neutralize the minefield; unfortunately, they have enough major ships gathered around the stargate that they could destroy our ships as we came through the stargate one at a time."

"How about going through two or three at a time?" asked Commander Anita Collins, the *Gulf's* executive officer. "Has that been tried?"

"No!" said Grand Admiral Michael. "Nor will it. In order to get the amount of ships that we would need in there, we would have to try to send four dreadnoughts through the stargate simultaneously. They wouldn't fit. Even if we only tried to send two ships at a time, the odds are nearly 100% that they would interpenetrate on their emergence. We will *not* attempt that."

"Then there must be something else that can be done," Calvin said. "You can't just sit here and wait for them to come to you!"

"That is exactly what we *must* do," said Grand Admiral Michael. "Our defenses are thickest here, and they will have to come in one at a time. Additionally, our shipbuilding industry is working to produce more ships, and we have recalled all of the ships we can from our outlying systems. We will meet them here, and we will do everything we can to stop them."

"We have virtually no chance of destroying their fortress," said Captain Raziel. He passed some reconnaissance photos down the table. As the photos reached Calvin, he saw that they were somewhat blurry, although he didn't know whether that was due to a limitation of the camera, or whether the Archons had blurred the photos to not give away any of their intelligence capabilities.

"Here's what we know," continued Captain Raziel. "First, the asteroid is covered in some kind of metal. We don't know how thick the armor is, but we believe the metal is extremely dense and at least several feet thick. They have weaponized it to a great extent, with five-meter anti-ship lasers and smaller anti-missile lasers mounted all across its surface. We have estimated there are over 500 of the larger lasers and at least 1,000 anti-missile lasers. There are also more than 500 hatches on the asteroid that we believe are for missile launchers; the number of missiles that the asteroid can hold is probably in the tens of thousands. Our fleet cannot hope to destroy it; all we can hope to do is destroy the rest of their fleet and buy some time for Mrowry aid to get here."

"I'm sorry, sir, but I do not believe there will be any aid coming from the Mrowry," said Lieutenant Rrower. If he was intimidated by being the most junior officer at the table, he didn't show it. "We were just at Grrrnow, and I spoke with my grandfather, the emperor. Something is driving the Ssselipsssiss into us, and they are pressing us like they never have before. We don't have so much as a frigate to send to aid the Terrans, and they were responsible for saving our crown prince."

"If thou could not send any assistance to a nation thou were honor-bound to aid," Grand Admiral Michael replied, "then it is unlikely that any will be coming to assist us. Without aid, unfortunately, there is little chance that we can stop the Drakuls. We are doomed."

"We can't just assume that," said Calvin, fighting the despair that threatened to overwhelm him. "We have got to do something about it. We can't wait for them to come here and attack us when they're ready, we've got to take the fight to them and hit them when they're not. We've got to hit them now!"

"Thou art asking us to do something that we have not been able to do in many years," Grand Admiral Michael said. "Thou art asking us to break into the Olympos system, a system that the Drakuls have reinforced like no other. We need to defeat their minefield, as well as the fleet that was assembled for the sole purpose of holding us out. Then, with all of the forces that survived, we need to go destroy an orbital fortress that is beyond our ability to destroy, even if we had the whole fleet. It cannot be done."

"I don't know about that," said Calvin. "I have an idea."

"An idea?" asked the grand admiral in disbelief. "Thou, who have little knowledge of the situation, little appreciation for the forces involved in this battle, and a minimal combat ability? Thou hast an idea?" He laughed. "By all means, mighty warrior, do tell us how thou thinks all of this is possible."

"Well, sir, I don't think that we can beat their minefield or fleet, and certainly our cruiser is not up to the task of destroying the asteroid in a stand up fight any more than your fleet is," Calvin replied. "You have already made it clear that confronting them head-on is the wrong way to go about it."

"And thou hast some other way?" asked Captain Raziel. The feeling of despair lightened a little as a wave of hope went through the room.

"I do," said Calvin. "I have a plan that I think will work; I just need a little time to discuss it with my commanding officer and our ship's AI."

CO's Conference Room, Archon Ship *Holy Word*, HD 10180, February 7, 2021

"We've looked at it extensively," said Captain Sheppard two hours later, "and I think that we may be able to take care of your problem."

"I am sorry," said Grand Admiral Michael, "but I still do not see how that is possible. How is one ship of 300 humanoids going to accomplish something that the biggest fleet assembled in over 5,000 years has been unable to?"

Captain Sheppard looked at Calvin. "It's your plan, Lieutenant Commander Hobbs," he said. "Why don't you go ahead and brief it."

"Sure thing, Skipper," Calvin said, nodding his head. For good or bad, they were committed. Now was not the time to be timid, regardless of who he was briefing or what emotions he currently felt. He looked at Grand Admiral Michael. "We're going to do it through a combination of stealth, audacity and trickery. Oh, yeah, we'd also like to use one of your battlecruisers, too, if you've got an extra one."

Grand Admiral Michael looked confused. "I am sorry; that did not translate. What is this trickery of which thou speaketh?"

Calvin began briefing his plan. After five minutes, Grand Admiral Michael stopped shaking his head. After another 15 minutes, he was nodding, a thoughtful look on his face.

"And that's the plan," said Calvin in conclusion. "We will destroy the asteroid for you, and in return you will assist us in defending our home system from the Drakuls. I know there are a lot of holes in how we're going to accomplish this, but we're going to have to fill them in as we go along. We don't have enough intel to have all of the answers now. Any questions?"

"I don't have any questions," said Grand Admiral Michael. "Although I find this plan unlikely to succeed, it is better than anything else we have come up with. If ye are able to destroy the asteroid, we will send some ships to help with your home system's defense." He paused, and the Terrans could feel Michael steeling himself to say what must be said.

"There are a couple of things ye must know before ye attempt this mission," he finally added. "First, if ye get the chance to wipe the Drakuls out, ye must do so. They are one of only two races ever to be issued the Final Directive. Even though it was issued more than 3,000 years ago, it still remains in force today, and for good reason."

"What is the Final Directive?" asked Captain Sheppard.

"The day we issued the Final Directive was the low point of the Alliance of Civilizations," said Grand Admiral Michael. "It was the day we admitted the Drakuls could not be redeemed. We attempted to change them, but failed. We tried to quarantine them, but that also failed. We were left with one last option, the complete destruction of their race. Genocide. Although we did not want to eliminate their race, not exterminating the Drakuls was a worse option for every other civilization. The Drakuls were too amoral and reproduced far too quickly." His eyes looked sad, but he stood up straight to make his pronouncement. "By the power of what remains of the Alliance of Civilizations, I charge you with destroying the Drakul civilization, wherever ye find it and through whatever means ye deem to be the most effective to ensure its complete termination. *That* is the Final Directive, and that is the directive under which ye must operate."

Captain Sheppard felt a tremendous weight fall on his shoulders. This went way beyond what the Terran government had charged him with and was a far greater responsibility than what he felt was in his mandate. The complete extermination of a race if he had the ability? He was glad he didn't have the ability, so he didn't have to deal with the consequences of that action.

Lost in thought, he almost didn't notice that Grand Admiral Michael was talking again. "I must get back to organizing our forces. The other thing thou must know is that even though thy plan is the best we have, I believe that its chances for success are minimal. If thou art not back in two weeks, we will do what we have to. We will bring all of our fleet through the stargate with the intention of destroying all of the Drakuls that we can. We will fight until our fleet is no more. We will fight and die, but we will do our best to defeat the Drakuls. I wish ye Godspeed and good luck in thy quest." With that, he got up and walked out. With heavy hearts, the Terrans realized that the meeting was at an end.

Shuttle Back to the *Vella Gulf,* HD 10180, February 7, 2021

"I'm just happy that we don't have to worry about committing genocide on the Drakuls," said Captain Sheppard to the rest of the group returning to the *Vella Gulf.* "We certainly weren't authorized to do that by the Terran government; in fact, our mandate was just the opposite. We were supposed to find new allies, not utterly destroy a race, no matter how much they may need killing. I don't want that on my conscience."

Most of the officers and enlisted present nodded their heads. "That isn't actually the case, sir," said Lieutenant Finn quietly. "The part about committing genocide, I mean. We actually *do* have the capability to destroy their planets."

Captain Sheppard's head snapped around to look at the lieutenant. "What do you mean?" he asked.

"I mean that there is a weapon in the replicator's database that is translated as the Doomsday Device," said Lieutenant Finn.

"You mean to tell me that we have been flying around on a ship that has the capability to destroy planets?" asked Captain Sheppard.

"Oh!...umm...no, not really," said Lieutenant Finn evasively, looking at the deck of the shuttle. "It wasn't in the *Gulf's* database. It was in the *Terra's*..."

"He is correct," said Lieutenant Rrower. "That weapon wouldn't have existed in a cruiser's database, even a Mrowry cruiser's. An Eldive vessel like the *Vella Gulf* would never have had it at all. The weapon was outlawed a long time ago, and it is a closely held secret that its pattern still exists in our replicator databases. Even then, the pattern can only be found in the replicators onboard battleships or dreadnoughts. These ships would normally have an admiral onboard to exercise the type of authority needed to employ the weapon. You would also need the emperor to authorize the use of the bomb, because only he knows the code necessary to unlock the blueprint. As a military member of the royal family, I am aware of the bomb's presence in the databases of some of our ships, but I do not have the code to unlock it."

"Obviously," Lieutenant Rrower continued after a pause, "we never thought about that when we handed over the *Terra* to you or we would have removed it. That type of weapon doesn't belong in the hands of such a young race." He turned to Lieutenant Finn.

"How did you know about it?" he asked. "That file was encrypted. Even the name would have been encrypted."

"Oh!...umm...yes, it was," replied Lieutenant Finn in a small voice, still looking at the shuttle's deck.

"So, you broke one of our highest military grade codes?" asked Lieutenant Rrower.

"Well, yeah, sort of," said Lieutenant Finn. "When I first saw the encrypted file, I thought it would be fun to try to decrypt the name of the blueprint. I didn't know what the file was, or I wouldn't have touched it. I was *much* happier not knowing that a weapon of this type existed."

"Well, regardless, that file's on the *Terra*, so we don't have to worry about it," said Captain Sheppard.

"Umm...well...not exactly," said Lieutenant Finn.

Captain Sheppard looked angry. "And why is that?" he asked.

"Well...umm...I sort of brought a copy of the database along with me, in case we needed to use any of the things in it," he said, looking miserable. "The Mrowry database had a *lot* of cool things that neither the *Vella Gulf* nor the Ssselipsssiss replicator had. I thought we might need them. I never thought we'd need Armageddon."

"I really wish you hadn't said that," said Lieutenant Rrower. "Even admitting to its existence is a death penalty offense on my planet. It would be best if everyone that just heard that forgot they did. That way, no one will be forced to kill you."

"Got it," said Captain Sheppard. "No one heard what Lieutenant Finn said. That's an order."

Everyone nodded their heads. They all understood the gravity of the situation.

Lieutenant Rrower tilted his head, looking at Captain Sheppard. "Now that you know it exists, what do you intend to do?"

"I don't know," replied Captain Sheppard. "I intend to do my absolute best *not* to ever use such a weapon; however, I guess we'll just have to burn that bridge when we come to it."

Chapter Fifteen

President's Conference Room, Terran Government Headquarters, Lake Pedam, Nigeria, February 8, 2021

"Attention on deck!" the aide called. Over two thousand people stood and snapped to attention as one. All conversation immediately died.

"Everyone please be seated," ordered Admiral James Wright, the head of Terran Fleet Command, as he walked into the room. He had been given permission to use the president's conference room for the afternoon, and he didn't want to waste a single moment. They had too much to do. The room was full, with the most junior officers, enlisted and civilians either standing in the back or sitting in the aisles. The fire marshal would have had a fit at how badly the room was overloaded if he had seen it. Admiral Wright didn't give a shit.

He surveyed the room as he walked to his seat. He saw the groups from the *Terra,* the *Pacific* and the *Septar* at the other end of the conference table, along with a contingent from Alice Springs. The *Atlantic* was conspicuous in its absence, but there was no time to dwell on its loss. On the left side of the table sat his senior staff officers and the head of Replicator Command; all of the senior extraterrestrials sat on the right. Senior officers from all of the Terran states filled the auditorium, as well as a few Mrowry and Domans. The Mrowry and kuji sat together in a section that had chairs modified for their tails. Although most of the former Terran nations had converted to the standard Terran Fleet uniforms, some of the poorer

159

nations still wore their legacy uniforms, making the auditorium look untidy to his military eye. He put that thought aside, too, as he sat down and nodded to his intelligence officer, Vice Admiral Sir James Lockery. "Why don't you give everyone a quick recap so that we all have the same baseline?"

Lockery nodded. "Yes, sir," he said. He could have gone to the podium, but everyone in the room had implants and could hear him as well as if he were sitting next to them. The admiral had said not to waste a minute, and he wasn't going to. "As everyone is aware, we have lost the Ross 154 system and the TSS *Atlantic.* Although we were forced to withdraw, we destroyed several of the Drakuls' ships and gave them something to think about. The Drakuls know that when they come through the stargate into the Solar System, we will fight them with everything we have. I expect that seeing the *Terra* gave them pause, which is why they didn't immediately follow us back here. Until now, they thought the largest ship we had was a cruiser; the battleship had to be a nasty surprise." An evil grin crossed his face, but it fled rapidly as he made his next point. "The problem is, of course, that no matter how well Captain Griffin and the *Terra* performed against the Drakul battlecruisers and battleships, they can't go up against a Drakul dreadnought in a toe-to-toe fight. The fact is, we don't have anything that can."

"We have run a number of scenarios with the *Terra's* AI, and one thing is clear: if we don't come up with a new plan, we will be unable to stop the Drakuls when they assault this system. Unless we can come up with a way to stop their dreadnoughts, we're going to lose. The purpose of this meeting is to figure out a way to do that."

There were a number of murmurs that could be heard through-out the room. The members of the Terran Fleet that had been in the

Battle of Ross 154 sounded uniformly negative in their comments. They had seen the dreadnought shrug off damage that would have destroyed several battleships and keep on coming. Worse, the Terran Fleet Command didn't have battleships; they had one battleship, which was still being repaired from its last fight. It wouldn't last long against the dreadnought without a tremendous amount of support.

The kuji princess raised her hand and was recognized. "Has the Terran government begun looking at evacuating the system and bringing the government to Domus?"

Admiral Wright's eyes narrowed. He did not want this meeting to go down the rabbit hole of despair. "Yes, Your Highness," he said, "there are other groups that are looking at both of those alternatives." He stood up, and his steel gray eyes swept the conference room. "I want to make it clear to every military person in this auditorium that I will *not* entertain that sort of defeatist attitude. President Nehru has decided that she will stay in the system, along with the billions of Terrans we cannot evacuate. We *have* to hold the stargate to protect our president and all of the civilians that can't be evacuated, including most of our own families. We have to hold the stargate. We *will* hold the stargate. From now on, everyone in this room needs to be focused on that." His eyes swept the audience again, avoiding any contact with the kuji princess. "Are there any questions about that?"

As expected, there were no questions. He sat back down. "Admiral Becker, the floor is yours."

"Thank you, sir," replied Admiral Becker, who stood and crossed to the podium. A German, he believed in doing things the correct way. Officers did not sit when leading meetings as important as this.

"As Admiral Lockery noted, the purpose of this meeting is to come up with a line of defense to stop their dreadnought-class and larger ships. Anything that we develop to stop a super dreadnought will function even more admirably against any of the smaller classes. I know that many of you have come up with ideas for how we can do that. We will get to all of them, and then we will work through as many spur-of-the-moment ideas as we have time for. Ladies and gentlemen, if you have an idea that you think will work, now is the time to voice it. We have a lot of work to do, so let's try to keep the discussion as focused as possible." He glanced down the table to the senior officer from Alice Springs. He hated to advertise that group's existence to the Mrowry, but it was unavoidable. "For those of you that are unaware of Department X, we created a special unit; its mission is to exploit all of the alien technology that we acquire. They will make the first presentation. Captain Sarkozy?"

The captain from Alice Springs stood up. Like many of his group, he was pasty white in complexion, despite working in the middle of a desert. They didn't get out much. "We have been through as much of the new replicator database as we could, and we have several ideas that we think will make a difference." He glanced at his notes. "The first is that we need to stop building major combatants and focus on building additional fighter craft. We have found some plans that will carry more missiles than our current fighters, making them far more effective."

"It won't work," said a voice from up the table.

"I'm sorry?" asked Captain Sarkozy, blinking his eyes. "Did someone say something?"

"I did," announced Andrew Brown, the civilian that ran Replicator Command, the unit that operated all of the replicators in the Solar System. "I said that it wouldn't work."

"It *will* work," said Sarkozy, annoyed that a lesser intellect would challenge his plan. "For the same amount of mass, you can make 56 fighters instead of one battlecruiser. Those 56 fighters have a combined launch capability of 280 missiles, which is sure to breach the dreadnought's defenses, especially if its shields are already down as a result of our minefield. For the price of two battlecruisers, we can make over 100 fighters that will fire over 550 missiles. We have calculated that a strike of this size *will* result in the mission kill of a dreadnought. If we have 150 fighters, we can achieve the mission kill of a super dreadnought." He smiled, sure that he had made his points plain enough that everyone should understand. Even civilians.

"And I still say that it won't work," repeated Brown. Seeing that Sarkozy was about to argue the point, Brown waved for silence. "I'm not debating your arithmetic or saying that many fighters shooting that many missiles won't kill a dreadnought or super dreadnought. I'm not a military expert. It probably would. What I *am* saying is that your plan won't work because *we can't make that many fighters*. There are two problems. First, every single advanced spaceship we make needs 100 pounds of protactinium for its fire control system, regardless of whether that ship is a fighter or a battleship. I think we currently have just over 200 pounds, total, so you're not going to get your 150 fighters. Give me a year to replicate the things we need to go to the asteroids and mine it there, or wherever it is that it exists in abundance, and I can do it, but right now or in the next six months? Forget it."

"The second problem is that all of the advanced fighters use a number of the rare Earth elements in their structural framing. As I'm sure you know, if you don't put those elements into the replicator, you don't get them back out again. When the replicator gets to an element it doesn't have, the replicator just stops and waits for you to add it. If we don't have the element, the whole production line just stops. Earlier this year, we didn't have enough protactinium to finish the battlecruiser we were working on, and the replicator was jammed up for nine days. *Nine days!* We didn't make *anything* for nine days while we waited for the protactinium. I don't want to start building fighters and find out that we don't have enough yttrium or dysprosium or whatever type of unobtainium it is, and jam up the replicators again. *We don't have time!*"

Brown turned to meet Admiral Wright's eyes. "We looked at this option ourselves. There are smaller fighters in the database that are even a better investment in the number of missiles they can carry per ton of mass expended to build them. Unfortunately *all* of them need various types of rare Earth elements, plus that damned protactinium. *It can't be done.* Not at this time. Our best bet is to continue to make more box launchers and missiles. The launchers aren't particularly economical, but they work, and we can build lots of missiles. But more fighters to carry them? It. Can't. Be. Done."

Captain Sarkozy sat down heavily. All three of their 'great ideas' had involved a variety of mini-spaceships shooting lots of missiles. The greatest minds in the Terran Fleet had failed utterly because they had neglected to look at their supply chain while thinking their big thoughts.

Captain Griffin raised her hand and was acknowledged. "What about modifying the fire control system? Can you either re-wire it with something other than protactinium or swap out the computer system with another one?"

"I wish," said Andrew Brown, shaking his head. "*All* of the advanced systems use that element, and they don't work right without it. Not having that element upsets the timing of the targeting information processing somehow, and the missiles launch without getting the entire targeting download they need."

"He is right," agreed the Mrowry officer sitting at the table. Originally a weapons officer on the *Emperor's Paw*, he had more hands-on knowledge of the advanced missile systems than all of the Terrans put together. "That element is plentiful on one of our home planet's moons, and is used in many of our systems. The fire control system won't work without it."

"What about putting some of our current fire control systems onto the space fighters, then?" asked Captain Griffin.

"We looked at that, too," replied Brown, "but there is an interface problem between the ship's computers and our legacy fire control systems, and there are still difficulties in getting enough of the rare Earth elements to build them. We're working to adapt them, but so far, no luck. We can pass our lessons learned to Captain Sarkozy's unit; maybe they can figure it out."

"All right," said Admiral Becker, seeing that the Department X ideas were dead ends, "we'll move on to the next option. I understand the *Terra's* crew has an idea they'd like to discuss?"

The afternoon wore into evening with no solution in sight. The only option that they had discussed that had any chance of working was the solution proposed by the commanding officer of the *Terra*, but that solution was almost too horrible to contemplate.

Admiral Wright realized that the conference had exhausted all of the ideas that had shown promise, as well as a large number of suggestions that were fanciful or farcical, and they were no closer to a solution. All of them either relied on something they didn't have or, on closer inspection, just wouldn't work. He knew they needed to take a longer break than the two 10-minute breaks they had already taken, but they were almost out of time, and his mind kept coming back to the first idea. They needed ships that would mount terrestrial fire control systems which would integrate with their computers.

He realized that there was a question that no one had asked. He raised his hand, interrupting a laser officer from the *Septar* who was proposing building a massive number of mirrors to create a giant solar-powered laser. The idea sounded like something out of a science fiction book. Admiral Becker gave the floor to his boss.

"We missed something," Admiral Wright noted. "No one ever asked whether our terrestrial computers and fire control systems can talk to the advanced missiles. Does anyone know if they can?"

"Yes, they can," replied Captain Sarkozy. "We looked at arming our air-breathing fighters with advanced missiles for the last-ditch defense of Earth. There were some coding changes involved, but one of our smart guys figured out how to make it work."

"What about space fighter engines?" asked Admiral Wright. "How are we set for making them?"

"Those I can make a dime a dozen," answered Andrew Brown. "The helium-3 engines don't use anything fancy in their construction, and there are now enough miners and mining equipment on the moon that we are getting a steady supply of helium-3. I think we have so much of it, in fact, that we just sent down enough to fuel the first couple of power plants on Earth."

"So we have missiles?" asked Admiral Wright.

"Yes, sir," replied Andrew Brown

"Engines?"

"Yes, sir."

"Terrestrial computers and fire control systems?"

"Yes, sir."

"It sounds like we just need some airframes, then," noted Admiral Wright.

"Yes, sir," agreed Andrew Brown. "Do you happen to have a couple hundred of those lying around?"

"I do, actually," replied Admiral Wright, "In fact, I have thousands."

National Museum of the Air Force, Wright-Patterson Air Force Base, Dayton, Ohio, February 9, 2021

"They want *this aircraft* out?" asked the assistant director, Major General (Ret.) Tom Bates, gazing up at the giant plane. "They know the bomber's way back here, and it's going to take several days for us to get it out and then get everything put back in again, right?"

"Yeah," said the director, Lieutenant General (Ret.) Bob Thompson, "they know that. Believe it or not, apparently the old girl is going to fly again, if what I hear is true."

"Really?" asked the assistant director. "They have a lot of things that they'll have to put back into her to get her to fly again."

"If they're really doing what I heard they're doing," said the director, "they're going to put a lot more into her than you'd ever believe."

309th Aerospace Maintenance and Regeneration Group (AMARG), Davis-Monthan Air Force Base, Tucson, Arizona, February 9, 2021

"They're going to do *what* with this?" asked Airman Kinsler as he hooked up the tow bar to the nose gear of Bureau Number 152591.

"I heard they're going to carry it up to the moon and turn it into a space fighter," replied Senior Airman Charles from the seat of the tow tractor.

"You've got to be shitting me," said Kinsler, gazing up at the metal monstrosity. He had only been at the boneyard for a few weeks and had a feeling that the senior airman was having a joke at his expense. An aircraft storage and maintenance facility, the AMARG was home to more than 4,400 aircraft that had reached the end of their combat lives but were still deemed too valuable to be sold for scrap. Like a giant auto junkyard, some were used as parts lockers for aircraft that continued to fly, saving the services the money they didn't have to pay for new parts to be made. Others were in various phases of preservation, ready to be called back to action if their nation ever needed them.

Their planet needed them now.

Chapter Sixteen

"Holy Word, *this is the* Vella Gulf, *we are beginning our transit*," transmitted the communications officer. Having made that announcement, the *Vella Gulf* began its run to the stargate. Calvin had decided to hit the stargate at about half the speed of light, or 335 million miles an hour. The *Vella Gulf* would take well over 11 hours to accelerate to that velocity at 375 G, and they would cover almost two *billion* miles during that time. The last three days had been busy, but they were finally ready. Everything was set and in place. Now the Terrans just had to thread the needle of the stargate at half the speed of light, turn before they ran into the star and, oh yeah, try to do it without being noticed. No problem.

But the plan was in place, and it was a good one, Calvin thought. The plan would work. It was too crazy not to. He glanced down at Steropes who stood next to him. "So, how am I doing?" Calvin asked.

"What do you mean?" Steropes asked.

"Well, I would bet money that you're still observing me as one of your hero souls or hero ghosts, or whatever it was," said Calvin. "Tell me you're not."

"The term was 'hero spirit,'" Steropes replied. "And it is hard to not evaluate your performance as such when you continue to be central to the events unfolding around you. For example, are you not the person who suggested flying through a stargate at half the speed of light, or do we have someone else to thank for the idea?"

"No, it was my idea," Calvin said. He paused, thinking. "Does that mean that this is going to work?" he asked finally.

"I don't know," Steropes said, "but the odds are good that it will not. Studies have shown that over half the time hero spirits fail to accomplish their mission. They risk much, which makes the consequences of failure that much larger."

"Take this attempt, for example," he continued. "If you destroy the asteroid, you will not win the war for the Archons. You will simply allow the status quo which existed beforehand to continue. The consequences of failure, however, are catastrophic. If we get caught before we destroy the asteroid, we will show the Drakuls that we know about the battle station and will make it nearly impossible for the Archons to save themselves from it. No," he said, shaking his head, "we cannot win the war with this attempt, but we can very possibly lose it."

"Then why didn't you say something to the Archons?" Calvin asked. "Why didn't you warn them that this is likely to fail?"

Steropes laughed. "You think that they don't know this is a huge gamble? That they don't realize this could cost them the war? The Archons know it as well as I do, and far better than you do, obviously. The only reason that they are going along with the plan is that having a hero spirit on their side gives them a chance, even if it is a small one. Their support of your plan is an indication of just how desperate they are."

"I didn't realize they went along with the plan," Calvin replied. "They wouldn't give us a battlecruiser; we had to have Lieutenant Rrower requisition it."

"Like I said, the fact they are letting us attempt this at all speaks volumes about how bad their situation is," Steropes said. "Maybe they didn't do everything for you that you wanted, but they agreed to let you try, even knowing what the consequences of failure would be. You couldn't do this without their help, remember? They *did* promise to move the asteroids in front of the stargate, didn't they? Hitting an asteroid at half the speed of light would really ruin our day, wouldn't it?"

"Uh, yeah, it would," said Calvin.

"So, to answer your original question," Steropes continued, "yes, I am still watching you. How could I not? It is the best show in town, as your people say. And it will continue to be so, right up until you make the mistake that kills us all."

Calvin had plenty of time to rest prior to their attempt at transiting the stargate, but he doubted that sleep would come very easily.

Bridge, TSS *Vella Gulf*, HD 10180, February 11, 2021

"This is kind of like landing on the aircraft carrier," commented Calvin to Sara and Steropes at the science station. "The carrier looks really tiny for the entire approach and then only expands for you to land on during the last few seconds." He looked at the front view screen. They were only 10 minutes out from the stargate but couldn't see it yet, even at the *Vella Gulf's* highest magnification. Probably because they were going *half the freaking speed of light*, Calvin thought.

"We're on course for the stargate," noted the helmsman. "10 minutes out."

"Understood," said Captain Sheppard. "Sound General Quarters."

"Sounding General Quarters," said the duty engineer, seated next to the helmsman. The alarm began sounding.

"I just hope that they moved the asteroids out of the way," said Calvin, "or things are going to get really rocky."

"Another pun like that," Captain Sheppard announced, "and you'll be confined to your quarters." He then smiled at Calvin to show that he appreciated the attempt to lighten the mood.

Time seemed to stretch to infinity as they continued toward the stargate.

This has got to be the dumbest thing I've ever done, thought Calvin. This is worse than landing on the aircraft carrier at night in a storm. Dumb, dumb, dumb. This is even worse because it was my stupid idea.

"Penny for your thoughts," said Captain Sheppard.

"Umm, I was just thinking that I'd like to go back to landing on the aircraft carrier at night and in bad weather," Calvin replied. "Where it's safer."

Calvin looked at the countdown timer above the view screen. One minute to go. The stargate still couldn't be seen on the screen. He also couldn't see whether the asteroids had been moved or if they were still in place. He decided he didn't want to know.

"How are we doing Solomon?" asked Captain Sheppard.

"We are nominal to profile," said the ship's artificial intelligence. "I estimate an 83.6% chance that we will pass safely through the stargate."

83.6% seemed like pretty good odds, thought Calvin, as long as you didn't play them too long. Eventually you were going to hit that

16.4% and crap out. Hopefully, this wouldn't be the time that he made his fatal error.

As the timer reached two seconds, the stargate seemed to leap forward at them, its black maw expanding to engulf them. The *Vella Gulf* hit the stargate at half the speed of light and made the jump.

Bridge, TSS *Vella Gulf,* 54 Piscium, February 11, 2021

The *Vella Gulf* emerged from the stargate going faster than any ship had ever jumped previously. Before even the Drakuls' automated systems could react, the *Vella Gulf* was past the minefield, and the forces arrayed to stop it. Thankfully, none of the defenses were directly in front of the ship. What *was* directly in front of the ship was 54 Piscium, an orange dwarf star which already covered almost the entire view screen. In the five seconds that it took for the people and systems to recover from transit, the star grew beyond the edges of the screen.

"Stealth on! Both ships!" ordered Captain Sheppard. "Separate ships! Evasive maneuvers!"

"Stealth is on!" replied the DSO. "Both ships!"

The duty engineer pushed a button. "Ships separated!" he replied as the *Vella Gulf's* clamps released the Mrowry battlecruiser that the *Vella Gulf* had been attached to when it entered the system. The Terrans immediately lost sight of the battlecruiser as they left the ship's stealth bubble, and they were left to hope that the ship's pre-programmed navigational system would function as programmed.

"Evasive maneuvers, aye!" replied the helmsman. In a softer voice he said, "Here goes nothing."

Clear of the battlecruiser, the *Vella Gulf* went to emergency power. Mounted backward in relation to the battlecruiser, the *Vella Gulf* was already pointed away from the star. Slowly the ship began to change its thrust vector. It was going to be close. The helmsman pressed a button and their expected impact point on the surface of the star was displayed on the view screen. Although only 76% of the Sun's mass and 46% of its luminosity, 54 Piscium was still hot enough to fry the *Vella Gulf* if the ship got too close. Steropes thought that the shields might protect them for a short while in the corona. Maybe. Slowly....ever so slowly, the impact point on the view screen began to change, moving outward from the center of the star toward the star's corona.

Steropes began a countdown, "Three, two, one, impact!" As he said "impact," there was a giant eruption from the center of the star as the battlecruiser ran into it with its engines set to full power, creating a massive solar flare that covered over 5% of the surface of the star. The flare reached out to the Terrans, but the *Vella Gulf* was already out of the way, and the flare did no damage.

"Geryon is on the other side of the star," Steropes noted. Geryon was the planet closest to 54 Piscium. The size of Saturn, the planet orbited closer to the star than Mercury orbited the Sun. Running into it at the speed they were traveling would have been just as bad, and just as fatal, as running into the star. Thankfully, the ephemeris information the Archons had given them was correct; the planet was currently on the other side of the star.

As Calvin watched, he saw the ship's projected impact point clear the corona. That was important, because the whole mission was based on stealth, and everything they had done was with the intention of fooling the Drakuls. He knew that the Drakuls would be aware that a ship had transited the stargate, and that they would have had about five seconds to see them. Calvin had hoped that by coming through so quickly, the Drakuls wouldn't have gotten a good look at them; their sensors wouldn't have been prepared for a ship coming through so fast.

Calvin gave them something to see by attaching the much smaller *Vella Gulf* to the former Mrowry battlecruiser *Halcyon*, requisitioned by Lieutenant Rrower when the Archons refused to provide a ship. Lieutenant Rrower had some sort of writ or decree from the emperor; Calvin wasn't sure how it worked, but all of the royal family was able to command any non-royal officer in the event of an emergency. Lieutenant Rrower determined that this was an emergency, and used his writ to take charge of the *Halcyon*, which had been passing through the system. Its commanding officer had *not* been happy to lose his ship, but gave it up after seeing Lieutenant Rrower's black pelt. The captain and crew of the *Halcyon* were on a transport back to Grrrnow that Terra would have to pay for at some point in the future.

About twice as long as the *Vella Gulf*, the purpose of the *Halcyon* was to hide the *Vella Gulf*. From the angles that the *Vella Gulf* could be seen, the Terrans painted both ships black, making the *Gulf* more difficult to distinguish by optical systems. The ships stayed attached to each other until the stealth systems came on; after that, the *Halcyon* was detached so that it could accelerate on its death flight into the star. Calvin figured the Drakuls would get a reading on the mass of the combined ships; the *Halcyon* accelerated so that its impact would have the same momentum as the combined ships would have at their original speed. Hopefully, the Drakuls wouldn't notice that the ship hit the star sooner than it should have, but there was only so much he could do. Although the Drakuls would probably have noticed if the *Gulf* had gone through the corona of the star, the *Vella Gulf* had avoided the corona and now...hopefully...they would be safe.

"Somebody talk to me about the forces at the stargate," said Captain Sheppard. "Are they coming toward us?"

"It doesn't appear so," said Steropes. "They appear to be resetting around the stargate."

"That's what I'm seeing, too," said the DSO, who had a number of passive systems at his disposal. "The Drakul ships are slowing down and moving back toward the stargate." He paused and then said. "I think they bought it, Skipper."

"Good," said Captain Sheppard. "Let's get a survey going of the system. Make sure that we stay well away from all Drakul ships and any stellar outposts."

Bridge, TSS *Vella Gulf*, 54 Piscium, February 12, 2021

"In addition to Geryon," said Steropes woodenly, "this system has three other planets. One of them, Olympos, is inhabited. I do not know how much of its indigenous population still resides there."

"You know you could go back to your cabin, right Steropes?" asked Captain Sheppard. "You don't have to stay here and do this."

"If I went back to my cabin," Steropes replied, "I'd have nothing but time to think of everyone and everything I've lost. At least this way, I am contributing to what I hope is the Drakuls' eventual downfall. I don't know what we can do to stop them, but if it's in my power to exact some revenge, I intend to."

"Revenge is somewhat down our list at the moment," said Captain Sheppard. "I'm not saying that we won't be killing plenty of Drakuls sometime soon, because I'm pretty sure that we will; however, any revenge needs to be done within the scope of our mission. We have a job to do, and we need to get it done. Am I clear on that?"

"Yes," said Steropes, "you are clear. I would, however, like to go on whatever combat missions we send out."

"We'll see about that," replied Captain Sheppard. "In the meantime, what else can you tell us about the rest of this system?"

"In addition to Olympos, which is a super-Earth type planet, there are two other super-Earth type planets that are beyond the habitable zone and are too cold to live on. These are named Pavonis and Pindus. The system has two other stargates, in addition to the stargate we came in through. These two gates lead to Kepler 68 and Gliese 876. The Kepler 68 gate leads to Hooolong space; the Gliese gate leads to the Drakul home world, as well as back to Earth. 54 Piscium also has a brown dwarf companion star, but it is too far away to affect our mission here."

Chapter Seventeen

Bridge, Drakul Ship *Destruction of Olympos*, Ross 154 System, February 14, 2021

It wouldn't be long now, thought Bullig, recently promoted to admiral to lead the next assault. Although he had enjoyed the sense of anticipation at first, he was ready for the attack to begin. Perhaps he should have allowed his crews to destroy another one or two of the Terran ships. If he had, they might have been able to capture some live samples of the new food source.

At least the Overlord was happy with the samples Admiral Bullig sent back to Drakon. Rather than making Bullig return for punishment, the Overlord agreed to send a few more ships from the 54 Piscium system to assist in the assault of the Terran home world. With the new battle station operational, the Overlord decided to pull some of the ships from the defense of that system to aid in the conquest of Terra. A cruiser had just entered the system to advise him that two more battleships, four battlecruisers and seven cruisers were on the way. It also brought a message from the Overlord. These ships were the only ones he was going to get. He either needed to take the system or die trying.

He voted for the former option.

He had already received a few ships from Drakon and had sent a few back; with the additional reinforcements, he had six battleships, 17 battlecruisers and 15 cruisers, in addition to his dreadnought. He had lots of battlecruisers and cruisers...so many, in fact, that a large percentage of them would be expendable in the upcoming fight, especially if that was required to spare Bullig's life. If only he didn't have to be on the first ship into the system, the assault would be easy. Since he did, though...hmmm...there must be a way that he could use them to his advantage...

Chapter Eighteen

"Dead slow ahead," ordered Captain Sheppard.

"Dead slow ahead, aye," repeated the helmsman. The ship moved forward at its slowest speed.

The Terrans had noticed that the size of the ship and the speed with which it entered the stargate were directly proportional to the electromagnetic pulse, or signature, the stargate made when the ship exited. Calvin hoped a relatively small ship, going extremely slowly, would make so minimal a signature on stargate exit that no one would notice. He asked Steropes, who confirmed that it was possible. No one did that, he was told, because it didn't make tactical sense. If your forces controlled the stargate, there was no need to worry about the pulse; if they didn't, you wanted to have a good amount of speed available in case there was a minefield or enemy ships waiting at the exit. Going slowly through a stargate made little tactical sense in most normal situations.

Being behind enemy lines during a war wasn't a normal situation, though; there was no reason for them not to try to suppress their signature. They didn't want anyone to know they were coming or going and didn't think there would be a minefield on the Gliese 876 side of the stargate. At least they *hoped* there wouldn't be a minefield, anyway. What would be the purpose? No race mined the interior

181

systems they held because no sane commanding officer wanted to navigate his ship through a minefield. It didn't matter whether it was an enemy minefield or a friendly one. Only bad things could happen in close proximity to that much high explosive.

But no one really knew how the Drakuls thought. They might have mined the exit side 'just in case.' In case of what, no one knew. But everyone worried about it, just the same.

The *Vella Gulf* was at General Quarters in case there were ships or mines. If there were, the odds were they wouldn't be able to escape back to the 54 Piscium system. If they were discovered, they were going to try to make a run for Earth, even though they didn't know where the stargates were in the systems they were going to have to pass through. The potential for things to get ugly was 'high,' to say the least.

"3...2...1...star—," the helmsman started to say but then everything stretched to infinity and they were gone.

Bridge, TSS *Vella Gulf*, Gliese 876, February 14, 2021

"Gate," finished the helmsman.

"Mine check!" ordered Captain Sheppard. "Stealth as soon as it's available."

"Checking for mines, aye," chorused Steropes and the DSO. "Stealth when it's available, aye," added the DSO.

"What do you think, Steropes?" asked the CO. "Do you think anyone will see our signature?"

"It is unlikely," replied Steropes. "Our transit signature was minimal, and there are no ships close to the stargate."

"We are stealthed," said the DSO.

"All ahead full," said Captain Sheppard. "Let's get away from the gate and see if we can go find this asteroid the Archons are so worried about."

Chapter Nineteen

CO's Conference Room, TSS *Vella Gulf*, Gliese 876, February 15, 2021

"The star in this system is Gliese 876," reported Steropes. "It is a red dwarf star that is about 15 light-years from Earth in the constellation Aquarius. Gliese 876 is only about 1/3 the size of the Sun and is significantly cooler, resulting in a luminosity that is only about 1.25% of the Sun's."

"The star has four planets," he continued. "The first two are a super-Earth planet about six times Earth's size and a gas giant. Both are too close to the star to be hospitable. The third planet is another gas giant almost twice the size of Jupiter, which orbits in the habitable zone. For Gliese 876, this is about the same distance as the Sun to Mercury. The final planet is a super-Earth that has about 14 times the mass of Earth, or similar to the planet Uranus. The system has two stargates, the one we came in through, and the other that goes on to Lalande 21185."

"*Captain Sheppard, I've got stargate emergence,*" commed the DSO, interrupting the brief. "*I've got multiple ships entering the system from the 54 Piscium stargate. At least one of them is a battleship.*"

"*Roger, DSO, I'll be right there,*" replied Captain Sheppard. He looked at Steropes. "Please continue. I believe you were going to tell us whether you had found the phantom asteroid that we were looking for? That *was* the military objective for coming here, right?"

"Yes," replied Steropes, "I was just coming to that. I did find the asteroid, and I am sorry to say it is already moving. They must have finished the battle station; it is headed toward the stargate from the position of the fourth planet. At the moment, the fourth planet is on the other side of the star from the stargate. We have a little bit of time to see what the ships that just entered the system are going to do before we have to decide what to do about the asteroid."

Bridge, TSS *Vella Gulf*, Gliese 876, February 16, 2021

"I've got an update on the Drakul ships," Steropes said. "They appear to just be transiting the system to the Lalande 21185 stargate. The group consists of two battleships, four battlecruisers, seven cruisers and a few smaller vessels."

"You're sure that they aren't headed toward us or the asteroid?" asked Captain Sheppard.

"No," Steropes confirmed, "they are definitely headed toward the stargate."

"Refresh my memory," said the CO, "what lies in that direction?"

"There are two stargates in the Lalande 21185 system," answered Steropes. "One of them leads to the COROT-7 system, which we believe is the home world of the Drakuls. The other leads through one more system to Terra."

"So they are either going to their home or to ours?" asked Captain Sheppard.

"It would seem so," replied Steropes.

"We've got to hurry," said Captain Sheppard. "I find it unlikely they'd be needed at their home world when the Drakuls are at war in at least two places. They must be headed to Earth."

"Yeah," said Calvin. "We need to destroy the asteroid and get back to the Archons. Like yesterday."

"That may be a little more difficult than we first thought," Steropes advised. "The asteroid has a battlecruiser flying alongside it." He pushed a button, and a picture of a small asteroid appeared on the front view screen. He zoomed in, and the Terrans could see just how large the asteroid was. The 2,200' battlecruiser flying along- side the asteroid was dwarfed by it.

"Damn," said Night, "that thing's huge."

"No kidding," Calvin agreed.

"The asteroid is a cylinder that is about two miles long and one mile in diameter," said Steropes. "It has missile and laser emplace- ments spaced fairly evenly across its surface."

Night looked at Calvin. "Trying to find the control room on that thing is going to be a bitch," he said. "A two mile long cylinder is a lot of volume for one platoon to search, especially if things start get- ting hot."

Before Calvin could reply, Steropes interjected, "Yes, the asteroid is large, but I believe the inhabited spaces are going to be more con- fined."

"Why do you think that?" asked Captain Sheppard.

"My guess is based on the orientation of the fighter and shuttle bays," said Steropes. He changed to another picture of the asteroid. Four large dark spots could be seen in a vertical arrangement at the front of the asteroid. "These four holes appear to be hangars for smaller spacecraft. They are about 400 feet high and 1,000 feet wide.

As you can see, they are all on the opposite side of the asteroid from where the engines are mounted." He pointed to the top one. "If you look at this bay, you can see what looks like the nose of a shuttle."

Steropes flipped to another picture that showed the other side of the asteroid. Although it was an oblique angle, the back ends of four engines could be seen sticking out of the asteroid. "As you can see, they have mounted four super dreadnought-sized engines on the back of the asteroid. It is interesting there are no missile or laser batteries within half a mile of the engines."

"What do you think that means?" asked Captain Sheppard.

"It is possible the engines are not clean," replied Steropes. "They may be producing something that is either radioactive or toxic in nature because there doesn't appear to be anything near them. I believe all of the inhabited spaces are located on the other side of the asteroid. If that's true, the volume that would have to be searched is much smaller."

"If 'ifs' and 'buts' were candy and nuts," Night said, "we'd all have a Merry Christmas."

"I agree with Night," said Calvin. "That's a lot of 'ifs' and 'it's possibles.'"

"True," said Steropes, "but I believe that if we go in through the fighter bays, I think we'll find the living spaces close by. Would you want to have fighter pilots travel two miles after they get back from a mission, or would it make more sense to have everything they need close by?"

"It *would* make sense to do that," allowed Calvin, "assuming the layout was put together by an aviator. Who knows what was important to the station's designers?"

"That is a good point," said Steropes; "however, I believe that if we enter through these bays, we will find the living areas close by, and then the operations spaces somewhere not much deeper from there."

"Well, we need to find the operations center," said Calvin, "or at least make sure we're close. If we can get inside and drop off a nuke close to the ops center, we'll make this thing unusable." He looked at Night. "What do you think?" he asked.

"Can you bring up the image of the front of the asteroid again?" Night asked. Steropes switched back to the requested picture. Night moved closer to the 3D screen and studied it for a minute, pursing his lips. Calvin walked up to join him.

"With the shuttle in the top bay, it's obvious that one is being used," Night said. "That's probably a good place to start. The problem is going to be spreading out enough to look for the ops center, while still staying close enough together to provide mutual support, especially against Drakuls. I'm thinking that we should send in one squad into the top bay, and the other squad into the bay underneath it. If the ops center is further down or deep inside, we'll just have to adapt on the fly."

"That's what I was thinking, too," agreed Calvin. "Why don't you take the Ground Force into the top bay, and I'll take the Space Force into the bay right below it?"

"That would work, sir, if we can get there," Night agreed.

Calvin looked at the picture again, and a strange look came over his face. "What's holding in the air?" he finally asked.

"It is being held in by a force shield," said Steropes.

"Can we pass through the shield?" asked Calvin.

"Yes, you should be able to pass through the shield," Steropes said; "however, it might disable the stealth features of your suits. The Drakuls will also probably get some sort of indication you have entered the bays."

"What do you suppose the battlecruiser will do once they set off the alarm?" asked Captain Sheppard.

"It will probably go to battle stations and try to find the ship that brought the troops," replied Steropes. "Obviously, our troops didn't just spring up from the asteroid; something stealthed must have brought them."

"They are going to know something is in the area," Calvin said, "so we need to build something into the planning to take out the battlecruiser before the troops land."

"Well, yes," Steropes agreed, "but then we have to worry about what the defenders on the asteroid are going to do when they see the ship is under attack. There are probably blast doors that they can shut on the bays that will keep us out. It *is* a battle station after all, and is built to resist intruders. Once they go to general quarters, we probably won't be able to penetrate it."

"OK," Calvin said, "so if I understand this correctly, we can either surprise the battlecruiser and alert the asteroid's defenders, or we can surprise the asteroid's defenders and alert the battlecruiser."

"That is correct," Steropes agreed.

"No matter which we attack first, the *Vella Gulf* is likely to be destroyed by the other," said Captain Sheppard. "Neither of those options is very good from my point of view."

"I'd say they both pretty much suck," said Master Chief in a stage whisper.

"Regardless," Steropes said, "those are the facts. You can probably attack either the asteroid or the battlecruiser and achieve surprise. If you try to do both, it is likely that you won't surprise either."

"My money's on surprising the battlecruiser," Captain Sheppard said. "That's the thing that can come after us."

"The asteroid, however, is more heavily armed," Steropes noted.

"We could go round and round on this all day," Calvin said; "the bottom line is that we can probably only surprise one of them. The asteroid is our main target; we've got to destroy it." He looked back at the picture. "We need to get onto the asteroid without anyone knowing or being alerted to the fact that the *Vella Gulf* is nearby." He looked back at Steropes. "Is the battlecruiser far enough away that we could get a stealthed shuttle up to the asteroid without it being noticed?"

"Yes, probably," Steropes replied. "However, they're going to know that you're there, regardless of whether you pull into the bay or walk into it."

"Without a doubt," Calvin replied. "We'll just have to not walk into the bay until our cover is blown. If we could get close to the bays, though, or maybe even inside the asteroid prior to them knowing we were there..."

"...we might just have a chance," finished Night. "Do you have a plan, sir?"

"I have the beginning of one," replied Calvin. "It will maximize our chances for accomplishing all of the things we want to do, but it's going to be risky. And there's also still the matter of the bomb."

Calvin looked at Lieutenant Finn, who had been sitting at the table listening to the discussion. "Is there anything in your database for blowing up a two mile long asteroid?" he asked. "Something that will break it up or at least render it unusable?"

"I'll go look and see," said Lieutenant Finn.

"Make two of them," said Night. Calvin raised an eyebrow. "We need a backup," Night explained. "If we have two, each of the cyborgs can carry one. Whichever squad finds the ops center first blows it up; that way, we don't have to worry about linking back up to accomplish the mission. We can both exfiltrate as soon as the bomb is planted."

"Sounds good," replied Calvin. "In that case, here's what I think we should do..."

Platoon Briefing Room, TSS *Vella Gulf,* Gliese 876, February 18, 2021

"Then we set the bomb in the ops center and egress from the asteroid," concluded Night. "Are there any questions?

"What are our rules of engagement?" asked the Ground Force Leader, Master Gunnery Sergeant Joan Kinkead. A former Marine Corps drill sergeant, she believed there was only one way of doing things, the right way. There were three loves in her life: her kids, her country, and her Corps. But not necessarily in that order.

"The rules of engagement?" asked Calvin. "Besides 'kill every giant frog that we see?'"

"No," said Kinkead, "I was wondering if we were trying to do this quietly, without firing our rifles, or are we supposed to blast everything that we see? Also, are we supposed to shoot anything that moves, or are there noncombatants that we need to worry about?"

"While I would like to go in as quietly as we can," said Calvin, "doing things quietly means getting close to the Drakuls, where they have a pretty considerable reach and toughness advantage over us."

"Reach, yes," said Kinkead. "As far as toughness goes, they may be tougher than some of these troops, but not me. I've always liked frog legs."

"What I meant is that they can take a lot more damage than we can," said Calvin. Seeing Kinkead about to speak again, he added, "Well, they can take more damage than most of us anyway. Regardless, we want to kill them as far away from us as we can because they have a propensity to pull off peoples' arms and legs."

"A propensity?" asked Bob, one of the kuji from the planet Domus. "What's that?"

"It means they like to tear you apart and eat you while they're still fighting you," said Night. "Kill them on sight, from as far away as you can."

"Got it," said Bob, showing his teeth in the kuji version of a smile. Seeing a six feet tall tyrannosaurus rex smile was...uncomfortable...to say the least. "Shoot them from long range."

"With regard to noncombatants," continued Calvin, "the Drakuls don't have friends. If you see creatures from a different race, they are probably neutrals, at worst, and might be friendlies. Exercise restraint on anything other than Drakuls; Drakuls you can terminate with extreme prejudice." He looked up and saw Lieutenant Finn walking into the room. "Do you have something for us?" he asked.

"Yes, I do," replied Lieutenant Finn. "I knew there were a variety of bombs and warheads in the database; I just needed to find the right one. I was looking for something that was big enough to destroy the station, yet small enough to be man-portable...or at least cyborg-portable," he said, looking at Staff Sergeant Randolph. "Can you guys carry something that weighs 200 or so pounds?" he asked.

Staff Sergeant Randolph paused, doing the calculations. "I think we can," he said, looking at Staff Sergeant Dantone, who nodded. "We will need to readjust some things and maybe take a smaller weapons load, but yeah, it can be done."

"Oh! Okay, that's great. There was this one bomb that they called the Mother of All Bombs," Lieutenant Finn said. "That would have done the job very well, but it was way too large to carry. It was about 1,000 pounds, which I didn't think would work." Both cyborgs shook their heads. "That was what I thought, so I went with the other one. There are three of them waiting in the replicator room. I made a third one, just in case."

"What are they?" asked Night.

"They are four-stage hydrogen bombs," said Lieutenant Finn. "Each of them has a yield of about 100 megatons. That is equivalent to almost 3,000 times the combined power of the bombs that destroyed Hiroshima and Nagasaki. Hopefully, that will be enough."

"*3,000* times the size?" asked Calvin. "Each? Yeah, that should do it..."

Platoon CO's Office, TSS *Vella Gulf,* Gliese 876, February 19, 2021

Calvin was putting on his suit when he heard a knock on his door. Looking up, he saw Steropes standing in the doorway. "Yes?" he asked.

"I had assumed I would be going on this mission, but I was just told that I'm not," Steropes said.

"That's correct," Calvin replied, going back to putting on his gear.

After a pause, Steropes asked, "Is there a reason why I'm not going?"

"Yes," said Calvin, "Several. The first is that you're not part of the platoon. You haven't trained with us, so don't know our tactics very well."

"The same could be said for you," Steropes said. "Before we left, you were gone so much that *you* probably don't know the platoon's tactics very well, either. In fact, I've probably spent more time with the platoon since we got back from our last mission than you have. If it comes right down to it, I'm better integrated into the unit than you are."

"Be that as it may, I'm their commanding officer," said Calvin. "I'm going."

"You don't have to go," Steropes noted. "Night could command the unit just as well as you could; with all of his training, he could probably do it better."

Calvin could see that there was no way to win the argument. "This discussion isn't about whether or not I'm going; I am."

"You're right, the discussion was about qualifications," replied Steropes. "You haven't said why I'm not qualified to go. If the unit gets into hand-to-hand combat, you know I'm better than you are. I'm a tai chi master and have been one for hundreds of years. How about you? Want to spar with me to see whether I go or not?"

"No, I have no desire to get into a ring with you so that you can kick my ass," Calvin replied. "I'll give you the point that you are better in hand-to-hand combat."

"So I can go?" Steropes asked.

"No," Calvin replied, "you can't."

"Can I ask why?" Steropes asked. "Obviously there is a reason. Is it that you don't trust me? Didn't I prove my worth in the coatl temple?"

Calvin sighed. "Yes, you proved your worth plenty of times while we were inside the temple." He paused and sighed again. "The problem is that I'm worried about you. You want to get into combat more than anyone else I've ever seen. It's almost like you're hoping to be killed. You said that you don't have the same death wish as the rest of your civilization, but I'm worried your feelings have changed since you found out what happened to your home planet. I know if Earth were to be destroyed, it might color my actions. I might even want to run off and get myself killed; I don't know. The bottom line is that I don't mind that much if you want to go off and get yourself killed, but I'm worried about what the collateral damage would be to the platoon."

"Collateral damage?" Steropes asked.

"I'm worried about how many of my men and women are going to get killed as a result of your getting killed," Calvin replied. "Until I know that you've adjusted to the new situation, I don't want to take you into combat. Let's just see how things go."

"What if my presence could have saved lives?" asked Steropes, playing his last card. "I have talents and knowledge your troopers do not. My skills and experience might be the difference between mission success and failure, from bringing everyone home safely to not returning at all."

"I can see scenarios where that may very well be the case," Calvin agreed.

"So I can go?" Steropes asked.

"Not this time."

Chapter Twenty

Shuttle 02, Asteroid Weapons Platform, Gliese 876, February 19, 2021

"This is combat reporter Bob 'Danger' Jones with the Frontline News Service. We're at the frontline of the news. Today, I really am at the frontlines, as I'm here with the Terran Space Marines during their assault of a Drakul battle station. With me is their commander, Lieutenant Commander Shawn 'Calvin' Hobbs. Can you tell me what we're going to do today, sir?"

"Sure, Bob," replied Calvin with the winning smile he'd been working on during the past two years of dealing with the media. "The Drakuls have converted an asteroid into a battle station and are moving it into position to attack our new allies, the Archons. We told the Archons that we would destroy the asteroid if they would help us with the defense of Earth. We're inbound to the battle station to do our part. We are going to get inside, set some bombs and blow it up."

"Hopefully, we're not going to blow up the fortress with all of us still inside it, right?" asked Bob Jones.

"No," replied Calvin, laughing good naturedly at the cameraman's joke, "I intend to have us far away when we detonate the bombs. There are three of them, each of which will explode with the force of 100 megatons, so we *don't* want to be close to them when they go off."

"Makes sense to me," Jones commented. He turned to the person next to Calvin. "And here we have the senior enlisted member of the group, Master Chief Ryan O'Leary. Master Chief, what's it like to lead this caliber of men and women into combat?"

"Jones, did I ever give you any indication I wanted to be interviewed?" Master Chief asked.

"Umm, no, but everyone likes to get their face on the news, Master Chief."

"You know that it's hard to walk with a camera shoved up your ass, right?"

"Perhaps I should interview someone else?" Jones suggested.

"Good idea," replied Master Chief.

He walked off in search of another interviewee but was interrupted in his quest. "*Two minutes to the LZ,*" Lieutenant 'Foxy' Fox, the shuttle's WSO, commed. His call let all the troops in the back know they were approaching the landing zone. This was the second time that the shuttle had stopped to drop off personnel; it had also stopped at the back of the asteroid for Night and Staff Sergeant Dantone to get off for five minutes to drop off a package. As Steropes had guessed, the back part of the asteroid was 'hot;' something inside it was radioactive as hell, and the radioactive material was being shunted over the side.

"Let's go," Master Gunnery Sergeant Joan Kinkead said, picking up her helmet. "Gear up and then check the soldier next to you."

"*It looks like they haven't spotted us yet,*" the shuttle's pilot, Lieutenant Matthew 'Exit' Kamins added. "*Everything is still quiet.*"

"*We're here,*" said Foxy a couple of minutes later. He seemed to speak softer, as if he were unconsciously trying to keep the Drakuls from hearing him. "*Ramp coming down.*" The boarding ramp started down, and the platoon got a closer look at the surface of the asteroid. Since they didn't know whether the asteroid would have any mass sensors on its surface, the decision had been made to have the shuttle hover over the surface of the asteroid rather than land on it.

The asteroid's surface was a metal plate; it appeared that some sort of molten metal had been poured onto its surface and allowed to cool during the asteroid's weaponization. The metal covered the surface of the asteroid as far as they could see, providing a protective shell against the weapons of its enemies. The asteroid's surface was barren, except for the battle station's laser mounts, and the closed hatches that guarded its missile tubes' outer doors. The troops could see two different types of lasers. There were a significant number of the enormous five-meter anti-ship lasers and an even bigger number of the smaller counter-missile lasers.

One by one, the members of the platoon dropped gently onto the surface of the asteroid. The Drakuls had an artificial gravity generator somewhere within the asteroid; the gravity on its surface was about 3/4 Earth-normal. Invisible to all but each other, they followed their internal tracking systems until they came to a hatch, which was different than the ones covering the asteroid's missile tubes. The platoon took cover in the outcroppings and laser pedestals surrounding the hatch and then signaled their readiness via their suits' laser datalinks.

Seeing that everyone was ready, Master Chief walked over to the closest of the laser defense arrays. As he neared the mount, he saw that the intelligence department had been correct. The defensive position was a fixed mount; it did not retract into the surface of the asteroid. With a smile, he cut the power cord that ran from its drive motors into the asteroid.

Forward Laser Control, *Death Station Alpha,* **Gliese 876, February 19, 2021**

Lieutenant Gralup sighed. It was bad enough that he had drawn duty during the feast and now this. "We have another fault on one of the lasers. Mount #241 is indicating that power is out to its drive motors."

"Damn it," Technical Sergeant Rikkub replied. "It probably got hit by a micrometeorite or some other piece of space junk." He sighed, too. It was a recurring problem with the configuration. "Whose bright idea was it to mount the lasers permanently on the surface of the asteroid, instead of having them on a telescoping platform that could be retracted into it?" he asked. "There's nothing to protect the mounts or keep them from getting hit by every piece of shit that we fly past. Even if they just put up a small piece of metal in front of the lasers, that would at least shield them from getting hit all the time."

"Some smart person in the high command came up with the idea, no doubt," Lieutenant Gralup said. "They wanted more missile storage. With over 500 laser mounts, keeping them on the surface freed up enough space for another 4,581 ready missiles in our magazines. Or so I've been told."

"I should have been a missile tech," grumbled Rikkub as he began putting on his suit. The lieutenant didn't go up on the surface. The one time the sergeant had suggested it had been...painful, to say the least. Now he just went outside to fix the systems without bitching. Out loud, anyway. "The missile techs' stuff is inside where it doesn't break as much and is easier to get to when it does."

"Cheer up," said the lieutenant. "Go requisition a food creature to do the work, and then bring it here on the way back. We'll have a treat for having to do the extra work."

The lieutenant will get the treat, the sergeant thought with a mental sigh. All *he'd* get would be the husk, once the lieutenant had drained the food creature of blood. Still, that was better than nothing. He'd just have to pick a race that had plenty of fat.

Asteroid Weapons Platform, Gliese 876, February 19, 2021

"Hey, Staff Sergeant," commed Havildar Ali Buzdar, "How long are we going to wait?"

"As long as the boss tells us to Ali," said Staff Sergeant Burke. "Now shut the hell up and be patient." Fat chance, thought Burke. The Pakistani sergeant was the least patient man he had ever met.

Before Buzdar could say anything else, the door they were standing by began opening. The outer hatches moved first, opening from a seam that went down the center and then rotating up and out. Once they had finished moving, another set of doors began moving up and out. Each a foot thick, they would have been a bitch to try to break into, thought Burke. It was very hospitable of the Drakuls to open up the doors for the Terrans.

Two creatures came up the stairs from inside the asteroid. The first looked to Burke like some sort of overgrown caterpillar, moving along in an upside down "U" like an inchworm. There were four arms? legs? that extended from the caterpillar's body from both the front and back parts of it. The creature would probably have reached six and a half or seven feet tall if it stood straight up. Before Burke could study the caterpillar any further, a second suited creature followed it up the stairs. As big as the monster was, it could only have been a Drakul. The thing was immense, topping well over 10 feet. The Drakul was about four feet wide, barrel-chested and easily weighed over 300 pounds. No, it was probably closer to 400, thought Burke.

The Drakul would take a lot of killing to bring down.

The path to the laser mount had a 90 degree bend. As the caterpillar turned the corner, Burke and the other four soldiers that were waiting had a clear shot. They fired as one, and the Drakul dropped. The two laser beams to the chest might not have killed it, but the three that penetrated its helmet certainly did. He dropped, surprising Burke with how long something that big took to fall. The 3/4 gravity played a part, surely, but only a part.

Sensing the Drakul had stopped following him, the caterpillar turned around to find out what had happened. The creature's four purple eyes widened in surprise to see Calvin standing over the dead Drakul, holding up both hands to show they were empty. The creature raised up on its back pad and slowly swayed back and forth, turning around in a full circle.

After completing the circle, the creature dropped down to both pads and shuffled over to where Calvin stood. The caterpillar put its faceplate against Calvin's so that the sound would travel and asked, "You came here with only 38 troops? 36 biologicals and two more that are robots? Cyborgs? Please tell me there are more I can't see."

Calvin stifled a tremor. As if having four purple eyes inches from his face wasn't creepy and disgusting enough, the creature's mouth was on top of its eyes. Up close, he could see that the creature's four arms each had four talons, with two opposing talons on each side of its 'hands,' somewhat like a bird of prey. It was as alien as anything he had ever seen.

Calvin's suit translated the creature's speech as high Hooolong. "How did you know there were 38 of us?" he asked. Of all the things he could have said, he realized that was one of the lamest.

"Sonar," the creature said. "You probably want your shuttle to move half a mile aft, too. The Drakuls are currently performing maintenance on the radar system, but when the radar comes back on, the Drakuls may see the shuttle where it is waiting."

"Um, yeah, I will do that," Calvin said. "Thanks," he added. Lame again.

"We're going to be missed before too long," said the creature, "especially when it doesn't check in," he added, indicating the dead Drakul. "Is this supposed to be a rescue, an assault, or did you just get lost on the way to a costume party?" It paused. "If this is a rescue, I am ready to leave."

Calvin took a deep breath, refocusing himself. "This is an assault," he said. "We are here to stop this fortress from making it to the front lines. The Archons are worried about the effect the battle station will have on the balance of power."

"As well they should be," said the creature. "This station was built with one purpose and one purpose only, to break into Archon space. Although there is a design flaw in having the lasers permanently extended, as you have noticed, this was done to allow extra missile space inside. This station's armor is layered and several feet thick. It protects the Drakuls against both blast and radiation damage, and will shrug off most mines, missiles and lasers. For all intents and purposes, the asteroid is indestructible once it shuts all of its doors."

"How do you know all that?" Calvin asked.

"Simple," said the creature. "I designed it."

"You designed this fortress for them?" Calvin asked. "Why the hell did you do that?"

"I didn't design it for them," clarified the creature. "I designed the battle station to be used against them. However, I was captured by them, and they can be quite...persuasive...when they want you to tell them something."

"I'm Lieutenant Commander Hobbs from the Republic of Terra," Calvin said. "We're here to destroy this thing." He paused and then added, "But we'd also be happy to take anyone off that wants to come with us."

"I would like very much to leave this place," said the creature. "As for who I am, unless you have sonar, my name is unpronounceable in your language. You can call me Smetlurge."

"Smetlurge it is," Calvin said.

"Just a second," said the creature, closing its eyes. "You must hurry," he said when he opened them again. "I was just contacted by the dead Drakul's lieutenant, who wants to know where it is. I told the lieutenant its radio was inoperable, and we would be finished in a few minutes' time. Judging by the lieutenant's reaction, it intends to kill me and eat me. Whenever beings are selected to help its section, they never come back."

"Any chance you could lead us to the operations center?" asked Calvin. "That would help us get out of here faster and would increase your chances of getting off the asteroid, too."

"I will help," the creature said, "under two conditions. The first is that we must stop and kill the lieutenant. Not only does the Drakul deserve to die, but if we don't, it will start looking for the soldier you killed, and will raise the alarm when it can't. The second condition is that we rescue any of the slaves here we can."

"We need to get in and out of here quietly," said Calvin. "If killing the lieutenant helps maintain our secrecy, I'm all for it. As far as a rescue mission goes, our primary mission is to place our bombs in or near the operations center and destroy this station, but if there are others of your kind onboard that we can take off without compromising the mission, we will."

"Fair enough," the creature agreed. "I see the two metal members of your group are bigger than the others. I would recommend using one of them to pretend to be the Drakul soldier when we go through the airlock. Your suits are similar to theirs, and I think that we can get everyone through, but we will need to make two trips. I will say that I left a tool on the surface, which is why we have to go back. We will continue the deception that the Drakul soldier's radio is out."

Chapter Twenty-One

The plan to get them inside the asteroid worked. The Hooolong slouched down to make Staff Sergeant Dantone seem taller, and the airlock technician from Central Control that looked at them in the airlock's camera hadn't noticed the difference. He had also believed the story that Dantone's face shield was blacked out, due to the same malfunction that had fried his radio. The process had taken a few minutes, but they were all inside and camouflaged.

The Hooolong didn't seem to care whether they were visible or invisible to normal sight; with his sonar, he saw them just fine. Calvin knew that was a flaw in the system he would have to address when they got back. If they got back. No, he thought, *when* we get back.

As they rounded the first corner, the Hooolong came face to face with a Drakul going the other way, and the platoon got its first good look at a Drakul. It was the stuff of which nightmares were made. Standing over 10 feet tall, the monster was a dark tan in color, and even stockier than the one in the suit had appeared. The Drakul was probably over 400 pounds, thought Calvin, and it had incisors in its upper jaw that were too long for its mouth; they extended several inches. The Drakul was one of the ugliest things Calvin had ever seen. As they were previously described to the Terrans, the creature *did* appear vaguely frog-like, with a white throat and big, red bug eyes on its flat head. Calvin would never have thought it possible, but he found that he preferred looking at the four-eyed Hooolong to looking at the Drakul. "Where is the technical sergeant?" the creature asked the Hooolong in a deep rumbling voice.

"He went to get a replacement for the radio in his space suit," Smetlurge replied. "He told me to come and report to you."

"Yes," the Drakul agreed with an evil grin. "There is something in the control room we need your help with."

Calvin didn't know whether Smetlurge was acting or whether he shivered because he was scared, but Smetlurge gave every indication of being afraid. He cowered on the floor and didn't appear to want to move.

"Come on," the Drakul said. "I have something I need you to assemble. I'm not going to eat you...unless you don't come along right now."

Smetlurge immediately began moving forward, once again reminding the Terrans of a giant inchworm. As they walked down the corridor, another Drakul came down the hallway in the other direction. The Terrans flattened themselves along the walls, but the Drakul following Smetlurge made a hand motion to the approaching Drakul, who turned and began walking alongside the first. Calvin saw the newcomer had the same insignia on its uniform and decided it was another lieutenant. Apparently the junior officers' buffet was about to open.

The procession stopped at a door on the right side of the corridor with a metal plate to the right of it. The first lieutenant unclipped an identification tag and swiped it along the plate. The door opened, and the lieutenant motioned for the Hooolong to precede him into the room. Smetlurge inched forward into the room, brushing up against Master Gunnery Sergeant Kinkead, who tried to sneak in while the Hooolong entered.

Smetlurge fell to the right and rolled around on the floor. "Sorry, sir, very clumsy of me," the Hooolong said. He continued to roll around while the two Drakuls laughed, allowing several other soldiers to enter the room. Finally, the lieutenant reached over and palmed the plate, shutting the door.

"I have not tried one of these before," said the new lieutenant. "Is the creature as tasty as it looks?"

"Yes," the first one replied. "The best part is that there is an artery on both ends, so that we can both feed at the same time."

"You said you wouldn't eat me!" cried Smetlurge.

"I lied," the first Drakul said. "Now come here and don't make me chase you, and maybe I will make this painless for you." It laughed. "Then again, maybe I won't, but at least there's a chance..."

Calvin saw on his display there was a cyborg behind each of the Drakuls. "*Go!*" Calvin commed.

Before either Drakul could move, both of the cyborgs punched the Drakuls in front of them. As their hands moved forward, both extended a spike from the center of their fists. Over 10 inches of steel entered the Drakuls' brains, killing them instantly.

As they fell to the floor, Smetlurge inched forward and spit a blob of orange goo on the first lieutenant. "Let that be a lesson," he said. "Never trust a Drakul."

Master Chief checked to ensure both Drakuls were dead. Looking up, he saw that Staff Sergeant Dantone was looking at his spike, turning his hand over slowly. Without facial expressions, it was hard to know what the cyborg was thinking, but just the way he moved indicated puzzlement. "Is there something wrong?" he asked.

"Yeah," the cyborg replied. "My spike won't retract."

"Hoppy, get over here and take a look," Master Chief ordered.

Sergeant Hopper walked over to the cyborg and inspected the cyborg's hand. "This'll just take a sec," he said. He sprayed the area where the spike came out of the cyborg's hand with a bottle that he pulled out of a pocket. The bottle was inside two separate containers. He counted to 10, and then he sprayed it with another bottle.

"What is that stuff?" asked Master Chief.

"Flesh eating bacteria," Sergeant Hopper said. "Don't get any on you; the bacteria will tear you up. My research showed that most combat 'borgs get deadlined from biological matter getting wedged in their crevices. Bone fragments are the worst. The bacteria I applied will clean any sort of biological material out, but then you have to spray the antibiotic to kill the bacteria. You *don't* want that shit running around. Nasty stuff. If the government on Earth ever finds out about it, the bacteria will be illegal faster than you can say 'lawsuit.'"

"Where did—" Master Chief started.

"Don't ask," Hoppy cut him off. "Long story." He surveyed the cyborg's hand, frowned, and sprayed some lubricant he pulled from another pocket. "Try it now."

The spike retracted silently.

Calvin surveyed the room while Night went to the door and let the rest of the platoon into the room. The laser control room was a 40' diameter circle with 16 operator stations along the wall. Each group of four had another station behind it. A command chair sat in the center of the room, overseeing the four supervisors. It appeared to be on a swivel so that it could face in any direction.

Calvin turned to look at Smetlurge. "So, what is this place?" he asked.

"This is the forward laser control station," said Smetlurge. "Each cluster of four stations controls the main lasers for a quadrant of the battle station. This group controls the lasers on the port side of the station," he said, pointing at the group on the left. "These others control the lasers on top of the station, its starboard side and on the station's bottom," he added pointing at the other groups in turn. "Each station controls 16 lasers, each group of four controls the quadrant's 64 lasers, and the whole forward laser center controls 256. There is an aft laser control station that controls the 256 main lasers on the back part of the ship. The counter-missile lasers are controlled from defensive stations scattered throughout the ship. There are also a forward and an aft missile control station as well as counter-missile missile batteries scattered throughout—"

"That's great," Calvin interrupted smoothly. "Any chance we could take out the battlecruiser that is flying alongside this asteroid before it gets a chance to respond?"

"Of course there is," Smetlurge agreed. "Remember, I designed this station. I have called others to come help. There are not enough of you to do everything that needs to be done."

"What do you mean?" asked Calvin. "We need to blow up the control center. There are enough of us to do that."

"If you like one-way missions, perhaps," Smetlurge said. "I, however, have spent enough time on this rock and would like to leave. That entails disabling the battlecruiser that is alongside...unless you have something that can do that...no? I didn't think so. This mission is the worst planned event I have ever seen. It is even worse than my sister's wedding, which is really saying something."

"OK, great, you're going to kill the battlecruiser," Calvin interrupted again. "Thanks."

"Yes," continued Smetlurge, "I also intend to disable this station's offensive and defensive weapons, so that we can get away in your shuttle. Unless you have a plan for that, which you haven't shared with me yet? No?"

"We are working on that," Calvin said. "The most important thing is to destroy this station. Our civilization has a lot riding on it. Completing our mission is more important than all of our individual lives."

"You can still destroy the station," Smetlurge said, "but my life is more valuable to me than your lives apparently are to you. I haven't kept myself alive this long just to die in your botched assault. You need to think bigger. Let us help, and we can also rescue a lot of the hostages held here. We'll also get ourselves away, which I don't think you are going to be able to do on your own."

There was a soft knock on the door.

"They're here," Smetlurge said. "What's it going to be?"

"We'll follow your lead, as you seem to know the station better than we do," Calvin agreed. "What do you suggest?"

Smetlurge didn't respond for a moment; instead, his eyes closed, and he began swaying side to side slowly. Calvin motioned for Night to open the door, and a collection of eight aliens entered the room. Although most of them were Hooolongs, there was an Archon who was missing his wings, and something that looked uncomfortably like a five-foot tall spider. Night shut the door behind them.

One of the unit's medics, Corporal Lawrence, went over to the Archon and began talking with him in a low voice, looking at his wing stumps.

Smetlurge's eye stalks opened, and his swaying changed to a nodding motion. "Here is what I would recommend," he said. He indicated the spider analog. "Bzzzeedlezzzzz is an excellent computer programmer, and the rest of my countrymen are weapons technicians. They can run the laser stations here." Four of the worms moved to stand near a weapons station in each of the four groups, while a fifth went to stand next to the command chair. "I would recommend leaving three or four of your troops with them to provide security. They are unarmed and don't know much about personal combat."

Calvin turned to Master Chief. "Pick four to leave as security," Calvin said.

Master Chief consulted his mental roster. "Sergeant MacKenzie, Corporal Hall, and Corporal Jones," he said, "with Staff Sergeant Burke in command."

Calvin nodded. "Make it so." He turned back to Smetlurge. "What else?"

"I think we'd be best served by splitting up," the alien said. "My son will lead one group to the operations center," he said, indicating the last Hooolong that had come to stand by him. "I will lead the other group to the airlock control room, where we will begin facilitating our escape."

"*What do you think?*" Calvin commed Night via laser link.

"*It's as good of a plan as we have,*" Night replied. "*At least this way, we have a guide to take us where we need to go. I'll take the Space Force with both cyborgs to go destroy the ops center, if you want to go take and hold our exit.*

"*Agreed,*" Calvin said. "Captain Train will go with your son to the ops center," Calvin said to Smetlurge; "I will go with you to the airlock."

"They should go first, then," Smetlurge advised. "They have further to go."

Night nodded and moved to the door. "Wraith, you've got point," he said to Sergeant Park. She moved to the door and went invisible. "Lead the way," Night said to the Hooolong. "We've got your back."

The Hooolong went through the door, followed by the rest of the Space Force. Each went invisible as he or she went through the door. Finally, just Night was left. "Hold the airlock for me," he said; "I'll be right back." He went invisible, and the door closed quietly.

"Master Gunnery Sergeant Kinkead, are you ready to go take an airlock?" Calvin asked.

"I am, sir," she replied. "It's the only way to get off this piece of shit rock." She turned to the remaining members of her squad. "Zoromski, you've got point. Don't let anyone eat the Hooolong."

Smetlurge nodded, which for him was a bend at the 'waist.' "The Hooolong in question would be very thankful for that." Smetlurge moved to the door.

Zoromski went invisible and opened it. Smetlurge followed him out, and the rest of the squad went invisible and followed. The Archon followed the last soldier out the door. "Keep them safe," Calvin said to the four troopers that were staying behind to guard the command center. "Captain Train will get you on his way back. If anything else comes through the door, blast it."

Calvin went invisible and left, closing the door behind him on his way out.

Task Force Night, Asteroid Weapons Platform, Gliese 876, February 19, 2021

The passageways were strangely quiet, and the squad made good time. Still, Night had a bad feeling. He didn't know if the battle station was fully manned yet or not, but he would have expected to see at least a *few* of the Drakuls moving around through the corridors. So far, nothing. They had met up with another one of the spider creatures, a couple more Hooo-longs, and some sort of leather-skinned flying creature, and they had sent them all to the airlock that they were planning on using, but no Drakuls so far. It was weird.

Night hated when things were weird. That usually happened just before they went to shit.

Task Force Calvin, Asteroid Weapons Platform, Gliese 876, February 19, 2021

Smetlurge stopped suddenly, and the Archon ran up to him. They spoke for a couple of moments, and then both of them looked back down the passageway and started waving frantically. Since there was no one else in the passageway for them to be waving to, Calvin moved forward. "There is a problem," Smetlurge said.

"What is it?" Calvin whispered.

"You don't have to whisper," Smetlurge replied. "The central computer can't hear us."

"What do you mean, the central computer can't hear us?" Calvin asked. "It looks like there is a monitor and audio pick up in the corner." He pointed to the camera, guessing that Smetlurge could see what he was doing.

"It isn't able to hear us," said Smetlurge. "Remember, I designed this station?"

Calvin nodded invisibly. Smetlurge seemed to have no problem seeing him.

"When I designed the station," Smetlurge continued, "I was also responsible for the computer's coding. I had Bzzzeedlezzzzz write the code so that the AI ignores any non-Drakul race. We can walk around and talk, and the computer won't see or hear us. None of our conversations are recorded or even noticed. The station's AI is *physically unable* to hear us. How do you suppose we got from the airlock to the control room unnoticed? Did you think your invisibility fooled the computer? That the computer didn't notice the temperature increase in the halls? The oxygen usage? The strange air currents? Of course the AI noticed! It then decided that those things were due to the presence of non-Drakuls and promptly forgot about them as being beneath its notice."

"So we can use our comm systems to coordinate, and the station's AI won't notice?" asked Calvin.

"I wouldn't, if I were you," replied Smetlurge. "The computer on the asteroid probably wouldn't notice or care, but the computer on the battlecruiser alongside us probably would."

"Aren't you worried about a Drakul coming around the corner and seeing you talking to yourself? Calvin asked.

"No," the Archon said, speaking for the first time, "that is the problem. All of the Drakuls not on watch are at a giant gathering to celebrate the station becoming operational. They are going to sacrifice about half of the remaining prisoners onboard for their feast."

"Shit," said Calvin, who could feel the horror emanating from the Archon. He spoke to Master Gunnery Sergeant Kinkead via laser link. "*We've got a problem.*"

Chapter Twenty-Two

Staff Sergeant Burke detailed Sergeant MacKenzie to watch the door and put Corporal Hall and Corporal Jones to work disassembling chairs and desks to build firing positions in case something showed up. The work was difficult, as the chairs were built to resist battle damage and remain in place, not come apart at the first bump that the ship took...or the first time a steel-toed boot kicked them.

Needing more situational awareness on the station, Burke walked over to the giant spider that was pushing buttons at the battle commander's station. Getting a closer look, he realized that the creature didn't really look quite like a spider. The body only had one circular section, from which all of the legs grew out, and that there were way too many legs. Burke couldn't count them all because they were continually in motion, but he could tell there were more than eight. A lot more. "Can I help you?" the creature asked, without stopping what it was doing. Burke jumped. He hadn't noticed previously that the spider had a set of eyes and a mouth on both sides of its body. Burke wondered if the creature had two brains, too; as it continued to work with one side while talking to him with the other.

"Um, hi," Burke said to the creature. "Can I ask what you're doing?"

"I am searching the computer system to watch for things that might give us away," said Bzzzeedlezzzzz. "When I find them, I erase them and make sure that the computer system forgets that it ever saw them."

"Can you see where the other groups are?" Burke asked. Watching it carry on a conversation while half of its legs worked so fast that they were a blur was...creepy...to say the least.

"Not exactly," said the creature. "I can usually tell where they've been, but can't be entirely sure where they are at any given moment."

"What about the battlecruiser?" Burke asked. "Can we kill it from here?"

"Yes," Bzzzeedlezzzzz said. "It shouldn't be a problem to destroy the ship if it moves forward into our zone of fire."

"That sounds more like a "no" than a "yes" answer," Burke replied. "Can we kill it or not?"

"Oh, we can absolutely destroy it," said the alien, "as long as it moves forward a little bit. Right now it is too far back for us to aim our weapons at it."

"Shit," Burke swore. "We need to destroy that ship."

"That will be important at a future time," Bzzzeedlezzzzz replied, "assuming that we are still alive."

"Why wouldn't we be alive in the future?" Burke asked.

"Because the Drakuls on watch normally change out now," the alien said. "The oncoming watch is approaching and will be here in less than a minute."

Burke looked over to where the soldiers were working on welding two desks together. "Load up, boys," he said. "We're about to have company."

Task Force Night, Asteroid Weapons Platform, Gliese 876, February 19, 2021

The Hooolong that Night was following crawled past two Drakuls standing at attention in front of a doorway, went around a corner and entered a storage room full of boxes and crates. The platoon followed him, becoming visible once they were in the room to conserve their batteries.

"The operations center is behind the door guarded by the two Drakuls," the Hooolong said.

"That's going to be tough to get into unnoticed," Master Chief observed. "They had their backs up against the wall and will be hard to take out silently. Anything we do has a good chance of alerting someone. That door is probably locked, too, so we'll have to burn our way in."

"Agreed," said Night. He looked at their guide. "Is that the only door?"

"Yes," the Hooolong replied, "that is the only doorway into the room."

"That can't be the only way in, though," Master Chief said. "There have to be air ducts or something like that going into the room, right?"

"Well, of course there are air ducts," the Hooolong said. "How else would anyone breathe in there? You didn't ask about them."

"All right," Master Chief said, his fists clenched, "I'm asking now. Are there *any* other means of access into the operations center, beyond using the door?"

"Yes, there are," the Hooolong replied. "You can use the air duct in this room to access the ops center." He indicated a grate in the ceiling. "If you can get up there, you can get into the ducting. I believe that the ceiling will hold your normal soldiers, but I do not think that it will hold your metal men."

"I don't think I want to go into an air duct anyway," said Staff Sergeant Randolph. "I've always been a little tense in close places."

"Before we decide anything," Night said, "let's get someone up there to take a look."

"I'll go," said Mr. Jones. "I'm probably the most qualified." A professional combat spy, Mr. Jones had been a SEAL and a Delta operator before being recruited by the CIA. He had been given the rank of Corporal when he joined the platoon, but everyone knew he had a much higher government service rating. He wouldn't say how high, but Night figured it was a lot higher than his own rank. Jones had always played the part of a corporal well, though, so it had never been an issue.

"I'll go with him," said Irina Rozhkov. Whatever Jones did in the CIA, Night knew Rozhkov did something similar for Russia's spy service (whatever the KGB had become in its current incarnation), and he knew that Rozhkov was equally qualified as a spy. She also had a history with Jones, although neither would talk about it. Whatever their relationship, Night knew they worked well as a team and could be counted on to get the job done. Any job.

"All right," Night said, making a quick decision, "you two go and take a quick look and come right back. No impromptu assaults. Got it?"

"Got it," they replied. The rest of the team moved the stores out from under the vent's entrance and formed a pyramid to get them up to the ceiling while the two spies stripped out of their suits. The two cyborgs formed the lowest level. Facing each other, they put their hands on each other's shoulders, forming a solid base. The two tallest members of the squad, Petty Officer Sherkov and Petty Officer Levine formed the next level, standing on the cyborg's shoulders. Sherkov removed the access plate on the ducting, and the two operatives were boosted into the ducting.

Mr. Jones turned on a small flashlight as he entered the ducting. He was pleased to see that the duct was a square about four feet on a side, plenty big enough to move around in. He knew a lot of air would have to be moved on a station the size of the asteroid, so he wasn't surprised that the duct was as large as it was, just happy. There also didn't appear to be any vermin living in it, which was another plus. Receiving a thumbs-up from Rozhkov, he started down the duct on his hands and knees.

Several passages went off in different directions, but he made it back to the operations center without much difficulty, stopping at a vent where he could see down into the room. He crossed to the other side and looked through the vent for about 15 seconds before giving Rozhkov a turn. When she looked back up, he whispered, "What have you got?"

"Circular room, about 30 meters in diameter," Rozhkov replied. "Looks like weapons control stations around most of the perimeter of the room, with overseer positions located behind them like we saw in the laser control room. Very narrow span of control, about four technicians to a boss. There are four groups of stations. At a guess, I would say one for missiles, lasers, counter-missile missiles and counter-missile lasers. One door out of the room. Big conference table underneath us that could seat about 20 of us or 10 of them. Overall, looked like about 28 Drakuls in the room. It'll be tough to get in there."

"Yeah, it's going to be a bitch," Jones agreed, shaking his head. "I had 29. Let's get back."

Task Force Calvin, Asteroid Weapons Platform, Gliese 876, February 19, 2021

"We can save them if we go now," Smetlurge urged, bobbing his head up and down in his excitement.

"What about the airlock?" Calvin asked. "Saving them doesn't do us any good if we can't get off this asteroid."

"That is truth," Smetlurge agreed, obviously not having given that part of it any thought in his haste to rescue the hostages. He paused and then said, "A small group should be able to take and hold the airlock. The rest of the force would probably be enough to go and rescue the prisoners."

"How many Drakuls are there?" Calvin asked.

"Well, there are over 500 that are waiting to be fed in the auditorium," Smetlurge replied. "You wouldn't have to fight them if we could make it down to the holding pens before the Drakuls begin taking the prisoners out." He indicated the Archon. "Ezekiel could lead you to where you need to go to rescue the prisoners while I take part of the force to capture the airlock. He can move much more quickly."

Damn, thought Calvin, who didn't want to split his forces again. This has the potential to end really poorly. Still, he knew that he couldn't let the Drakuls eat all of those civilians if he ever wanted to feel good about himself again. He just couldn't. "Master Gunnery Sergeant Kinkead," he said. "I want you to take the Three Caballeros and Corporal Lawrence and go secure the airlock. You're our way out; you need to take it and hold it, for as long as is necessary. I'll take the rest of the squad and see if we can rescue the civilians."

"Yes, sir," said Kinkead. "We'll keep the light on for you; just try not to stay out too late, OK sir?"

"We won't be long," said Calvin, "but when we come, we'll probably be in a hurry." He became visible so that Ezekiel could see him. "Lead on," Calvin said. "Let's go get them before the Drakuls do."

Task Force Kinkead, Asteroid Weapons Platform, Gliese 876, February 19, 2021

Master Gunnery Sergeant didn't have far to go after the squad split up.

"The airlock control room is the next door on the left after this corner," said Smetlurge, stopping in the middle of the passageway. "How do you intend to capture it?"

"I haven't decided," replied Master Gunnery Sergeant Kinkead. "How many Drakuls are in it?"

"Usually, there are two in the room," answered Smetlurge. "It is not very big...maybe a 20' square."

"In that case," Kinkead said, "I intend to apply superior firepower from a position of advantage and a condition of surprise." She smiled. "You're going to get them to open the door and then quickly move out of the way. After you move, we're going to shoot them in the face."

"Don't miss, please," Smetlurge said. "They will be very angry."

"Don't worry," Kinkead replied. "We're Terran Space Marines. We don't miss."

"Hmph," Smetlurge said. "Everyone misses some time. I'd appreciate it if you just didn't miss *now*." He walked to the door and watched with his sonar as the five soldiers lined up behind him, with Master Gunnery Sergeant Kinkead on the left end and a little closer to get a flanking shot at the second Drakul when the door opened.

"Ready," said Kinkead, getting a green light from all of her group.

Smetlurge reached up and pressed the button next to the door's access panel. After a short pause, a voice said, "What do you want, minion?"

"I have a message for you," replied Smetlurge.

"OK," the voice said. "Give it to me." The door didn't open.

Oh, crap, thought Kinkead. I hope he has a Plan B.

Smetlurge shuddered. "The message was that the general was sorry you missed his presentation," Smetlurge said, "and I was supposed to make up for it. The lieutenant that sent me said you'd know what that meant."

The door slid open and a Drakul filled the doorway. It was huge, nearly 10 and a half feet tall and well over 400 pounds. Saliva dripped from the two fangs that protruded from its mouth. Before Smetlurge could move, the Drakul reached out and grabbed him. It picked Smetlurge up and inspected the Hooolong, trying to figure out the best place to bite it. "Yes," he said, "I know exactly what the general meant."

"Hey!" said a voice from inside the room. "Save me some!"

The Drakul looked over his shoulder and said, "You can have what's left when I'm done."

"Help!" yelled Smetlurge. He struggled to get away, but his struggling form only blocked the troopers' shots as he flipped back and forth in front of them.

The Drakul looked back at Smetlurge, and Kinkead could see the creature smile as the Drakul decided where it wanted to bite Smetlurge. She had no shot, so she did the only thing she could. She charged. Taking two running steps forward, she planted a foot on the Drakul's knee and used it to jump up and head butt the Drakul on the chin with the top of her helmet. She wrapped her arms around the Drakul's neck as the creature fell backward into the room, stunned.

The Drakul released Smetlurge, who landed on one of his ends and bounced out of the way down the corridor.

The second Drakul jumped up from the control panel as its superior fell backward into the room. "What? Did it bite you first?" the Drakul asked with a laugh. The question was cut off as the first Drakul hit the floor. With a clear line of fire, all four of the other soldiers fired. Three lasers hit the Drakul in the face, and the creature dropped. Corporal Lawrence's shot went high and right, hitting the monitor that showed the airlock. It disintegrated in a shower of sparks.

As Kinkead and the Drakul hit the ground, she could feel the monster regaining its senses. The Drakul couldn't see her, but it could feel her, and it grabbed her around the waist. Face to face with the Drakul, she smashed her helmet into its face again, head butting the creature between its bug eyes. The Drakul didn't flinch; instead, it shifted its grip and grabbed her shoulder. The monster pulled her off, made a fist with its other hand and punched her, hitting her in the facemask. A long crack appeared; it only grew worse as the Drakul hit her again.

Her head rocked back, and she saw stars from the impact. The Drakul rolled to its side and slammed her into the floor, knocking the wind out of her. Gasping for breath and seeing two images of the creature in front of her, she drew her laser pistol as the Drakul lifted her back up to slam her again.

She fired at the image on the right and was rewarded with a splash of blue from its eye. The Drakul slammed her to the floor again, but not as hard as the first time. Her facemask shattered as she went face first into the floor. Her suit short-circuited, and she became visible.

The Drakul smiled as she came into view, and its remaining eye gleamed. Holding her with one hand the creature reached out toward her face with the other. She struggled in the Drakul's grasp and tried to push away the claw, but the creature was too strong. Firing wildly with her pistol, she swung in the monster's grasp, kicking it where she could, but she couldn't stop the Drakul from reaching into her helmet and palming her head.

Already concussed, Kinkead saw a white light of pain as the Drakul squeezed her head. She fought to keep from passing out from the pain, but suddenly the squeezing stopped, and the Drakul released its grip on her. Her pistol fell from numb fingers, and she reached up and pulled the Drakul's claw from her helmet. Rolling over, she looked at her enemy, and found that it now had a large knife sticking out from its second eye.

Corporal Lawrence materialized next to the Drakul's head. Stepping on the creature's forehead for leverage, she retrieved her kukri. Blue blood and part of its eye dripped back down onto the remains of the Drakul's face. With a sob, she dropped the weapon back onto the creature.

Kinkead got to her feet. She was woozy from the pain, but managed to stand. Stumbling over to Corporal Lawrence, she put a hand on her shoulder, part for comfort, part for stability. She could see tears on Corporal Lawrence's face behind her facemask, and she realized that the Drakul was Lawrence's first kill. "Thanks," she said. "You had to kill it. I wouldn't have lasted much longer if you hadn't."

"I know," Corporal Lawrence said with a sniff. "Fucking bastards." She kicked the Drakul in the head, and her kukri fell to the floor. Kinkead bent over and picked the large knife up. She wiped it off on the Drakul and handed it back to Corporal Lawrence handle first.

"Thanks," she said. She took a deep breath and slid the kukri into its sheath. "I'm OK," she said, standing a little taller. While Kinkead watched, her face transformed back to the one she had known for the last few months. Lawrence was a soldier again; determined, focused and ready to do what needed to be done. Whatever the cost. "So, what do we do now?"

"First, we shut the door so that no one knows that we're here," said Kinkead. "Then we wait for the cavalry." She paused and looked at Corporal Lawrence. "While we wait, I'd also appreciate it if you could check me out. I think I've got at least two broken ribs, and my suit is busted and won't give me any pain meds. If you could come up with some, I'd even let you call me Master Guns. Once."

"I can do that, Master Guns," the medic said with a chuckle as she reached into one of her pockets.

Kinkead sat down heavily as the pain threatened to overwhelm her.

"Should I begin assembling my people to leave?" asked Smetlurge.

"Yes," Kinkead said through her teeth as Corporal Lawrence applied some antibiotic to a slash down her cheek. *I am* tougher than the Drakuls, Kinkead thought...but not by much. Next time, shoot them from a distance.

"*All prisoners proceed to Airlock #1 for evacuation,*" Smetlurge transmitted. "*There is a shuttle here to take off everyone that can make it to the airlock RIGHT NOW. DROP WHAT YOU'RE DOING AND COME!*"

Chapter Twenty-Three

Bridge, Drakul Ship *Butcher*, Gliese 876, February 19, 2021

"That's odd," said the defender. "I just picked up a transmission saying that prisoners were going to be evacuated from an airlock to a waiting shuttle."

"What the hell is that all about?" asked the *Butcher's* commanding officer, Captain Frang, as he walked over to the defender's station. "Do you show a shuttle anywhere in the area?"

"No, sir, I don't," said the defender. "The transmission was weak, though...perhaps it came from somewhere else in the system?"

Captain Frang hit him in the back of the head. Hard. "Do you know of any other place in this system that might be sending out such a transmission?" the CO asked. "There is none! If there is a shuttle anywhere around, it is stealthed. Call the operations center on the asteroid and see if they know what is going on."

Operations Center, *Death Station Alpha*, Gliese 876, February 19, 2021

"Sir, the *Butcher* is asking if everything is under control here," said the communicator. "They said they just picked up a transmission that mentioned taking the prisoners off in a shuttle."

"What?" asked Commander Shrang, the officer in charge of the operations center. "No, no one is taking anything off of this asteroid. There are no scheduled flights. Call primary flight control and see if they know anything. No shuttles get in or out."

"Sir, the *Butcher* made it sound like there was some kind of waiting shuttle," added the communicator. "It didn't sound like the shuttle was one of ours."

Commander Shrang looked confused. "Have any of you detected any sort of shuttle or enemy ship?" All of the weapons systems' lead officers replied in the negative. Commander Shrang shook his head. "Well, the transmission they intercepted didn't send itself. Call down to all of your subordinate commands and see if any of them noticed anything out of the ordinary. If there is an enemy ship out there, it is obviously stealthed. Tell them to report any spurious indications that they get." He paused thinking. "Oh," he added, "and put all of the radars to high power. We'll see if we can't burn through whatever cloaking they have."

Task Force Calvin, Asteroid Weapons Platform, Gliese 876, February 19, 2021

"C*alvin, Foxy,*" the shuttle's WSO commed. Calvin had told them to stay off the radio; he knew this wouldn't be good. "*Go ahead,*" he replied.

"*They just lit off every radar they've got on high power,*" replied Lieutenant Fox. "*We were down in between the radar platforms, so I don't think they saw us, but when we come to get you, they probably will see us.*"

Damn it, thought Calvin. As if I don't have enough problems right now. He was so close to the Drakul auditorium that he could hear their screaming and hissing. They sounded like demons. *"Understood,"* he replied. *"We'll see what we can do."* He paused. *"Night, Calvin,"* he called.

"I heard," said Night. *"We'll adapt the plan and work something out. Five minutes 'til the fireworks start."*

"Got it," replied Calvin. *"Five minutes. Thanks. Calvin out."*

Task Force Burke, Asteroid Weapons Platform, Gliese 876, February 19, 2021

"They are here," said Bzzzeedlezzzzz from the master console. His legs continued to manipulate the keyboard on the side away from Staff Sergeant Burke.

"How many are there?" asked Burke.

"There are three," replied the alien.

"All right," said Burke, turning toward where the men were hiding, "let them get into the room and then blast them. MacKenzie, you've got the first one through the door, Corporal Hall, you kill the second, and Doc Jones, you've got the third. I've got any leakers or additional enemies that show up."

The door opened, and three Drakuls entered the control room. Seeing Bzzzeedlezzzzz sitting in the master console, the first Drakul in the group, its officer, drew up short. "What are you doing in the controller's seat?" the Drakul asked, confused. "Where is the duty officer?" The Drakul didn't seem angry or worried; secure in its position atop the hierarchy, the creature was more curious than mad. The third Drakul walked through the door.

"Now!" called Staff Sergeant Burke, and two rifles fired. All three Drakuls fell to the floor, the officer crashing through a table next to the staff sergeant. The first and third Drakuls were head-shot by lasers; as the second Drakul hit the ground and rolled, Staff Sergeant Burke could see a bowie knife protruding from its right eye.

"Too good to use your rifle, Hall?" Burke asked, sarcasm heavy in his voice. "It was too easy a shot, and you needed something to make it a little more challenging?"

Corporal Hall became visible and walked over to the Drakul. "You said to kill it," he said with a shrug, "so I did. You've seen me on the range, Staff Sergeant. You were on the other side; did you want me to shoot in your general direction?"

"No, you're right," said Burke. "Good call on the knife."

Bzzzeedlezzzzz gave off a high pitched "Tweep!" and jumped back from the keyboard. "Staff Sergeant Burke, the operations center is asking for a status update from all stations and just used a security code that is not in the computer system. What do you want me to tell them?"

"Tell them what General McAuliffe said at the Battle of the Bulge when the Germans asked him to surrender," replied Burke.

"What is that?" asked Bzzzeedlezzzzz.

"Nuts," said Burke.

Task Force Night, Asteroid Weapons Platform, Gliese 876, February 19, 2021

"Something's got them going all of a sudden," said Mr. Jones, as Night looked down into the operations center. "There wasn't this much activity before."

"Any idea what's going on?" asked Night, who had returned to the vent with Mr. Jones and most of the squad.

"No," replied Mr. Jones. "When I got back, they were already rushing around. Something's going on, but I can't hear well enough to tell what it is." He paused and then asked, "Since they are at a higher state of readiness, would we want to just bring the bombs up here? They would certainly do the job as well in this air duct as they would have down on the floor."

"No," said Night. "I don't think that this duct will hold both the bombs and us. Besides, moving 300-pound bombs through a duct isn't my idea of fun...Just a sec." He listened for a couple of seconds and then added, "The guys in the laser control room have been discovered. That's probably at least part of what's got them in a frenzy. We need to take them out so that we can disrupt their command and control. We'll go in as planned." He switched to his comm gear. "*Space Force, we go on three. One...two...*"

Bridge, TSS *Vella Gulf,* Gliese 876, February 19, 2021

"Sir!" the DSO called. "All of the radars on the asteroid just came on. The battlecruiser's radars just came on, too. It looks like they are on their highest power settings. They may be looking for us!"

"No," said Captain Sheppard, "we're way too far away. There's no way they could have noticed us. What is more likely is that they got some sort of reading from the shuttle and are trying to lock in on it."

"What do you want me to do?" asked the DSO. "Send the fighters?"

"No," said Captain Sheppard, "there's nothing we can do. If we show ourselves now, we'll give up the element of surprise and have to fight the combined might of both the battlecruiser and the battle station. We couldn't take on either one of them normally, much less with half of our weapons unusable because of the stealth modules. We can't help them. Whatever they got themselves into, they'll have to get themselves back out of."

Task Force Calvin, Asteroid Weapons Platform, Gliese 876, February 19, 2021

"This is as far as we can get without them seeing me," said Ezekiel, who didn't have a suit. "Around this corner is the hallway that leads to the kitchens and the holding pens. There will be a door, which will probably be guarded."

Invisible, Calvin leaned out into the corridor. 50 feet away, two guards stood in front of a massive metal door that was at least eight feet wide. Both guards were holding laser rifles, and both looked ready. This wasn't going to be easy.

Calvin was down to just five soldiers. The squad had crossed a major passage that led to the auditorium, and he left the Gordon twins and Corporal Westbrook there to keep a lookout. There were guards about 75 feet further up the cross-passageway, watching whatever was happening in the auditorium. From the howls and screams, he didn't think that he wanted to know. At the first sign of trouble, the Gordons were supposed to fire antimatter rounds into the auditorium that were big enough to fry all of the Drakuls in attendance. Judging by the smiles on the Gordon brothers' faces when given their orders, Calvin didn't think he wanted to be in the vicinity when they did it.

"*There are two Drakuls 50 feet down the hallway,*" Calvin commed, leaning back in from the corridor. "*Tiny, you think you can take both of them?*"

"*Yes, sir,*" replied Corporal Steve 'Tiny' Johnson, the platoon's sniper. "*I've got a silencer on my rifle. I can take both of them before they even know what's hit them.*" Calvin knew that Tiny's .95 caliber rifle fired shells equivalent to 20mm auto cannon rounds. They left *big* holes in whatever they hit.

"*OK,*" said Calvin, "*move into the passageway and get ready. When I give the signal, you shoot them, and then we will charge down the hallway. Once there, we'll get the door open, find what hostages we can and get the hell out of here. The other squad is about to attack; we don't have much time.*"

"*Ready,*" said the sniper, holding the crosshairs of his rifle steady on the Drakul on the right.

"*On three,*" said Calvin, "*One...two...*"

Chapter Twenty-Four

Operations Center, *Death Station Alpha*, Gliese 876, February 19, 2021

"What?" asked the communicator. "*Really?*" He turned to Commander Shrang. "Sir, the *Butcher* said they are now picking up enemy transmissions from inside the station."

"How is that possible?" asked Commander Shrang. "Why haven't you picked them up?"

"I don't know," said the communicator. "The only communications that the computer is showing me are the transmissions between the *Butcher* and us."

"Do you want me to sound battle stations?" asked the defender.

"Not yet," said Commander Shrang. "If we disturb the general's presentation unnecessarily, he will have all of us skinned alive and then killed. Why aren't we picking any of this up? What is the status of our systems? Missiles?"

"All clusters manned and ready!" replied the missile commander.

"Lasers?" asked Commander Shrang.

"All clusters manned and ready except for Forward Laser Control," said the laser commander. "There is something strange going on there. They were not answering for a long time and then they just said 'nuts.'"

"Nuts?" asked Commander Shrang. "What does that mean?"

"It was a translation from some other language," replied the laser commander. "Apparently, it is an expression of contempt or derision."

"That is where they are," decided Commander Shrang. He turned to the defender. "Send a security team to the forward laser control station. They are probably wearing combat suits, so turn on the jammers that defeat their suit's invisibility. They may be in other places throughout the ship. Set battle stations."

The defender flipped two switches on his panel and began talking into his microphone.

Door to the Operations Center, Asteroid Weapons Platform, Gliese 876, February 19, 2021

"*What the fuck?*" Master Chief swore as he leveled his weapon and fired. His group had been sneaking up on the door guards in front of the operations center when they suddenly became visible. Marginally more prepared for combat than the Drakul he was aiming at, he got off five shots before the Drakul could move. At least three of them were killing shots, including the bolt through the center of its forehead. The Drakul fell backward and began sliding down the door.

The other Drakul was faster. Seeing Staff Sergeant Dantone materialize in front of it, the Drakul dove to the right and avoided Dantone's initial burst of shots. Hitting the ground, the creature rolled and turned back to fire at the cyborg. Unfortunately for the Drakul, it rolled right up to Staff Sergeant Randolph's feet, and the cyborg fired eight shots from his .50 caliber Desert Eagle into the monster's head before the Drakul could bring its weapon to bear. The reports from the pistol's firing echoed down the halls as the Drakul collapsed in a heap.

"Well, if they didn't know we were here before," Master Chief noted, "they do now." In counterpoint to his statement, a horn began blowing, blue lights began flashing, and a deep voice said, "Intruder alert, intruder alert, battle stations for an intruder alert!" Master Chief sighed. Things just got a lot harder.

Task Force Night, Asteroid Weapons Platform, Gliese 876, February 19, 2021

"*Three!*" commed Night, and he and Mr. Jones began firing tridents into the operations center below them. They walked the triple-strength grenades across the room from one side to the other, the air pressure from the blasts pushing them back up and away from the opening. They paused for a second to allow Petty Officer Levine and Petty Officer Sherkov to drop through the opening onto the table below. Switching to their laser rifles, they began firing at individual movement as the two petty officers advanced on the Drakul bodies.

"Cover!" yelled Night, and the two men dove behind consoles as two other troopers dropped into the room. "Go, go, go!" Night yelled, and the four soldiers began advancing again.

Petty Officer Levine saw the way to the door was clear and ran over, pushing the button that opened it. As the door opened, the Israeli had to jump backward to avoid the Drakul that fell inward. He shot the creature several times in the head by force of habit, prior to realizing the Drakul was already dead. He turned to cover the room as the cyborgs and Master Chief charged in. Within seconds, all of the Drakuls were dead.

"Think you can silence the alarms?" Night asked Mr. Jones, the platoon's computer expert.

"I don't know," he said, "but I'll do my best." Dropping into the room, Mr. Jones walked over to one of the consoles and flipped the two switches that he had seen the Drakul throw just before the horn began sounding. The first turned off the flashing blue lights in the corridor, and the second blessedly turned off the horn. "They're off, for what it's worth," Jones said, "but I think it's pretty obvious they know we're here."

"No shit," said Master Chief. "We're going to have to hurry. Cyborgs, get the bombs in here and set up ASAP. Jones, Rozhkov, see if there's anything salvageable from their computer system." Smoke was coming from most of the consoles, but it didn't hurt to look. "Use what you can, destroy the rest. Karimov, Tereshchenko, go down the hallway to the right and set up a perimeter. Al-Sabani, Wazir, you've got the hallway to the left. Andrews, Hopper, go get the Hooolong and bring him back here. Everyone else, cover the main corridor. As soon as the bombs are set, we're out of here."

Task Force Calvin, Asteroid Weapons Platform, Gliese 876, February 19, 2021

"On three," said Calvin, "One...two..."

Corporal Johnson saw the Drakuls stiffen as he became visible. His rifle coughed, and the .95 caliber bullet hit the right Drakul between the eyes. The Drakul's head bounced backward against the door, and it crumpled to the floor. As Johnson retargeted, the other Drakul brought its rifle up. A veteran of many battles, Johnson knew it wasn't a matter of who shot first, but who shot best. He centered the laser dot on the Drakul's nose holes and squeezed the trigger. He watched through the scope as the Drakul's head exploded in a fountain of blue mist.

It was only then he felt the pain in his left shoulder.

"You're hit!" exclaimed Corporal Mike Bachmann, his spotter, as the rest of the squad surged forward.

Johnson looked down to find the Drakul's laser had torn a bloody chunk from his left shoulder; the heat of the laser caused the water in his upper arm to boil, expand and rip the surrounding tissues apart, much like a high velocity bullet impact. "Yup," he said, "but he's hurt worse." Johnson commanded a painkiller from his suit's pharmacopeia and ordered the suit's nanobots to stabilize the wound.

"Why don't you go back to join the Gordons?" Calvin asked. "They're going to need help with close cover, and you could do that with your pistol."

"I'm good, sir," said Corporal Johnson. "I'll make it work."

Calvin turned back in time to see Sergeant Zoromski open the door. As it cracked open, he took a peek through and quickly withdrew his head. Calvin's suit registered several laser bolts that came through just after his head moved. Shit. There were more of them on the other side.

Before Zoromski could pull the door open fully, someone or something on the other side slammed the door shut. As Zoromski grabbed for it, they heard the locking bolt move into place.

They were locked out.

Chapter Twenty-Five

Staff Sergeant Burke watched as the blowtorch's cut line worked its way around the door. It wouldn't be long until the Drakuls had the door open.

"The battlecruiser is moving forward," said Bzzzeedlezzzzz. "If you could just keep them out another five minutes, I will be able to shoot."

"Five minutes, huh?" asked Burke. At the rate they were going, the Drakuls would be through the door in about three. He looked at the door and then around the room. "Quickly," he said, "grab every thin piece of metal you can find."

Burke turned the chair next to him on its side and began stomping on one of the metal legs. After three strong kicks, the leg snapped off at the top. Running over to the door, he dropped the chair leg in front of the door. The other soldiers joined him with similar pieces.

"When I say 'now,' Doc," Burke said to Corporal Jones, "I want you to open the door." He gave Corporal Jones the badge that opened the door and then pulled out two grenades from one of his leg pockets. "After I throw these, shut the door again *really* quickly. MacKenzie, you and Corporal Hall shoot anything close by." He pulled the safety pins from both of the grenades. Burke looked at the door. The Drakuls only had about two feet left to cut. It was now or never.

"Now!" he yelled, and Doc swiped the badge, opening the door. At least 20 Drakuls stood in the hallway watching the two Drakuls operating the blowtorch. Both of them jumped back in surprise; most of the rest recoiled slightly at the Terrans' unexpected appearance.

Burke threw the first grenade into the mass of waiting Drakuls and lobbed the second behind the two Drakuls operating the blowtorch. One of them was already falling backward, a smoking hole in the center of its forehead from a laser bolt; the other reaching weakly for the knife protruding from its left eye.

Doc swiped the door shut as the second grenade left Burke's hand, and twin detonations tore through the hallway just after it closed. The top portion of the door listed inward slightly with the blasts; the door only held in place by the latch and the last two feet that hadn't been cut.

Burke grabbed the chair leg and jammed it into one of the cuts in the door, filling the cut. "Quickly," he said again. "We don't have much time. We need to secure this before they get reorganized." The door rang as one of the Drakuls outside the room kicked it. The door held. Barely. "Hurry!" He grabbed his laser rifle and tore off the safety interlock. Aiming the laser at the chair leg, he fired a long blast, using the rifle as a laser welder to melt the metal and seal the cut. Seeing what he intended, MacKenzie and Jones followed suit, using strips of metal they had torn off the weapons consoles.

"I'll get more metal," Corporal Hall said, seeing there wasn't enough room for him to work.

"Good," grunted Staff Sergeant Burke. He looked at the energy readout of his rifle and flinched; the power level was already down 10%. Their rifles wouldn't last long as welders. Hopefully, the grenade had damaged the Drakul's blowtorch...or maybe they had killed the only two Drakuls that knew how to use it. Please, Lord, thought Burke, just give me a little break here.

The light from the Drakuls' blowtorch appeared just above where he was working and began slicing through the chair leg. With the metal still hot, the blowtorch was able to cut through the chair leg much faster than Burke could weld the door shut.

They were in a losing race.

Task Force Calvin, Asteroid Weapons Platform, Gliese 876, February 19, 2021

Calvin shook his head. They didn't have anything that would be able to get through the door before reinforcements arrived. Before he could tell the troops to fall back, he saw Sergeant Hattori 'Yokaze' Hanzo waving at him.

"Just a second, sir," Sergeant Hanzo said. "I have an idea." He reached into his pocket and pulled out a handful of things that looked like 10-inch long pieces of plastic with plungers attached. He held one to the wall, pushed on the rod sticking out, turned it and then released the apparatus. The plunger stuck to the wall, with the plastic piece sticking straight out from the wall. He stuck several more to the wall, and then began climbing up his impromptu staircase. He reached the ceiling just below a vent and wedged himself between a foothold and the ceiling to hold himself in place while he took off the vent's cover.

Looking down, he said, "Mouse, come join me." He pulled himself up and through the opening in a somersault.

Havildar Rajesh 'Mouse' Patel went up the 'stairs.' Although he wasn't as smooth as Yokaze, he made it to the top. As he reached for the opening, Yokaze reached out and grabbed his arm, helping him into the ducting.

"This way," the ninja said, leading Mouse in the direction of the bolted door.

Task Force Gordon, Asteroid Weapons Platform, Gliese 876, February 19, 2021

"Fuck," the Gordon twins said simultaneously as blue lights began flashing, and a horn began sounding. The screams from the auditorium paused as the Drakuls processed what the lights and horn meant.

That was all the time the brothers needed. As they had discussed, Corporal Austin 'Good Twin' Gordon fired an antimatter round at the guards that stood 75 feet down the hallway. Corporal Jamal 'Bad Twin' Gordon also fired a grenade, but his continued past the guards and into the open area of the auditorium. 50 micrograms of antimatter contacted an equal amount of matter and exploded with the force of a ton of TNT. What little the brothers could see of the fireball was impressive...until it came racing down the hall toward them. Both of them dove to the side in the cross-passage, and the flames went past them down the corridor.

"Sweet!" yelled Bad Twin, who noticed that his voice sounded funny. Or maybe his hearing had been damaged, he wasn't sure.

"My turn!" Good Twin yelled as he launched a 50 microgram antimatter grenade into the auditorium. If one was good, two was better.

"Dude!" said Bad Twin, picking himself up off the ground again after the second fireball had passed. "Let me know before you do that again. Like this. Austin, I'm about to nuke the shit out of the Drakuls." He leaned out into the hallway and saw that a couple of Drakuls were silhouetted in the doorway. Somehow they had survived the first two explosions. They didn't survive the third one, which detonated 30 feet behind them, cooking them in their own juices.

"I could really get to like doing this," said Good Twin. "My turn!"

Task Force Calvin, Asteroid Weapons Platform, Gliese 876, February 19, 2021

Yokaze looked down through the grate at the largest Drakul he had ever seen. He guessed that the creature was the Drakuls' head cook; if not, the creature was dressed like one, holding a giant cleaver and wearing a blue overcoat spattered in a variety of colors of blood. The monster also appeared to be an officer or senior enlisted the way it ordered the other Drakuls around.

"You two," the Drakul said to the two near the locked door. "Do not let anyone short of the Overlord through that door." It turned to look in the other direction. "You two, kill all of the prisoners! We'll show them what happens to minions that revolt!"

"*Mouse, we don't have time to get the others,*" said Yokaze. "*We've got to stop them now before they kill the civilians.*"

"*I agree,*" Mouse said, "*but there are at least five of them and only two of us.*"

"*You're right,*" Yokaze agreed, nodding his head, "*we've got them vastly outnumbered.*"

"*That is* so *not what I meant,*" the Indian soldier said with a sigh. He shrugged. "*OK, what's your plan?*"

"*I'll drop down, kill the cook and you shoot the two guarding the door,*" Yokaze said. "*Then, while I kill the other two, you let the rest of the squad in through the door.*"

"*Got it,*" Mouse said. "*Anything else?*"

"*Yes,*" said Yokaze. "*Don't delay. We are in a bit of a hurry at the moment.*"

Mouse looked dumbfounded. "*A hurry?*" he asked. "*You think?*"

Yokaze smiled as he silently removed the grate. "*Just lightening the mood. Ready?*" he asked standing up.

"*Yes,*" Mouse said, "*remember, we're in a hurry.*"

"*On three then,*" the ninja said. "*One...two...*" he dove through the gate.

Task Force Burke, Asteroid Weapons Platform, Gliese 876, February 19, 2021

"I'm out," said Sergeant MacKenzie as his rifle shut off. MacKenzie's second battery had lasted the longest; the other three soldiers' rifles were already out of power. Staff Sergeant Burke had tried using his laser pistol, but it didn't have the same power output as the rifle. The blowtorch began cutting the last segment.

"One minute more," said Bzzzeedlezzzzz. He held his grasping appendage over a blue button. Burke was sure that at least 10 minutes had passed since the alien had asked for five. "I've got it from here," the giant spider said to the Hooolongs, and they left their stations to hide behind the furthest station from the door. Looking at the way they cowered, Burke could tell that they wouldn't have been much help in a fight, even if they had weapons.

"Fall back," Burke ordered, and the men withdrew to the consoles on the other side of the room from the door and crouched behind their makeshift firing positions. Burke watched the blowtorch finish the last several inches, and then the door fell into the room with a loud metallic 'clang.'

Immediately, Drakuls began pouring into the room, firing as they came. Experienced combat troops, they spread out as they entered, diving forward and taking cover. The Terrans returned fire with their laser pistols and remaining grenades, but they were outnumbered and outgunned.

"The ship is in range," noted Bzzzeedlezzzzz without looking up from his console. His statement drew the attention of several of the Drakuls, and he was hit by three laser bolts before he could push the button.

With a cry, MacKenzie fell, hit in both the head and chest. In his display, Burke saw MacKenzie's life signs quickly going to the red. MacKenzie was dead.

Burke fired twice more, downing one of the Drakuls that had been getting close. They couldn't hold out long against the Drakul force, but they *had* to kill that battlecruiser. It was the only way the platoon could get off the asteroid. *"Can either of you get to the weapons console?"* he asked over their comm circuit. *"We've got to take out that ship!"*

"I think I can," said Corporal Hall. *"Cover me!"* He ran in a crouch toward the console, but only got two steps before he was hit by some type of big weapon that one of the Drakuls was carrying. About three times the size of the Terrans' rifles, the weapon killed Hall with a single shot. Burke's suit identified the weapon as a Drakul blaster.

Burke took a quick look and saw that the Drakuls were almost on them. *"On three,"* he commed, *"go for the console, Doc, and I'll draw their attention. One, two, three!"* Burke stood up and charged the Drakuls. "FOR TERRA!" he yelled. Firing at the Drakul holding the blaster, he ran screaming at the enemy forces. Outgunned, he only took five steps before the Drakuls recovered from their surprise and focused their weapons on him. Burke went down, hit by seven rifle shots and a bolt from the blaster that put a three inch hole in the center of his chest.

As Burke went down, the Drakuls saw Corporal Jones running for the center console, and all of them fired at him. Most of the shots missed, but two hit him in the chest and another in the leg. He took one more step and dove for the console. Reaching out, his right hand slapped the blue button in the center, pushing it closed. He started to smile in spite of the pain, but was killed by a blaster shot to the head. He slid down the console and crumpled to the floor.

The battle station's 118 five-meter lasers that were in view of the battlecruiser fired as one. Although some of the energy from the lasers was absorbed by the battlecruiser's shields, and 17 of the lasers missed, over 100 lasers hit the battlecruiser from close range, over-loading its shields. Almost 50 of the lasers hit the ship after its shields collapsed, holing it like a sieve.

Chapter Twenty-Six

"Dammit!" yelled the shuttle's pilot, Lieutenant Matthew 'Exit' Kamins as the lasers all around him suddenly re-targeted on the Drakul battlecruiser and fired without warning. The shuttle jerked, but Exit quickly brought it back under control.

"What the hell was that?" asked Lieutenant 'Foxy' Fox, the shuttle's WSO.

"The asteroid just shot the battlecruiser," said Exit. "It would have been really nice to know that they were going to do that ahead of time; one of the lasers singed our tail!"

"Are we OK?" asked Foxy. "How bad are we hit?"

"Yeah, we're OK," Exit replied shaking his head. "A few feet further one way or the other, and we'd have been toast."

"No kidding," agreed Foxy. "A five meter laser is not...WHOA!" he exclaimed as the battlecruiser blew up with a flash. "I guess they hit something vital."

"I guess so," agreed Exit. "Well, at least we don't have to worry about the battlecruiser anymore."

Task Force Calvin, Asteroid Weapons Platform, Gliese 876, February 19, 2021

Yokaze somersaulted through the air and landed on top of the cook's shoulders as he had planned. What he hadn't planned was for the cook to turn around to say something else to the Drakuls guarding the door. Instead of landing on his back, he landed with the Drakul's face between his legs.

Yokaze, bowed to his enemy, saying nothing as he drew two eight-inch tanto knives. As the Drakul opened his mouth to bite him, Yokaze jabbed a blade into each of the Drakul's ear holes and into its brain, swirling them slightly to ensure maximum damage. The Drakul started to collapse, and Yokaze somersaulted backwards off of the creature, landing on the balls of his feet facing the two Drakuls that were talking to the cook. Yokaze took a step forward and threw both of his tantos at the Drakuls, hitting them both. Reaching over his shoulders, Yokaze drew his wakizashi and katana, and he dropped into a ready pose.

One of the Drakuls charged him while the other drew its rifle.

"Any time, Mouse," Yokaze said, focused on the enormous creature running toward him.

"Got it," Mouse replied under his breath, squeezing the trigger of his laser rifle. The Drakul with the rifle stopped suddenly as the laser bolt drilled through its left eye and into its brain.

Disdaining weapons, the Drakul charging Yokaze threw away the small knife that the ninja had hit him with, and the Drakul reached forward as it approached the ninja, hoping to grab him. Yokaze dove forward and to the right, turning his dive into a roll that eluded the Drakul's grasp. Yokaze used the momentum of the roll to stand up, and he slashed behind him to the left with the longer katana, severing the tendons in the Drakul's left leg. The Drakul went down. Yokaze was on it before the Drakul could get back up again, stabbing the creature through the back with both swords. Not knowing where a Drakul's vital organs were, he stabbed several times more, trying to ensure that he hit at least some of them. He must have punctured something vital; the creature collapsed.

Yokaze jumped back up and ran down the corridor in the direction that the other two Drakuls had gone. "Open the door!" he yelled over his shoulder as Mouse dropped into the corridor. A short man, the drop down to the corridor floor was a long distance for the Indian soldier, who rolled forward to break his fall. Getting up, he ran to the door and worked the mechanism that locked the door.

Opening it, he said, "Yokaze and the hostages are this way."

Sergeant Zoromski ran through the doorway. Taking in the dead Drakuls on the floor he asked, "Where's Yokaze?"

Mouse turned around. Yokaze was gone.

Shuttle 02, Asteroid Weapons Platform, Gliese 876, February 19, 2021

"Hey, there are some kind of wormy looking things that have come onto the surface of the asteroid," Foxy said.

"Can you tell what they're doing?" asked Exit.

"They look like they're waving to us," Foxy replied.

"How can they see us?" asked Exit. "Aren't we still stealthed?"

"Yeah, as far as I know we still are," Foxy replied. "I've got no idea how they can see us, but it sure looks like they can. Wait...they're motioning for us to land...what the hell's going on?"

Foxy paused. "Oh, wait, there's one of our guys," he added after a few seconds. "The wormy things must be all right; he's telling us to land, too."

The inside of the shuttle resounded with a '*bong!*' as a piece of the battlecruiser bounced off of it. "I was wrong," said Exit. "We do still have to worry about that stupid battlecruiser. Hurry up and get them onboard. There are a lot of pieces of the battlecruiser flying around; I'd hate to see any of those things skewered by one."

"Roger that," agreed the WSO.

Task Force Night, Asteroid Weapons Platform, Gliese 876, February 19, 2021

"**B**ombs are set, sir," Master Chief said.

"Good," Night replied. "Let's get the hell out of here. Wraith, you've got point; get us back to the airlock as quickly as you can. Randolph, you've got our backs."

"Roger, sir," Randolph said, moving to rear guard. Wraith didn't say anything; she just silently took the point and headed out.

"You're with me," Night said to the Hooolong. "Try not to get lost, OK?"

"I will stay by your side," the creature agreed. "I do not have a weapon, so I will not be going off on my own."

"Do you want one?" Master Chief asked, pulling out one of his backup pistols. On their previous mission, the platoon had been hit by an electromagnetic pulse that wiped out all of their electronics; now, just about everyone carried some sort of backup mechanical pistol.

"I do not know how to use that," the Hooolong said. "I would be just as likely to hit you as I would the Drakuls."

"Never mind, then," Master Chief said, putting the pistol back in his pocket holster. "Just stay close."

The squad started off down the corridor. Once again, the hallways were strangely quiet. Where were the Drakuls?

After about 30 seconds, there was an explosion from behind them. It wasn't the bombs they had left going off; that would have been far more catastrophic to them.

"What was that?" asked Night.

"They must have gotten into the ops center," replied Mr. Jones. "Irina and I left some booby traps. I'm guessing that was the bomb in the intercom transmitter. The next person who goes in the room will have a hard time using the transmitter...or anything within about 10 feet of it."

"*Movement from the rear,*" commed Staff Sergeant Randolph. Night could hear the cyborg's pistol fire several rounds. "*Looks like they may be massing for an attack.*"

"*Wraith?*" asked Night.

"*I heard,*" she replied. "*I'm going as fast as I can.*"

Task Force Calvin, Asteroid Weapons Platform, Gliese 876, February 19, 2021

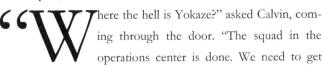

"Where the hell is Yokaze?" asked Calvin, coming through the door. "The squad in the operations center is done. We need to get the hell out of here!"

"I don't know," Mouse replied. "He was right behind me, but when I opened the door and turned around, he was gone. Two of the Drakuls went down the passageway; he must have followed them."

"Dammit, we don't have time for hide and seek," Calvin said. "*Yokaze, where are you?*"

"*I am freeing the prisoners,*" the ninja replied. "*If you would continue down the passageway, you'll find me. Hurry! They are coming.*"

Yokaze didn't say who the 'they' were, but from the tone of his voice, they weren't friendly. "Let's go," Calvin said to the remaining members of his group. "Quickly!"

They charged down the passageway, which turned to the left after about 50 feet. Rounding the corner, they found the first dead Drakul, a throwing knife in its right eye. "Well, at least we can follow the trail of bodies," Calvin said.

"Yeah, hopefully it doesn't end with Yokaze's," Mouse said.

The passageway turned back to the right, and they came to a hallway with a large number of doors down both sides. 100 feet further down the passageway, they could see Yokaze fighting four or five Drakuls, his swords flashing in the harsh glare of the passageway's lights. Although Yokaze continued to give ground and weave back and forth across the passageway, it was only a matter of time before one of the Drakuls grabbed him. The Drakul sitting behind the group wouldn't be grabbing him any time soon; the creature was missing both of its hands and was trying to stanch the flow of blue blood coming out of them like a small fire hose. The Drakul seemed perplexed that it couldn't figure how to do it without an opposite hand.

"Open fire!" Calvin ordered, aiming his rifle. The Drakuls stood more than four feet taller than the ninja, so the Terrans had a good view of their heads and upper chests; within seconds, the Drakuls were down.

"Thank you," said Yokaze. "That was a couple more than I wanted to handle by myself." He pulled out a key card from his pocket. "I took this from the cook; it seems to open the doors."

"Great," said Calvin. "Hurry up and get them open. We need to get the hell out of here. Zoromski, you and Mouse go to the end of the hallway and set up a perimeter while we get the hostages out."

"Yes, sir," the two troopers said, turning to jog down the passageway in the direction indicated.

Calvin turned to see one of the giant spider creatures coming from the doorway that Yokaze had just opened. They needed to get the hostages moving before they blocked the passageway. "Tiny, BTO," Calvin said to the sniper and spotter, "you guys show the hostages where to go. Let's get them moving. Fast!" Calvin turned to look down the hallway as a grenade blast was heard from the direction of Zoromski and Mouse. "The faster, the better."

Chapter Twenty-Seven

A doorway opened as Staff Sergeant Randolph went past it, and the cyborg went down as six or seven Drakuls poured out, tackling the cyborg to the ground. The rest of the Terrans wanted to fire, but were worried about damaging the cyborg. Before they could decide what to do, holes began appearing in the Drakuls as Randolph fired upward through the pile.

Staff Sergeant Dantone walked up and shot one through the head and pulled it off the pile. Most of the Drakuls had been shot several times by this point, and the rest of the squad joined Dantone in administering killing shots.

Randolph pushed the last couple of bodies off and stood up. He was a mess, covered in blue goo and missing a number of chunks of his artificial flesh. He stood up, stomping on the head of one of the Drakuls that twitched.

"The stupid things were biting me on the bottom of the pile," Staff Sergeant Randolph said, sounding disgusted. "Really? *Who tries to eat a cyborg?* Stupid Drakuls." He ejected both magazines from his pistols and slammed new ones into them. He turned around and shot one of the dead Drakuls lying on the floor in the head. "Stupid Drakuls."

"Maybe they were iron deficient?" asked Sergeant Hopper.

Randolph snorted. Night had never heard a cyborg snort before. It sounded like the air brake on an 18-wheel transport truck. "Well, I know one thing for sure," Randolph said. "They just got their fill of lead."

Task Force Calvin, Asteroid Weapons Platform, Gliese 876, February 19, 2021

"Zoromski, Mouse, fall back," Calvin commed. "We've got all the hostages, and we're out of here!"

"Roger that," Zoromski replied. "Looks like lots of them coming." Calvin heard two grenades explode from down the hall, and then Zoromski and Mouse came running toward him.

"Now would be a good time to be leaving, sir! Zoromski commed. "Fast as you can!"

Calvin turned and began running back toward the airlock, following the mass of prisoners. They weren't going to be moving fast. He had a bad thought. "Hey, Master Gunnery Sergeant," he commed, "Are there any spacesuits for all of the aliens that we have coming? There are at least 10 of the Hooolongs, three Archons, four or five of the giant spider-looking things, three things that look like pteranodons or whatever the hell the flying dinosaur was, and two or three other things that I can barely even describe."

"Stand by, sir, I'll ask," Kinkead replied. Calvin hoped it was the comm system; she didn't sound very well.

Calvin caught up with the hostages as they reached the cross passage where the Gordon brothers were standing, firing grenades down the hall into the auditorium. The passageway looked like it had seen better days; it was charred, and smoke filled the air.

"Hey, sir," said Bad Twin, "can we go take a look at the auditorium? We were kind of curious how many Drakuls were in there."

"What?" Calvin asked. "No! Do you see these hostages? We're leaving! This isn't the time to count who killed the most aliens. Help Zoromski and Mouse with rear guard. Let's go!"

"Lieutenant Commander Hobbs, Master Gunnery Sergeant Kinkead," the return call came, "that's a negative. There are no suits for the alien life forms. We already used the suits that the Drakuls had here. Apparently, this is a one-way trip for most of them. They only had a few suits for some of the techs that had to go out on the surface of the asteroid. Unless they are Hooolongs, Smetlurge says there probably aren't suits for them."

"Understood," Calvin replied. "Just how the fuck did he think we were going to get the hostages off this rock, then?"

"He said he wondered how long it would be until you realized that," Kinkead replied. "He also said there was no reason to bother you with that detail until you actually rescued the hostages. Since you were successful, he says that you need to have the shuttle pull around into the second shuttle bay from the top of the asteroid."

"You've got to be fucking kidding me," Calvin said, earning a curious look from Good Twin, who continued to fire grenades into the auditorium as the last of the soldiers went past.

"On the good side, he says it's not far from here," Kinkead added. "We can meet here and go in one group."

Great, thought Calvin, an even bigger clusterfuck. He switched to the platoon comm channel and added the shuttle crew to the network. "Everyone, listen up. There's been a change of plans. We have a bunch of friendlies that don't have spacesuits. We are going to join up at the airlock and go to the shuttle bay. Break. Break. Shuttle 02, did you copy that? It's the second bay from the top."

"Roger, boss, we copied," replied the shuttle's WSO. "We'll go take a look."

Chapter Twenty-Eight

Task Force Night, Asteroid Weapons Platform, Gliese 876, February 19, 2021

Night checked the map in his head. Their pace had slowed considerably after the Drakuls started attacking them, and he realized they were in danger of getting bogged down and not making it back to the airlock.

The end was in sight, with only two big cross passages to go; unfortunately, the cross passages were where the Drakuls seemed to be hitting them the hardest. Lacking central control with the destruction of the ops center, the Drakuls somehow still seemed to be getting the word that they needed to stop the Terrans.

They made it through the intersection, although there was a definite increase in incoming fire. The rear guard, Staff Sergeant Randolph, continued firing as he walked backward down the hallway. Reaching the intersection, he came up short. "*Damn it,*" he commed, "*I'm broke.*"

"*Talk to me, Randolph,*" Master Chief replied, "*What do you mean, 'you're broke?'*"

"*Something must have happened to me when I got dog-piled by the Drakuls earlier,*" Randolph said. "*I ran a diagnostic, and there's something wrong with my primary motivator. No kidding, I can't move, and I'm hard down if you can't do anything.*"

"*I think I've got one,*" Sergeant Hopper commed. "*They had extras at Sierra Army Base before we left, and I picked up a couple.*"

Sergeant Hopper looked out at the cyborg standing in the middle of the passageway as laser bolts flashed off of him. One of the groups of Drakuls had gotten smart, and all of them were shooting at the same spot on his left knee. Wisps of smoke and the smell of burning rubber filled the passageway as they melted off the pseudo-flesh that wasn't supposed to melt. The metal underneath glowed red hot. It wouldn't be long until the metal failed; even if it didn't, the Drakuls would probably bring up something heavier soon, and then the cyborg would be dead.

But they needed the cyborg's weaponry.

He made up his mind. "*Cover me!*" he commed as he ran out into the passageway. It seemed like World War III had just broken out as the rest of the squad came back to pour fire down the three separate passageways. Realizing what was happening, and that the cyborg must be important, the Drakuls increased their fire, hoping to take it out before Sergeant Hopper could fix it. Even though he had the cyborg's bulk for cover, Hoppy was still hit several times in the arms and legs, although most of them were glancing shots that barely penetrated his suit.

Willing himself to ignore the pain of a laser bolt that had caught him in the left leg, Hoppy popped open the access plate on the back of Staff Sergeant Randolph. "Fuck," he said under his breath. "*The rod is bent, and it's catching as it spins,*" Sergeant Hopper commed. "*It got caught on a couple of wires and yanked them out.*"

"*Can you fix it?*" Master Chief asked.

"*Yeah, I can fix it,*" Sergeant Hopper replied. "*But it's going to take me a minute.*" He paused a moment as another laser bolt singed his right leg. "*Think you could push them back a little? It's hard to-fuck!-concentrate when you keep getting zapped.*" He looked down and saw his suit was smoking or charred in several new places since the last time he had looked. The laser bolt that hit his right arm had penetrated and *hurt*. A lot. He triggered another pain killer from his pharma and all of the rest of his nanobots.

"*Stand by,*" Master Chief said.

"*I'm not going anywhere,*" Hopper said. "*Hey Randolph, how about you?*"

"*Nope,*" agreed Randolph. "*All systems are pretty much stopped here.*"

"*COVER!*" Master Chief yelled after a moment. Hopper plastered himself to the back of Staff Sergeant Randolph. He was sure he'd take some ribbing for the way he was up against the cyborg later when they got back. If they got back.

There was a pause, and then two antimatter grenades arced down the left passageway into the heaviest concentration of enemy fire. The detonations were enormous in the confined space, and the cyborg rocked to the side. Hopper braced himself and pushed the cyborg back up as two more grenades went down the hallway to the right and two more straight ahead. Hopper locked his suit and was able to keep the cyborg vertical in spite of the blasts.

Fire from the Drakuls slowed noticeably.

"*Thanks,*" Sergeant Hopper commed. "*That's a lot better.*" He pulled one of the wires out. "Now maybe I can get some of this shit fixed."

Shuttle 02, Asteroid Weapons Platform, Gliese 876, February 19, 2021

Exit flew the shuttle around to the front of the asteroid where the crew could see into the shuttle bays. As they got their first look, the flight crew noticed movement. Too much movement.

"*Calvin, Foxy,*" the shuttle's WSO commed. "*I've got good news, and I've got bad news. The good news is that the bay you said to meet you in is open; the two bays below it have their blast doors shut so they would have been a 'no go.' The bad news is that it looks like there's a welcoming party of Drakuls waiting there for you. There are six Drakuls setting up an ambush in the shuttle bay. Want us to do something about them?*"

"*Foxy, Calvin,*" he replied, "*yeah, if you can thin 'em out for us, that would be helpful. We've already got a few casualties, and now we've got a bunch of civilians in tow.*"

"*Roger that, sir,*" Foxy replied. "*We'll take care of them.*"

"Can you tell what they're doing?" Exit asked.

"I think they figured out that the platoon is bringing the hostages to one of the shuttle bays," Foxy replied, looking at his targeting scope that gave him an enhanced view, "They're setting up a heavy weapons position to shoot anything that tries to enter the bay from the interior of the asteroid. It probably won't hurt us, but it'll make a mess out of the platoon and the hostages if we let them."

"How about this?" asked Exit. "Let's not let them."

"Sounds good to me," Foxy replied. "I'll bet there's a force screen that will reflect our laser if we try to shoot them from outside the bay, so we'll have to go in. The only problem is that we'll probably lose our stealth when we do. Give me a second to get ready." He switched his laser system on and brought up the targeting system.

"OK," Foxy said, "I'm ready when you are."

"I'm ready," Exit replied.

Foxy turned on the armament panel that allowed him to fire. "Master Arm switch is 'on,'" he said; "the laser is hot."

"Here we go," said Exit, maneuvering the shuttle into the bay. As expected, the force screen recognized a shuttle and allowed it to enter. As they also expected, the ship became visible as it contacted the force screen. Two of the Drakuls happened to be looking when the shuttle became visible; both jumped back in surprise.

"Firing," said Foxy as he triggered the laser at one of the Drakuls looking at the shuttle. Developed to defeat incoming anti-ship missiles, the laser was devastating to flesh. The first laser shot hit the Drakul where its right arm joined its body, blowing it off and spinning the creature around. "One down," commented Foxy, "and *man*, could I get used to doing this!" He missed with the next two shots as the Drakuls ran around looking for cover, but blew apart another enemy soldier with his fourth shot, and then a third Drakul with the shot after that.

The rest of the Drakuls began firing their laser rifles at the shuttle, but they were not powerful enough to penetrate the ship's hull. Standing still to shoot at the shuttle also made them excellent targets for return fire.

"That's it," said Foxy as he killed the last one. 40 seconds had gone by since his first shot, and all of the Drakuls were down. All of them were in at least two pieces, if not more.

Task Force Calvin, Asteroid Weapons Platform, Gliese 876, February 19, 2021

"The hangar bay is clear," commed Foxy. "We're waiting for you in it."

"Copy, thanks," Calvin replied, "We just made it to the airlock and are waiting for the other squad to get here, and then we'll be on our way."

Calvin looked around at the group milling around in the passageway. Before he could say anything, Master Gunnery Sergeant Kinkead came out of the control room. It only took two seconds for her to assess the situation, and her face to go purple. "What the hell is going on here?" she yelled. "Who told you to take a nap in the middle of an assault? What, your mommy isn't here to babysit you, so you all forgot how to be soldiers? What the hell is all this standing around bullshit?"

No one wanted to interrupt her, but it didn't matter. She had worked herself into a full-fledged rant. "That'll teach me to take five minutes to get medical attention. See if I ever do that again! Zoromski, why haven't you taken charge of this nightmare? Start earning your fucking sergeant's pay, damn it! Owens, Stump, Cuillard! Get our alien guests into the control room so they're out of the way in case the Drakuls show up. Keep them there and get Corporal Lawrence to treat any of them that got shot. I don't care if she knows their anatomy; tell her to fucking figure it out!"

"Gordons, damn it, stop fighting with each other and get down the hallway to the right. We don't have any friends in that direction; shoot anything that moves. Hanzo, Patel, go find the Hooolong called Smetlurge and find out where the shuttle bay is. Scout out as far as you can in that direction so we know where we're going. Westbrook, Buzdar, set up a perimeter 50 meters down the passageway in the center. BTO and Tiny, you've got the passageway to the left. Watch out for friendlies; the other squad is coming from that direction, and the captain does NOT want to get hit with a .95 caliber slug. Jones, if you don't get that damn camera out of my face, I'll feed you to the fucking Drakuls myself! Now, did I miss anyone? No? Good! Get to work! I, for one, have no intention of dying today, so let's fucking look alive!"

Task Force Night, Asteroid Weapons Platform, Gliese 876, February 19, 2021

"O*ne more-fuck!-wire to connect,*" commed Sergeant Hopper. The Drakuls were pushing in again, and his suit's nanobots were running full-out trying to repair the continued damage he was taking. He was going to have to go to emergency override to get any more painkillers; the suit said that he had already received his recommended daily allowance in just the last 10 minutes. Even with all of that, the laser burns still hurt. A lot.

He continued to do the best he could to ignore the pain. They needed the cyborg; he had to get it running again.

"*There. That's got it,*" said Hoppy. "*How do you feel—*" His voice cut out suddenly.

"*I'm good,*" Staff Sergeant Randolph replied. He turned to see three Drakuls coming down the left passage. Two of them had the standard large Drakul laser rifle; one had a weapon with a larger tube that he was reloading. Randolph killed the Drakul carrying the tube with several well placed rounds. The other two Drakuls fried off some more of his combat skin while he killed them. The enemy taken care of, Randolph looked down at Sergeant Hopper and saw that the tubular weapon was some sort of flechette thrower; Hopper had four large metal slivers that protruded from both the front and back of his suit. Two more were stuck in the lower part of Randolph's left leg, but they were not impinging on anything critical. Randolph was fine; Hopper was dead.

Chapter Twenty-Nine

Shuttle 02, **Asteroid Weapons Platform, Gliese 876, February 19, 2021**

"Hey, Exit," Foxy said, "do you see that Drakul up there in the window?" He pointed up to a large window that overlooked the hangar bay.

"I do now," Exit replied. "That's gotta be the hangar bay control room. What do you think he's doing?"

Foxy watched him for another few seconds. "No idea. I'd shoot him, but the laser won't aim high enough for me to target him."

"That sucks," Exit said. "I doubt he's doing anything to help us." He saw motion out of the corner of his eye. "Shit! The hangar bay doors are closing!" The aviators looked back up at the window. The Drakul was looking back down at them. When he saw that he had the Terrans' attention, he began waving.

Task Force Calvin, Asteroid Weapons Platform, Gliese 876, February 19, 2021

"Calvin, Exit," the pilot commed, "there is a Drakul in the hangar bay control room, and it looks like he just started closing the hangar bay doors. Should we stay in or get out?"

277

"Stay in," Calvin replied. "Give me a second." He ran into the airlock control room. "Hey, Smetlurge, are there backup power systems for when the main engines receive battle damage?"

"I don't understand," said the Hooolong.

"I'm about to blow the main engines," said Calvin. "Are there backup systems to provide life support if I do?"

"Yes, of course there are," Smetlurge said. "It would have been dumb to build something this large without them."

"Master Chief, Lieutenant Commander Hobbs," Calvin commed, "I need you to detonate the explosives on the main engines, right now! All hands, brace for shock and prepare for dark!"

"Roger that, sir, I'd be happy to," Master Chief replied, ducking a flechette round as he pulled out the remote detonator. "Going dark in three, two, one, boom." He pushed the button, and a massive jolt was felt through the asteroid, knocking several of the aliens and a couple of the Terrans off their feet. They had to pick themselves up in the dark as all of the lights went out. It also got quiet as the life support systems cut out, eliminating the background noise of the air handlers.

After five or six seconds, emergency lighting kicked on in the passageways, and the sound of air moving could again be heard. "Exit, Calvin," Calvin commed, "did that kill the doors?"

"Yes it did," the pilot confirmed. "The doors are still open far enough for us to get out. The bad news is that the Drakul that was waving at us just left, so I'm guessing it went to go get help. I'd sure appreciate it if you could get here before he comes back."

Task Force Night, Asteroid Weapons Platform, Gliese 876, February 19, 2021

"Captain, Wraith, I just met up with BTO. We're at the airlock."

"*Great,*" commed Night; "*be right there.*" He jogged up to the front to find Calvin waiting for him.

"Hi, sir," said Night. "Funny thing happened on the way to our ride home."

"No kidding," Calvin replied. "Did you get everything set up?"

"Yeah, we're good," Night said. "Thanks for turning out the lights. They were about to pin us down, and it let us break contact. We've already lost Hoppy; we need to get moving before they re-group."

"*Master Chief!*" commed Calvin. "*Get 'em moving to the hangar bay. You've got combat ops. Master Gunnery Sergeant Kinkead, you're our shepherd; make sure our guests make it in one group.*"

"*You heard the man,*" Master Chief said, "*let's get moving. Wraith, you've got point with Yokaze. Get us there as quick as you can. Wall, you're in the middle to provide fire support for the aliens if we get jumped. Randolph, Zoromski and the Gordons, you've got rear guard; keep 'em off us. As the boss would say, the liberal use of high explosives is authorized. Move out!*"

Shuttle 02, Asteroid Weapons Platform, Gliese 876, February 19, 2021

"Shit!" said Exit, and Foxy felt the ship come off the ground. "They're trying to sneak around behind us." He spun the shuttle around in time to see three Drakuls setting up a crew-served weapon.

It was the biggest weapon Foxy had ever seen. "Master Arm is on, laser's hot," he called. He brought the anti-missile laser to bear, but the Drakuls were faster, and a shot went just over the cockpit glass.

"Holy shit!" Exit said. "That laser's huge! *Shoot 'em! Shoot 'em now!*"

Foxy fired, hitting the ammunition bearer in the chest. He blew backward in several pieces. The gun fired again, hitting the poly-glass right in front of Exit. He could see the bolt drilled a hole part of the way through it. "No, shoot the gunner! Shoot the gunner!"

Foxy retargeted and fired, hitting the gunner in the head. The Drakul fell backward as his head exploded in a spray of blue. The Drakul gun fired again, but its aim was off as the gunner fell backward. The assistant gunner pushed the gunner's body out of the way and grabbed the firing mechanism, but he was not fast enough; Foxy shot him in the chest. Foxy fired several more times into the gun, hoping to render it inoperable.

As he ceased, they heard a noise from the top of the shuttle. "You don't suppose there's one on the roof, do you?" asked Foxy.

"I thought I originally saw four of them," Exit replied. "How many did you kill?"

"Three. Shit."

"Yeah, shit," said Exit. "Flip you for who goes out to try and shoot him off?"

"No," Foxy replied, "we need you to fly this tub. I'll go." He unbuckled his harness and got up to go to the back.

"Wait a sec," said Exit, "I've got an idea. Besides, we need to check out the hole that they almost put in the window."

Foxy slid back into his seat and began strapping in as Exit flew the shuttle out of the bay. "I don't think any of them had suits," Exit said. "Let's find out." As the nose started through the force shield, several yellow lights started blinking on his dashboard. "Must go faster," he said, feeding in more power. "The bastard must have some sort of cutter or blowtorch; it looks like he just cut some of our steering."

As the shuttle cleared the force shield, Foxy asked, "So how long do you suppose the Drakul can last in vacuum?"

"I don't know," Exit replied, "but I'm willing to give it several minutes to find out. I think a human can do it for a minute or so, as long as he doesn't try to hold his breath."

"There's no telling how long a Drakul can hold its breath," said Foxy. "I'd give it five minutes, just to be sure." Exit rolled the craft twice, hoping the centrifugal force would throw it off. "That'll help, too," Foxy added.

Task Force Calvin, Asteroid Weapons Platform, Gliese 876, February 19, 2021

"I*'m in the hangar bay,*" Wraith commed, "*and there's no sign of the shuttle. There are some dead Drakuls scattered around, but no shuttle.*" They had made good time...only to reach the hangar bay and find that the shuttle had disappeared without a word.

"Shuttle 02, *Calvin,*" he commed, "*where the hell are you guys?*"

"*Calvin, Foxy*" the WSO replied, "*sorry, we had a Drakul on the shuttle, and we took it outside for a breath of fresh air. It cut up some of our controls, so we were testing them. We're on our way back.*"

As Calvin entered the hangar bay, he heard explosions behind him. The Drakuls had been pressing them harder as they got closer to the hangar bay. Turning back around, he saw the shuttle entering the hangar bay. It was noticeably wobbling. "*Is that thing flyable?*" he asked.

"*Yeah, barely,*" Exit replied. "*I don't want to have to wait around any longer, or I'd call for the other shuttle to come and get you. If there was any way to transfer the passengers in space, I'd do that, too. As it is, we'll just have to make it work.*" He brought it in to a stop, and the boarding ramp came down.

"Load 'em up!" Calvin yelled. "We're out of here as soon as everyone's aboard."

"*Hey sir,*" commed Sergeant Zoromski, "*you're gonna want to hurry. There's a whole pile of them back here, and they don't seem to be taking 'no' for an answer.*"

"I heard him, sir," called Master Gunnery Sergeant Kinkead. "We're going as fast as we can." She shook her head, watching the menagerie of different aliens board the shuttle. It wasn't quite like Noah boarding the animals two by two...but Noah only had to worry about rain, not 10-foot monsters that wanted to eat them.

Calvin saw the last aliens heading up the ramp. "*We're loaded. Fall back to the shuttle. Foxy, cover them with the shuttle's laser.*"

"*Got it, sir,*" replied Foxy.

The Gordon brothers came through the door, followed by Sergeant Zoromski. Staff Sergeant Randolph was the last through the doorway. He had borrowed Staff Sergeant Dantone's Hooolong pulse rifle to go with his Mrowry auto cannon and paused to fire both of them for nearly five seconds on full automatic, sending over one hundred 20-millimeter rounds down the corridor. He turned to see the other soldiers running toward the shuttle and began lumbering toward it, as well.

The shuttle laser fired, and he turned back around, ready to defend himself.

"*Sorry,*" the shuttle's WSO said. "*I was just doing a ranging shot to make sure I was on target.*"

Randolph turned and ran the rest of the way to the shuttle, shaking his metal head. As he climbed the boarding ramp, the door opened, and two Drakuls came through. Already on target, Foxy shot them as the shuttle lifted off, turned and wobbled its way out of the hangar bay.

As they rose above the asteroid, the shuttle jerked as a counter-missile laser hit its right wing.

"Shit," swore Exit, "I forgot we weren't invisible anymore."

"Just a second," replied Foxy. He turned the stealth generator off, waited a couple of seconds, and then turned it back on again.

Exit turned the ship hard to the left, and the laser missed with its next shot. Several other lasers began firing, but they were aimed in the shuttle's original direction and also missed. Exit applied full power, and the shuttle left the asteroid behind.

Calvin came up to the flight deck. "Impressive light show," he noted, watching as the computer showed where the lasers were firing. "Happily, I can do something about that." He switched to his comm system. "*Master Chief, blow the asteroid,*" he ordered.

"*Yes sir,*" replied Master Chief. "*Detonation in three...two...one...*" Fire from the asteroid ceased as the nuclear warheads detonated. Although the battle station's metal covering was thick and built to withstand a tremendous amount of damage, it was shaped to repel damage from the outside, not to withstand a 200 megaton blast from inside the station. With an enormous flash, the metal covering the asteroid fractured, exploding violently into thousands of large pieces and millions of smaller shards. The asteroid itself shattered into billions of rocky pieces that rocketed outward in all directions.

Exit smiled. "Thank you, sir," he said. "That'll help."

Chapter Thirty

"I can't fly like this," said Exit five minutes later. "We'll never make it back." After the asteroid had been destroyed, the shuttle's flight control system had become progressively worse. Exit wasn't sure what happened, but it felt like something else had failed in the spacecraft's control system.

"What's up?" asked Calvin, who had been called back up to the cockpit to discuss the shuttle's problems.

"I can't turn right," replied Exit. "Something's cut or jammed in the flight controls. In order to go right, I have to turn left and come all the way around to the heading I want. If I miss the heading, I have to do another circle. I'm never going to be able to dock with the ship like this."

"Got any idea where the Drakul was when the flight controls were damaged?" Calvin asked.

"Yeah, he was not too far behind the cockpit up on top of the shuttle," said Foxy.

BANG!

"What was that?" Calvin asked.

"That was a piece of the asteroid," said Exit. "We haven't been able to fly fast enough and straight enough to avoid the debris field. Some of the pieces are still flying around out there." He moved the stick. "Shit! Whatever just hit us finished off the flight controls; now they're not working at all. Someone's going to have to go up top and take a look at it. Got any mechanics in the back?"

"I don't know," Calvin replied, "I can go see."

"I hope you've got a couple; if not, we're not getting back any time soon," said Exit. "What's worse is we never planned on bringing back this many guests, or we'd have brought extra oxygen. We're going to be running pretty thin on air before long. I've commed the ship, but we're a long way out. It will take two and a half hours for the other shuttle to get here."

"How much air do we have left?" Calvin asked.

"Two hours."

"I'll go find a mechanic."

"Thanks," said Exit, "that'd be helpful."

Shuttle 02, **Stuck in Space, Gliese 876, February 19, 2021**

"*There's the problem,*" commed Staff Sergeant Randolph. With the death of Sergeant Hopper, the cyborg had more experience with mechanical things than anyone else in the platoon. He was also less likely to be injured than the 100% biological humans, so he had led the way to the top of the shuttle. Corporal Lawrence was assisting him, as she also had mechanical experience, having designed her own DNA sequencing machines. She was carrying the tools, while trying to stay behind the cyborg; each of the troopers had seen several pieces of the destroyed asteroid whip past.

"*What's the problem?*" asked Exit.

"*There's a panel cover missing and some torch marks,*" replied Randolph, "*as well as a spray of blue. Looks like your Drakul bought it in the end. Oh, yeah, the writing around the panel says, 'Caution, Flight Controls.' I'm in the right spot.*"

"*Can you tell what's wrong with them?*" Calvin asked.

"*Not at the moment,*" Randolph said. "*I'll have to move the rock that is sitting on them first.*"

"*Rock?*" asked Exit.

"*Yeah,*" said Corporal Lawrence, "*a big rock. Looks like part of the asteroid. It would probably weigh several hundred pounds in standard gravity.*" She moved out of the way. "*Stand by; we'll see if the big boy can lift it out of the way. Staff Sergeant?*"

Randolph braced himself and pulled, and the rock went flying off into space. "*The rock wasn't stuck,*" he said. "*It was just sitting on top of the panel, and I was able to move it.*" He looked down. "*Ouch,*" he continued. "*Yeah, I see what the Drakul did. It made a mess of the wiring. I think I can temp fix the cables that the Drakul cut, but it's going to be a really sloppy repair. There will probably be a lot of extra play in the flight controls.*"

"*That's fine,*" said Exit, sounding relieved. "*Just get me a little bit of control back, and you'll be my hero.*"

"*Don't thank me yet,*" Randolph commed. "*You haven't seen how awful the repair is going to be. Between not being able to hold onto the cables very well and the small area that the wires have to run through...just don't thank me yet. We'll see how it goes. Corporal, let's start with a pair of wire cutters.*"

"*How is the repair coming?*" Exit commed 15 minutes later. "*We're getting to where I'm going to have to make some hard decisions.*"

"*Doing good, sir,*" replied Staff Sergeant Randolph; "*in fact; I'm just finishing up. Two minutes.*" He finished installing heat-shrink tubing over the solder joint. He just needed to heat it, and he'd be done. *"Hand me the heat gun, please,"* he said without looking up. His hand remained empty. *"Today? Kinda like to get out of here, and it sounds like the pilot is getting antsy."* Corporal Lawrence still didn't reply. Randolph looked up in annoyance. *"Could you PLEASE hand me..."* Corporal Lawrence wouldn't be handing anyone anything ever again. A two-inch wide sliver of metal from the asteroid was protruding from her facemask, which was rapidly filling up with blood. A thin red mist sprayed out into the vacuum from where the metal breached the facemask. As she slowly spun to the side, Randolph could see that it protruded from the back of her helmet as well. "Shit," Randolph said. *"The thrusters are fixed,"* Randolph commed, *"but we just lost Corporal Lawrence."*

Chapter Thirty-One

Bridge, TSS *Vella Gulf*, Stargate to 54 Piscium, Gliese 876, February 21, 2021

The stargate spread out in front of the *Vella Gulf*. It looked close enough to touch, but didn't seem to be getting any closer. "This is the hardest part," noted Captain Sheppard, "knowing that the Archon attack is imminent, and that we need to get back as quickly as possible, but being unable to go quickly because we'll give ourselves away."

"Yes it is," agreed Calvin, as conscious of the passage of time as anyone else. He could feel it slipping away from them.

"Dead slow ahead," ordered Captain Sheppard.

"Dead slow ahead, aye," repeated the helmsman. The *Vella Gulf* started forward and jumped.

Bridge, TSS *Vella Gulf*, 54 Piscium System, February 23, 2021

"That's a lot of stuff waiting for the Archons when they attack in two days," said the OSO, using the long range viewer to catalog the Drakul forces at the stargate to Archon space. "They've still got a lot of ships there, even without the task force we saw leave, but what's going to kill them are the mines. I've never seen a minefield so dense. Even if the Archons use those robot ships, there's still going to be a ton of mines waiting for them." He paused, trying to count all the mines he could see in one area. "Damn," he finally said. "There's got to be something we can do to make their entrance easier." His weapons-release finger twitched unconsciously. The sense of urgency driving the Terrans to do something, *anything*, was at an all time high.

"What we really need to do," said Ensign Sara Sommers, "is something for the rest of the Psiclopes left on Olympos."

"I wish we could," said Captain Sheppard. "However, we don't know how many Psiclopes still exist, and there's no way to get them off even if we could sneak in there and get them."

"I realize that," said Ensign Sommers. "It's just that I can't think of anything worse than sitting around, waiting to get eaten. It would almost be a mercy to put them out of their misery."

"It *would be* a mercy," said Steropes, as he entered the bridge. "I know it's what I'd want."

"Steropes, I know this has to be tough on you," said Captain Sheppard. "Why don't you go back to your cabin or to the gym or something. We'll take care of this."

"Anywhere I go, I'll only think about it," said Steropes. "Besides, there ought to be a Psiclops involved in determining the fate of the planet, don't you think? What are you going to do?"

"We were just working on that," said Calvin. "The problem is that we have a couple of things we'd like to do, but probably can't do either of them very well."

"What are they?" asked Steropes.

"As you already heard, we are trying to work out what to do about the remaining Psiclopes on the planet, for one," said Captain Sheppard. "We'd also like to do something about the fleet orbiting the stargate if we could."

"What can one cruiser do against all of that?" asked Steropes, indicating the holographic display of the enemy forces. "We couldn't take them on normally, much less with half of our missile tubes covered with stealth modules. We'd get slaughtered."

"Well, we would have surprise on our side," said the OSO, "and we could probably get in a few shots before anyone reacted. Maybe we could go back into cloak again after that and get them to chase us? We could probably lead some of them away from the gate..."

"No," said Captain Sheppard, "We don't have enough throw weight to make a difference. All we'd do is piss them off and let them know that we're here. There's got to be a better way that we can use our stealth and the element of surprise."

"Hey," said Calvin, looking at the tactical map of the system. "What's this thing orbiting Olympos' moon?"

"It's a Class 8 replicator," said Ensign Sommers. "The last time I looked, the replicator was making a super dreadnought. I think the ship was almost complete, too."

"Can we get a visual?" Calvin asked.

"Yeah, the replicator is just coming around to our side," she said.

She put it up on the screen. The replicator happened to be pointing at the *Vella Gulf* as the replicator orbited the moon of the second planet. So did the nose of the super dreadnought, tied up alongside it.

"Oh, shit, the ship's finished," said the DSO. "That's one more super dreadnought that the Archons will have to destroy."

"Not if we take the ship first," said Calvin. "That would also take care of one of our problems. We could do some real damage to their fleet with one of those things."

"You have got to be kidding me," said Captain Sheppard. "How exactly are you going to capture the ship? And once you take it, how are you going to crew it?"

"Well...what if we take half of the *Gulf's* crew over there?" asked Calvin. "I mean, we'd take them over once the platoon secured the ship, of course. The ship has to have some sort of AI, right? We wouldn't need to have a full crew, just enough to assist the AI in running the crucial systems."

"If the asteroid is any indication," said Night, "there may also be some other races onboard the ship that could help to capture the ship or to man it afterwards. If they're building the ship, they must know at least a little bit about running it."

"Hmmm...You're right," said Captain Sheppard. "Maybe we *could* operate it, at least in a minimal status. The problem remains, though; how are you going to capture the ship? You do know that it's almost three miles long and masses almost ten million tons, right? And you've only got like 30 troops to capture it, right?"

"Yes, I know," said Calvin, "but if the ship is like the Mrowry dreadnought, the ship is mostly just empty space used to mount really big weapons. There are the crew's living areas and a few other areas that are manned to run the ship, but much of it is empty, especially if they don't have any marines, or whatever they use as marines, onboard yet."

"That's our biggest problem," Captain Sheppard said. "We don't know if the ship is manned yet, and if so, how many of them there are aboard."

"Hey, Sara," asked Calvin, "do you have any indications of whether or not the ship is manned? How about energy usage? Are any of the ship's systems operational?"

Ensign Sommers looked at her system. "The ship is currently operating at a minimum power setting," she said. "The ship's engines are running, but only enough to provide basic life support. I don't think there are too many Drakuls onboard."

Steropes nodded. "I concur with that assessment," he said. "It is unlikely that there are many life forms of any type onboard with that low of a power reading."

"I wonder if any of the people we brought back from the asteroid have any experience on the replicator or would be able to help with manning the ship," Calvin said.

"I don't know," said Captain Sheppard. "I think that most of them were so relieved at being liberated that they went to sleep as soon as they got here. Most of them haven't been out of their cabins much since. I doubt Intelligence has debriefed any of them yet."

"It would be helpful if we knew," said Calvin, "but it's going to take too long for us to go door-to-door to get the information we need." He paused and then had a thought, "But we don't need to; Solomon can ask them for us. Hey, Solomon, could you please query the folks that we brought back from the asteroid and see if any of them has experience crewing a ship? We'd also like to know how the Drakuls operate their replicators, and if any of them has experience with that."

"I will ask them," the AI answered.

"While Solomon is surveying our guests," said Lieutenant Finn, "I know how to take out the planet."

"Would that be your previously mentioned Doomsday Device?" asked Captain Sheppard. "If so, I strictly forbid the use of any weapon that is going to wipe out a planet. I forbid it. That was not in our mandate, despite what the Archons say. I *will not* be responsible for the complete destruction of a planet."

"Well, in that case," replied Lieutenant Finn, "the answer is both a 'yes' and a 'no.' Yes, in that I would use one of those types of bombs, but no, I wouldn't use it as a Doomsday Device. It has other methods of employment that you can use. I looked earlier, and most of the Drakuls seem to be clustered near the capital. In fact, I'm sorry to say it, Steropes, but it looks like the Drakuls have emptied all of the other cities on the planet. I can use the device in its secondary mode, which is a nuclear option, and create a burst big enough to wipe out all life in the capital area. Would that be good enough? The rest of the planet would still be habitable."

"Somewhere up above," said the Mrowry, "the gods are laughing at us right now."

"Why is that?" asked Captain Sheppard.

"You are familiar with Arton Churther, correct?" asked Lieutenant Rrower. "He was a Psiclops scientist who devoted his life to understanding black holes and how stargates worked. One of the things he invented was the Churther Box, the device that allowed the Drakuls back into this universe. He was also responsible for another major invention. That creation has many names. The Churther Bomb. World Ender. The Doomsday Device. They're all names for the same thing, a weapon that makes it possible to destroy a world. It is ironic that the person who made it possible for the Drakuls to come to this universe is also the person who will help us get rid of them again."

"What do you mean?" asked Lieutenant Finn.

"Have you read any of the documentation on the bomb?" asked Lieutenant Rrower.

"Yes," said Lieutenant Finn. "As I understand it, there are two modes of employment. One is a nuclear option that generates something on the order of a 200 megaton nuclear explosion. The other option, which I didn't understand fully, was the option to destroy the planet. The way that mode worked was unclear."

"It is intentionally left unclear so that no one can design one of them," replied Lieutenant Rrower. "I'm no physicist, so I can't explain the way it works, even if I wanted to. In general, though, the weapon has a massive nuclear/antimatter starter detonation, which is the 200 megaton bomb that you mentioned. That is actually just the primer phase for the other part of the bomb. The purpose of the starter bomb is to compact a mass of material into a state that is more dense than almost anything else in the universe."

"Almost anything else?" asked Lieutenant Finn. "What? Are you talking about a black hole?"

"Yes," said Lieutenant Rrower, with a nod. "Churther found a process to make a microscopic black hole. Happily, the artificial gravitational singularity that is formed is unstable and will eventually disappear; however, before it vanishes, it has the capability to devour about six times the mass of the Earth."

"It...eats the planet?" asked Captain Sheppard.

Lieutenant Rrower shrugged, a habit he had picked up from his association with Terrans. "Like I said, I'm not a physicist," he replied, "nor have I ever seen it used. 'Eat' may not be the right word. Maybe it opens a gate to another world or universe or time, and the things just go through it, like they did with his Box. *I don't know.* All I know is that the one time the bomb was used, the planet that it was used on disappeared, along with three spaceships that were in orbit."

"That's just....just...wow," said Calvin.

"Isn't it?" asked Lieutenant Rrower. "There's one other bit of historical reference. The one time the bomb was used was against the Drakuls. The fact that we are now contemplating using it to rid this universe of them for a second time is, I think, ironic. The bottom line is that if you only want the nuclear option, use the blue button. Don't touch the red button with the guard over it. That is the doomsday switch."

"Oh! OK," said Lieutenant Finn. "I got it; don't touch the red button."

"You say that as if you think you will be going on the mission, should we choose to send one down," said Captain Sheppard. "I was unaware that you were a combat trooper."

"I'm not a combat soldier," said Lieutenant Finn. "I am, however, just about the only person on this ship that understands at least a portion of how this bomb works. I am also someone that is not required for the assault on the dreadnought. I can accomplish this by myself if you just give me a shuttle and a crew."

"What has to be done?" asked Calvin.

"I can put the bomb onto an anti-gravity pallet," replied Lieutenant Finn. "I'd just need a shuttle to get me to the surface for a couple of minutes to drop it off, and then we could take back off and detonate it remotely from orbit. No problems."

"There are always problems in combat," said Calvin. "Nothing goes as smoothly or easily as you planned, mostly because the enemy has a say in what you're doing, and he generally doesn't want your plans to succeed." Calvin looked at Captain Sheppard. "We only need one of the shuttles for the dreadnought assault. We could send the other with Lieutenant Finn to drop off the bomb. We'd also probably want to send a security detail of at least three soldiers just in case."

"That makes sense," replied Captain Sheppard. "Do you have three troopers that can be spared?"

"Yes, we do," Night said. "I've got three in mind. They don't have as much training in special operations, so they wouldn't be as helpful in the other assault. This is the perfect mission for them." He paused. "There's no doubt we can do this," he said, "but are there any other options that we haven't considered? Is there any other way that we can do it without sending people down to the surface of the planet?"

"I could nuke them from orbit," said the OSO.

"No," said Lieutenant Finn. "We couldn't be sure that would work. I analyzed the defensive systems surrounding the planet, and they are quite robust. Anything that we launch from orbit will most likely get shot down, in addition to giving away our presence to the forces in orbit and at the stargate."

"We definitely don't want that," said Captain Sheppard, "especially if we're going to have to get through the forces at the gate. No. Let's go with sending the bomb down to the surface in a stealthed shuttle."

"I have completed the survey that you requested," interrupted Solomon; "however, before I give you the results, I have to note that they may be somewhat skewed."

"Skewed?" asked Captain Sheppard. "How so?"

"Many of the individuals I had to contact were sleeping at the time of the survey," said Solomon. "Some of them reacted quite poorly to being awakened."

"Noted," said Captain Sheppard. "What were the results?'

"There is a Hooolong that has engineering experience on super dreadnoughts including their design," replied Solomon. "There are another 10 that have crewed starships at various times. As far as working on a Drakul replicator, there is only one, but he worked on the replicator that you are discussing assaulting."

"Would it be convenient for the engineer and replicator technician to come to the bridge?" asked Calvin.

"They are already on their way," replied Solomon. "I anticipated you would like to talk to them, so I asked them to come to the bridge. They will be here in approximately three seconds."

The doors to the bridge slid open almost exactly three seconds later. The first figure that walked onto the bridge looked like all of the Archons that had been rescued from the asteroid.

"Your wings!" said Sara. "What happened to your wings?"

The Archon gave a sad smile. "I was in the hands of the devils for some time," he said. "They treated me somewhat less well than what I was used to as an officer in the Archon navy."

Although he had lost his wings, it didn't do anything to affect his projection aura, and all of the Terrans were hit with a wave of sadness and loss. "I'm sorry for your treatment at their hands," said the CO. "I am Captain Sheppard, the commanding officer of the *Vella Gulf*."

"Stop that," said the Hooolong that followed him onto the bridge. Calvin was somehow not surprised to see that it was Smetlurge. "We're free now," Smetlurge continued. "You should be projecting happiness and confidence to help us, not boo-hooing. What's done is done. Get over it."

"Greetings, Mr. President," said Steropes, who bowed to the Hooolong. He looked at Calvin with a raised eyebrow. "You didn't tell me that you had rescued the Hooolong president. This will be very helpful."

"Mr. President?" Captain Sheppard exclaimed, giving Calvin a less than favorable look. "I'm sorry, but I wasn't aware that you were a dignitary. We would have tried to find better quarters for you. Maybe we could put you into a certain lieutenant commander's quarters..."

"I didn't know," said Calvin. "Nobody told me."

"He is telling the truth," agreed Smetlurge, "I never told him who I was. Besides, if there is no Hooolong civilization left, am I really the president of anything?" His eyes looked at the Archon, Captain Sheppard, Steropes and Calvin simultaneously, daring them to contradict him. "Like I already said, what's done is done. Our society was a technocracy; as the senior and most accomplished scientist on the planet, I was elected president, against my wishes. Now that the majority of my civilization has been destroyed, I am free to be a scientist again. I assume that is why you asked us to the bridge? You needed help with something?"

"Yes," agreed Captain Sheppard, "we need your help." He looked at the Archon. "I understand that you worked on the replicator here in the 54 Piscium system?" he asked.

"Yes, I worked on the replicator here," said the Archon. "I worked there until the demons found out I was a laser expert and sent me to work on the asteroid's defenses. My name is Azrael."

"We are considering assaulting the replicator," Calvin said. "What can you tell us about it? How many Drakuls would be aboard? How many will be onboard the dreadnought that just came out?"

Azrael paused to consider. "If the dreadnought just came out of the replicator, the ship will not be manned by its crew yet. Normally, there is a two or three day period where the crew of the replicator works with the artificial intelligence onboard the ship to run the initial diagnostics. When that is complete, the crew will transport up from the planet." He looked at Calvin for a moment and then asked, "Why doth thou want to know?"

"We're thinking of commandeering the dreadnought, as well," Calvin replied. "How many Drakuls do you think will be onboard the replicator and the ship, total?"

"Hmmm...Somewhere around 100, I would guess," the Archon replied. "That's just a guess. There will also be a variety of other races aboard, most of which will be friendly if you can separate them from the Drakuls."

"Which ones are allied with the Drakuls?" Captain Sheppard asked.

"Allied with the Drakuls?" Azrael asked with a laugh. "Thou don't know the Drakuls very well. No one is allied with them. Who would ally with them when they are just as likely to tear off parts of thy body and eat them as look at thee? Still, many of the races will be afraid of reprisals if they help you, so ye will have to make them believe that ye can win."

"What about a way to get onto the replicator unnoticed?" Night asked. "Is there any way to get aboard the replicator or, even better, the dreadnought?"

"Thy best chance of getting onboard unnoticed is to go through the replicator," Azrael answered. "There may be an open hatch somewhere on the dreadnought, but that is a lot of area to cover. I can get you onto the replicator easily, unless the Drakuls have changed the codes."

"You can?" Calvin asked.

"Why, yes," Azrael said. "I used to have to go outside to work on the laser systems of new ships, so I used the hatches on numerous occasions. For all of their viciousness, most of the Drakuls are not extremely intelligent. Are they sly? Yes, most of them are quite cunning, but as a race they are not overly bright. The code on most of the hatches is 1-2-3-4."

"No shit?" asked Night. "You've got to be kidding me."

"I am telling thee the truth," Azrael replied, "The codes were never changed the whole time I was there. What would be the reason? They would never expect anyone to come here and try to steal a ship. It should be easy to get into the station, and I would be happy to show you the way. Once ye are in, though, things will get decidedly more difficult for you."

"Why is that?" Calvin asked.

"As I already said," Azrael repeated, "they are quite vicious, and ye will be fighting them at close quarters. They like to tear things off of the people they are fighting. I don't know how many soldiers ye have, but there are probably a hundred of them. I wouldn't think ye had enough troops to fight them on a ship this small."

"We may not have enough to go toe-to-toe against them in an open area," Calvin replied, "but if we can get in and out without raising an alarm, I think we can pull it off. How many do you suppose will be on the station, and how many will be on the ship?"

"There will probably be about half on the ship and half on the replicator," Azrael answered. "If ye could capture the bridge on the ship and the control station on the replicator, ye could keep the alarm from being raised. No one would know ye had captured them. Ye could also use the controls to lock up some of the Drakuls in various rooms, where ye could deal with them separately. Maybe even pump out the atmosphere and let them die of their own accord." He smiled at the thought.

"That wouldn't bother me any," Calvin said.

"More important to the success of the plan, you also have us," added Smetlurge.

"No offense, but you didn't seem too fond of combat on the asteroid," Calvin replied.

"Me?" asked Smetlurge. "Of course not. I'm not going to fight any of the Drakuls, nor would any of the other Hooolongs. Some of the other races might fight, but we wouldn't. You have seen what they do to Hooolongs; they pick us up and drain us dry. No thanks. We absolutely will not go into close combat with the Drakuls. However, if you can get us into the control room, we will run the computers for you and make our presence felt that way, as long as you provide security for us. Also, if you succeed in taking it from them, we will crew it for you. As we no longer have a planet, I would request the ship be given to us to serve as our home, along with any of the other prisoners of war that want to join us."

"That is fine with me," agreed Captain Sheppard. "If circumstances allow it, we would like to lay claim to the replicator, should we manage to capture it, but the ship is yours."

"Solomon, how many of each type of alien do we currently have aboard?" Calvin asked.

"Currently onboard the *Vella Gulf* are 41 Hooolongs, 12 Depsips, three Xanths, three Quugeerts, two Clranks, three Archons, one Mrowry and one Psiclops," Solomon noted.

"Can any of them fight?" Night asked. "We're down a few soldiers after the assault on the asteroid, and we could really use a hand if we're going to try to take both the replicator and the ship."

"The Depsips might fight," said Smetlurge. "They have automatic crossbows that they use in combat that fire poison arrows."

"The Depsips?" asked Calvin. "What race is that?"

"They are the creatures with lots of legs and two heads," said Smetlurge, "like Bzzzeedlezzzzz on the asteroid. They are also very good with computer network operations and computer network attack."

"Oh, the ones that looked like giant spiders," Night said. "They didn't impress me as being the most fierce..."

"Generally, they are not," agreed Smetlurge, "unless they are defending their homes or children."

"Which they wouldn't be," noted Calvin. "Maybe they'd be better running the replicator control room if we can get them there, rather than taking them into combat with the Drakuls. Any others?"

"The Xanths are quite warlike, although small," added Smetlurge. "They can fly, but there won't be enough room to use them as aviation units where they would be at their best. Perhaps if they were given laser pistols, they might be of use. If nothing else, they would be hard for the Drakuls to catch."

"I, too, will fight on thy side," said Azrael. "I believe that the Drakuls and I have some unfinished business over the removal of my wings."

"You already know that you can count on me," added Lieutenant Rrower. "I'm in."

"That still leaves us pretty short," said Calvin. "I just have the feeling that we're going to need more troops..."

Platoon CO's Office, TSS *Vella Gulf*, 54 Piscium, February 24, 2021

Calvin looked up at the sound of a knock. "You asked for me to come by?" Steropes asked. "Am I to be allowed to go with the force that is going to the planet?" asked Steropes.

"I'm sorry," said Calvin, "but no. The group that is going there is just going to the surface of the planet, dropping off the bomb and then coming back. You'd just be in the way." He paused, looking closely at Steropes. "We're also getting ready to launch an assault on the dreadnought..."

"And you're going to tell me that I can't come," Steropes interrupted.

"Actually, no," said Calvin, "I wanted to talk to you about coming along."

"Really?" Steropes asked, hope in his eyes.

"When I said that I didn't want you to come with us on the asteroid assault, I wasn't being entirely truthful," Calvin replied. "Part of the reason *was* that I didn't want you trying to get yourself killed, but that was only part of it."

"Was it because we lied to you, and you didn't trust me?" Steropes asked.

"Maybe that was a little bit, too, but once again, not the main point," Calvin replied. Instead of interrupting again, Steropes waited for Calvin to explain.

"The main reason I didn't let you go," Calvin said after a short pause, "was the matter of your redemption."

"My redemption?" Steropes asked.

"Yes, your redemption," Calvin agreed. "I have heard you say several times that you wanted to redeem yourself for the wrongs that you have committed, thereby hoping to reunite with your wife in your next lifetime."

"I didn't think that you believed in reincarnation," Steropes said.

"I don't," agreed Calvin, "but that doesn't mean that I can't respect your belief in it. Who knows? Maybe you are right. I wouldn't want to cheat you out of what you were working toward. The reason I didn't take you is that it looked like you wanted to go and give your life for us, thereby acquiring some sort of kharma points that would let you move up the ladder in your next lifetime to be with Parvati."

"That is my hope, yes," admitted Steropes.

"Then you are going about it all wrong," said Calvin. "A deity wouldn't fall for that. You are trying to take the easy way out, just like your civilization did when it started this war. You didn't want to be responsible for your actions then; you just wanted to blame all of the bad things on someone else. You're doing the same thing now. Rather than actually helping us, you're just hoping to go get killed. The thing you don't see is that going out on a mission just to get killed isn't going to earn you the points you want, because you're not really helping us. If you want to earn the kharma points necessary to make up for the things you've done, you have to do that by *struggling* to do good, by staying alive and giving us the benefit of your thousands of years of experience. Nothing worthwhile is ever easy, and salvation is one of the hardest things to achieve, no matter what your religion or belief system."

"If you want to achieve your goals," Calvin continued, "you do that by staying alive and striving with every fiber of your being to do the right thing, not by taking the easy way out. You do that by going down to that dreadnought with us and kicking the shit out of every Drakul we see, without letting them kill you in return. You help us get back to the Archons with the support needed to beat the Drakuls on this front, so that they can come help us defend Earth. We need your help. You want redemption? *Then earn it.* Stop being a baby, stop whining about what might have been, get off your ass and come help us kill some Drakuls. We need you, but we need the tai chi master, not someone that's just looking to die."

Steropes looked up. There was a light in his eyes that Calvin hadn't seen in a while. Steropes nodded. "You are correct," he said. "It is often easier to see what is better for others than to analyze yourself." He nodded. "I agree. Take me on the assault. I will give you my all."

Chapel, TSS *Vella Gulf,* 54 Piscium, February 24, 2021

Calvin knocked on the doorframe to the ship's chapel, interrupting Father Zuhlsdorf who was cleaning up something on the altar. He looked up in surprise to see Calvin standing in the doorway. "Come in, come in," he invited. "Are you still struggling with who you are, and who you think you should be?"

"No," Calvin said. "For the first time since the war with China, I think I'm finally at peace with myself; my problem today is more of a physical nature."

"Yes?" Father Zuhlsdorf asked. "What is it?"

"We are about to try to capture a replicator and a ship from the Drakuls," Calvin replied; "however, the platoon is a little thin. Heck, we'd be a little thin if we tried to do this with a full battalion; the ship alone is over two miles long. On our last mission, you helped out in combat against the coatls...I wanted to ask if you'd consider coming with us to help out with the assault. We need everyone we can get."

"The Lord works in mysterious ways," said Father Zuhlsdorf. "I was due to be replaced prior to this cruise, but the replacement chaplain ended up with an appendicitis and was delayed. As it turns out, I still have all of my gear onboard. I can be ready in 15 minutes."

Spacehawk Ready Room, TSS *Vella Gulf*, 54 Piscium, February 24, 2021

"OK," said Lieutenant Phil 'Venturi' Ventura, the shuttle's WSO, "that's the plan. We fly down, try to avoid detection for as long as possible and then land in this valley 12 miles outside the capital city. Lieutenant Finn will egress and place the bomb, while the security team provides cover from any wandering Drakuls in the area. Surveillance shows the area to be clear, but we're still a long way off. Once the bomb is set, Lieutenant Finn will call for egress, and everyone will board the shuttle. At that point, it is up to Boom Boom, I mean Lieutenant Sean Ventura, the pilot for the mission, and I to get us safely back to our rendezvous with the *Vella Gulf*. Once we're outside the blast radius, you can detonate the weapon. Any questions?"

"Do we know anything about their defenses?" asked Boom Boom. Although an aviator, he had picked up his call sign in Afghanistan on a detached duty. The locals started calling him "Boom, Boom" after the sounds his boots made as he ran across the roofs of buildings, trying to chase down mujahedeen infiltrators.

"Yeah," said Venturi, "I just got the download from Intel. It looks like the Drakuls are there to stay. They have set up a planetary defense center as well as several orbital command posts. They've also got a shitload of missiles, lasers and other defenses. Intel didn't know if the orbital command posts would be able to penetrate our stealth shield. They didn't think so, for what it's worth."

"That's great," Boom Boom said with a snort. "I feel safer already."

"Yeah, no kidding," Venturi agreed. "Regardless, we won't know until we get there. If we lose the stealth module, it's going to take a great crew to get the shuttle down in one piece. Don't worry, though. We're the best. If anyone can do it, we can."

"For our part," Corporal Craig Cuillard said, "we may not be quite as good as the Terran operators at special forces missions."

"We may not have all of the experience that the rest of the unit has," said Corporal John Stump.

"But we *can* do this," said Corporal Weldon Owens. "We *will* keep the Drakuls off of you long enough to get the bomb set up, and for us to get back in to the shuttle. If you can get us down, we'll do the rest."

Platoon Ready Room, TSS *Vella Gulf*, 54 Piscium, February 24, 2021

"We'll be ready in two minutes," Master Chief said, scanning the controlled chaos that was the platoon's gear room. Similar to a sports team's locker room, each of the soldiers had a cubicle in which to store his or her combat gear.

"You recommended moving Sergeant Zoromski up to replace Master Gunnery Sergeant Kinkead?" Calvin asked.

"Yeah," said Master Chief, "I did. He's the senior person in the Ground Force now that Staff Sergeant Randolph's been detached to the other squad."

"Everyone's talking about me like I'm dead," said Master Gunnery Sergeant Kinkead from the doorway. "Is there some reason you're giving away my spot when it's obvious the troops need my leadership so desperately?"

"Besides the broken ribs and other various injuries that have the medibot saying that you're confined to your quarters?" asked Calvin.

"It sounds like this is pretty much an 'all hands on deck' effort," Kinkead said. "I'm a hand, and I'm on deck. I'm coming."

"Well, there's no doubt that we need your leadership," agreed Calvin, ducking as one of the Xanths glided by.

The Xanths looked like smaller versions of Earth's prehistoric pteranodon, with leathery wings and skin, although they didn't have the pteranodon's crest. They stood slightly less than three feet tall, with wingspans just under 10 feet. The Xanth landed at the cubicle the three of them were sharing, Staff Sergeant Burke's. They were going to wear an oxygen mask in the assault shuttle, but would take it off once they made it onboard the replicator so they could fly.

The two Depsips were standing at the lockers of the two medics. Each was large enough to need a locker to itself. No suit ever made could contain the spidery Depsips; they would also wear specially-made masks in the shuttle.

What a mess, thought Calvin, who didn't feel like he knew enough about all of the aliens to command them in battle. Although he had talked with the Xanths and the Depsips for a few minutes, he barely understood their capabilities and limitations. He knew he couldn't count on the Hooolongs for combat support. While the race had once been warlike, that time was centuries past. They promised to operate the ship's systems if he could get them onboard, but driving the creatures along in their inchworm-like pace was somewhat like trying to herd cats. They were slower than cats, but more prone to stopping and looking at something suddenly. Just watching them 'walk' was disconcerting. At least all of them had implants so they could talk to each other. He had the platoon on one frequency and the extraterrestrials on a separate frequency so they didn't compromise the combat capabilities of the squad.

Hearing a whirring sound, Calvin turned to find Bob 'Danger' Jones, the combat cameraman, filming their preparations. He was using a digital 3D camera, so there was no need for the noise. Danger just liked the sound because hearing it made him feel like an old-time war correspondent. He was dressed in combat gear, although Calvin didn't see a weapon on him. "Hi, Bob," Calvin said to the combat cameraman. "As you can see, we're a little thin today. Any chance of getting you to be more 'combat' and less 'cameraman' today?"

"I guess I can," said Jones, with his award-winning smile, "especially if it's what's needed to get the story back to my public."

"Good," replied Calvin. "Go see Master Chief and have him issue you a laser rifle."

"Hey, uh, sir," Jones said, putting out a hand to stop Calvin as he turned to leave, "I've always been more of an explosives kind of guy. Can I get one of those tridents instead? That way, I don't have to be quite as accurate."

"That's fine," agreed Calvin. "Just don't shoot it near me."

Bridge, TSS *Vella Gulf*, 54 Piscium, February 24, 2021

"Both shuttles launching," said the communications officer.

"Roger, both shuttles launching," Captain Sheppard repeated. "Good luck, boys and girls..."

Chapter Thirty-Two

Shuttle 01, Approaching the Replicator, February 24, 2021

"A little further to the right," Azrael said, pointing. "See that hatch? That's where we want to go."

"Got it," said the pilot, Lieutenant Rob 'Thing 1' Mees, "Couldn't pick an easy one, huh?" The hatch was in a recessed area where it would be hard for the pilot to 'hover' the shuttle.

"Nice and easy," advised his WSO and cousin, Lieutenant Paul 'Thing 2' Mees. "It's just like the third simulator flight in flight school."

"Yeah, except that the simulator flight didn't have live Drakuls that would come pouring out to shoot at you if you clanged the shuttle into it," replied Thing 1. He worked a couple of minor corrections into the controls. "OK, this is as close as I can get. Send them in."

Thing 2 pushed the button to put down the ramp. He could see from the camera that Thing 1 was holding the shuttle less than a foot above the replicator, despite his earlier comment. "_Gluck ab!_" he commed to the troops as they stepped down onto their objective.

Shuttle 02, Descending to 54 Piscium, February 24, 2021

"**S**hit!" said Venturi. "I don't know how they did it, but they're onto us." He paused, looking at his scope. "Yeah, they definitely know we're here. All of their command posts just went on high alert. I've got missile systems warming up in orbit and on the planet."

"*Hold on in back,*" commed Boom Boom to the troops in the cargo bay. "*It's going to get rough.*" He began a series of evasive maneuvers as he pushed the nose of the craft down toward the planet to hasten their descent.

"At this rate, we're going to exceed the recommended heat limits on the nose of the shuttle," said Venturi.

"Yes, we are," agreed Boom Boom, "probably by quite a lot." He jerked the shuttle to the left. "If I can get us down and back in one piece, though," he said, "they can bill me." In counterpoint, a laser beam from one of the orbital defense stations flashed through the space he had just vacated.

Within seconds, more lasers were firing, and it wasn't long before the ground lasers began firing as well. The shuttle took a glancing blow from one of the large orbital lasers, and their stealth module failed.

"We're visible," said Venturi. "On the good side, the stealth module absorbed some of that last shot, so we took less damage. On the not-so-good side, you're now going to have to fly the shit out of this thing."

"No kidding," Boom Boom grunted as he wrenched the shuttle around to the right.

Task Force Calvin, Onboard the Replicator, February 24, 2021

"Let's go, ladies," growled Master Chief, using his suit to look behind him while he ran. "Try and keep up." Tasked with capturing the dreadnought, his squad was sprinting toward the replicator's docking tube to the warship. At least he didn't have the worms slowing him down. The only aliens that had been added to his squad were the three flying ones, and they could keep up, even if they were hard to control since they didn't have suits on. The high ceilings were helpful for one thing; they gave the Xanths room to fly above the middle of the squad, since they were too small and light to be good shock troops. Of course, the pain in the ass photographer had also been added to his squad, but at least he could keep up. So far.

Wraith had the lead, with the two kuji in close pursuit. Although they had other failings, when they put their heads down, they could run for long periods. Master Chief was right behind the kuji, and the rest of the platoon was spread out behind them. The two that worried him the most were the squad's cyborgs, Staff Sergeant Dantone and Staff Sergeant Randolph, who had been added to his squad for the assault. Built more for combat power than speed, they kept falling further back.

Before he could order a halt, Wraith rounded a corner and ran headlong into a Drakul that was approaching from the other direction. Running with their heads down, the kuji ran full speed into her, tripping and going face first into the rest of the Drakuls that were spread out across the passageway. There were five Drakuls returning from some errand or work detail.

"*Contact!*" Master Chief called, drawing up short of Wraith. His laser rifle was already in transit to the firing position as the rest of the squad started to bunch up behind him.

Lords of their domain, the Drakuls had no need for weapons and were unarmed. Although they initially drew back slightly in surprise from the invisible creatures that ran into them, they immediately began moving forward again, and the Drakul in the front reached down to grab Wraith. Lying back on her hands and feet, she spider-crawled away from its grasp. Before it could grab her, Bob, one of the kuji, leapt forward. Too close for his rifle, the miniature tyrannosaurus rex had several rows of sharp teeth inside his mouth that he could use, and he clamped his jaws shut on the Drakul's forearm. The Drakul roared in pain.

Master Chief shot the closest Drakul to him between the eyes, momentarily blocking the passageway. As the Drakuls behind it pushed the slumping Drakul out of the way, the three Xanths flew overhead, screeching their hatred. Although they blocked the firing lines of some of the back members of the squad, the Xanths had great angles of their own, which they used to shoot the other Drakuls that were in the back of the pack. They only had laser pistols, but they also had great aim. All three were down before they could get close to the Terrans.

The last Drakul continued to roar as it swung the invisible kuji back and forth at the end of his wrist. Bob's teeth shredded the skin and meat at the end of the Drakul's arm as Bob was thrown from side to side. Seeing the impact Bob was having, Doug leapt forward, fastening his teeth on the other forearm of the Drakul. The weight of the second kuji overbalanced the Drakul, and it was pulled forward.

Feeling itself drawn down, the Drakul leaned forward to bite whatever had fastened itself to its arm. It opened its mouth, but only got a mouthful of Wraith's laser rifle as she jammed it between its jaws and pulled the trigger. The laser fired, the bolt frying the roof of the Drakul's mouth and continuing upward to boil its brain. The Drakul twitched a couple of times before falling forward, dead.

Bob spit out the arm he had been chewing on and then vomited out several pieces of flesh in a blue spray onto the dead body. "That is the *worst* thing I've ever tasted!" said Bob, who was known to like everything, even the *Vella Gulf's* version of food. "That's even worse than swamp rat."

"Nothing's worse than swamp rat," Doug replied. He spit out a piece of Drakul flesh. "Bleh. Except Drakul."

"If you two food critics are done," Master Chief said, "we still have a ship to capture. Wraith, if you're OK, lead on."

Task Force Night, Onboard the Replicator, February 24, 2021

"I*t's this way,*" commed Azrael, pointing to the right at the "T" intersection. Lieutenant Rrower bounded off in the indicated direction, invisible to everyone who didn't have a suit. Down a number of people due to casualties on the asteroid, Lieutenant Rrower joined the Ground Force and volunteered to take point. Night let the natural-born hunter have it.

"*How much farther?*" asked Night. Their advance was painfully slow, having to wait for the Hooolongs. It was a rapid advance...in slow motion.

"*About 100 yards or so,*" Azrael replied. "*We're almost there.*"

"*Drakuls!*" called Lieutenant Rrower. "*Four coming your way.*"

"*Understood*," repeated Night. "*Four inbound.*" He set up a firing line across the passage as the four Drakuls made their appearance. "*One, two, three!*" he commed. The soldiers fired, and all four Drakuls dropped. One wasn't dead, though, and it pulled out a little box and said something into it before Night could finish the creature off.

The box was obviously some sort of transmitter, as blue lights began flashing, and a voice began repeating over the replicator's intercom, "Intruder alert! Intruder alert!" Behind them, a door began rolling across the passageway, sealing it off. With an electrostatic 'pop,' all of the soldiers became visible as the suits' stealth modes died.

"Quickly!" cried Smetlurge. "We must get to the control room. It's just a little further on the right." He began an end-over-end method of travel that the Terrans hadn't seen before. As one of the end pads of the creature touched down, the other end pad flipped up and over. As the end came over the top, the end in contact with the ground pushed off, giving the Hooolong a bouncing effect as it vaulted down the corridor. The creature moved so quickly that the Terrans were left behind; the only member of the group able to keep up was Lieutenant Rrower, who bounded after the Hooolong in four-legged pursuit.

Smetlurge didn't have far to travel, and stopped in front of a closed door about 50 yards farther up the passageway. "This is the control room," he said. "I am in contact with a Hooolong in there. The Drakuls are killing all of the non-Drakul races. He will open the door for us when we are ready, but we have to hurry; they are discussing killing him, too.

Master Gunnery Sergeant Kinkead took charge of the entry. "Zoromski, you're in first and go left. I'm second and going to the right. Sergeant Hanzo in and left, followed by Corporal Westbrook, who goes in and right, followed by the twins and everyone else. Ready? Let's go!"

"Open the door!" said Night.

"Stand by..." said Smetlurge. "They're looking at him...They decided to kill him...Door opening!"

The door opened, and Sergeant Zoromski charged into the room in time to see a Drakul picking up a Hooolong, with several other Drakuls looking on. He didn't have a shot at the Drakul holding the Hooolong, so he fired at the one closest to him, hitting it in the chest.

Master Gunnery Sergeant Kinkead followed Zoromski into the room. She saw that the Drakul would kill the Hooolong before anyone could get into a position to shoot it, so instead of going right, she charged it. Again.

Seeing her coming, the Drakul tossed the Hooolong to the side and opened its arms, ready to grab her. Kinkead put her head down and launched herself at the creature, driving her head into its stomach. She had hoped to knock the wind out of it, but it didn't have that effect on the Drakul. Instead, it latched onto her and rolled to the side, using her momentum against her as it threw her to the ground. Momentarily stunned, the Drakul dove on top of her; she felt her ribs re-break inside her and something vital tear. Momentarily stunned, she watched as the Drakul tried to bite her through her helmet, but only succeeded in leaving slobber trails from its fangs down her face mask.

Regaining her senses, Kinkead drew her laser pistol from her leg holster and began firing into the creature's side. The Drakul shuddered every time she fired, but still drew its knife from a sheath. Kinkead saw it coming, and her eyes widened in horror; the oversize knife was as big as a Terran short sword. Kinkead struggled to get her pistol arm free from under the Drakul, but it had her pinned. She fired as quickly as she could pull the trigger, the pistol growing warm in her hand. She could tell that the pistol was having an effect as the monster's actions slowed...but it didn't stop the Drakul from grasping the knife in both hands and driving it into her chest.

Night entered the room with the second rank of soldiers, diving forward and then rolling up against the feet of one of the Drakuls. The creature looked down in time to see Night's rifle come into alignment. Night fired, killing it with a shot through its right eye. Pushing the falling Drakul to one side, Night propped himself up on a knee and surveyed the room. He fired one more time, killing the last Drakul standing. Jumping up, he went to assist Master Gunnery Sergeant Kinkead, who was trying to push off the Drakul that was on top of her. He could see where she had shot it repeatedly on one side; half of its internal organs were open to view, and most of them looked cooked.

Pushing the dead Drakul off her, he saw why her motions were weaker than they normally were. The Drakul had left its knife buried in her chest. Checking her life signs in his monitor, he saw that she was fading fast. Her suit showed dark red, fading to black. She struggled to get her helmet off; he helped her remove it.

"Told you..." she said, "tougher than...stupid frog." Her head fell to the side, and her suit went black in his monitor. She was dead.

"I am sorry for the loss of your soldier," said the Hooolong, who had come over to thank her for saving its life. "I will do anything I can to help you."

"Good," growled Night. "Show us what we have to do to take over this damn station."

Chapter Thirty-Three

The laser fire was nearly continuous now, and the terrestrial missile batteries had opened up as well. *"30 seconds to go,"* commed Boom Boom. In the back of the cargo bay, Lieutenant Finn's eyes darted wildly from side to side with every near miss. The troopers riding alongside him could see the sweat pouring off of him and knew he had never done a combat drop before. It was their first combat drop, too, but they had the training and knew what to expect. Finn didn't.

With the loss of the stealth module, it seemed like every missile and laser had opened up on them at once. The troops in the back were slammed from side to side as the Venturas tried to defeat the weapons aimed at them. Knowing that the terrain would help hide them from the enemy's radars, Boom Boom dove for the ground and the mountain range just to the east. The nose of the shuttle glowed a bright cherry red as it overheated, moments from failure.

Without warning, they were hit by an orbital anti-ship laser, which put an 11-foot diameter hole through the starboard side of the shuttle and glanced briefly off the bomb, melting the straps that held it to the bulkhead. The air screamed explosively from the cabin, and Lieutenant Finn watched in horror as the Doomsday Device fell onto its side with a clang. He held his breath, but the weapon didn't detonate. The ship maneuvered again, and the weapon rolled off the pallet, giving Lieutenant Finn a look at where the laser had hit. All of the external equipment had been slagged, and all of the covers to the buttons, dials and gauges down the side of the bomb were melted off.

"Crap" he said. "*I think we just lost the ability to remote detonate the bomb,*" he commed.

"*We're kind of...fuck!...busy up here,*" replied Boom Boom. "*What does...bastard!...that mean to the mission?*"

"*You'll have to drop me off and run,*" Finn replied. "*I'll have to manually detonate the bomb. Hopefully the arming mechanism hasn't been destroyed, too.*"

"*Roger that,*" said Venturi. "*We will set down in as clear an...bitch!...as clear an area as we can find. As soon as you are off the shuttle...damn it!...we'll take back off and try to lead them away.*" He paused as he fired the shuttle's anti-missile laser, detonating a missile just outside its effective kill range. The blast rocked the shuttle. "*It's pretty hairy out there,*" Venturi continued. "*They're everywhere.*"

The WSO paused as there was another blast close aboard. The shuttle began to shake violently. "*Stand by,*" said Venturi. "*10 seconds.*" The shuttle's boarding ramp started down. Finn didn't think it possible, but the ramp's movement made the shuttle's swaying even more violent and uncontrolled. The bomb rolled toward the opening, but got stuck on the corner of Finn's seat.

Lieutenant Finn's shoulders slumped, and tears threatened to break free from his eyes as he saw the weapon up close. "The remote receiver *is* melted," he said. "I'm going to have to detonate it manually."

"Manually?" asked Corporal Cuillard. "As in, set it off while you are standing next to it?"

"Unfortunately, yes," replied Lieutenant Finn, looking destiny straight in the eye. "That's not the worst part. It looks like the arming mechanism is going to need some work, too. It will probably take me five minutes once we get on the ground before I will be able to set it off."

"We will stay with you to make sure you have enough time," said Corporal Stump. "The Three Caballeros do not leave men behind."

"And the Three Caballeros always win," said Corporal Owens, as if it were one of the tenets on which the universe was built.

"Gluck ab!" all three chorused.

"Well, I won't say that some company wouldn't be appreciated," said Lieutenant Finn with a small sniff that he did his best to hide. "I can't work on the bomb and defend myself...especially from 10-foot tall monsters."

"That is why we will be staying," said Corporal Owens. "We have been taught by Lieutenant Cristobal Contreras that duty and honor are important, but honor most of all!"

"We will not leave an officer to fend for himself," added Corporal Cuillard. "You fix the bomb; we'll kill the Drakuls."

"*Crash positions,*" commed Venturi. "*This is going to be violent.*"

Finn looked out and saw the ground rush up to meet them. As the pilot applied power to brake their descent, there was another blast close to the shuttle, and the troops winced as shrapnel sprayed in through the ramp opening. Hot metal pinged off the inside of the ship, but the shuttle was already so damaged it didn't appear to cause any additional harm. Finn felt something hit his seat and looked down to see a six-inch sliver of metal sticking out of the seat between his legs. If it had been four inches higher...he didn't want to think about it.

As the shuttle touched down, there was another explosion behind and to the right, causing the back of the craft to swerve violently as its landing skids hit the ground. The shuttle slid to a stop, its sideways motion causing it to tilt down to the left, and the right skid to lift off the ground. Before the shuttle could begin to roll, the pilot activated one of the thrusters, and the shuttle crashed back down, coming to a halt. *"Thank you for flying Devastation Air,"* called Boom Boom. *"All ashore who's going ashore."*

Finn hit the quick-release buttons on his harness and the bomb pallet. As the chains fell away, he rolled the bomb back onto the pallet and activated the pallet's anti-gravity system. The corporals charged down the ramp, taking covering positions behind large rocks in the landing zone. Finn continued to work the controls, and the pallet moved forward. It picked up speed as the pallet reached the ramp and gravity helped pull it toward the planet.

"They're clear," said Venturi, watching the cargo compartment monitor.

"Good," said Boom Boom. He reached across his body to advance the shuttle's throttles to full with his right hand. Venturi looked over and saw that the lower portion of Boom Boom's left arm hung at a strange angle. "Let's get the hell out of here."

He yanked back on the stick with his good arm, and the shuttle lifted. He immediately rolled the ship 90 degrees to the left so that they stayed within 50 feet of the ground. Using a mountain range to shield the shuttle from the majority of the missile systems around the capital, he continued to accelerate; hoping to build up enough speed to avoid the missiles he knew would come when they climbed.

The crew never saw the Drakuls in the small gully, nor the missile that was launched at the shuttle. A heat-seeking missile, they didn't get any indication that it was coming until the automatic defense system opened fire. Boom Boom tried to jink, but it was too late.

The missile hit, and the shuttle's right engine exploded, cart wheeling the damaged craft through the air and sending pieces raining back to the planet below. The shuttle hit the ground and rolled, tearing off its wings and rupturing the craft's fuel tanks. The ship finally came to a rest at the bottom of a small knoll. Unconscious, neither of the aviators had a chance to get out. It exploded.

The Three Caballeros had their own problems. As Lieutenant Finn disassembled the arming mechanism, they saw a group of at least 10 Drakuls heading their way. "So much for leading them away," sighed Corporal Stump.

"Think you could thin them out some?" asked Corporal Owens, looking at Corporal Cuillard, who had the group's sole trident. "I don't mind sharing, but I think there are more in that group than we really need."

"My pleasure," said Corporal Cuillard. He leveled the trident and began firing antimatter grenades into the approaching Drakuls. Most of the Drakuls got back up from a barrage that would have killed all of them...if they'd been any other species. "This is going to take a little work." He tripled the strength of the antimatter mass and fired again. The force of the blasts pushed the corporals backward. This time only a couple got up; they were finished off by the other two corporals' rifles.

"Behind you!" yelled Lieutenant Finn, looking up from the bomb. The corporals turned and saw two groups of three coming from different directions; both of the groups were wearing some kind of armor. The corporals fired their rifles as fast as they could at the new groups, and Cuillard threw explosives where he could. Lieutenant Finn glanced back down at the bomb. He couldn't get a hold of the wire with his suit on. "Damn it," he swore softly as he quickly stripped out of his suit. Bare-handed, he grabbed the loose wire that had eluded him. "One more minute," he yelled to the corporals.

As he started to wrap the wire around the terminal, the sounds of lasers firing picked up again. He forced himself to finish connecting the wire, counting on the corporals to do their jobs while he did his. As he tested the circuit, there was a scream of pain. Knowing that Drakuls didn't scream, he unintentionally looked up. One of the corporals was on the ground, unmoving. Judging by the pool of blood he was lying in, he probably wouldn't be moving again. It was Corporal Owens, missing a leg. Two Drakuls each held onto one of Corporal Stump's arms, and he was suspended in the air while they used him like a human wishbone. He screamed again as they pulled him apart. Corporal Cuillard was trying to fend off a third Drakul with his sword and laser pistol. The Drakul was missing a hand on one arm and several fingers on the other, but that didn't seem to bother it. As the Drakul reached in one more time, Cuillard blocked its hand with the sword and shot the monster several times in the chest. The Drakul finally went down, and Cuillard started shooting at the ones pulling on Corporal Stump.

Lieutenant Finn looked back down to the bomb, connected the last wire and ran a circuit test. Success! The bomb would finally work. He cycled it to 'on,' and heard it start to run through its boot up process.

"Look out!" Corporal Cuillard yelled.

Finn looked up to see a Drakul stumbling toward him holding one of Corporal Stump's arms. The second Drakul was down, and Cuillard continued to shoot at the Drakul approaching the officer. Finn drew his pistol and tried to aim at the Drakul, but found his hand wouldn't hold still. He fired once, missing to the left of the

Drakul's head and then a second time, missing to the right. As the Drakul got within 10 feet, its eyes suddenly rolled up into its head, and the monster fell forward. The Drakul's head came to a stop between Finn's feet, a smoking laser hole in the back of its head.

"Ha!" said Corporal Cuillard. He put his fists on his hips and boasted, "the Three Caballeros always win." He didn't see the Drakul behind him rising to its feet.

Finn screamed a warning, but Cuillard only had time to turn before the monster was on him. Lacking hands, the Drakul stepped on his right foot and pushed. Finn could hear Cuillard's leg bones shatter as his leg dislocated. Cuillard screamed in pain as he fell backwards. Barely able to see, Cuillard fired at the Drakul and saw it collapse. Again. He fainted.

As the last Drakul went down, Finn breathed a sigh of relief. The bomb was still going through its boot-up process, so he started forward to check on Corporal Cuillard. He had only taken two steps toward the downed soldier when something grabbed his left wrist and lifted him off the ground. As he dangled, he spun slowly, eventually coming eye to eye with the Drakul holding him.

Before he could break free, the Drakul reached forward with his other hand and grabbed Lieutenant Finn under his left arm. Holding him steady, the Drakul twisted the lieutenant's arm with its other hand, dislocating it at the shoulder. The Drakul then ripped Finn's arm out of the socket and tore it from rest of his body.

Lieutenant Finn screamed as he fell to the ground, blood spurting from where his arm used to be. In shock, he stared up at his tormentor. The Drakul looked down at him, considering, before finally stepping forward to stomp on his chest with a massive foot. Finn screamed again as he felt things inside him shatter. He coughed up a gob of blood and realized the end was near.

With the Terran pinned beneath him, the Drakul paused to look at Finn's arm. It took a bite out of the meaty part at the end and then looked back down at Finn.

Pinned like a butterfly on a mounting board, Finn was done. Even if he had a way to get the Drakul off of him, he knew he couldn't reach the bomb before he died of blood loss, either from his arm or the perforated organs in his chest.

Feeling faint, he looked up at the Drakul standing over him. The Drakul looked back down, inspecting him with its three eyes. It took a few precious seconds before Finn realized that Drakuls only had two. Just long enough for the Drakul to start to fall backward.

"Ha!" a voice said thinly from the side. Lieutenant Finn's head rolled over to where the three corporals lay amidst the pile of dead Drakuls. Corporal Cuillard was up on one elbow, Corporal Owens' laser rifle resting in the dirt in front of him. "Three Caballeros...always...win." Spent, he fell forward into the dirt.

That only left him to arm the bomb, thought a dazed Lieutenant Finn. Shit, he thought, swearing for only the second time in his life. He looked at the weapon, but the bomb was six feet away. He didn't think that he had it in him. He *knew* he didn't have it in him. One step, he thought. If I can get up and take one step, I can fall forward to it.

He rolled over, screaming as his mangled shoulder hit the ground. When the pain had receded enough that he could see again, he managed to get up on his knees and his remaining hand. He looked down and saw his blood was starting to pool. Got. To. Do.

This. He managed to get one foot under him and then most of the other. Pushing off, he stood up weakly.

Lieutenant Finn coughed up another gob of blood as he tried to stanch the flow of blood from his left shoulder. The shoulder seemed more important, although he didn't know why. The Doomsday Device beeped once, indicating its readiness to be activated. Remembering his purpose, he took a step toward it and then collapsed in the dirt. His combat suit would have helped stabilize his shoulder, but it was lying in a pile on the other side of the bomb.

Raising his head, he looked at the device. The bomb was only four feet away. It might as well have been a mile. He took his hand off of his shoulder and used it to pull himself a foot closer. Blood spurted anew from the hole where his arm used to be.

He lay face down in the dirt. Although the planet was hot and damp, he was cold. So very cold.

It won't be long now, he thought, the edges of his vision going gray. He pulled himself forward again with his remaining arm. Two feet away, the button was still just out of his reach. Rolling onto his left side, he stretched out his right arm. The pain that shot through him as his left shoulder hit the ground cleared his vision for a few seconds, and he pushed off with his right foot. Pressed into the dirt, maybe his shoulder wouldn't bleed out quite as fast.

He fell short of the button again. Only a couple of inches more. As he pushed forward, he saw motion through the gray in the periphery of his vision. Looking over, he could see several Drakuls approaching. From his vantage point at ground level, they looked immense. And fast, they were moving way too fast. He wouldn't make it.

The first Drakul drew a rifle and aimed it at Lieutenant Finn. Finn closed his eyes, waiting for the inevitable. The Drakul had him; he wouldn't make it. When the expected blast didn't come, he opened his eyes again. He only had vision in the center of his sight, but could see two Drakuls fighting over the rifle. The second one must have recognized the device was a bomb and was worried about setting it off.

He pushed off with his foot again, moving another couple of inches closer. With a shout, a third Drakul ran around the two fighting for the rifle and sprinted toward Finn. All Finn could see was a dim outline of the bomb. Reaching out, his hand slapped at the side of the device, just as the Drakul grabbed the bomb and tried to pull it out of reach. The Drakul succeeded in turning the weapon slightly, and Lieutenant Finn missed the blue button.

His hand hit the red button with just enough force to activate it. His pain vanished in a flash of light.

Chapter Thirty-Four

Bridge, TSS *Vella Gulf*, 54 Piscium, February 24, 2021

"Break orbit!" yelled Ensign Sommers from the science station. Although they were orbiting around the planet's furthest moon, she wanted to be even further from the planet. "Now! Now! *Now!*"

"Uh, what?" asked the helmsman. "To go where?"

Captain Sheppard looked over. "What's going on?"

"Sir!" Ensign Sommers said. "My system just picked up an anomaly from the planet's surface. It looks like there is a black hole forming!"

"Dammit!" growled Captain Sheppard. "They weren't supposed to do that!"

"Sir, it doesn't matter whether they were *supposed* to do it or not," Ensign Sommers said. "They *did it*. There is a black hole forming, and if we don't move, *we're going to be caught in it!*"

"Shit!" said Captain Sheppard, wrapping his mind around the problem. "Break orbit! Maximum speed away from the planet!" He paused to ensure his orders were being obeyed, and then had another thought. "What about the shuttle? Will it be caught in it?"

"Sir, I haven't had communications with *Shuttle 02* for a while," said the communications officer. "They reported they were taking heavy fire as they lifted off. Since then, I haven't heard a word. They aren't overdue yet, but I haven't heard from them."

"I think we have to assume they have been destroyed," said Ensign Sommers. "If they aren't in orbit now, they will be caught in the gravity field. We only just avoided it. *Shuttle 01* should be OK; the replicator should be outside the black hole's area of effect."

Chapter Thirty-Five

Task Force Calvin, Onboard the Dreadnought, 54 Piscium, February 24, 2021

Calvin looked back as the access tube to the replicator clanged shut, blocking out the flashing blue lights in the replicator. "The other group must have been discovered," he said as the squad became visible. He glanced back to Master Chief. "You know where the bridge is; let's get there ASAP."

"Aye aye, sir," Master Chief replied. "I've got point; everyone, follow me."

Before they could move, the door next to Calvin opened, and a Drakul filled the doorway. Seeing the soldier in front of him, the Drakul clubbed Calvin to the floor with a fist. Moving quickly despite its bulk, the Drakul drew a giant knife. Raising it over his head, he stabbed down toward the officer. Lying semi-conscious on the ground, there was no way for Calvin to avoid it. As the knife started down, though, a metallic hand flashed out and grabbed the Drakul's wrist, stopping its downward travel.

"Not today, froggie," said The Wall, reaching up to punch the Drakul in the face with his free hand. Although smaller than the Drakul, the cyborg had as much mass and rocked the Drakul backward with the punch. The punch only stunned it for a second or two, however, and the monster reached for The Wall with its free hand. Seeing that it intended to grapple with him, The Wall grabbed its other hand, momentarily holding it at bay.

The Wall looked down at Calvin, still on the floor between them. "Hey Skipper," he said, "it would be kinda helpful if you would move please." The Drakul, taller than the cyborg by two feet, had moved in on him and was beginning to use its leverage to force The Wall's arms down and apart.

Calvin slid out from under them and back to the rest of the group. The Wall's hydraulics were not quite up to the task of holding the Drakul, and he saw a smile, or what he thought was probably a smile, begin to form on the Drakul's face. The Drakul could see that it was winning their wrestling match. In another few seconds, the Drakul would force the cyborg's arms far enough apart that the monster could step in and break them off.

The Wall gave a small smile of his own. "I'll bet you don't have one of these," he said. With a thought, an eight inch blade sprang from the toe of his right boot. Bracing on his left foot, he kicked the Drakul as hard as he could in its knee, driving the blade all the way into the joint. The Wall twisted his foot and the blade, pre-stressed to do so, broke off in the knee of his enemy. The Drakul crumpled to the side as its knee gave out. Seizing his advantage, The Wall dove onto the 10 feet tall monster, and his added weight collapsed the Drakul's leg the rest of the way. The Drakul fell to the ground with The Wall riding it down, both knees on its stomach.

The Drakul thrashed around on the ground, but was unable to throw off the 450 pound cyborg. After a few seconds its motions became less violent, finally going still. As The Wall climbed off of the now motionless creature, the rest of the squad could see why; matching eight inch long blades protruded from both of his knees. The entire stomach area of the Drakul had been pureed. "Stupid frog,"

The Wall said, wiping a wad of blue from his right knee blade. "Now I'm going to have to get disinfected again when I get back."

The Drakul twitched as he started to walk away. Without looking back, he drew his pistol and fired once, hitting it between the eyes. It went still.

"I got it!" said Bob 'Danger' Jones, looking up from his camera. "My audience is soooo gonna love that!"

"Wonderful," said Master Chief, sarcasm dripping from his voice. "We've still got a ship to capture. Space Force, *follow me!*"

He took off at a lope down the larger than normal corridors. The ceilings were four feet higher and the passageways four feet wider than any Terran ship he had ever been on; there was plenty of room to run, especially since the Drakuls hadn't set general quarters or gone to any kind of higher alert status.

Blue lights started flashing in the passageway, and a voice announced the intruder alert.

"Damn it to hell," Master Chief grunted. In a louder voice, he said, "Faster! We've got to get there before they lock the bridge."

The stairs were right where Azrael had said they would be, and he began climbing. As he reached the second landing, there was a pounding from above, and he could see two sets of oversized boots coming down. Hiding behind the stairs, he waited until they were right above him and then stuck a hand through the gap between the stairs and grabbed one of the Drakul's feet. Pounding down the steps as fast as it could, the Drakul couldn't get its balance and went head-first down the last five steps. There was a loud 'crack' as it hit the deck and lay motionless. From the angle of its neck, it wouldn't be getting up. The other Drakul hadn't seen Master Chief's hand come out, and it stopped at the bottom of the stairs, looking at the Drakul on the deck.

Staff Sergeant Dantone firmly but silently pushed Master Chief out of the way and went to stand next to the Drakul. "Too bad," he said in Drakul.

"He was an ass..." the Drakul started to say as he turned. He was cut off as The Wall shoved 15 inches of steel up through his throat and into his brain.

Dantone pulled out the short sword, and the Drakul fell to the floor. He swept out a hand toward the stairs. "All yours, Master Chief," he said.

Master Chief ran up the last flight of stairs and looked carefully into the passageway. One Drakul could be seen going away from them. It went through a door and was gone.

The doorway to the bridge was just to their left. It was ajar; the last person in hadn't noticed that a piece of plastic, negligently discarded as part of the replication process, kept it from closing all the way. It sounded like a beehive of activity on the bridge, with contradictory orders being shouted by a number of voices.

"Cast us off!" a voice yelled.

"We can't!" another voice replied. "We don't have a qualified engineer."

"I don't give a shit," the first voice answered. It looked up in surprise as two cyborgs strode onto the bridge.

"I love a target rich environment," said Staff Sergeant Randolph, firing a burst of 20mm shells from his Mrowry auto cannon into the Drakul that was trying to take charge.

"Plenty of 'em here," agreed Staff Sergeant Dantone, putting a burst of 20mm shells from his pulse rifle into the other Drakul that had been arguing with the first. The eight other Drakuls on the bridge stopped what they were doing at the sound of gunfire and began pulling out weapons.

"Just another day on the target range," Randolph said, shifting targets from his second target to his third. The second no longer had a head; it seemed a waste of ammo to continue shooting it.

"Save some for me," Dantone said, shifting to his own third target. The second had a huge blue hole in its chest, and most of its internal organs were now external.

A laser beam glanced off Staff Sergeant Randolph, but Master Chief killed the Drakul before it could shoot again. As the rest of the squad poured onto the bridge, the remaining Drakuls were quickly put down.

"Now *that* made the whole cyborg conversion process worthwhile!" Randolph said in glee.

"Yeah, it did," agreed Dantone. He turned toward Calvin. "What next, sir?"

"Guard the door," said Calvin, as he got an incoming comm.

"*Calvin, Night,*" his XO transmitted.

"*Go ahead,*" Calvin replied.

"*We've got the control center,*" Night commed. "*You're never going to believe this, but all of the doors lock from here. The replicator was built to have a minimal staff, so all of the passageway doors and damage control stations can be controlled from here. We've locked the Drakuls down. Assuming they don't have a torch or a space suit, they're not going anywhere. There are also cameras in most of the spaces, so we can tell where they are and what they're doing.*"

"*Good,*" replied Calvin. "*Take whatever steps you think are necessary to secure the replicator. We've got control of the bridge here, but there isn't any sort of camera system onboard, so we don't know where any of the Drakuls are. I am*" *going to send a group to secure engineering. If you get some extra hands, please send them over. This thing's huge!"*

"I'll send what I can," agreed Night, *"but I could use a cyborg to help with clearance for a short while."*

"I'll send Staff Sergeant Dantone back," Calvin replied. *"Anything else?"*

"Yeah," Night said. *"One more thing. Azrael recommends making an announcement over the ship's intercom. He says to tell everyone onboard that you have taken the ship and that anyone that wants to kill Drakuls is free to do so. If they don't want to kill the Drakuls themselves, tell them to call you on the bridge, and you'll send a unit down to do it for them. There should be a large number of non-Drakuls onboard; put them to work for you."*

"Roger, that," replied Calvin. *"Good info, we'll give it a shot. Calvin out."*

He glanced around the bridge at the array of consoles. "Jones, Rozhkov, see if you can find the intercom system. We need to talk to the crew."

"Me?" asked Bob 'Danger' Jones. "I've got a microphone, but have no idea where to plug it in here."

"No, dipshit, he meant Jones the spy, not Jones the reporter," said Master Chief. "As far as plugging it in goes, I'm sure I can help you find somewhere to shove it, if that's an issue."

"Nope, not an issue, Master Chief," said Danger. "I'll just be over here out of the way if you need me."

"Found it," called Irina Rozhkov, standing next to a dead Drakul that was wearing the remains of a headset on the remains of its head.

"Really?" asked Mr. Jones, walking up.

"Da," Rozhkov said, pointing at the panel. "It is just like the one in the asteroid." She pushed a couple of buttons. "Testing, odin, dva, tri," she said in Russian.

"They can hear you in the hallway," said Staff Sergeant Dantone from the doorway as he left to join the group on the replicator.

Rozhkov pointed to a green button. "Just push the button and talk, sir," she said.

Calvin took a deep breath and pushed the button. Using his implant to translate into the Drakul language, he said, "Attention throughout the ship! This is Lieutenant Commander Hobbs of the Terran Space Force. We have captured this ship, and I am declaring open season on the Drakuls. If you are not a Drakul, feel free to either kill any of them that you see, or call the bridge, and we will do it for you. If you are a Drakul, you have five minutes to come to the bridge and turn yourself in; otherwise, we will consider you an enemy combatant and shoot you on sight. If you choose to exercise this option, place both hands on your head and walk to the bridge. You have five minutes; your time starts now." He repeated the message.

"Think any of them will give up?" asked Master Chief.

"No," answered Calvin, "I don't. Would you, in their place?"

"Hell, no, I wouldn't!" replied Master Chief. "I'd figure out a way to overload the engines and...holy shit."

"Yeah, that's what I thought, too," said Calvin. "That's why I want you to take Randolph, Wraith, Witch, Mr. Jones, Miss Rozhkov and Jet and go make a sweep of the engine rooms. I have a feeling that you'll find the rest of the Drakuls on the ship down there. Go stop them."

"Can I go, too?" asked Bob 'Danger' Jones. "It looks like that's where the story is."

"Sure," said Calvin with a smile, knowing Master Chief wouldn't want the cameraman along. "Be my guest." He turned to find Master Chief looking at him with a pained expression.

"You know the engine rooms are well over a mile from here, right?" asked Master Chief.

"Yep," replied Calvin. "They're probably closer to two. That's why you'd better hurry. Good thing you're in shape; I'd probably pass out along the way." He paused, then raised an eyebrow at Master Chief and asked, "Are you waiting for an engraved invitation?"

"No, sir, damn it, I'm not," replied Master Chief. "Randolph, Wraith, and every other damned person he just said, let's go." Calvin heard him mumble as he went out the door, "A fucking master chief's job is never done."

Calvin smiled. A grumbling master chief was a happy master chief.

Task Force Rrower, Nearing the Engine Room, 54 Piscium, February 24, 2021

Lieutenant Rrower surveyed the collection of exterminators spread out across the passageway. He couldn't call them 'soldiers,' as one was a priest and another was a Psiclops civilian. For that matter he was part of the Mrowry fleet, and therefore technically a sailor, not a soldier. Regardless of their normal occupations, they all looked focused and ready. "*Open the door,*" he commed.

The giant steel door that went across the passageway opened from the left. As the door reached the half-way point, two Drakuls came from behind it and charged down the passageway. Their charge surprised no one, as the same thing had already happened three times previously.

The two Drakuls only covered half of the distance before they were exterminated. It helped a lot that Staff Sergeant Dantone had come over to join them. His 20mm pulse rifle was very helpful in killing Drakuls.

"*Two hostiles down,*" Lieutenant Rrower commed, "*Proceeding up the passageway.*"

"*Your destination is just past the next blast door,*" replied Azrael from the control center. "*All of the cameras have been destroyed beyond the door, so I can't tell you what's there.*"

"*Understood,*" Rrower said.

Rrower knew the Terrans wanted the Drakuls cleared out of the replicator before they could do anything to destroy it. If things worked out for them, the Terrans hoped to take the replicator home with them at the end of the war. Assuming there was still a Terra to take the replicator home to.

He looked again at the group he commanded. In addition to Dantone, Father Zuhlsdorf and Steropes, he only had Sergeant Zoromski and Havildar Rajesh Patel. It wouldn't be enough if they ran into a big group of Drakuls.

The group continued up the passageway to the next door, and the group took their positions without being told. "*Ready for the next door,*" he commed.

The giant steel door rolled aside to reveal an empty passageway that ended in a door.

"*You said the cameras are out beyond here?*" asked Lieutenant Rrower.

"*That is correct,*" Azrael replied. "*There must be Drakuls somewhere beyond there.*"

"Well, they're not in the hall," noted Rrower, *"so they must be in the room at the end of the passageway. Any idea what's in it?"*

"It's marked as a storeroom," Azrael answered, looking at a schematic in the control room. *"There could be almost anything in there. Rare metals for the replicator, food, other stores for the crew..."* His voice trailed off.

"What about weapons and explosives?" asked Rrower.

"There could be some of those, too," Azrael admitted. *"Like I said, there could be almost anything in there."*

"I guess it's too much to hope for that the storeroom contains a lack of Drakuls?" asked Sergeant Zoromski out loud.

"I expect so," Rrower said. "Something in there destroyed the camera. Any guesses?"

"Divine intervention?" asked Zoromski, raising an eyebrow at Father Zuhsldorf.

The priest shook his head. "I don't think so," he replied.

Lieutenant Rrower inspected the door. It was a damage control door that had a round handle which had to be spun to open it. Whatever was inside the door would know they were coming. Not good.

He moved half of his force to each side before spinning the unlocking mechanism. Nothing happened, and the door unlocked; so far so good. Stepping to the side, he pushed it open with the muzzle of his rifle and was rewarded with five or six laser bolts that passed through the space where he would have been standing. Obviously, there were creatures inside that wished him ill.

"Staff Sergeant Dantone, I don't think they want us to come in," he remarked. "Perhaps we didn't announce ourselves well enough. Could you throw a few calling cards into the room?"

"Yes, sir," replied The Wall. He walked up to the side of the door, unclipping grenades from his combat harness. Special grenades that had been modified for cyborgs, he could hold each with a finger. He loaded four into his right hand and pulled the pins on them. "Fire in the hole," he warned as he swung his arm into the doorway, releasing each finger sequentially to send the grenades out in a spread pattern. There was a cry of alarm from the room, and then the grenades exploded, blowing a spray of some kind of white fluff back out the door.

"Me first?" asked Dantone.

"Be my guest," replied Lieutenant Rrower.

Drawing a mental breath, the cyborg stepped into the doorway with his pulse rifle ready in his right hand and a laser pistol in his left. He surveyed the mess he had made for a couple of seconds, prior to stepping into the room. The majority of the storage space had been used for storing bedding, and pieces were everywhere, with some sort of downy material floating like a snowstorm throughout the room. There were scorch marks and hotspots scattered throughout the 50 foot square room; at least four places were on fire.

He stepped forward, looking for other heat spots that indicated Drakuls that were still alive, but it was difficult to find them with the fires burning in the room. One Drakul rose up at the back of the room; he dispatched it with a burst of five 20mm rounds through the center of its chest.

The rest of the group charged in to see the Drakul falling backward. "Is that it?" asked Lieutenant Rrower, who had been expecting more resistance.

"It appears so," replied Staff Sergeant Dantone as he walked further into the room.

"Well, let's search the room and make sure they're all dead," replied Rrower. "There must have been something here they wanted."

The group spread out, trying to discover what the Drakuls had been doing.

"*I found one,*" said Father Zuhlsdorf. "*I can see a Drakul leg sticking out of a pile of bedding. Lots of blood all around it.*"

Staff Sergeant Dantone moved to stand next to the priest and pulled out his short sword. "*Yep, looks like a frog leg,*" he said. "*Want me to cut it off or throw off the bedding and shoot it?*" he asked.

The rest of the group came to stand nearby. "*Why don't you cut it off and see what happens,*" said Lieutenant Rrower, looking at the blue puddle. "*That way, we have the initiative. It looks like it's already lost a lot of blood.*"

"*It would be my pleasure,*" Dantone said. Raising his sword, he chopped down on the foot, which fell out from under the mattress with about six inches of leg still attached. "What the hell?" he asked.

"Ugh," said Father Zuhlsdorf, the breath driven from his body. He looked down to find a foot long piece of pipe sticking out of his chest. "Help..."

The group turned to find a Drakul on its knees behind the priest, having risen out of the pile of bedding where it had hidden. It pulled the sharpened length of pipe back out of the priest and swung it like a baseball bat, hitting him in the head and knocking him aside. It turned to swing the pipe at Staff Sergeant Dantone, who blocked it with his left hand while stabbing forward with his sword.

As Dantone stabbed the creature, he saw it was the Drakul missing its foot. Already weak from loss of blood, it fell backward into the pile of bedding with Dantone's sword stuck through its throat.

Lieutenant Rrower didn't have one of the Terran helmets that showed squad member's health status, but he could tell the priest was mortally wounded. As he leaned down to inspect the wound, he saw movement at the corner of his eye. Turning his head, he saw a Drakul running toward to the door, holding something in its arms. "Look out!" he yelled.

The only member of the group who was close was Steropes, who had shouldered his rifle. Knowing he didn't have time to bring it to bear, he bent over and grabbed one of the pieces of piping scattered throughout the room. Without standing up, he threw it underhand at the Drakul as it reached the door. Although it didn't hit the monster, it went between his legs and tripped him up as the ends caught on the doorway.

Whatever the Drakul had been carrying went flying down the passageway as the Drakul went headfirst out the door. Trying to follow up on his advantage, Steropes charged the creature, drawing his sword as he ran. Reaching the Drakul, he swung, but the Drakul had already drawn its knife and blocked Steropes' slash. Catching Steropes' sword on the knife's guard, it pushed upward, and Steropes fell back, giving the Drakul time and space to get up.

Steropes saw the Drakul edging toward the object it dropped, and he ran to block the Drakul from getting to it. "The Drakul's mine," said Steropes as Dantone stepped into the doorway with his pulse rifle drawn. "Leave it to me."

While he was talking, the Drakul made a backhand slash that Steropes barely dodged; the Drakul's knife connected with his sword, knocking it from his hands. Steropes jumped back, dodging as the Drakul reversed its stroke, trying to take the Psiclops' head off. The Drakul moved forward to continue its attack, stopping to laugh as

Steropes pulled two six-inch knives from his sleeves. The laughter stopped as the point of one of the throwing knives embedded itself in the Drakul's right eye.

The Drakul pulled out the knife, blue blood dripping from the tip. Throwing the knife to the side, the Drakul charged at Steropes. Over twice the size of the Psiclops, he swung awkwardly at Steropes, who surprised the creature by diving forward through its legs.

The Drakul roared in frustration and turned on Steropes, swinging its knife. The monster narrowly missed as Steropes dove backward. Turning his dive into a back flip, Steropes came to a standing stop next to the knife that the Drakul had thrown away. Reaching down, he flipped it up into the air. Catching the knife by the blade, he threw it at the Drakul's other eye. Blind in one eye, the Drakul couldn't judge the distance so it put up a hand to block the throw. The knife embedded itself in the palm of the creature's hand.

The Drakul roared again, infuriated by the little creature tormenting it.

The monster fastened its teeth on the knife handle and pulled the weapon out of its palm, more of its blood dripping off the blade.

The Drakul advanced slowly on Steropes, not wanting to make the same mistake of charging him again. Instead of slashing, the Drakul used thrusting attacks that would not be as hindered by the creature's lack of depth perception.

Steropes kept moving to his left, taking advantage of the Drakul's missing eye, as the creature advanced on him. He timed the Drakul's attacks, noting that it thrust and recovered the same way every time. Realizing that he couldn't avoid the Drakul's attacks forever, he decided to try to end the fight, one way or another.

He feigned a stumble, drawing the Drakul in as it thrust at him. He caught the blade of the Drakul's knife on the blade of his throwing knife and guided it to the side, reaching in to take hold of the creature's sleeve as it pulled back. The move was unexpected, and the Drakul pulled him closer by reflex.

Steropes used his momentum to take another step toward the Drakul and then ran up the Drakul's leg and plunged his knife into the Drakul's other eye, blinding it. Somersaulting backward, Steropes jumped down and away from the Drakul as it slashed in all directions, trying to kill him.

"I think you can kill it now," Steropes said to Staff Sergeant Dantone.

"It would be my pleasure," The Wall said. He aimed and put five 20mm rounds into the Drakul's head, putting it out of its misery.

Steropes went over to look at what the Drakul had been carrying. "We're going to want to do something about this," he said.

"Why's that?" asked Staff Sergeant Dantone.

"Because it's a bomb."

"Really?"

"Well, it may not be a bomb," replied Steropes, "but it definitely looks like explosives and has something that appears to be counting down. If that's not some sort of timer, I don't know what it is."

"What's going on?" asked Lieutenant Rrower as he bounded up.

"It looks like they made a bomb," replied Staff Sergeant Dantone.

Lieutenant Rrower looked at the stack of explosives on the deck. He cocked his head and then reached over and pulled out the timer/detonator.

"How did you know that you could do that and not have the bomb explode prematurely?" asked Staff Sergeant Dantone.

"I didn't," said Lieutenant Rrower. He tossed the device down the passageway, where it detonated impotently. "But the timer only said six seconds, so it was either do that or watch it blow up in our faces. I didn't think they had enough time to make a sophisticated bomb, so I decided to try pulling out the detonator instead of running from it."

"Good choice," said Steropes.

Chapter Thirty-Six

Task Force O'Leary, Nearing the Engine Room, 54 Piscium, February 24, 2021

Master Chief stopped to consult the maps that the dreadnought's AI sent and saw they were finally nearing Engine Room #1. The group had only found one live Drakul so far, although they had found the bodies of four others, as well as the bodies of several Hooolongs, an Archon, and several other things that Master Chief didn't recognize. It was obvious that the other creatures had given their lives to kill the four Drakuls. The amount of hate required to attack something so much bigger than you must be incredible, he thought. Then again, he never lived under the threat of being eaten every day, so what did he know.

The only living Drakul walked past them with its hands on its head, but once it was past, the creature turned and drew a laser pistol. Although Staff Sergeant Randolph killed it with a burst of auto cannon rounds, the Drakul was able to get off a shot that hit Jet in the leg. Although his suit was working to repair the damage, he was still limping badly.

"*We're approaching Engine Room #1,*" Master Chief commed Calvin.

"*Roger that,*" replied Calvin. "*Be careful. We just had a Drakul pretend to surrender. Once he got in close, he attacked Sergeant Tereshchenko. Tereshchenko's dead.*"

"*One did the same thing to us,*" replied Master Chief. "*Jet got shot in the leg, but he'll be all right.*"

"*The five minutes are long over,*" Calvin said. "*If you see a Drakul, regardless of what it does, kill it immediately.*"

"*Got it,*" Master Chief replied; "*we will kill them all.*"

Master Chief surveyed the troops waiting by the door. This was the third engine room they had checked. Aside from the Drakul they killed, there hadn't been any organized resistance so far.

This door felt different.

He didn't know why, but for some reason he could feel danger lurking on the other side of the door. He shook his head, trying to make the feeling go away. Let's go, damn it, he thought to himself. We're not getting paid by the hour, and we've got a lot more of this damn ship to search.

"I got a bad feeling about dis one," said Sergeant Margaret 'Witch' Andrews. The Jamaican woman's feelings were usually right on the mark. "I tink dey be here."

Having Witch confirm his suspicion didn't make Master Chief feel better; if anything, it only made his feeling worse. "All right, let's stay sharp," he said. "I don't know why, but I've got the same feeling. We know there were Drakuls onboard, and we haven't found them yet; they may well be in here. Jones the spy, in and right. Rozhkov, in and left. Randolph and I will follow and take the center. Everyone else spread out behind us. Look for cover; check your corners. Everyone ready?"

He saw everyone nod their assent. The door had four metal 'dogs' on it, one in each corner. Each dog was a metal handle on both the inside and outside of the door that could be pulled down to seal the door in place. He pulled the dog in the upper left open. It appeared to have been greased recently; its movement was smooth and silent. Taking hold of the dog in the lower left, he pulled it clear.

Its movement mirrored the first. He pulled down on the handle in the upper right. It moved, but with a '*screeeeeeeeech*' that would have woken up anyone inside the room. Even if they were dead.

Although everyone was already focused and ready, the noise caused the soldiers to instinctively point their weapons with a hyper-focus known only to soldiers in combat. He winced. "Sorry," he grunted with a smile that didn't reach his eyes.

He took hold of the remaining handle and checked to make sure everyone was still ready. They were; he pulled on the handle. It didn't budge. He tugged again, pulling with all of his augmented strength. "Wow," he commented, "this one's stuck." He rubbed his gloved hands together and approached the handle another time. "Here goes," he said.

He took hold of the handle, but before he could pull on it, the handle was thrown open from the inside with a force that shattered his right wrist and launched him, airborne, to the right. The door swung inward to reveal a Drakul with a laser pistol. The creature was unprepared for the number of soldiers waiting for it, though, and the Drakul was driven back under the lash of five lasers and a burst of 20mm from Staff Sergeant Randolph. The Drakul toppled backward, allowing the Drakuls in the room to fire at the soldiers. Laser bolts flew through the doorway.

Although the Drakuls didn't kill any of the soldiers with their ambush, it effectively destroyed their sequence of entry into the engine room and trapped them on the outside. Seeing the impasse, Staff Sergeant Randolph waded into the onslaught, knowing that he could probably survive a few bolts...as long as they didn't hit something vital.

Randolph entered the room, Mrowry auto cannon in his right hand and one of his Desert Eagles in his left. A Drakul leaned out from cover to see where the cyborg was and took a burst of 20mm in its forehead. The creature went down, brains flying out in a blue mist.

The amount of fire was a little higher on the right, so he went in that direction. That allowed the other members of the group to go left on entering the room, where there was cover behind several pieces of machinery. Just like the other two engine rooms, Engine Room #1 was over 150 feet long by 100 feet wide. Judging by his thermal scan, there were also at least nine more live Drakuls. No, make that 10; one was down behind a piece of very hot machinery in the back of the room. Randolph couldn't tell what the creature was doing, but the fact that the other nine seemed to be guarding it told him that the Drakul was doing something the Terrans didn't want it to do.

Seeing that the rest of the force had entered the room, Randolph paused behind a large metal junction box to allow the smoking and bubbling patches of his proto-skin to cool. *"I've got 10 hostiles in the room,"* he commed. *"Nine of them are screening the tenth, who is at the back of the room behind some machinery that is* really *hot."*

Master Chief consulted a schematic. *"That is probably the antimatter conversion unit,"* he replied. *"We've got to stop whatever it's doing."*

"I could put a mortar round on top of it," Randolph said, calculating the bounce angles.

"And set off the antimatter next to it?" asked Master Chief. *"No thanks. I don't know how much antimatter is in there, but I imagine you could effectively write off most of the aft end of the ship if you break the containment. Besides, that's probably what it's trying to do in the first place."* He paused.

"*Randolph,*" he added, "*you're going to have to lead; my wrist is broken. The suit is working to stabilize it, but we don't have time to wait.*"

"*Got it, Master Chief,*" Randolph replied, taking charge. "*Wraith and Witch, work your way around to the left. If you stay low, they probably won't see you. I'll circle right and draw their fire. There are three that are about 25 feet in front of you. Rozhkov, Jones stay low and see if you can work your way up the center. As tall as they are, they probably won't think to look at the floor.*" He stood up to take another scan and was rewarded with a laser bolt that set his red hair on fire. The good thing about being a cyborg, he thought as he pulled off the burning wig and threw it to the metal floor, was that you didn't have to smell burning hair if you didn't want to. He continued to work his way to the right, staying just high enough to continue drawing their attention and, periodically, their fire as well.

Sensing movement to the side, he turned and trained his Desert Eagle on the motion. His finger came off the trigger milliseconds before firing on the cameraman.

"*You didn't tell me where to go,*" said Bob 'Danger' Jones, "*so I thought I'd follow you and see if I could help.*"

"*Don't come too close to me,*" commed Randolph, "*I'm trying to draw their fire.*"

"*Uh, yeah, I can sort of tell,*" replied Danger, pulling out a camera to film the cyborg. "*You should see yourself. You've got skin hanging off in about six places, scorch marks on the top of your head, and there isn't enough of your suit left in any one spot to put an eight-inch crease in.*"

"*Just stay low, OK?*" asked Randolph.

"*You can count on it,*" replied Danger. "*Can I borrow one of your pistols?*" he asked, pointing at the one holstered on Randolph's right side. "*All I've got is a trident, and I don't want to use it in here.*"

Randolph handed the pistol to the reporter, along with another magazine for it. "*I want these back,*" he said.

"*No problem,*" Danger agreed.

Randolph didn't have any more time or attention to spare on the cameraman. Bending low, he crossed further right behind the cover of another piece of machinery. "*Everyone ready?*" he asked.

Receiving a chorus of affirmatives, he stood up and fired a long burst of auto cannon fire at the Drakul he had flanked. The Desert Eagle was loud in the enclosed space as he fired off its last four rounds into another Drakul. Ducking behind the machinery again, he asked, "*Status check?*"

"*I got two,*" said Wraith.

"*One here,*" added Witch.

"*I got one, too,*" Mr. Jones reported.

"*We're down to four then,*" Randolph said, putting another magazine in his pistol. "*Unfortunately, I lost one of my eyes, and it was the one with the thermal sensor, so I can't see much better than you. With all of the moving machinery in here, my radar isn't as good as it normally is, either.*"

If the Drakuls hadn't moved, Randolph knew there was only one more of them left between him and the back wall, as long as he stayed along the outside wall. He saw a flash of movement ahead of him behind a piece of machinery. Yep, the Drakul was still there.

There was an open space of about 25 feet to get there. He'd have to be more careful; he couldn't afford to lose his other eye. He searched the rest of the room, looking for the other two shooters. He couldn't see them or the other members of his group. Feeling motion at his side, he looked down to see what the cameraman was doing, but instead it was Master Chief, holding his laser pistol in his left hand. His right arm was suit-locked to his chest.

Master Chief nodded toward the generator ahead of them. "*You go to the left,*" he said, "*and I'll go to the right. Whoever gets there first kills the Drakul. If it gets me, you're in charge. Stop them from damaging the engine.*"

"*Stay here,*" replied Randolph. "*I can take it, and then the path will be open to get to the other Drakul.*" He pointed to where the suspected saboteur was hiding. "*It's over there.*"

"*That's nice,*" said Master Chief, "*but we go together. On three. One...two...*" he stopped as a loud gunshot rang out in front of them, and the Drakul fell out into the open, unmoving. Danger came around the side, holding Randolph's Desert Eagle.

"*I got him!*" he crowed, pumping his arm. "*It's safe—*" Six inches of metal burst forth from his chest in a spray of blood, and he was lifted off the ground by the Drakul holding the knife.

Danger dropped back to the ground as Randolph put a burst of 20mm rounds into the Drakul's chest. Jones stood weakly, before dropping to his knees and then falling onto his side. Watching for the other two Drakuls, Master Chief and Randolph ran up to the reporter. Master Chief rolled him onto his back while the cyborg kept watch. Danger's suit showed damage that it wouldn't be able to repair.

"What the hell did you do that for?" asked Master Chief, removing Danger's helmet.

"Wanted to...help the team," Danger gasped. "Knew that...Randolph couldn't take...much more. I was...expendable." He pulled his camera from a leg pocket, but didn't have the strength to hold it up. "Take my...camera," he said, a line of blood running from the corner of his mouth. "Worth... millions." His head fell to the side, and Master Chief's monitor showed that Danger was gone.

Putting the camera in his pocket, Master Chief looked down at his frequent tormentor. "Thanks," he said, nodding to Danger in salute of his sacrifice.

Master Chief stood up. "Let's go finish this," he said to Randolph.

"*One more down,*" Rozhkov reported.

"*That should only leave the saboteur,*" Randolph commed. He got up and sprinted to where he thought the last Drakul was hiding. Coming around the corner, he saw a Drakul with its back to him stand up from whatever it was working on.

The Drakul sensed motion behind it and turned to face Randolph. The cyborg saw that the Drakul was holding a box with a button. Seeing the Terran soldier, the Drakul made a 'glub, glub, glub' noise, and Randolph realized that it was laughing. The Drakul's hand moved toward the button. Seeing that the Drakul intended to push the button, Randolph took two steps and dove for the Drakul. Randolph's left hand covered the Drakul's hand on the box as it pushed the button.

Randolph clamped down, pinning the Drakul's finger and holding the button down. As he fell to the floor, Randolph extended a knife blade from his right wrist and cut off the Drakul's hand in an explosion of blue. Retracting the knife, Randolph pushed off the ground with his empty hand, spinning around to kick the Drakul in the stomach. Without getting up, Randolph drew his remaining Desert Eagle as he turned back toward the Drakul. Gushing blue from its missing hand, the Drakul reached toward him, desperate to get the box back. Randolph triggered off five shots in quick succession, and Master Chief added several more as he came around the corner.

The Drakul fell backward to lie still on the floor. A blue puddle began to grow from a number of holes in its body.

Master Chief walked over and inspected the Drakul. "Nice grouping of your shots," he noted.

"Thanks," replied Staff Sergeant Randolph. "We've got a problem. See this big bomb?" He pointed to a pile of red bricks that appeared to be wired together. A light flashed ominously from a metal box wired to the middle of it.

"That's a bomb?"

"Yeah, that's Alliance of Civilizations' advanced plastic explosives," Randolph replied. "I saw it once at explosive ordinance disposal (EOD) school. Once the stuff is armed, it's extremely sensitive to movement."

"And that little blinking light..." Master Chief asked.

"...means that that the explosive is armed," finished Randolph. "I've got the detonator," he continued, showing Master Chief the box and Drakul hand he was holding. "The button has already been pushed, which armed the bomb; if I let go, the bomb will detonate."

"We've got to get it off the ship," Master Chief said. "We need to wrap the button with some tape or something to keep it from going off."

"I always knew this would happen," Randolph said. "This is why I wanted *out* of EOD. I only had one more week when my partner blew us up." He shook his head. "I can't let go of this box, nor can I get any further than about 10 feet from the bomb, or it will explode. I'm pretty fucked."

"There's got to be something we can do," Master Chief argued.

"There is," agreed Randolph. "You can *very carefully* pick the bomb up for me and then cycle me through the airlock. Anything else will result in the bomb exploding and wiping out this engine and most of the aft end of the ship."

"If we let you go out the airlock, what are your intentions?" asked Master Chief.

"I'm going to jet as far as I can away from the ship prior to letting the bomb detonate," stated Randolph. "It's the only thing I can do. Trust me. I'm no hero; that's the only possible option."

"There's got to be another way," Master Chief said.

"No," Randolph disagreed, "there's not. I have to do it, and I have to go *now*. I don't know how long I can hold this box. The Drakul's hand makes the box damn hard to hold onto, especially with a mechanical hand." He looked at the bomb again. "You'll need help lifting it. The bomb has to be kept level or it will detonate. You'd better hurry. There's also probably a countdown timer in there somewhere, too. It's what I'd do."

"Jones, get over here and give me a hand," Master Chief ordered. With a twinge, he realized that he didn't have to differentiate between the spy and the cameraman any more. *"Everyone else, get the hell out of here and close any blast doors you can find."*

The two men lifted the bomb and put it under Randolph's right arm where he could carry it. "I don't care what you think," said Master Chief as the cyborg walked carefully to the engine room's airlock, "you're a hero in my book."

"Thanks," said Randolph as he walked into the small enclosure. He turned around. "Do me a favor, would you?" he asked. "Go save the world?"

"We will," replied Master Chief as the door slid shut. "We will, indeed."

Chapter Thirty-Seven

Bridge, Drakul Dreadnought, 54 Piscium, February 24, 2021

"There was nothing else we could do," replied Master Chief. "We let him go out the airlock, and he jetted a couple of miles away from the ship where he blew up. We saw the flash; he's gone."

Calvin sighed. He had called all of the senior officers and enlisted together on the bridge of the dreadnought to take stock of their situation, prior to reporting back to the *Vella Gulf*. He turned to Night. "Who did we lose taking the replicator?" he asked, dreading the answer. He didn't see Master Gunnery Sergeant Kinkead, who should have been in attendance. He knew they had taken casualties, too.

"We lost Master Gunnery Sergeant Kinkead to a surprise Drakul attack during the initial assault," Night said. "We also lost Father Zuhsldorf during mop-up operations afterward. The Drakuls tried to blow up the replicator and set a trap."

Calvin shook his head. "Damn," he said with a sigh. "I should never have asked him to come."

"You said it yourself," Night said. "We didn't have enough people. He came willingly, wanting to do his part."

"He had a message for you," Lieutenant Rrower added.

"He did?" asked Calvin.

"Yes," Lieutenant Rrower said. "I was with him at the end. His last words were, 'Tell Calvin to go to confession.'"

"That sounds like him," Calvin said, feeling a little better. He turned to Steropes. "I heard that you fought a Drakul in hand-to-hand combat," he said. "Feeling better?"

"I am ashamed to say I thought it would help," Steropes replied; "however, it did not. I remember Francis Bacon saying that, in taking revenge, a man is but even with his enemy; in passing it over, he is superior. I am better than the Drakuls, so I have decided to let go of my feelings of revenge. I need to be the person I was before the Drakuls came into my life. I need to be me. It will be better that way."

"It always is," agreed Calvin.

"I am sorry for your losses," interrupted Smetlurge, "but we need to figure out what we are going to do. We, the remnants of the Hooolong society, along with various other allies, would like to take this ship as our new capital. We have no home world; we have no other members of our civilization that we are aware of. We do have over 350 Hooolongs onboard this ship, along with another 175 members of the Depsips civilization, the Xanth society, the Clrank Confederation and the Quugeert nation. If you will allow us to, we will fight this ship in the upcoming battle."

"How are you going to do that?" asked Night. "This thing must take a crew of 3,000 or so."

"3,500, actually," Smetlurge corrected. "We do, however, have some outstanding computer programmers among the Depsips. They are already modifying the computer to allow more functions to operate autonomously. The Psiclops may have put aside his feelings of revenge; we have not. When the Archons attack, it is our intention to aid them. We have a plan."

"You have a plan?" Calvin asked.

"Indeed," Smetlurge said. "I used to design weapons systems before I became president, remember? I have a plan. We just need you to let us have this ship. You need to hurry, too. There are a large number of Drakul ships coming."

"What?" Calvin asked. "Why?"

"Apparently you Terrans do understand revenge," Smetlurge said, nodding his agreement.

"What do you mean?" asked Calvin.

"You unleashed a black hole on the Psiclopes' home world," Smetlurge replied, "despite saying that you would not. Olympos is no more. The ships are coming to find out where it went. The Drakuls are not happy."

Bridge, *Vella Gulf*, 54 Piscium, February 24, 2021

"So, all we need to do is let the Hooolongs have the ship, and they'll use it to fight the Drakuls?" asked Captain Sheppard.

"Yes sir," replied Calvin. "They also have a plan to deal with all of the ships that are headed this way after you guys wiped out Olympos."

"I don't know why they did that," said Captain Sheppard. "I specifically ordered them *not* to use the black hole generator on Olympos. Please pass on my sympathies to Steropes."

"Steropes is fine with it," Calvin informed him. "In fact, I think that was his preferred option all along. The Hooolongs are also impressed with our resolve. Azrael said that his people will think more highly of us because we 'did what we had to do.' The Xanth and Depsips are scared of us and think we're too warlike. That doesn't change much, since they were already scared of us and thought we were too warlike. Only Lieutenant Rrower is unhappy. He says that there may be problems with the Mrowry."

"Well, we're not going to have problems with anyone unless we get aid back to Earth," replied Captain Sheppard, "and the only way we're going to do that is by helping the Archons. We don't have enough manpower to operate both the *Vella Gulf* and the dreadnought, and we don't know how to run it in any event. Tell Smetlurge the ship is theirs and to please kill a lot of Drakuls with it."

"Will do, sir," Calvin said. "I don't think they'll have a problem with that."

Bridge, *Hooolong's Revenge*, 54 Piscium, February 24, 2021

Calvin watched the conversation between the Drakul captain and the Drakul admiral on a side monitor.

"Yes, admiral," answered Captain Vlad. "When I saw the planet eaten by the black hole, I knew there were enemies in the system, probably with some sort of stealth ship, so I took charge of the new dreadnought and launched it. I did not want it to be destroyed or to fall into the hands of the enemy to be used against us."

"That was good thinking," replied Admiral Kralg. "How is your manning? Should we send you additional crew?"

"That will not be necessary," replied the captain. "Just before the planet was destroyed, we received two shuttle loads of crewmembers. We have enough crew to operate it until we can get the rest of the crew from Drakon."

"Good," the admiral said. "Bring the ship to the stargate for integration with the fleet. I cannot believe that the destruction of Olympos is anything other than a precursor for an Archon invasion. We need to be ready. The fleet is at its highest alert status. We could use your firepower at the stargate, especially since we had to send the battle group to assist in the pacification of the new food source."

"We are on our way," noted the captain.

Calvin smiled as the conversation terminated, and Smetlurge ceased being a Drakul captain; the Drakuls had fallen for it. As Smetlurge had said, the Depsips had proven to be excellent programmers, and the hologram program they had designed for him had worked to perfection.

Now they just needed to get close enough to give the Drakuls a little surprise.

Bridge, *Vella Gulf,* 54 Piscium, February 25, 2021

"How much longer until we're within weapons range?" Captain Sheppard asked.

The OSO consulted his display. "About two more hours at this speed."

Captain Sheppard nodded. "And how long until the attack commences?"

"Four hours," said Ensign Sara Sommers, "according to the schedule that the Archons...wait! *I've got stargate emergence!*"

"Talk to me, Sara. What have you got?"

"The ships are small," she replied, "and there are quite a few of them that just entered." The Drakuls began firing on them, confirming her guess. "They're the mine clearance vessels," she said. "They've started the attack."

"I thought that they weren't supposed to attack for four more hours," said Captain Sheppard.

"They weren't," agreed Sara. "They're early."

"Well, we're not going to let them start the party without us," Captain Sheppard said. "Flank speed!"

Bridge, *Hooolong's Revenge*, 54 Piscium, February 25, 2021

"The attack has commenced," noted Steropes from the science station. "The robot mine clearance vessels just transited into the system."

"We're getting a message from the fleet admiral," advised the communications officer. "He's telling us that there is an incursion by the Archons and is asking us to come to flank speed to get there as quickly as possible."

"We wouldn't want to keep the good admiral waiting, now, would we?" asked Smetlurge from the captain's chair. "All ahead flank," he said to the helmsman. Captain Smetlurge turned back to the communications officer. "Please tell the admiral that we are on our way."

Bridge, Drakul Ship *Destruction of Depsi*, 54 Piscium, February 25, 2021

"The super dreadnought's captain confirms that his ship has come to flank speed," said the communicator.

The admiral looked at the plot and did some mental calculations. If the Archons attacked as normal, the new super dreadnought would arrive just after battle was joined. Its arrival would be a nice surprise for the Archons, he was sure...if their minefield didn't kill all of the Archons first.

Bridge, *Vella Gulf,* 54 Piscium, February 25, 2021

"Sir, do you want me to send the fighters ahead to attack?" the OSO asked, "or would you rather I hold them back until we're in range?"

"Hold them back for now," Captain Sheppard said. "Their biggest advantage will be their surprise. We've only got one shot with them; I don't want to waste it before the fighters are needed."

"Captain," Ensign Sommers called. "The attack has begun. The *Holy Word* just entered the system. There are three dreadnoughts and several battleships already firing."

"That's not what's going to kill it," said the DSO. "There are still far too many mines that didn't get cleared by the robot vessels. The *Holy Word* is about to go into the field, and it's going to get annihilated!"

"Not today," replied Captain Sheppard. "Not while they've got friends here. Tell the *Revenge* to pass on the good news."

"Yes, *sir,*" said the communications officer. "It would be my pleasure."

Bridge, *Hooolong's Revenge*, 54 Piscium, February 25, 2021

"We just got the word," announced the communications officer. "The *Vella Gulf* says to shut them down."

Smetlurge nodded to the Xanth officer seated at the ship's defender position. "Turn them off, if you would, please."

The Xanth bobbed its head and reached forward with a wing claw to turn a dial on its panel, and then its primary digit pushed the button that the Depsip technician had circled in blue an hour earlier. "It is done," said the Xanth, continuing to bob its head in obedience.

"And here's where the ship begins to earn its name," said Smetlurge.

Chapter Thirty-Eight

Bridge, Drakul Ship *Destruction of Depsi*, 54 Piscium, February 25, 2021

"Why aren't the mines destroying the invaders?" asked the admiral. The ship shuddered as the first super dreadnought through the stargate hit it with another volley of missiles. "That ship will be the end of us! Take it out now!"

"Sir, I'm unable," replied the defender. "All of the mines just went into maintenance mode for some reason. I won't be able to bring them back online for at least an hour."

"Who did that?" screamed the admiral. "What imbecile is responsible for this?"

"I think the order came from the new super dreadnought," the defender said.

"Get them on screen!" shouted the admiral. "Now!"

The ship rocked again, harder this time. "Shields down," the defender called.

The front screen changed to the captain from the new ship. "You idiot!" the admiral yelled. "You just put the mines in maintenance mode. What the hell were you thinking?"

"I'm sorry, but the person at the defender position is brand new to the job," the captain said. "In fact, we're all pretty new to the job."

"My attacker says that you are in range," noted the admiral. "Fire your weapons and help us salvage this battle!"

"You would like us to fire our weapons?" asked the captain. He made a motion off screen, and his appearance transformed into a member of the tasty worm race. "It would be my pleasure." He looked off screen. "All weapons, *FIRE!*"

Bridge, *Vella Gulf*, 54 Piscium, February 25, 2021

"That's our signal," said Captain Sheppard as the *Revenge* launched a full broadside of missiles at the command dreadnought. "Launch the fighters. Fire!"

Bridge, *Holy Word*, 54 Piscium, February 25, 2021

"Sir, the super dreadnought that is joining the battle just fired upon the command dreadnought," said the OSO. "Fighters! Fighters just came out of stealth and are launching at the command dreadnought! It must be the *Vella Gulf*, sir." He paused, watching the missiles track inbound on the Drakuls' command dreadnought. "The *Vella Gulf's* fighters just destroyed the dreadnought's engines!"

"Good," said Grand Admiral Michael. "Let's put another volley of missiles into them and send them to hell!"

"Admiral!" interrupted the communications officer. "The super dreadnought that just joined the battle is trying to raise us. The ship says that its captain is Hooolong President Smetlurge, sir."

"On screen," replied Grand Admiral Michael.

"Welcome to 54 Piscium," said the figure on the screen. Grand Admiral Michael couldn't tell if it was President Smetlurge or not, but it was definitely a Hooolong. "I am Smetlurge onboard the Hooolong's Revenge. We've turned off the minefield for the moment, but it will come back on shortly. I recommend moving the fleet clear of the minefield while you destroy the rest of their ships."

Bridge, *Hooolong's Revenge*, 54 Piscium, February 25, 2021

"This won't take much longer," noted Smetlurge as another battleship came apart under the missiles and lasers of the *Revenge*. He bobbed his head in satisfaction.

After the Alliance ships destroyed the Drakul command dreadnought, the cohesive Drakul defense fell apart. Instead of concentrating their fire on high value targets, they began firing at the ships closest to them. With the Drakul fire spread out, most of the Archon ships were able to keep their shields up, and the combined might of the Archon dreadnoughts and super dreadnoughts, along with the *Hooolong's Revenge*, was applied to ship after ship of the Drakul fleet.

It was a slaughter.

Bridge, *Vella Gulf*, 54 Piscium, February 25, 2021

"Contact the *Holy Word*, please," ordered Captain Sheppard.

Within moments, the flowing locks of Grand Admiral Michael appeared on screen. "We could not have won this battle without thee," said Michael. "I can't wait to hear how thou captured a Drakul dreadnought. I will tell thee, the battle would have been substantially different if the minefield hadn't been turned off. We were down to 3% on our shields when the *Hooolong's Revenge* fired on the command dreadnought. If any of the mines had hit us, the entire battle might have been lost."

"It was our pleasure, and I look forward to discussing it over drinks sometime," said Captain Sheppard; "now, however, isn't that time. We need to leave immediately for Earth."

"If ye must leave," replied Grand Admiral Michael, "then leave with my blessing, as ye were instrumental in our victory today."

"You are missing the point," said Captain Sheppard. "We did what you asked of us. Now you need to honor your part of the bargain and come help us."

"Aye, we will," agreed Michael, "but it is a far wiser choice to pursue the Drakuls to their home world and eradicate them first."

"Perhaps for your society, and from your viewpoint, it may be," argued Captain Sheppard, "but in the time that it takes to do so, *our civilization may be wiped out.* While we were fulfilling our end of the deal, we saw a battle group transit through the next system over. It was either going to Drakon or to Earth. If it was to Earth, it was large enough to defeat the fleet units we have and destroy our planet. Do you want that blood on your hands? Do you want to be known as oath breakers?"

"It would not be breaking our oath if we stopped to attack Drakon on the way to Earth," disagreed Michael. "We would just be pursuing the logical course of action, which has the greatest chances for long-term success."

"Perhaps," Captain Sheppard agreed again, "although it could be catastrophic for our society if you did." He paused, thinking furiously. "I think you're missing a key strategic point that makes it extremely important to go to Earth. If you go to Earth first, and you destroy any forces that are attacking there, you will have trapped all of the Drakul forces on Drakon. If you go to Drakon first, some of their forces could escape down Earth's chain of stargates. If they get out that way, you may not find them again until they are strong enough to overwhelm you. Next time, you won't have us around to help you, either. It makes strategic sense to honor your agreement. We need your help, and we need it *now*."

Chapter Thirty-Nine

Bridge, Drakul Ship *Spurting Blood*, Ross 154 System, March 03, 2021

It was time to begin the glorious conquest. If Admiral Bullig waited any longer, he risked someone else trying to take over. He was sure that at least one of the captains had orders to kill him if he showed any sign of cowardice. His eyes scanned the bridge and stopped on the one sign of movement, his new executive officer, whose fingers were unconsciously toying with the butt of his laser pistol. He probably had orders from the Overlord to kill Bullig if he refused to lead the assault; it's certainly what Bullig would have done in the Overlord's place.

"Are the ships in formation?" he asked.

"Yes," replied the attacker. "All ships are in formation and show they are ready."

Bullig had moved over to the battleship *Spurting Blood*. The battleship was a little smaller, which would let it fit through the stargate with its flanking squadron of cruisers. The battleship had a cruiser on both sides, as well as three more cruisers in formation both 'above' and 'below,' with the middle ones centered on his ship. Admiral Bullig would go through first, but he was going to surround himself with a screen. He knew that there was a possibility that some of the ships might interpenetrate on emergence, but gave it no further thought; the cruisers were expendable. He figured his life expectancy was measured in minutes on the other side of the stargate with the cruisers surrounding him; without them, his life span would only be measured in seconds. The dreadnought *Destruction of Olympos* was close behind his ship; he hoped that the dreadnought would draw the Terran's fire as soon as it emerged from the stargate. *"Admiral Bullig to all captains,"* he transmitted. *"Commence the attack! Full speed ahead!"*

Bridge, TSS *Terra*, Solar System, March 03, 2021

"Stargate activation!" called the DSO. "Holy shit! I've got six...seven...eight...no, *nine* ships just transited at the same time. Two interpenetrated, but there's still a battleship and seven cruisers!"

"*Terra to all ships,*" radioed Captain Griffin, *"concentrate fire on the battleship! Let's take it out!"* The battle they had been dreading was upon them, and they would have to fight it without outside aid. Captain Griffin didn't know why the ships had come through in the strange formation, but if they were trying to protect the battleship for some reason, then she wanted that ship *dead*. The first mine flared against the screen of one of the remaining cruisers as missiles began launching from her ship.

"Do you want to commit the bombers?" asked the OSO.

"Not yet," replied Captain Griffin. "I think we can handle these by ourselves."

She looked at the tactical plot and saw that all three battlecruisers were firing at the battleship, as well as some of the automatic missile canisters, but no more Drakul ships had entered the Solar System. This was the long-anticipated attack? After the losses they took at the battle in Ross 154, surely the Drakuls would have known to send more ships than this...

Bridge, Drakul Ship *Death Blow*, Ross 154 System, March 03, 2021

"Destruction of Olympos, *are we not going to follow them into battle?*" asked the captain of the battlecruiser *Death Blow*. The Drakul formation was based on all of the ships keeping station on the dreadnought; when the *Destruction of Olympos* had flipped and started slowing after the *Spurting Blood* made the transit to the new system, all of the other ships were forced to flip and slow down in order to keep their spacing. Unprepared for the dreadnought's maneuver, the *Death Blow* was unable to stop in time and passed the dreadnought, changing their order of entrance into the next system.

"*We will follow them momentarily,*" replied the captain of the *Destruction of Olympos*. "*My orders from the Overlord are to ensure that Admiral Bullig does his part for the empire.*"

In other words, thought the captain of the *Death Blow*, he is to die after personally absorbing as much of the system's defenses as possible. That's fine, he thought. It leaves fewer missiles for us.

After 15 minutes of waiting, the captain of the *Destruction of Olympos* finally announced, "*All units, advance!*" The dreadnought resumed its course toward the stargate, along with the rest of the ships in the fleet.

"10 seconds to transit," noted the *Death Blow's* helmsman. "Five...four..."

"Gate activation!" called the defender. "Multiple activations from the gate behind us..."

The *Death Blow* transited.

Bridge, TSS *Vella Gulf,* Ross 154 System, March 03, 2021

"It appears that we are too late," said Grand Admiral Michael from the view screen. "The Drakul attack on thy system has already commenced. For all we know, it may already be over. Our time would be better served by proceeding to the Drakul home world while their fleet is occupied with thy system."

"It may *not* be too late if we hurry," Captain Sheppard said. The last Drakul battleship winked out on the tactical plot as it made the jump to the Solar System. They were too late. He shook his head. Damn it, no, *they were not going to be too late.* Not on his watch. He had *not* flown thousands of light years to get back too late. If nothing else, he'd run that last battleship down and shove the *Vella Gulf* straight up its ass. He looked down at the helmsman. "Helm, flank speed. Give me everything it's got!" He looked back up to the view screen. "With you or without you," Captain Sheppard said, "my home world is being invaded, and I intend to do everything I can to save it. The defenses may still be holding. Hopefully, you'll honor our agreement and follow us. If not, *I'll see you in hell!*" He pushed the button that ended the transmission. "Please be holding," he begged under his breath.

Bridge, Archon Ship *Holy Word,* Ross 154 System, March 03, 2021

"Their transmission ended," noted the communications officer.

"Shall I proceed toward Drakon?" asked the helmsman.

"No," said Grand Admiral Michael. "They honored their word to us and helped save our system; we wouldn't even be here without their help. If there is any way to assist them in their hour of need, we owe it to them to do so." He switched to the battle group's communication network. "*All ships, follow the Terran ship. Flank speed!*"

Chapter Forty

Bridge, TSS *Terra*, Solar System, March 03, 2021

Between the mines, the box launchers and the fire from the Terran ships, the Drakul ships were finished, thought Captain Griffin. Two of the cruisers had interpenetrated on arrival. What was left of them wasn't pretty. Four of the cruisers were floating hulks, victims of the Terran minefield. One more had intercepted a volley of battleship missiles intended for the Drakul battleship, just after its shields failed. That cruiser was wrecked beyond repair. Only the battleship and one of the cruisers were still in the fight. Both were hit and staggered like punch-drunk fighters, but continued to trade missile and laser fire with the Terrans. The amount of fire from the battleship had fallen way off, and the ship appeared to be finished. The Terrans were going to carry the day. A small smile came to Captain Griffin's face. It didn't last long.

"Gate activation!" called the science officer. "It's a battlecruiser...More activations... Battleship!... *Dreadnought!*"

The real fleet had arrived. They were doomed.

Bridge, Drakul Ship *Spurting Blood*, Solar System, March 03, 2021

It's about time, thought Admiral Bullig, who had been wondering whether he was going to be left to die in this system. Without the rest of the fleet, it would have been inevitable. With the emergence of the *Destruction of Olympos*, though, all of the fire shifted to the larger vessel. The *Spurting Blood* was free of the minefield and drifting toward one of the Terran battlecruisers. "All weapons, cease fire!" he said.

"All weapons cease fire, aye," replied the attacker.

"We will let them think that we are finished," said Admiral Bullig, "and then we will hit them from minimum range."

Bridge, TSS *Terra*, Solar System, March 03, 2021

Captain Griffin stared with horror at the tactical display. In addition to the dreadnought, at least 10 battleships and 15 battlecruisers had entered the system, along with countless smaller vessels. There was no way they could stop them all.

"Now would be a good time for the bombers," Captain Griffin said, not allowing any of the terror she felt to enter her voice.

"Yes, ma'am," replied the OSO, keying in the orders. "Calling the bombers."

Lancer 01, Solar System, March 03, 2021

"All bomber aircraft, this is Skywatch," announced the Space Operations Center, "We have indications of multiple major combatants transiting into the system, including at least one dreadnought and four battleships. Stand by for activation!"

"Lancers copy," replied Colonel Judy Khalili, Lancer 01's WSO. She switched to the squadron frequency. "All Lancers, heat 'em up!" The pilots of 37 modified B-1B Lancer spacecraft brought the power levels up on their helium-3 fusion reactors. The leader of the Lancers, Colonel Khalili had the squadron's one tactical display, computer, radar, and fire control system. She wished more of the craft had them, but there hadn't been time.

"Has everyone checked in?" asked her pilot, Colonel Darrell Larson.

Colonel Khalili nodded. Concentrating on her system display, she didn't realize Larson couldn't see her nodding in her spacesuit. "All of the Lancers are up and ready, except for 24. Their weapon system is showing some sort of fault. They're troubleshooting it."

"It's amazing that only one aircraft is having problems," Colonel Larson said. "As fast as they slapped these things together, I'm surprised any of them work at all. Pull old aircraft out of preservation or museums, refit them with helium-3 engines and then carry them up to the moon to be put back into service? The whole idea is ludicrous, and Admiral Wright's an absolute genius for thinking of it."

"The planes aren't much more than shells from which to hang missiles," agreed Khalili. "The control systems for flying them are minimalistic, the avionics are a joke, and the life support is non-existent. If it weren't for the spacesuits, we'd be dead within seconds.

God bless the men and women of the Air...what used to be the Air Force, for making it all work."

"No kidding," said Larson. "I heard over 2,000 former mechanics showed up within two days of the call going out to help convert them. They lived in tents in the desert at Davis-Monthan Air Force Base so that they could spend all their time working on the aircraft."

"The Spirits are reporting in..." said Khalili. "Looks like all 20 of the B-2 bombers are up. They should be; all of them were operational aircraft, so the conversion process was a lot easier for them. I think half of ours were previously retired. Did you hear where our plane came from?"

"No need," replied Larson. "It's aircraft 84-0051. I used to fly the plane before it was retired. In fact, I was the pilot that flew it to the National Museum of the Air Force. This jet was in the Cold War Gallery the last time I toured the museum."

"OK," said Khalili, staring at the system display, "looks like 24 of the 26 B-52s are up and ready, and 33 of the 35 A-6E Intruders. The Russians aren't doing so hot...only 10 of their 14 Bears are ready and nine of the 12 Backfire bombers. Let's see...the B-1s have 24 of the new missiles, the B-2s have 16, the B-52s have 12 and the A-6s have five. I think the Russian Bears have 16, and the Backfires have 8. That makes...1,869 missiles, each with a one megaton warhead."

"All bomber aircraft, this is Skywatch," said the Space Operations Center. "Stand by to launch on my mark!"

"Think 1,869 missiles will be enough?" asked Larson, advancing the engine to full.

"I don't know," said Khalili. "I hope so, but I don't know..."

Intruder 502, Solar System, March 03, 2021

"All aircraft, this is Skywatch," announced the Space Operations Center, "We have indications of multiple major combatants transiting into the system, including at least one dreadnought and four battleships. Stand by for activation!"

"Wake up, damn it," said Commander Walton 'Salty' Wells, reaching across the cockpit to shake his pilot. "It's almost time to go."

"I'm awake," replied Commander Rick 'Lindy' Lindenmeyer. "I was just resting my eyes."

"How you can sleep at a time like this is beyond me," remarked Salty, shaking his head. He pointed to the flashes that could be seen in front of them. "Drakuls are in the system, people are dying...and you're sleeping."

Salty thought he could see Lindy shrug inside his suit. "If I'm going to die today, at least I'm going to do it well rested." He stretched, incredibly stiff after sitting in the close confines of an A-6E cockpit in a spacesuit for two days. The plane was a two-seater, with a small space for the pilot and another for the bombardier. There wasn't much space beyond that to move around in, and his right leg had been cramping all day. Adding to his misery, their spacesuits were supposed to recycle their air, but Lindy's wasn't working very well, and he could smell his own stink.

A particularly big flash came from in front of them. "So you think this is going to work?" asked Lindy, betraying his nervousness. They had been over this several times while they waited. There wasn't much else to talk about.

"I don't know," replied Salty. "The AI in the Terra said that it had a good chance of working. At 50,000 miles from the stargate, we're too far away from the stargate to look like mines to the Drakuls, and too close to look like missile launchers. We're too small to be ships, and we aren't flying fast enough to be fighters. The AI thought that we would look like anomalies and would be ignored by the Drakuls...at least until we fire our missiles. Hopefully by then they'll have other problems and won't worry about little ol' us. That's the theory, anyway."

"All bomber aircraft, this is Skywatch," said the Space Operations Center. "Stand by to launch on my mark!"

"Here we go," Lindy said, advancing the engine throttle. He was watching Intruder 501, the lead aircraft of the Intruder formation, out the left side of the cockpit. Since only one spacecraft in 10 had a full system, the rest of the converted aircraft would fire in the same direction their leader was pointing. In theory, all of the missiles would go down the same line of bearing into the vicinity of the stargate. With five bomber groups coming from five different directions (the two Russian squadrons were grouped together), they hoped to hit the maximum number of targets possible. It was the best the Terrans could do with what they had.

"Intruder Flight, this is Intruder 501," commed the lead aircraft-turned-spacecraft as Skywatch transmitted the launch code, "stand by to fire on my mark. Three...two...one...Fire!" All down the line, missiles blasted off their rails and went in search of the enemy.

Bridge, Drakul Ship *Destruction of Olympos*, Solar System, March 03, 2021

"Captain, I am picking up new power sources approximately 50,000 miles out from us," said the defender. "They weren't there previously, or if they were, they were operating at minimal power."

"Are they weapons?" asked the commanding officer.

"Not like any I have ever seen," the defender answered. He paused while the ship shuddered from a mine that detonated close aboard. The *Destruction of Olympos'* shields were holding, so far, although they were down to 54%. "They are too far to be mines and too close to be missiles."

"Then concentrate your fire on the mines," the commanding officer ordered. The ship shuddered again, harder this time. "That one was far too close!"

"Yes, sir," the defender said. He glanced at the shield readout. 31%. Far too close indeed.

"Do you know what the new power sources are?" the captain asked the attacker.

"No, sir," replied the attacker. "They just started moving in our direction, but they are only accelerating at a couple of Gs. They are unlike anything I have ever seen before."

"Missile separation!" called the defender. "The new power sources are some sort of new missile launcher!"

"Defend the ship," the commanding officer ordered, "and destroy those things...whatever they are."

Bridge, TSS *Terra*, Solar System, March 03, 2021

"The bombers are launching, ma'am," said the OSO. "The computer estimates that over 1,800 missiles were just launched."

"That'll help," replied Captain Griffin. "Our 30..." she paused as a dreadnought missile detonated on the *Terra's* shields, shaking the ship. "Our 30 launchers aren't going to be enough."

"Shields at 23%," said the DSO. "More missiles incoming. Counter-missiles firing."

"Are the bomber missiles going to hit?" Captain Griffin asked.

"Looks like most are on target," said the OSO. "Some are being intercepted, some are going after ships that have already been destroyed, and some are just going to miss, but most are headed for the Drakul fleet." After a couple of seconds he added, "Aw, shit. The Drakuls just launched counter-missiles on the bombers. Those guys are going to get pasted."

The ship rocked. "Shields are down!" called the DSO.

"Laser hits forward, midships and aft!" added the duty engineer. "Damage control crews responding."

Please hit them, thought Captain Griffin, and please hit them soon.

"Another hit aft," said the duty engineer as the ship skewed violently. "Main engine room 2 is decompressing!"

Sooner would be better...

Bridge, Drakul Ship *Destruction of Olympos*, Solar System, March 03, 2021

"Captain, several of those slow craft are transmitting something," said the defender. "They may be the leaders of the five groups."

"Good," said the commanding officer. "Kill them first."

Lancer 01, **Solar System, March 03, 2021**

"Mother fucker!" exclaimed Colonel Khalili. She stared at the screen as if she hoped it would change.

"What is it?" asked Colonel Larson.

"We just lost *Lancer 16*. The Drakuls must have decided that we were legitimate targets after we launched on them," Khalili replied. "The counter-missile batteries that don't have incoming missiles to defend against are mopping up the bombers." She switched to the squadron frequency. "*All Lancers, evasive maneuvers!*"

"How are they going to find their way home if we get separated?" asked Colonel Larson. "We're the only Lancer with a tactical system. They'll never find their way back."

"If we win," Colonel Khalili replied, "each bomber has a locator beacon, and hopefully there'll be a shuttle left that can run around and collect everyone. If we lose..." she let the thought trail off.

"If we lose, it might be a lot more comfortable just running out of oxygen here among the stars than it would be succumbing to the 'tender mercies' of the Drakuls."

"Yeah," Khalili replied, "that's pretty much what I thought—" The rest of her sentence was lost as a 5.25 meter laser struck *Lancer 01's* cockpit, vaporizing both members of its crew.

Intruder 502, Solar System, March 03, 2021

"All Intruders, take evasive action!" their lead, Intruder 501 commed. It immediately went through several sharp turns and was lost amid the backdrop of the stars.

"What the fuck was that?" asked Lindy. "Take evasive action, and then they bolt out of here? I lost *501*. We're never going to find it again, either. How the hell are we going to find our way home?"

"Beats the hell out of me," replied Salty. "They never said—"

The crew never saw the counter-missile missile that destroyed the aircraft formerly known as Bureau Number 152591. Developed to intercept missiles that could fly at a sizable portion of the speed of light and employ a number of countermeasures, the Terran aircraft wasn't a challenge to the missile's targeting system; it impacted the cockpit canopy and detonated, killing both men instantly.

Chapter Forty-One

Bridge, TSS *Terra*, Solar System, March 03, 2021

"The bomber flight was a success," said the OSO. "It looks like we destroyed eight of their 10 battleships, most of their battlecruisers and almost all of their cruisers. All of the group leaders have been destroyed, though, and the remaining aircraft are scattered throughout local space. It's unlikely we'll ever find them all...assuming we survive to look for them."

"Did we get the dreadnought?" asked Captain Griffin.

"I don't think so, ma'am," replied the OSO. He glanced at his system display. "No ma'am, we didn't. There was a battleship in between the dreadnought and one of the attacking groups, and it intercepted the majority of the missiles. There isn't much left of the battleship, but only a few missiles got by it to hit the dreadnought. The dreadnought's shields are down, and it's wounded, but it is still in the fight."

"Damn," said Captain Griffin softly. "I really hoped I wouldn't have to do this." Growing up, Captain Griffin had watched a movie where one of the characters had to make a painful decision, based on the needs of the many outweighing the needs of the few. She had never wanted to be in that position, but she knew the power of the dreadnought. She couldn't hope to match it with the *Terra* or anything else that Terra had remaining in its arsenal, which is why she had made her suggestion at the meeting.

Kamikazes.

People under her command that would sacrifice themselves at her word for the good of the race. Just like the Japanese at the end of World War II, it was their last card, played in desperation, and their only remaining hope to even the odds.

In a previous battle with the Ssselipsssiss, she had seen the effectiveness of kamikazes against ships that had turned off their drives. A stealth fighter pilot could attack from behind and drive his or her fighter into the engines of the enemy ship. While fatal to the pilot, if it was done correctly, it would also be fatal to the ship, as it would take out all of the power to its offensive and defensive weapons systems.

"Holy shit!" cried the DSO, watching the ball of expanding plasma. "The dreadnought just hit the *Septar* with a broadside of missiles and lasers, ma'am. The *Septar's* gone."

If the dreadnought wasn't neutralized immediately, all hope was lost. Hell, all hope was probably lost, anyway, with the dreadnought and smaller ships that were still in play. The converted bombers had closed the odds but hadn't been enough to even them. You play the cards you're dealt, she thought with a mental shrug, and she still had this card to play. Sending people to certain death broke her heart, but it was the only weapon she had left.

"*Kamikaze flight, go, go, go!*" she commed. "*Get the biggest ships you can!*" A tear rolled down her cheek. She didn't think that she would ever be the same again.

Kamikaze 01, Vicinity of Stargate #1, Solar System, March 03, 2021

Damn, thought Lieutenant Sally Watts, I'm really going to have to do this. She didn't want to die; in fact, she wanted nothing more than to watch her two-year old son Stevie grow up. She had everything to live for. In a world that's free, though, not in a world ruled by Drakuls. When the call had gone out for volunteers, the intent of this mission had been very clear. Fly a stealth ship into the engines of a major combatant and blow it up.

Chance of survival: 0%.

Her mother had tried to talk her out of it, a little bit, but her mother understood the meaning of sacrifice. Her father had left when Sally was just a little girl, and her mother had spent most of her life sacrificing for Sally. Sally's life was a circle; she had been left with a baby boy herself when her latest bad choice walked out on her.

This was where she broke the circle and made it better.

She had volunteered to lead the five stealth fighters. Her task force was a small group, but that was all the ships they'd been able to make and get stealth modules for. Although there weren't many of the fighters, it was hoped that their sacrifice would have a much bigger effect on the outcome of the battle. She looked over at her WSO, Lieutenant Jon 'Angel' Aniello, who was assigning targets to the other four members of the group. He pushed the button that transmitted the instructions and turned to look at her.

"Time to go save the world," he said. He gave her a half smile; like Sally, he was a single parent trying to make a better world for his child. "The dreadnought's ours, let's make it count."

Sally tried to smile back, but couldn't. She thought about her son one last time. Yes, it would be hard on Stevie growing up with only a grandmother and no parents, but Sally's mom would make it work. She always did. Knowing that all of his needs, including college, would be paid for helped. Was it enough? Sally didn't know, but she hoped so. It was the best she could do to ensure his survival and future success.

"Kamikaze 01, *copies*," she commed. Steeling herself, she looked at Angel and gave him a half smile. It was all she could do. "*We're on our way.*"

Chapter Forty-Two

Bridge, TSS *Terra*, Solar System, March 03, 2021

"Ma'am, the *Pacific's* engines just blew up!" called the DSO. "The lead Drakul battleship wasn't out of the fight, they were just playing dead. They opened up on the *Pacific* from in close and shredded it. The ship is unpowered and venting."

Captain Griffin looked at the system display. "*Bastards!*" The battleship was trying to sneak around for them next and hit them when they engaged the dreadnought. "Helm, full power," she ordered. "Aim to cut in front of the battleship!"

With a final broadside at the dreadnought still trying to extricate itself from the minefield, the *Terra* began turning toward the battleship. "We're going to finish off that bastard if it's the last thing we do." With the dreadnought almost out of the minefield, it probably would be, she added to herself.

Bridge, Drakul Ship *Spurting Blood*, Solar System, March 03, 2021

Admiral Bullig watched in satisfaction as the Terran battlecruiser detonated under the hammering of his weapons. As he hoped, the Terrans had shifted their fire to the bigger threat when he stopped firing at them. When he fired again, it had been from minimum range, with all of his lasers and missiles targeted on the engines and engineering section. Most of the last 1/3 of the ship was now reduced to scrap metal, and the ship was dead in space. There would be food stock to pick up from it later, once the last couple of Terran ships were destroyed. *That* was how you killed an enemy ship.

"Sir, the enemy battleship has broken off attacking the *Destruction of Olympos* and is moving toward us," the defender said.

"Shift fire to the battleship," he ordered. "All lasers and missile systems."

"Shifting fire," the attacker said. "Missile tubes at 30%."

"Noted," Admiral Bullig acknowledged. If he could just kill the battleship or hold it off until the *Destruction of Olympos* was clear of the minefield, the battle would be won. He wasn't worried about the other battlecruiser.

Bridge, TSS *Terra*, Solar System, March 03, 2021

"There goes the *IO!*" called the DSO. The crew of the Terran battlecruiser *Indian Ocean* had exceeded expectations. Commissioned just two days prior, its crew was inexperienced but had lasted far longer than he would have thought possible. They managed to fire plenty of their missiles into the Drakul armada and had done incredibly well, in fact...until the dreadnought freed itself from the minefield. Able to turn whichever way it needed to take the Earth's defenders under fire, it made short work of the battlecruiser. One volley from the chase armament in the dreadnought's nose knocked down the *Indian Ocean's* shields; the first broadside the Terran ship received destroyed it beyond salvage.

The DSO winced as the dreadnought began turning to present its broadside to the *Terra*. With the ship's shields already down, and one of its engines out, he knew it wouldn't take more than one or two volleys before the *Terra* was out of the battle...and they were dead. There would be nothing left to stop the Drakuls' advance on Earth.

"Firing counter-missiles," the DSO said. "Tubes at 20%." Hopefully they'd last long enough to take out the battleship that had destroyed the *Pacific*. That would at least give them bragging rights in hell.

"Missiles launching at the battleship," said the OSO as the Drakul warship came into view of the *Terra's* broadside. "All weapons firing." The battleship had already been hit a number of times and its shields were still down. The *Terra's* weapons ravaged the aft section of the Drakul vessel, destroying its engineering spaces.

The DSO glanced at the dreadnought. It had reached a firing position on the *Terra*, and the first of its lasers fired.

"Laser strike in the galley," reported the duty engineer. "It's open to space, and we're venting atmosphere. Several crewmembers went overboard. Damage control crews are responding." The ship shook violently and went dark. After a few seconds, the emergency lighting came on. "Missile strike near engineering. All motors are out. We're operating on emergency power."

The OSO pushed the button that, if powered, would have launched the last barrage of missiles needed to destroy the Drakul battleship. He pushed it again, but it remained unpowered. "Damn," he sighed, "I really wanted to kill that bastard."

"What's the dreadnought waiting for?" asked Captain Griffin. "Why doesn't it finish us off?"

"Ma'am!" shouted the communications officer. "Skywatch just called. *Kamikaze 01* took out the dreadnought's motors, and two of the other kamikazes were successful in hitting the battleships. Skywatch isn't sure how long the dreadnought will be unpowered...if we can get our motors back online, we've got a chance to destroy her!"

"*Engineering, Captain Griffin,*" the CO commed, "*can you give me an ETA on getting a motor back online? The dreadnought is dead in space, and we could destroy it if we could get some weapons operational.*"

"*Ma'am, it's going to be a while,*" the assistant engineer replied. "*The chief engineer is dead, along with half of the crew that was in Engine Room #2. That space is open to vacuum and Engine Room #1 isn't much better. #3 and #4 are a little better, but not much.*"

"*Just give me a graser, as soon as you can,*" pleaded Captain Griffin.

"*It's going to be at least 10 minutes,*" replied the assistant engineer.

"*Try and make it eight,*" said Captain Griffin.

Bridge, Drakul Ship *Spurting Blood,* Solar System, March 03, 2021

"Get me power!" screamed Admiral Bullig. "Their battleship is defenseless. This battle is won if we can kill that ship. Give me some missiles or some lasers; I don't care what, just give me something!"

"It's going to be at least 10 minutes," replied the engineer.

"Make it sooner," ordered Admiral Bullig, "or I'll come back there and kill you myself!"

Bridge, TSS *Terra*, Solar System, March 03, 2021

"Power coming up," said the assistant engineer. "We've got enough for three grasers. If you try to use more, you're going to overload the grid, and we'll go dark again."

"Understood," said Captain Griffin. "Nice work." She turned to look at the OSO. "You've got three grasers. Using anything else will cause the power to fail. Within those constraints, destroy that dreadnought!"

"Yes, ma'am," replied the OSO. "Grasers firing!"

"I've got gate activation," called the DSO. "It's a big ship...not one of ours...holy shit, super dreadnought incoming!"

I'm sorry Earth, Captain Griffin thought. *We were so close, but we've failed you.*

"Lasers firing from the super dreadnought," announced the DSO. "They're eliminating the rest of the mines." He gazed at his tactical display, hoping it would change. It didn't. "Won't be long now," he muttered as an afterthought. The last few mines in the vicinity of the stargate were destroyed. As if those would have mattered much against a ship that large.

"Wait a minute," said the OSO, as the super dreadnought fired again, "the new dreadnought just shot one of the Drakul battlecruisers that was near the gate. What the...?"

"Attention all Terran forces," commed the newcomer, "This is the Archon super dreadnought Holy Word. We are here to help ye in thy fight against the Drakuls. Please deactivate the rest of thy mines around the stargate at this time. More forces are incoming."

"Ye? Thy?" asked the OSO. "Who the hell talks like that?"

"Anyone that wants to come kill Drakuls can call me 'ye' all day long if he keeps pounding on the Drakuls like that," replied the DSO. He switched to his radio. "This is the battleship Terra. The minefield has been deactivated. You are free to maneuver at will."

"We thank thee very much," replied the Holy Word, turning to take the Drakul dreadnought under fire, while destroying the remaining battlecruisers with its chase armament. Although the Drakul dreadnought was still without power, the Archons didn't know when the Drakuls might get it back again, and they were taking no chances. Missiles the size of frigates began pouring from the Holy Word like water, washing away the defenseless dreadnought.

"I've got another gate activation," said the DSO as the first round of missiles detonated on the dreadnought. "It's a much smaller ship...it's the Vella Gulf! The Gulf's back!"

Bridge, TSS *Vella Gulf,* Solar System, March 03, 2021

The *Vella Gulf* transited into the system just behind the *Holy Word*. Missiles were already arcing out from both sides of the *Holy Word*. With the enhancements provided by the view screen, the Terrans could see the power of the super dreadnought in action. Lasers and grasers reached out to starboard to envelope the closest battlecruiser, whose screens had already been flattened by its initial missile launch. Counter-missile lasers were still focusing their attention closer in, scouring the area close by the ship of mines...just in case.

"Launch all fighters!" ordered Captain Sheppard. "Weapons free! *Blast the bastards!*"

"Weapons free, aye," replied the *Gulf's* OSO. "Opening fire! Helm, bring the ship 50 degrees to the right!"

"Coming right 50 degrees," said the helmsman.

"Chase mounts firing!" said the OSO. The missile launchers at the front of the *Gulf* launched their first volley at the cruiser to their left. As the ship turned further right and the main batteries on the port side unmasked, the first volley leapt out to follow the missiles from the chase mounts.

"Mines close aboard to starboard," called the DSO. "Counter-missile lasers firing!" The mines wouldn't know the difference between the Terran ship and the Drakuls; once armed you didn't go through them. No sense taking chances.

"Sir, the *Terra* is calling," said the communications officer. "They are asking if we'd finish off the Drakul battleship that is alongside them."

"Tell the *Terra* it would be our pleasure," replied Captain Sheppard. He turned to the OSO. "You heard the lady," he said. "Kill the bastards."

"Yes sir," the OSO replied. "I'm on it." Nine missiles roared downrange, accompanied by the 10 grasers in the *Vella Gulf's* broadside. The weapons hit home on the *Spurting Blood* before its crew could get their ship's shields back up. Its magazine breached, the Drakul ship exploded, killing all aboard.

Chapter Forty-Three

**President's Conference Room, Terran Government
Headquarters, Lake Pedam, Nigeria, March 04, 2021**

"Grand Admiral Michael, I wanted to pass on the grateful thanks of a very frightened population," said Terran President Katrina Nehru to the figure on the view screen. "If not for your assistance, the Drakuls would be overrunning the planet right now."

"We were happy to assist thee," replied Grand Admiral Michael, "especially since thy ship Vella Gulf was instrumental in helping us to make significant gains against the Drakuls in our war against them. We must be going, however. We currently have the Drakuls on the run and need to keep up the pressure. If we can trap them in their system, we will end this war, once and for all."

"I understand completely," said President Nehru, "and I look forward to talking with you under better circumstances. The Vella Gulf is the only ship we have that is operational, but we will happily send it with you."

"Wow," she said after Grand Admiral Michael had signed off; "he looked just like an angel…"

Chapter Forty-Four

Bridge, TSS *Vella Gulf,* Lalande 21185 System, March 12, 2021

The force was the biggest that Captain Sheppard had ever seen, although he was admittedly a bit of a novice at major interstellar battles. They had rendezvoused with a fleet from Archonis and now had two super dreadnoughts, four dreadnoughts, five battleships, seven battlecruisers and five cruisers. When they had entered the Lalande 21185 system, they had also found the *Emperor's Paw* waiting for them, along with another dreadnought and the brand new spacecraft carrier *Night Strike.* The Terrans' contribution of a single cruiser looked pathetic compared with the other star nations, but the *Terra* had been in too bad a shape to join them, and the rest of the fleet was scrap that was currently being fed into Terra's replicators to make new ships. There would be a nice sized fleet once they got all of the wreckage around Saturn cleared out, but that was a long time in the future.

With the *Terra* sidelined for major repairs, it was up to the *Vella Gulf* to carry the flag of the Republic of Terra into the climactic battle with the Drakuls. No one really expected the Drakuls to have *too* much in the way of capital ships left; the alliance forces had already exterminated two whole Drakul fleets.

"*All ships, this is Grand Admiral Michael,*" the Archon transmitted as the ships approached the stargate to COROT-7 and the planet Drakon, the home world of the Drakuls. "*We are faced with an enemy*

405

that has attacked us from the very bowels of hell. They shall not stop us, for our mission is true. Our faith is pure! Let us advance and send these demons back to the hell from whence they came. For God and Archonis!"

"For God and Archonis!" replied the rest of the fleet.

"Here we go," said Captain Sheppard as the first mine clearance vessels transited the stargate. Robot ships led the assault into the next system. After transit, they launched a number of decoys for the mines near the stargate to attack. The Archons expected a *lot* of mines and had used all 20 of the mine clearance ships they had available. The *Holy Word* would follow them in, followed by the *Emperor's Paw* and the *Vella Gulf*, and then the rest of the fleet.

"Leaders lead," Captain Yerrow had said, with the Mrowry equivalent of a shrug, when Captain Sheppard had asked why Yerrow had requested the honor of following the *Holy Word* into the system. It seemed like suicide to him, but when the Mrowry officer had asked if the *Vella Gulf* would follow them, Sheppard had said, "Certainly; I wouldn't have it any other way." Captain Sheppard shook his head in remembrance. His mother had always warned him that his mouth would be the end of him; it appeared that her prophesy had finally come true. All he could hope for was that the Drakuls would be too worried about the *Holy Word* to bother with his little cruiser.

He watched the front view screen, waiting for the lead ships to begin the assault. The key was to follow the mine clearance drones closely enough that the enemy couldn't bring up any additional mines after the drones did their job, but not so closely that the warships intercepted mines that were still headed for the drones. The *Holy Word* began advancing toward the gate.

"All ahead full," said Captain Sheppard. "Maintain separation from the *Emperor's Paw*."

The *Emperor's Paw* made the jump in front of them. It seemed like forever, and yet no time at all, for them to reach the gate. They made the jump...straight into hell. Although the drones had eliminated most of the mines around the stargate, they had done nothing to reduce the Drakul fleet waiting for them, a fleet that was considerably larger than expected.

"Launch all fighters!" ordered Captain Sheppard. "Weapons free!"

"Holy shit!" muttered the OSO as he started targeting the enemy forces. "That is the largest ship I have ever seen!" Even bigger than the *Holy Word*, the flagship of the Drakul fleet was a full three miles long, brimming with missiles and lasers. Three other super dreadnoughts only slightly smaller waited at the stargate, as well as five dreadnoughts, six battleships, 12 battlecruisers and more cruisers than he could count.

The *Holy Word* had immediately been trapped between the biggest super dreadnought and one of the other super dreadnoughts when it entered the system, and it was trading fire with both. The carrier *Night Strike* entered the system after the *Vella Gulf*, and fighters began launching from all four of its catapults. Every Alliance ship was taken under fire as it entered the system.

Captain Sheppard counted the number of ships showing on the tactical plot and didn't like the totals. "I'm not sure we can win this one," he said in a low voice to Steropes.

"Did you see the courier ship the *Holy Word* just launched?" Steropes replied. "They're probably thinking the same thing. I believe they are sending it back to let their rulers know."

"Ummm...wouldn't we want to retreat to the last system and wait for reinforcements?"

"I don't know what the Archons are thinking," replied Steropes; "however, it is my guess that Grand Admiral Michael is trying to take advantage of catching them all here. If by some chance we could destroy them all, including their replicator, then the rest of the forces could come and finish them off before the Drakuls can get off planet again. I imagine that he doesn't want to have to chase them through the universe in order to eradicate them...again."

The Alliance forces traded missiles and energy weapons with the enemy fleet. Although they gave better than they received, it didn't appear the alliance forces were going to win the battle. While the *Holy Word* wasn't out of the battle after the first 15 minutes, it was close; air and fluids streamed from it in more places than the Terrans could count. Still, it wasn't done, and the smaller of the two super dreadnoughts that it was fighting blew up as Captain Sheppard watched. The biggest Drakul ship looked like it was in the same shape as the *Holy Word*. Both ships were wrecked; their captains were just too stubborn to admit defeat.

"Sir," said the OSO, "another super dreadnought has changed directions and is headed toward the *Holy Word*."

"If they take out the *Word*," said Captain Sheppard, "they can deal with the rest of us at their leisure. Comm the fighters. See if they can hit the super dreadnought before it can get to the *Word*."

Asp 01, COROT-7 System, March 12, 2021

"Asp 01 *copies*," Lieutenant Sasaki 'Supidi' Akio replied. *"We're inbound to the target."* He punched the new target into the system. *"That's our target,"* he said to Calvin.

Calvin looked over at Supidi's system. *"Big one,"* he grunted. They were a long way off, but he could still see it in the long range viewer.

"Yeah," said Supidi, *"they want us to shoot the engines out of it."*

"Wonderful," said Calvin. *"This is going to suck."* He switched to the squadron frequency. *"All Asps, join on me. We've got a high priority target. They need us to take out the motors of the super dreadnought in front of us."*

"Do you suppose they'll even notice we're here?" asked Lieutenant Martyn 'Tinman' Sinclair from *Asp 08*. *"Their missiles are bigger than our fighters."*

"They'll notice when we shove a few megatons of explosives up their ass," replied Calvin. *"Follow me!"*

Bridge, TSS *Vella Gulf*, COROT-7 System, March 12, 2021

"New contacts!" the OSO called as the ship shuddered from another missile strike. The *Gulf's* shields were down, and they had already been hit several times. One of their engines was out, and Captain Sheppard could see flashes from the ongoing battle through the window-sized hole in the bridge. "Sir, I've got ships coming from around the other side of Drakon. They must have been hiding there with their power turned down. There are five more dreadnoughts and eight more battleships accelerating toward us!"

"Damn," said Captain Sheppard. "We were close to pulling this off, but there's no way we can beat all of them."

"Sir, I have an incoming transmission from the *Holy Word*," said the communications officer.

"On screen," replied Captain Sheppard. The ship shook as another missile hit it.

"Missile hit in officer berthing," said the duty engineer. "Damage repair crews responding."

"Ye must all retreat," Grand Admiral Michael ordered from the front screen. "We do not gain anything further from thy destruction. We will stay as a rearguard and hold them off as long as we can. Get back to Alliance space and mine the stargate. Perhaps ye will have time to rebuild the fleet before they attack again."

"Helmsman, proceed to the stargate," Captain Sheppard said.

"Head to the stargate, aye," confirmed the helmsman.

"We're not going to run, are we?" asked Steropes.

"We're not running," replied Captain Sheppard. "We are retreating, as ordered by Grand Admiral Michael."

"They just called in the Mrowry fighters," the OSO noted. As he watched, all six squadrons launched simultaneously, and over 350 missiles streaked inbound toward the super dreadnought approaching the *Holy Word*. "That's going to leave a mark."

Chapter Forty-Five

Drakon, COROT-7 System, March 12, 2021

The Overlord hated the stupid Archons. If their wings didn't taste so good, there wouldn't be any reason for keeping a single one of them alive. As it was, he was going to have to teach them a lesson. After he destroyed this pitiful fleet, he would send out the Home Fleet and wipe them out, all the way up the star chain to their home world.

With the Home Fleet committed to the battle, it wouldn't be long. He could sense that they were about to break. No...it wouldn't be long at all.

Bridge, TSS *Vella Gulf*, COROT-7 System, March 12, 2021

"Sir, Captain Smetlurge is hailing the fleet," said the communications officer.

"On screen," replied Captain Sheppard.

The front view screen changed to a live feed of Smetlurge from his bridge.

"Everyone else may do as they desire," he said. "As for us, we have a different mission. We have experienced the rape of our system by the Drakuls, and we will not suffer it again. Hopefully our versions of the afterlife will line up, Grand Admiral Michael. I would very much like to talk strategy and leadership with you some time.

411

Captain Smetlurge, out." The front screen returned to the tactical plot.

"Sir, he just cut off the transmission," the communications officer said.

"The Hooolong ship is moving out of formation," Steropes noted. "It has begun accelerating toward the new Drakul fleet."

Captain Sheppard looked stunned. "He can't hope to take on that big of a force."

"I do not believe that is his intention," Steropes said. "The Drakuls ended his civilization. I know what that's like, and how the need for revenge burns within you. I don't think he intends to do battle with the Drakuls. I have analyzed his vector, and I believe he intends to destroy the planet."

Asp 01, COROT-7 System, March 12, 2021

"Asp 01 copies," Supidi commed. He looked at Calvin. "The Gulf says that the super dreadnought's shields are down, courtesy of the Mrowry. Something's going on, and we need to give the Holy Word time to get back into the battle.

"Attack Plan Red," Calvin said without hesitation.

"Really?" asked Supidi. Attack Plan Red involved splitting the squadron into two-fighter sections to attack a target from a multitude of angles. It kept the target from turning to protect a vulnerable spot, but left the attackers extremely vulnerable to defensive fire, as they were no longer massing their attack along a single axis. It would be a death sentence for many of the squadron's crews.

"Do it," ordered Calvin.

Supidi switched to the squadron frequency. "All Asps, Attack Plan Red. I say again, Attack Plan Red." When all the rest of the squadron indicated that they heard, Supidi transmitted, "Execute!" and the squadron, which had been flying in a 12-fighter formation, flew apart into six sections of two. Staying outside of the range of the dreadnought's defensive weapons, the squadron maneuvered into position.

"They're ready," said Supidi, looking at his plot.

Calvin switched to the squadron frequency. "This is where we earn our pay," he transmitted. "We've got to keep the super dread-nought off of the Holy Word. If the Word goes, we're done for. The Drakul ship's shields are down, and we need to take out its engines. Commencing attack run...now!"

As one, the 12 fighters turned inbound toward their target. The crew of the super dreadnought had obviously been watching the fighters set up, because the ship began turning, trying to keep its vulnerable engines away from the threat. There was nowhere to hide, though, as the fighters attacked from all sides.

"It looks like they just launched a missile from every launcher they have," said Supidi as the fighters entered the dreadnought's mis-sile range. "This is going to be ugly." The warship fought with a fe-rocity born of desperation. Relatively new to the fight, the dreadnought's missile racks were nearly full, and its crew flushed them all to try and stop the fighters.

"Evasive measures!" Supidi commed to the squadron. "All coun-termeasures on!"

Calvin began to maneuver the fighter randomly and violently as they closed with their target, and the fighter's anti-missile laser fired at the missiles targeting them.

"Launching countermeasures," Supidi announced, toggling the switch that released a pattern of decoys. "Full spread."

Calvin continued to maneuver the fighter as the decoys launched. Some ran off in front of the fighter to draw off the incoming missiles, while others dropped behind it. Some reflected radar, creating a larger image; others burned fiercely to decoy missiles that used infrared seekers.

Calvin could feel a slight vibration in the fighter's controls as the defensive laser fired, and then a shudder as a missile blew up close to them. A high pitched whistle could be heard in the cockpit as the air left through the hole that had materialized next to Calvin's head.

"Damn," Calvin said. "That was too close."

"30 seconds to launch," noted Supidi, turning on the missile launch panel. "Master Armament panel is 'on,'" he advised. "Damn!" he added, "the dreadnought is turning toward us. Our missiles won't get the engines. 07 and 08 are behind it; looks like it's going to be up to them. Here goes...roll out."

Calvin stopped maneuvering and gave the system two seconds to align and download the final targeting information. A green light illuminated on his heads-up display, and he pulled the trigger. Missiles detached and roared off toward the super dreadnought. "Asp 01, Fox One!" he called, indicating missile launch.

The last missile launched, and Calvin put the controls hard over as he began maneuvering again. "Let's get the hell out of here," he said.

Asp 03, COROT-7 System, March 12, 2021

"**H**ow are we looking?" asked *Asp 03's* pilot, Lieutenant Rob 'Thing 1' Mees.

"*Shitty,*" swore *Asp 03's* WSO, Lieutenant Paul 'Thing 2' Mees. "*It just turned. We're in its broadside. We're—*" He was interrupted as a 5.25 meter laser from the dreadnought speared through the cockpit, killing both officers and destroying the fighter.

Asp 07, COROT-7 System, March 12, 2021

"**L**ooks like it's going to be up to us," said *Asp 07's* WSO, Lieutenant Brett Dylan 'Foxy' Fox.

"*Oh, yeah?*" asked his pilot, Lieutenant Matthew 'Exit' Kamins, pulling the fighter around hard.

"*Yeah,*" replied Foxy. "*The dreadnought just turned away from us. We're the ones with a shot at its motors.*"

"*Good,*" replied Exit, "*Let's nail it, and then get the hell out of here. It's getting awfully—*"

Designed to attack dreadnoughts, the anti-ship missile was so large that Exit actually saw it a fraction of a second before it hit. Many times the size of *Asp 07*, there was nothing left of the fighter afterward.

Asp 08, COROT-7 System, March 12, 2021

"**T**hat was a big one!" noted Lieutenant Terry 'Guppy' Gupton, the pilot of *Asp 08*, as a flash lit up space to his left. He continued maneuvering for all he was worth.

"*Yeah, that's what it looks like when an anti-ship missile hits a fighter,*" replied his WSO, Lieutenant Martyn 'Tinman' Sinclair. "*We just lost 07.*"

"*So it's just us?*" asked Guppy.

"*Yeah,*" agreed Tinman. "*We're the only fighter left with a shot from behind the ship, and they're launching everything they've got at us. Even the big shit, the anti-ship lasers and missiles.*"

"*The anti-ship missiles?*" asked Guppy. "*Didn't you say that those things were bigger than our fighter?*"

"*Yeah, they're a lot bigger,*" confirmed Tinman. "*Trust me; you're a lot happier that you can't see what they're shooting at us.*" The ship rocked as another missile exploded close to them. "*Last countermeasures pattern being used.*" Normally he'd want to save some for the egress, but he'd had to use up all of them on the way in. There was just too much shit trying to kill them.

"*10 seconds to launch,*" said Tinman, turning on the missile launch panel. "*Master Armament panel is 'on.'*" He turned off the notifications he was receiving about missiles and lasers targeting his fighter. At this point, he was happier not knowing.

Guppy continued to yank the fighter back and forth randomly, pulling even harder when he felt the anti-missile laser firing from underneath the craft. He didn't know if it affected the targeting system of the laser, but if there were missiles close enough for it to fire, he wanted to be somewhere *else*.

"*Stand by for launch,*" said Tinman as Guppy completed an especially violent maneuver. "*Roll out!*"

Guppy obediently rolled the wings of the craft level, and the missiles received their targeting information. He saw the green light and pulled the trigger. The missiles launched, seemingly in slow motion.

"Asp 08, *Fox One!*" Tinman called.

The last missile came off, and Guppy began a pull to the left to get clear of the target area. It was too late; an anti-ship missile as big as a small frigate impacted the fighter, obliterating the smaller ship.

Chapter Forty-Six

"The dreadnought's dead in space!" yelled the DSO. "The fighters did it!"

"That's great," said Captain Sheppard. "Focus. Fight the ship."

"Yes, sir," said the DSO, calming himself.

"That's odd," interjected Steropes. "The Hooolong ship just swerved a little to port, but then resumed its heading toward the planet."

"Why would Smetlurge do that?" Captain Sheppard asked.

"I do not know," Steropes replied. "Just a second...Oh, I understand now."

"What?" Captain Sheppard asked.

"I believe that they still intend to ram their ship into the planet," Steropes explained; "however, on their original trajectory, they would have missed the replicator that is in orbit over the planet. On their new trajectory, they will drive straight through it on their way to hitting the main city on the planet."

"Will they destroy the planet?"

"Probably not," Steropes said, estimating the impact. "The Chicxulub asteroid that hit Mexico's Yucatan peninsula was about six miles long, and it didn't destroy the Earth, although it did make the dinosaurs go extinct. As the ship is smaller than the asteroid, it is unlikely that it will destroy the planet...but it *will* inflict severe devastation. It looks like they're going to miss the capital by several miles, but that won't make much difference to the Drakuls there."

Drakon, COROT-7 System, March 12, 2021

The Overlord stared at the tactical plot. "What is that ship doing?" he asked. It had originally looked like it was going to try to hold off the Home Fleet by itself, so that the Archons could run away. According to his senior advisors, the Archons would have had to start running a long time ago in order to have a chance of avoiding the Home Fleet. They had no chance of making it out of the system now. They were his...and he expected to have Archon for dinner tonight. Whatever the dreadnought was doing was a side show; there was no way that it could expect to hold off, much less defeat, the ships arrayed against it.

"Overlord!" exclaimed the admiral who led the High Command. "You need to go to the bunker. I believe that the dreadnought intends to ram the planet."

"What?" asked the Overlord. "What does he hope to accomplish with that?"

"I do not understand the food source's thought processes," the admiral replied, "but its trajectory impacts the planet just outside the capital. I expect that the crew of the dreadnought is hoping to kill you."

"*It must be stopped!*" shouted the Overlord. "I will not allow the food source to damage our planet. All ships are to stop what they are doing and *destroy that ship!*"

"Do you mean all of the ships involved in combat at the stargate, or just the ships of the Home Fleet?" asked the admiral, who had learned to ensure that he followed the Overlord's directives to the letter. His two predecessors had been less meticulous, making his ascent to his current position possible.

"*I mean every ship of the fleet!*" screamed the Overlord. "Every ship in our fleet is to chase that ship down and destroy it before it can hit our planet! *Do it now!*"

"Yes, Overlord," the admiral said with a mental sigh. It was too bad, he thought. We had the battle at the stargate won.

Bridge, TSS *Vella Gulf*, COROT-7 System, March 12, 2021

"They're not going to catch the Hooolongs," judged the DSO. "I don't know why they broke off the battle; they can't catch the *Hooolong's Revenge.*"

"They're not?" asked Captain Sheppard. "What about the second fleet?"

"I don't think that the second fleet is going to be able to stop the Hooolongs, either," determined the DSO. "The ship is going so fast now that it's going to blow right through their missile and laser envelopes. They'll get a chance to shoot at the *Revenge*, but I don't think it will be enough to stop it."

"The *Hooolong's Revenge* is transmitting to the fleet," announced the communications officer.

"On screen," said Captain Sheppard.

Smetlurge appeared on the front screen wearing a uniform. With no shoulders, his insignia flowed down his side. Whatever rank he was dressed as had a *lot* of stars.

"As a race, our time is over," he transmitted. "3,000 years ago, it took the selfless devotion of a race to eradicate the Drakul menace the first time. The Eldives gave their lives to make sure that the Drakuls were destroyed. Unfortunately, the Drakuls were allowed back into our universe, and now a similar sacrifice is necessary. We do this for you, that the universe may be a better place, and that no other race might have this stain on their hands. When you remember the Hooolongs, please remember us well." The transmission ended.

"10 seconds until the Hooolongs impact the replicator," Steropes noted. "Five... Four... Three... Two... What the...?"

"What?" asked Captain Sheppard. "What happened?"

"The impact didn't happen the way it should have," Steropes said. "It was almost like the Hooolong ship ate its way through the replicator...the impact was far less than it should have been. The replicator is following the ship down toward the planet, as if there had been an impact, but it was weird..."

"Weird how?" asked Captain Sheppard, starting to get frustrated with Steropes' lack of information.

"Well, it was almost like the ship was pulling the replicator along, and not that the ship actually hit the replicator," replied Steropes. He paused and then said, "*Black hole!* They set off a black hole device and are going to hit the planet with it!"

"What?" asked Captain Sheppard. "A black hole? You mean like the black hole we set off on Olympos?"

"Just like that," replied Steropes. "No...this one is even bigger. I don't know if this one will go out on its own...we might want to back up from the planet even more."

"Back up?" asked Captain Sheppard. "Aren't we already a lot further back than we were for the one that was set off at Olympos?"

"We are," agreed Steropes; "however, this black hole is bigger than the one that we set off on Olympos. I don't know what the Hooolongs have done; this one may not self-extinguish. Smetlurge was their preeminent weapons scientist, and it appears that he has done something to the design of the weapon, or has set off several of them simultaneously. I can only postulate that he hoped that the black hole would last long enough to eat the replicator and still make it down to the planet."

"Is it going to catch the Drakul fleet?"

"That is unknown at this time," replied Steropes. "If they keep chasing him, it will be very difficult for them to get away."

"Well, at least we know what he was talking about when he said the stain would be on their hands," Captain Sheppard said. "I guess the implication is that what we did to Olympos isn't going to look very good on our record once all is said and done."

"That is true for some of the minor races," Steropes said. "Many will fear you for having done it. The Archons, however, will likely see you as a race that is not afraid to make the hard decisions, or to do what must be done. The Mrowry will be less enthusiastic, because their population is afraid of the device. On the good side, the Aesir will love it. They were the first race to come up with an expression along the lines of 'an iron fist in a velvet glove.' They are not afraid to use force when it is required...and sometimes when it's not."

He paused before adding, "The universe is filled with races that would rather run and cower than make a difficult decision and follow through. You will be seen as a race that is willing to do its part. There may be some skittishness that such a young race has possession of the bomb and has shown a willingness to use it, but others will approve."

Captain Sheppard shrugged. "I guess it doesn't matter; what's done is done. What was it that Stalin said? 'A single death is a tragedy; a million deaths is a statistic?'"

"I don't know if he was ever proven to have said that," replied Steropes; "however, when he was asked how long he intended to continue killing people, he said, 'As long as it is necessary.' With the Drakuls, that quote goes a long way."

"Holy shit," mumbled the DSO. "The black hole just went off, and the Drakuls are gone. With the exception of the unpowered dreadnought off the starboard bow, they're *all* gone."

Epilogue

"Ooooh," Princess Merrorritor said as Calvin pulled the rod out of his backpack. The rod glowed a bright cherry red. "That's pretty! What else is it going to do?"

"I don't know," Calvin said. "I wasn't told what would happen once I brought it here, only to find rock formations like this one and bring the rod to them. The alien that gave me the rod said that I would know what to do."

"Do you?" she asked.

"Do I what?" Calvin replied.

"Do you know what you're supposed to *do*, you silly," she asked.

"If it was supposed to just flash into my head," Calvin said, "I must have missed it." He turned the rod around in his hands and inspected it thoroughly. The only thing that seemed different was that one of the buttons was now glowing, too.

"Maybe you should push that button," the princess suggested. "Was it glowing before?"

"No, the button didn't glow before now," Calvin replied. "I'm going to push it, but before I do, I'd like you to move back a little ways, in case something bad happens."

The princess laughed. "You really are silly," she said. "A computer that is millions of years beyond you gives you something, and you're worried that it's going to hurt us? If the computer had wanted to kill you, or even just to hurt you, couldn't it have done that to you while you were on its planet? Why would it send you on a quest, just to kill yourself?" She laughed again. "Daddy is right; you humans *are* funny."

Calvin's face went a little red at having his wisdom chastised by a child. "When you put it that way," he said, "it does seem a little silly. Still...could you just move back a couple of steps, just in case?"

The princess sighed but moved a few paces away. She growled in frustration; now she couldn't see as well. "I moved," she said, tapping her foot as Calvin continued to look at the rod. It *seemed* warmer, but he couldn't tell if its temperature had risen, or if he was just imagining it.

"Are you going to push the button, or just look at it all day?" She looked around. "We're going to have to go soon, or it will be dark before we get back. We'll be in trouble if we aren't back in time for dinner, too."

"OK," Calvin said, "Stop bugging me. I'm pushing it now." He pushed the button, holding the rod at arms' length. The glow faded.

"That's it?" asked the princess in disappointment. "It didn't *do* anything."

Calvin looked at the rod more closely. It looked the same as it had before the trip to Clowder Rock, except..."Hey, there's a new symbol glowing on it," he said. The symbol was located next to the button he had pressed, in between the button and the end of the rod. It looked like two wavy lines, one on top of the other.

"What does that mean?" the princess asked.

"No idea," Calvin replied. "Maybe Steropes will be able to interpret the symbol."

"Well that's lame," said the princess with a sniff.

They walked back toward the house, the princess asking questions throughout. Once she decided that Calvin really didn't know any more about the rod than what he had told her, she started asking questions about what life was like on Earth, and if there were any fun animals to hunt.

As they rounded the final bend in the pathway, Calvin almost ran into Steropes, who was hurrying to meet them. "You have a visitor," he said. "An Aesir is here to see you."

"I love the Aesir!" the princess said. "They are so much fun! Well, they're not really very much fun at all, when you first meet them. They're all boring and...distant...yeah, that's the word daddy uses. They're all boring and distant when you first meet them, but after you get to know them, they can do sooooo many cool things. They are so much fun...even if they are still kind of distant."

Steropes held up a hand to get the princess to stop. "The princess is correct in that the Aesir do tend to keep to themselves," he said. "Even at the height of the alliance, they only interacted when they needed to, and foreigners weren't welcomed on their planets. They are a very honorable and peaceful society, but they are also very private. It is extremely rare for one to come here; his mission must be of the utmost importance."

"In that case," said Calvin, "we ought to quit wasting time and get back so we can find out what it's all about." He began walking toward the emperor's estate house. As Calvin looked toward it, he saw the Aesir come out and begin walking in long strides toward them. He looked humanoid in appearance, although shorter and thinner than was normal for a Terran. The Aesir's pale green skin was a giveaway that the creature was definitely *not* a Terran.

"Oh," Steropes added, "there's one other thing that you should probably know about the Aesir before meeting them..."

Calvin saw one of the Aesir's ears, poking through the long blonde hair that he had drawn up in a ponytail. The ear was very definitely pointed.

"...they're elves."

* * * * *

The following is an
Excerpt from Book 1 of the Codex Regius:

The Search for Gram

Chris Kennedy

Available from Chris Kennedy Publishing

eBook, Audio Book, and Paperback

Excerpt from "The Search for Gram:"

Princess Merrorritor stared open-mouthed at the flame dancing on the Aesir's hand. "Why doesn't it burn you?" she finally asked.

The Aesir smiled. "The flame doesn't burn me because it is my friend," he said. "Hold out your hand," he instructed, "and you can hold it, too."

"You don't have hair on your hands," said the princess, "but I do. Won't it catch my hand on fire?"

"No," said the Aesir, "it won't burn you. It is a special flame." He put his hand next to the Mrowry's paw and blew gently. The flame hopped over to the princess' paw and began to dance rhythmically but did not burn the young Mrowry.

"See?" the princess said, holding the flame out to Calvin, "I told you the Aesir were neat!"

"OK," said the Aesir, scooping the little flame out of the princess' hand after a moment, "I need to talk to the adults, and it is time to let the flame go back to his world." He cupped his hands around the flame and blew gently into them; when he opened them again, the flame was gone. Despite the different cultures, everyone could tell the look on the princess' face was one of abject disappointment.

"Run along, Mimi," said the emperor. "You can talk with our guest later."

"If I have to..." she said as she walked to the door with her head down, dragging her feet.

"You can sit next to me at dinner," said the Aesir, "if your grandfather allows it."

"Can I, grandfather?" she asked, life coming back to her voice.

"Yes, you may," replied the emperor. "Now, *run along.*"

431

Happy again, the princess bounded out of the room on all fours, stopping only to close the door.

"What can I do for you?" Calvin asked.

"We have met a foe that is beyond us," replied the Aesir. "Our elders conducted a divination and it was determined that we needed to look outside our realm for aid. All of the signs point to you...we need your help."

ABOUT THE AUTHOR

A Webster Award winner and three-time Dragon Award finalist, Chris Kennedy is a Science Fiction/Fantasy author, speaker, and small-press publisher who has written over 30 books and published more than 200 others. Get his free book, "Shattered Crucible," at his website, https://chriskennedypublishing.com.

Called "fantastic" and "a great speaker," he has coached hundreds of beginning authors and budding novelists on how to self-publish their stories at a variety of conferences, conventions, and writing guild presentations. He is the author of the award-winning #1 bestseller, "Self-Publishing for Profit: How to Get Your Book Out of Your Head and Into the Stores."

Chris lives in Coinjock, North Carolina, with his wife, and is the holder of a doctorate in educational leadership and master's degrees in both business and public administration. Follow Chris on Facebook at https://www.facebook.com/ckpublishing/.

* * *

Connect with Chris Kennedy Online

Website: http://chriskennedypublishing.com/

Facebook:
https://www.facebook.com/chriskennedypublishing.biz

* * *

Find out what's coming from CKP! Meet us at:

https://www.facebook.com/groups/461794864654198/

Made in the USA
Las Vegas, NV
15 January 2023

65683172R00243